The Quisling Orchid

by

Dominic Ossiah

ISBN: 978-0-9568829-9-8

There was once a maid
who loved a man
with a splinter of her heart;

her soul she gave
to the village she adored

and the blind Jewess
she took to the mountain.

A POEM BY ERIK BRENNA

1

My interview with Oscar Strande lasted for three minutes and four questions. While he interrogated me, he drank a mug of espresso, sweat waterfalls, and injected himself from the insulin syringe he kept in a shoulder holster.

Can you make real coffee?

How about tea?

Ever used a typewriter?

Can you make coffee, or did I ask you that already?

He thought he was a journalist of the old school: a white pin-striped shirt, bright red braces, and a cigar he rolled from one side of his mouth to the other. He carried his girth and his failing pancreas like a boxer carries a prize belt; they were his rite of passage, the sacrifices he'd made in return for his position at the *Trondheim Echo.*

He gave me the job without listening to a single reply or sparing me a look. He scribbled down notes, which I'm sure had nothing to do with the interview, and told me I could start that afternoon if I wanted.

'I am warning you though, Miss…?'

'Ersland.'

He looked up, staring at me over the top of his spectacles. He knew the name was a lie, so it was down to how much he cared. For the first time since I'd stepped into his office he took a good look at me and found things that didn't seem to fit: I wasn't wearing makeup; my shoes were scuffed and worn, and the dress – my only dress – had faded with age.

'Ersland,' he said.

I nodded.

He raised an eyebrow. 'Would you like to try again?'

I shook my head.

His brow furrowed and he tapped his teeth. His eyes dipped so he could look at my legs.

Monica was right; this was a terrible idea. I was about to get up and leave when Strande leaned forward with his hands clasped in front of him.

'I will do *you* the courtesy of being honest. Only three people applied for the job: a woman in her forties, a man – if you can believe it – and you. If there were someone more suitable, I'd take them in a heartbeat. But let me warn you, young lady, you will find this the dullest, most unrewarding job you will ever have. I should know; I was doing it at your age.'

And look at you now.

'I only need to know one thing: would it be a mistake to hire you. Think carefully. I am not a forgiving man.'

I told him I was hardworking, didn't have a criminal record and wasn't wanted by the police. I think that's all he wanted to know.

He stared into my eyes; I stared back without blinking. Finally, he sniffed loudly and sat back in his seat. 'Fine,' he said. 'Mine's black, four sugars.'

* * *

Strande hadn't lied. The work was dull, repetitive and mostly unappreciated. Only Rodrek, a junior reporter, ever thanked me for the coffee. But I did like being there. There are few places I can go where I just fade into the wallpaper.

'You take far too many risks,' Monica said over a late breakfast. We were sitting in a small café, a short walk from the *Echo,* at the table closest to the door. Monica kept one eye on the entrance and berated me again for my spectacularly poor judgement. 'A newspaper? I think you've lost your mind.'

'I'm hiding in plain sight; that's what you called it, isn't it?' I smiled and spooned ice cream into my mouth. 'No one recognised me. The biggest paper in Trondheim and not one journalist, photographer or editor has looked at me twice.'

She lit a cigarette and craned her neck to blow smoke at my eyes. 'You think we're forgotten, don't you?' She put the cigarettes back into her bag without offering one to me. 'And you're looking at me like that again.'

'Like what?'

'Like this is all my fault.'

'I never said that. I *have never* said that.'

'You never say half the things you're thinking.'

'Would it make any difference if I did?'

'A newspaper for God's sake. I mean, you can barely read.'

'Now that *is* your fault,' I said, lighting a cigarette of my own.

Monica widened her eyes. 'Excuse me?'

'You're my mother. If not you, then who?'

'Well – how about your fucking father!'

The other customers stopped eating to look at us.

'We have to fly low, Brigit,' she whispered, her eyes searching for an assault from any quarter. 'One day we won't have to. One day, Norway will—'

'Yeah, I know. "Norway will forget."'

The mantra changed a while ago. She used to say 'Norway will forgive.' But it's been thirty years since the war ended, so forgiveness was clearly off the table.

'We could leave,' I said. 'We could just leave and settle somewhere where they've never heard us. Switzerland maybe. Or America.'

'America? You're joking. They're up to their necks in Viet Nam, and don't get me started on all that "free love" crap...' She stubbed out the cigarette with the same gravity someone else would use to load a gun. 'No,' she said. 'Norway is our home.'

'Norway doesn't seem to think so.'

'Then Norway will have to learn.'

'Mrs Quisling must've said the same thing.'

She looked at me as though I'd accused her of drowning kittens. 'You're comparing me... to her.'

'That's not what I meant.'

'Right,' she said. 'Fine.' She stood up, threw her napkin on the table and walked out. The other customers were staring at me; some smiled sympathetically, some shrugged – others frowned while they back-tracked through our conversation, perhaps trying to piece together our lives from a single snatched word:

Quisling.

An old man, sitting alone in one corner, gripped the arm of a passing waiter. He whispered in his ear and pointed in my direction. I guessed he was a Survivor. We ran into them frequently, or their relatives, or their descendants, or people with no lives of their own and nothing better to do than hound us. Strange when you consider there were only a few hundred people in that village to begin with.

I'd been recognised so it was time to leave. I left money next to the ice cream dish and hurried back to the *Echo*.

A shame – I really liked that café.

* * *

Back at the *Echo*, Oscar Strande was throwing chairs.

'Impact!' he screamed.

Another chair bounced off the wall.

'Where is my *fucking* impact?'

The editors and journalists crammed into his smoke-filled office looked at each other and then back at Strande. He was purple, a very deep purple. I moved amongst the rigid bodies, quietly taking orders for the afternoon coffee run.

'We are three days out from the new year,' Strande said, pressing his fists into his desk. 'Three days from the most significant event in—'

'A year,' said Marte Henning, and I was so glad I wasn't her. She smiled weakly and a ripple of laughter flowed around the office. Oscar Strande stared at her and rolled his cigar from the left side of his mouth to the right – the angry side.

The ripple stopped.

'We'll speak later, Marte,' he said. 'But for now, just get out.'

'Oh come on, Oscar. She was just trying to lighten—'

'And you can go too, Thomas. In fact, both of you, leave the building and don't think of coming to the New Year party. Now does anyone else have a little year-end humour they'd like to share? No? Good, I thought not.'

Marte left in tears, and Thomas slammed the door on his way out.

'Quite honestly people, the Special, as it currently stands, is shit. It is worse than shit.' Strande looked to the ceiling for a suitably barbarous metaphor. 'If shit stepped in our Year-End Special then shit would hop to the nearest patch of grass and scrape its shoe.

'There is nothing emotional here, people. Norway during the war – check. Norway and its nascent welfare system – check. Norway's future oil wealth – check. Yes, we know all that! All you idiots have done is add "as the end of the year approaches" in front of every sentence! And that, dear friends, is shit.'

'Oscar, if I may speak—'

'No Jens, you may not. Norway is just a slab of land which God saw fit to place next to an oil slick. What makes our country is the people who built it. Did no one think to speak to the family of Edvard Grieg? What about Quisling's relatives? Yes, he is the most reviled man in Norwegian history, but his actions lit a fire of righteousness that still burns in every one us. You! Yes, you – coffee girl.'

I hiccoughed, dropped my pad and stood to attention.

'You're young,' he said accusingly. 'What will 1969 mean to you, and don't you dare mention free love or the fucking Beatles!'

Rodrek pushed the notepad back into my shaking hand and whispered in my ear: 'Say something. Anything.'

'Don't help her, Rodrek. She's not a retard. You're not a retard, are you?'

'It's the year I stop waiting for things to change,' I said with nothing to follow it with.

'And can you tell me what the fuck you mean by that?'

I swallowed so loudly I swear everyone heard it.

'Well,' I began, 'it's just another year, isn't it?'

Strande's cigar returned to the angry side of his mouth.

'Korea's ongoing,' I said. 'Viet Nam is heading towards another fuck-up that'll cost millions of dollars and millions of men. We might put a man on the moon, we might not. Even if we do, the aliens won't drop by and Jesus won't come back.'

'So what you're saying is…?'

'What I'm saying is that I don't care about any of that. I just want to know how to get out of this crappy job and get one like yours. I want to know where I'll find a man when they're still in short supply, and when I'll have babies. I want to know how I can have a career while I'm caring for my family. I think I want it all, Mr Strande, and I think the New Year Special should tell me how can I get it.'

The silence wasn't quite what I'd hoped for. The journalists looked at each other. I think the women wanted to applaud. Most of the men probably wondered if Strande would fire me with violence, or just fire me.

'The youngsters will love it, Oscar,' Rodrek ventured.

Strande rolled the cigar to the left side of his mouth. 'Have something that ends with "this year I'll change things myself" on my desk by tomorrow morning.'

'Me?'

'You do want to be a journalist, don't you? I mean that's why you took this crappy job, isn't it?'

'I don't know if I can—'

'Good, an article by tomorrow morning, and if you value your life, I'd better not see the phrase "as the new year approaches".'

I nodded while everyone stared at me.

'You'd better get started then, Coffee Girl, and before you do, mine's a double espresso, four sugars. The rest of you should take a cue from her. Now fuck off back to your desks, and give me people, not bullshit.'

* * *

Around nine o'clock, after the rest of the newsroom had gone home, I realised Monica had been right all along.

Write a piece on the coming year from the perspective of a twenty-three-year-old Norwegian woman. It would have been easy except for one small problem: I can't write. When you spend your life running from one town to the next, things suffer. You make no friends, develop no social skills. You don't spend long in school so you say goodbye to college, university – you say goodbye to pretty much everything.

I looked at the blank paper; it looked back. I glanced at the clock: nine-forty-six. I turned around and snatched a glance at Oscar Strande sitting in his office. He was reading from a brown folder, his eyes scanning quickly across the pages, stopping every so often to look at me. He smiled, and not in an endearing way.

I desperately rattled out a few words on the keys, hearing the door to his office open then close. When I turned around again, he was perched on the edge of a desk six or seven feet away. The folder was resting against his thigh, the rictus smile stretched across his jowls. I could hear him wheezing.

Seven words altogether. The journalist's equivalent of 'It was a dark and stormy night.'

'I'm sorry,' I said, and I meant it. 'I can't do this. I just can't.'

'Hmm.'

'If I had some more time, and a little help – from Rodrek maybe…'

He dropped the folder on my desk.

'What is it?'

'Take a look.'

He licked the perspiration from his upper lip. He looked nervous, and that made me nervous. I opened the folder. Inside it were a few sheets of paper, copies of old documents from the Nuremberg trials, and a large photograph. The black-and-white picture was of Erik Brenna, taken just before the end of the war. He was dressed in black woollen trousers and a chequered shirt. He was smiling. I'd never seen the picture before. My mouth went dry and my hands started to shake. It occurred to me that I had his nose.

'I didn't know who you were at first,' Strande said. 'Which begs the question, what sort of reporter am I? I mean, the daughter of the second-most reviled man in the history of Norway walks into my humble establishment, and I don't even recognise her.'

'Mr Strande, I—'

'Just be quiet.'

He closed in behind me, pressing down on my shoulder with one hand. 'I gave you a chance, Brigit. I asked you if I could trust you.'

'You can. What my father did has nothing to do with me.'

'Can you see how embarrassing this is for *the Echo*, for me personally?'

I said I was sorry, and he started massaging my shoulder, pushing his thumb into my collarbone.

'I'm sure you are. I mean, you're not a bad person, are you, Brigit?'

I heard him undo his zip.

'No, I'm not. I should have told you.'

'Yes, and now we have to think of a way to make this right, don't we?' His hand left my shoulder and I could breathe again. Then it snaked inside the collar of my dress. I froze. He leaned closer. He smelled like raw onions. 'When people find out that I've taken on the daughter of a missing war criminal, I'll be a laughing stock.' He started kneading my breast. 'But I'm sure we can come to an arrangement that'll benefit us both.' He used his free hand to draw my dress to the top of my thighs. I tried to pull at the hem to cover myself. He gently moved my arm out of the way. 'We can say that you came here to tell your story, to see justice done, to see your father answer for his crimes.' He pressed his hand between my thighs and spread his fingers, forcing my knees apart.

'Mr Strande, please…'

'Do you know where your father is, Brigit?'

He fumbled between my legs and I snapped to my senses. I grabbed hold of a paperweight and swung it over my right shoulder. It connected, though I wasn't sure with what. I heard him cry out and stumble backward; he tripped, landing heavily on the floor.

I was on my feet, holding the paperweight out in front of me with both hands, like a gun.

Strande was on his knees, doubled over, his chest rattling and blood running from his nose and mouth. 'You cut me, you… little… bitch.'

'I swear to God I'll kill you if you come near me again!' I gave the paperweight a threatening shake. Strande got up, staggered back to his office and closed the door.

It took a few minutes to get myself together. My right breast hurt; it was probably bruised. My tights were ripped and I'd managed to fold a fingernail back on itself; there was blood running from the cuticle. I drank what was left in the water cooler and wiped my eyes with napkins I found in Rodrek's desk. I thought Strande might have ripped my dress because I could feel a coldness around my shoulder blade. When I reached round to check for the hole I found the dress wasn't ripped – it was damp. I used the rest of the napkins trying to wipe my back.

I thought about calling the police, but Monica doesn't trust them, and so instinctually, neither do I.

Strande sat upright when I threw open his door. His shirt was covered in blood and he hadn't made any attempt to staunch the flow from his nostrils. I'd managed to break one of his front teeth.

He glared at me then looked down at his desk, rubbing the palm of his hand with his thumb.

He said, 'I appear to have misread the situation.'

'Yes,' I replied, 'yes, you did.'

'But the offer stands. Tell me where your father is hiding and I will make sure—'

'I want money. Everything in the safe, all of it.'

He blinked rapidly before narrowing his eyes. 'You're blackmailing me?' he said, loosening his collar. The top button of his shirt popped free and landed on the desk. He looked at it as though he had no idea where it could have come from.

'Empty your pockets.'

He slid down in his chair and started wheezing, pearls of white sweat already congealing at his hairline. 'No one will believe you.'

'Perhaps.' I dipped my eyes towards his wedding ring. 'But a man like you… I don't think you can take the chance.'

There wasn't much: his wallet, a pair of museum tickets, a small notebook and a silver cigarette case. I took all his cash, even the change, about three thousand kroner all together. And I kept the cigarette case, which seemed to upset him more than the money. 'That was a present from my wife.'

I lit a cigarette and gratefully filled my lungs.

He opened the safe which landed me another thirty thousand kroner, and I took his wedding ring because it was worth more to me than it meant to him.

'Do you know why Norway hates you?' he asked.

Fastening my coat and feeling bulletproof, I told him I didn't care.

'You see, I think you do. Don't you wonder what makes you different from the descendants of other war criminals?'

'He's alive,' I said. 'He's alive and he hasn't paid for what he's done, so they take it out on us. I expected better.'

'That's only part of it. Yes, Quisling paid for his crimes, but his atrocities were slow, they were measured, meted out over time. Your father...' He shook his head. 'A whole village wiped out in one terrible day. Two hundred men, women and children – gone. He will never be forgiven, and in his absence neither will you.'

I made for the stairs before he could see me cry.

'Enjoy your life, Brigit,' he shouted after me, 'such as it is.'

2

When I got home I found Monica sitting cross-legged in the middle of the living-room floor. We had furniture, which was something of a luxury for us. Most of the places we rented came with nothing but a single bed and a refrigerator.

She had a large tapestry resting in her lap, which she was stabbing at with a needle. Her fingertips were covered in tiny red dots and there were more spots of red on her blouse. The tapestry hadn't fared much better; it was supposed to be a vase of white orchids. Some of them looked decidedly pink.

'You should call if you're going to be late,' she said without looking up. 'I was worried.'

'Problem at work.' I dropped my coat on the floor – then remembered there were hooks behind the door.

She looked up with one eyebrow raised and then carried on with her needlework. 'Were you recognised?'

'Yes.'

'Told you.'

'He had a file on us.' And if I'd been thinking straight I would have taken it with me.

'A file? From a journalist? Who would have guessed?' She'd only recently discovered the joy inherent in sarcasm, probably the only thing she'd learnt from me. 'So did he call you the accursed spawn of a traitor and fire you on the spot?'

'More or less.' My voice cracked and Monica picked up on it. She stopped torturing the canvas and gave me a long penetrating look. I let myself exhale and took a step towards the kitchen.

'Do you remember Mr Fiske?' she said suddenly.

I did. Fiske was a thin ugly whip of a man who rented out a cottage he'd built on his farmland. We'd only seen him twice during our time there: once when we arrived and again, a year later, when he came with a rifle and his son to throw us out.

'That was 1961.' I couldn't remember the exact date. 'Just outside Lesja.'

'It was the Summer of '62,' Monica said. 'And the farm was in Lom, not Lesja.'

She was right of course. She kept a meticulous mental record of our life as pseudo-fugitives for the book she was planning to write when… Well, I'm not sure when she planned to write it or with what. She even had a title; she was going to call it 'Repentant' even after I'd pointed out we had nothing to be repentant about.

'Fiske came to see me the night we left.'

We hadn't 'left'. We were kicked out at gunpoint with the words 'traitor scum' burning in our ears. Monica's sewing became more frantic and even more careless. 'He said we could stay another week if I did something for him.'

I remembered returning to the cottage that night. I was excited; I'd made friends, and one of the local boys had asked me to join them on a hike the following day. I'd walked in and the farmer pushed past me on his way out. Inside, I'd found Monica at the kitchen sink, drinking dish soap.

I thought she'd finally cracked.

She'd washed out her mouth and spat into the sink. *Pack your things,* she'd said. *We're leaving.*

'Shit!' Monica dropped the needle and began sucking blood from her thumb.

I took the tapestry from her and threw it across the room. 'Give me your blouse.'

She looked at me quizzically, like the child neither of us had ever been.

'Give me your blouse. If I soak it now I can get most of the blood out of it.'

'There are three types of people in this world,' she called after me as I went through to the kitchen. 'Those that hate us, those that don't care and those that don't care but think they can use us in return for their silence.'

I ran water over the spots of blood and prayed she'd stop talking.

'I take it your boss at the *Echo* was a type three.'

'I didn't let him near me, if that's what you're asking,' I said.

'Good,' she said. 'Because I didn't let Fiske near me. As well as being ugly, type threes are always liars.'

I went back into the living room where I found her sewing the tapestry again. She was sitting in the same place, facing the door; it was though the tapestry had leapt back into her hands as soon as I'd left the room. Her skin stretched in a translucent layer over her ribs, and her shoulder blades stood proud from her back.

'So you didn't let that old farmer touch you,' I said, wondering when she'd gotten so thin.

'Of course not. You remember him; he was disgusting.' She said this without meeting my eyes. I returned to the kitchen and started wringing out the blouse.

'Self-respect, Brigit,' she said. 'It's one of the things in life we must hang on to.'

Though honesty wasn't, it seemed.

* * *

She slept soundly that night, while I lay awake facing her, watching the slow rise and fall of her breasts, listening to the purr of her breathing. There were times I thought I was very lucky; not many women get to my age and are still able to share a bed with their mother. Most nights she ran a little too warm for comfort, a by-product of being raised in the mountains she said, so I slept on the very edge of the mattress.

Sometimes I would lie there and wonder what would happen if we just stopped, if we just turned around and said, *Enough. We're sorry, but it wasn't us. And it was twenty-five years ago for God's sake; leave us alone.*

Strande was right. We were hounded because Norway had been cheated of its pound of guilt. My father had escaped, and in his absence we shouldered the blame.

So we run, and because we run our countrymen find even more reason to despise us.

But what if we just stopped?

I switched on the bedside light.

'Brigit? What is it? What's wrong?' She drew herself upright and looked at the clock. 'It's three in the morning.'

'Do you know where he is?'

'Who?'

'You know who. Where is he?'

'What makes you think I have any idea?' She ground the heel of her hand into her right eye.

'I don't know. I thought you might be protecting him from—'

'Protecting him? Why would I do that?'

'Out of some misguided sense of loyalty. Or maybe you've started to enjoy this running and hiding. Perhaps it's what makes you feel special – different. Maybe you've forgotten what it's like to just—'

I wasn't surprised when she slapped me. I would have most likely done the same. Of course it wasn't the first time she'd hit me, but it was the first time she'd hit me for something I'd said rather than something I'd done. She clenched her fists and I turned the other cheek. Her frail body trembled as she fought to reassert the indifference she needed to survive.

I asked again, softly this time: 'Mother, do you know where he is?'

She reached for her cigarettes, taking the last one from the pack and lighting it. 'Do you have any idea how much this country has spent trying to find him? This tolerant, forgiving nation of ours? Three million kroner. Quisling's widow lived a comfortable, anonymous life while we're chased and hated and—'

'Quisling was executed.' I wondered if I'd ever get an answer from her.

She drew on the cigarette and jetted smoke from her nostrils. 'What has that got to do with anything?'

'Justice was done. In the case of my dear father, justice is still waiting.'

'And you think that justifies what has been done to us? We didn't murder Fólkvangr, Brigit.'

'No, we didn't, but we run and hide as though we did. We're hounded because we behave as if we're guilty.' I took a breath. 'Because we believe we are guilty.'

My mother stubbed the cigarette on the bedside table. 'You're saying I wanted this life.'

'No. It's just that you're used to it. Twenty years ago, the wound was still raw. But now? Norway isn't hounding us, Mother. She's just giving us what we want: penance.'

For a moment I thought she was going to hit me again; her jaw set and her eyes narrowed until I could barely make out the whites.

'So,' she said finally, 'guilt is hereditary. Who would have guessed?' She ran her fingers through her hair and looked at me. 'You're leaving me.'

It wasn't a question. I half-wondered if it was a request. I swallowed and said, 'I think we're out of places to run. And when Norway tires of us, what will we do then?'

She nodded. I had expected anger, tears, any one of a hundred emotions. There was nothing. 'Where will you go?'

'To find him.'

Again she nodded. She beckoned me to come to her. She put her arms around me and kissed the top of my head; her bones pressed into me.

I said, 'I've never even seen a picture of Fólkvangr.'

'There aren't many around.' She relit her cigarette. 'But as far as I remember, it was very pretty.'

The Friends of Fólkvangr

(8th April 1940)

Dear friends, welcome!

We have reached something of a milestone; this week marks the 50th edition of the Friends of Fólkvangr newsletter. To commemorate this most momentous of occasions we will be running not one, but two competitions! Yes friends, alongside our regular Hunt the Goat contest, we will also be offering a special prize for anyone who can guess the weight of Jon Ohnstad's most extraordinary Pearl Onion. This wondrous vegetable will be entered in the Bergen fete next week. Good luck, father! The hopes of Fólkvangr travel with you!

On a more sombre note, Kvist Gundersen reports that a ladder was stolen from outside his cottage, Tuesday last, while he tended to his hanging baskets.
Has it come to this, my friends? But a year has passed since the declaration of war in Europe, and already we tear at each other like rabid wolves. We are of Fólkvangr! We are bound to each other through honour and history. We do not take from one another, my friends; we do not! I myself have spoken to Kvist,

and he has agreed that if the ladder is returned by the week's end, no more will be said.

And I'm afraid there is more bad news. It is with the most profound regret that I must tell you that my good friend Helga Bratvold will be leaving our fair village to take a position with a small book-keeping firm in the town of Lillehammer. Many of you will remember Helga as the runner-up in the Fair Maiden pageant at last year's fete. We have been friends for many years, Helga and I, and this bond between us remained strong, even after my unanimous victory over her at that very same pageant.

Though I cannot think why anyone would leave Fólkvangr for the festering streets of Lillehammer, I would like you all to join me in wishing her well and reminding her that there is nowhere better than home.

And now friends - on with the festivities!

3

Silje chewed on the end of her pencil, sighed, and put a line through the word *festering*. She wrote *suppurating* in its place and drew air through the spaces between her teeth. She exhaled, gasped, crossed out *suppurating* then wrote *festering* above it.

'Yes, festering,' she whispered to herself. '"Lillehammer's festering streets."' She groaned and leaned forward, parting her knees further. 'Do you think…' She gasped again. 'Do you think I should have mentioned that I beat her in the pageant?'

'No.'

'Oh.' A spasm of pleasure rattled her spine; she tried to squeeze her thighs together.

'Ow.'

She said 'Sorry' and closed her eyes, leaning back and clawing her fingers into the bark of the chestnut tree. 'Does it sound mean-spirited?'

'What?'

'Mentioning the pageant. It sounds mean-spirited.'

'Yes.'

'Mmm.' She ran a line through the offending sentence. 'Though I find it hard to believe people would think that of me.'

'Silje?'

'Mmmm?'

'Silje, is that your notebook resting on my head?'

'No,' she replied, gently sliding the notebook from his crown.

Erik swore under his breath and sat back on his haunches, wiping his mouth. 'I thought you liked it when I did that.'

'I did,' she said without thinking. 'I mean, I do. I am just… preoccupied, that is all.'

'Preoccupied with your stupid newsletter.'

'Please don't sulk, Erik.'

'I am not sulking!' He jumped to his feet and walked away, distancing himself from her with long, disgruntled strides.

The late spring had cast a blanket of bloodroot and lilies far beyond the forest, spreading their petals of white across the meadow – which all but smothered his indignation. Silje bit her lip to stop herself from laughing. She pushed her skirts down over her knees and got up from the grass.

'I am sorry,' she said, chasing after him.

'What for?'

He was his most handsome when he was angry, which to Silje's mind was a great shame. Even a mild rage brought colour to his othertimes sallow complexion, a regality to his slightly receding chin. To her shame, Silje often found herself making him angry just to bring a gentle savagery to his bearing.

'For not…' How to say this, she wondered. 'For not showing my appreciation.'

He stopped, mid-stride. 'Showing your appreciation,' he echoed. 'I was attempting to pleasure you, Silje, not mend your gate.' He turned west, heading for the line of sparse beech trees that separated Fólkvangr from the meadows and the hills. The flowers and the grass faded away, replaced by stony earth and patches of mud.

'Erik, I'm wearing a dress!'

'Then take the path back to the village you love so very much.' He disappeared into the trees.

'So you're not even going to walk me home.'

'I could,' came back his disembodied voice, 'but I wouldn't want you to feel the need to show your appreciation.'

'You are being ridiculous,' Silje shouted, but there was no answer. 'This is the end for you and me, Erik Brenna. Do you hear me?'

If Erik did hear, he chose not to reply.

She sighed and pulled her coat tightly around her. Night would fall soon, leeching away what little remained of the day's warmth.

The true path to the village, the path suitable for a young lady in a pretty dress, cut through the tree-line at its narrowest point. Silje walked about half a mile before stopping at a knoll covered in lichen. She took off her shoes and climbed to the top from where she could see her village, nestled in a recess of stone and ice, and the town of Bergen at the foot of the mountain. She often came here to write and watch the Allied warships steaming away to patrol the seas around Scandinavia. But today the harbour was empty, save the small, squat lines of Bergen's tugboats and fishing vessels. Silje reached into her bag and took out the old box camera that had belonged to her mother. She peered down into the viewfinder, focussing on the horizon beyond the harbour.

She could see smoke, just off to the east. She stood motionless and held her breath. Her heart was racing. As she pressed down on the shutter, the sound reached her, carried on the winds from the sea: a metallic thud, like thunder striking inside a steel box. She put away her camera, slipped her sandals on her feet, and ran down the mountain path as fast as she could.

* * *

She stopped to catch her breath where the path widened and Fólkvangr's plateau began. The track became a cobbled street that ran the length of the village from north to south, beginning just beyond the stone archway and a sign bidding visitors 'Welcome'. The sign said the population of the hamlet stood at two hundred and three.

Two hundred and two, Silje thought, if one considers the treachery of Helga Bratvold. She heard bootfalls on the stones and looked to see Jonas Kleppe limping towards her. He carried a short wooden ladder on his shoulder and an oil can swung from a hook on his belt. Mr Kleppe – and he would always be Mr Kleppe to Silje – dressed in a flamboyant tweed oddly matched with black hiking boots and thick woollen socks. His beard was reputed to be the most magnificent across the mountains, the envy of every male villager over the age of fifty. Silje often dreamt of stealing into his home in the dead of the night and spinning his whiskers into yarn.

'Ho there, Silje,' Jonas Kleppe said. He raised a long clay pipe to his lips and struck a match against the oil can. 'Dragging your feet again, I see. And such a face, child. Did someone shoot your goat?'

'Hello, Mr Kleppe,' she said, pointing back the way she'd come. 'I heard an explosion, out at sea.'

He tapped her on the nose with the wet end of his pipe. 'You must learn to call me Jonas, child.'

'Jonas then. And Baldur thrives, thank you for asking, but I heard an explosion! Like a cannon.'

Mr Kleppe said 'Ah' and puffed gently on the pipe. He studied her face until Silje was quite red. 'Your young man, Erik, came by me just a few moments ago, wearing that very same face. You can catch him if you—'

'Thank you, I have no wish to see Erik now. But you must tell everyone; I think the Germans are preparing themselves.'

'Ah,' Mr Kleppe said. Something appeared to be amusing him. 'You young people turn love into such a battlefield. It is not as hard as you make it, certainly no more difficult than teaching a goat to fetch a stick.'

Silje smiled painfully.

'But when I think on it, Mrs Kleppe and I were the same at your age.' He relit his pipe and squinted at the sky. 'Though of course I would give anything to have her here today, shouting at me for not trimming the hedges or thatching the roof, or for spending far too much time at the tavern, instead of being at home tending to her womanly needs.' He puffed savagely on his pipe.

'I really should go, Mr Kleppe. I should warn everyone that—'

'Death,' he continued. 'is a most odd thing, even when it is expected. You build a suit of armour for yourself so that when it happens you can stand tall and true. You do not think that thirty, forty, fifty years on, the pain will come to you in the night when your armour has long since rusted away.' His eyes clouded and he seemed to fade, as though his soul were escaping.

'Mr Kleppe?'

He came back to her with a start. 'Right, yes,' he said. 'Must get on. These lamps won't light themselves.' He coughed and waved his pipe at the metal stalks that lined the path far into the hills. 'And if you want to do something useful, young Silje, then use that newsletter of yours to find more volunteers. Since Lars passed, God rest his soul, I have been doing this all by myself.'

'I will do that, Mr Kleppe.'

'Jonas!'

'And until we find someone, I shall help you every other day.'

'It is no job for a young lady,' Mr Kleppe said firmly.

'Of course it isn't.' Silje stood on her toes and pecked him lightly on the cheek. He reddened like a furnace as soon as her lips touched him. 'But I will help you all the same.'

'Then your help and your company will be very much appreciated,' he mumbled. 'Now off with you. Darkness is almost upon us. And I should warn you, your father's former wife is lurking by the orchids.'

'I shall try my best to avoid her, Mr Kl—'

'Jonas!' he said, climbing to the next lamp.

Silje's heart felt lighter as she took the path towards the village circle. She heard a short cry of surprise, and felt a burst of heat at the back of her neck. 'And you are still using far too much oil, Mr Kleppe.'

'Apparently so.'

'We may soon be at war, you know.'

'Thank you, child. I will bear that in mind.'

She had not taken three steps when another thought struck her. She stopped and turned. 'Mr Kleppe?'

'Mmm, yes my dear?' he replied, wiping the soot from his face.

'Is that a new ladder?'

* * *

The village streets were uncommonly quiet for a late afternoon. There was a flower and vegetable market every Tuesday, running from the small hours until dusk – every Tuesday since Silje could remember.

And today it was not there.

Silje marked time by the movement of Fólkvangr. When she was very young, her mother had told her the village was the metronome of her soul. Silje had stared at her with wide fathomless eyes, fearing she would break some magical spell if she asked what a metronome was.

Towards the centre of the village the single road divided, making room for a large circular dais formed of the same cobblestones as the town streets. Indeed, it looked for all the world as though the dais had grown from the road itself. Four narrower paths led away from the Monument, and at the point where each began, the first stone carried an inscription.

For Emily.

The centre of the stone circle was filled with orchids, each with petals of gossamer white and a heart-shaped mouth the colour of blood. Thirty-four blooms on slender stems, one for each year her mother was alive.

Silje put down the ladder and searched her pockets for a handkerchief.

'You weep for her, child.' The old woman moved from the shadows to stand between her and the Monument.

'Leave me be, Marit,' said Silje. 'I have little time for you this evening. There has been an explosion out at sea and I must warn the village. And yes, I weep for my mother, as would you if God had seen fit to furnish you with a heart.'

Marit Ohnstad laughed. 'You expect me to cry for her. You expect me to shed tears for the whore who stole my husband. You think me ungenerous.'

'I think you unforgiving, and your soul fouled with bitterness.'

The old woman stepped forward until their noses were almost touching. 'She stole him from me. She stole him and sired him twins, bastards in the eyes of God. By all that is right you and your brother should have been mine.'

'You should have left. You should have left Fólkvangr and found a new life. Instead you stayed to torture us. Look at you. My father did not do this to you. You did this to yourself.'

'You are a whore. Just like your mother.' Marit smiled, showing a mouth full of near-perfect teeth. 'Do you think I do not know why you take that boy into the hills? Do you think the whole village does not know?'

'I am twenty-three years old, and you are an old woman twisted by self-hatred,' Silje said mildly. 'All I need do is outlast you.'

Marit Ohnstad trembled. She opened her mouth but found herself unable to speak. Instead she turned to the Monument and plucked a single orchid from the circle.

Silje's heart screamed.

'I remember your mother. She was much as you are now: tall and beautiful with skin the colour of goat's milk. Such a delicate creature, spoilt by such a dreadful disease.'

'You are not fit to speak of my mother.'

'You and Magnus were too young to remember, I suppose; that thing that started as a tiny mound on her throat, and then grew until it had taken her face. And it was such a pretty face, so much like your own.'

'Shut up! Shut up!' Silje snatched the orchid from her and pushed her away.

Marit cried out and fell sprawling to the ground.

'You are evil, Marit. Spiteful and evil. That is why you were abandoned. And the few short years my father spent with her were worth a thousand spent with you!'

Silje wiped her eyes with her sleeve, then she hauled the ladder to her shoulder and hurried away without looking back.

4

Night had fallen when she reached the doors of *The Mottled Goat*, the most popular and least salubrious of the public houses serving the hamlet of Fólkvangr. Like most of the taverns in the mountains, *The Goat* had begun life quite by accident. The building was a large cottage occupying a narrow street to the north-east of the main thoroughfare. It was conferred the honour of being a public house because one of its previous owners, in its dark and frozen past, had realised the cottage had a parlour that was not only larger than most but also faced out onto the street.

Silje placed the ladder against the wall and dried her tears. Meeting her father's former wife always left her flayed and aching; it had done so since she was five years old. Magnus had long outgrown Marit's baiting, and Silje felt ashamed she was unable to do the same. She cleared her throat, prepared her announcement and pushed against the doors.

She was met by an opaque wall of pipe smoke and the silhouettes of men huddled in the mist. The smoke she was quite familiar with; indeed, she was quite fond of it as it furnished her with memories of a future yet to come: sitting in a cottage of her own, weaving a small tapestry while her husband slept in the armchair and her six grandchildren played at her feet. She coughed and her eyes watered as she strained to find her father. The tavern was uncommonly silent and the patrons unusually still. From behind the bar, Silje could hear the wireless at full volume.

'I have just come from the mountains,' she announced.

'Be silent, child. And close the door; you are letting in the cold.' Her father's voice.

'There is a sea battle,' she continued, annoyed that the patrons seemed to be ignoring her, 'less than two miles out. We should be prepared. I think the Germans are planning an assault on our shores.'

It was her brother who spoke, so close he startled her. 'The Germans are already here, Silje. They have landed troops along the coast: Trondheim, Bergen and Oslo.' And on hearing the smooth baritone of his voice, Silje found herself strangely conflicted: torn by the joy of having him home, and the sense of foreboding at what lay ahead.

Magnus Ohnstad stepped from the smoke and stood before her, a taller, steadfast, dependable version of herself. Beneath his greatcoat he wore the vestments of a priest-in-training.

'Magnus!' Silje threw her arms around him, pressing herself against his chest. 'You're back! When did you return? Why did you not come find me?'

He returned the embrace with the smile of a Norse god. 'I would have, but I had a fair thought where you'd be: in the hills, under the chestnut tree, with Erik perhaps.' The smile broadened to a grin, and Silje wrestled herself from his arms. 'How dare you!' she cried with feeling, and a furtive glance towards her father.

Jon Ohnstad remained where he sat with his back to them, hunched over a mug of ale. He may have trembled but Silje could not be sure. She scowled at Magnus and put a finger to his lips. 'You swore...'

'That I did, Sister. But it is not my words that will give you away.'

'We are trying to listen to the radio,' Jon Ohnstad said sternly. He reached for his mug and drained it in a single mouthful. 'And the whole tavern can hear you.'

'And hello to you, Father.' Silje took Magnus's hand and led him away. 'What did you say about the Germans?'

'I said that they are here.'

They joined the crowd, six people deep, that encircled the tiny wireless from which a lone and sombre voice addressed them in sharp, precise sentences.

'And who is that?' Silje whispered.

Magnus looked horrified. 'You do not recognise him? He is the most hated man in all of Norway. How could you not know Vidkun Quisling?'

'Does he farm land in the mountains?' she asked plainly.

'Of course not, but what does that have to do with—?'

'Can he rear onions and orchids as well as Father can?'

'No, but—'

'Can he milk a cow?'

Magnus folded his arms. 'I assume not.'

'Can he bake? Can he brew mead from honey and apples?'

'I imagine he cannot, no.'

'Then why should I have heard of him?'

Magnus shook his head. 'Silje, I love you dearly, but I sometimes worry that you are perhaps not as worldly as you might be.'

'If by "not as worldly" you mean I did not abandon my village and my family and run off to Stavanger to become a priest, then yes, I am not as worldly and I am glad of it.'

'You could not have,' Magnus said glumly. 'There is no such thing as women priests.'

'I know that,' Silje snapped, realising why she'd never seen one.

'The puppet Quisling.' Kvist Gundersen spat upon the floor. 'He tells us this is not an invasion, but a liberation. He tells us that the Nazi scum have come to free us from Allied oppression.' He was about to spit again when a large cloth struck the side of his face.

'You can clean that up, Kvist Gundersen,' said Grette, *The Goat*'s formidable barkeep, whom many swore was a man in a previous life, and also perhaps in this one. 'You know the rules about spitting in my tavern.'

'And I have found your ladder, Kvist,' Silje said to him. 'I left it outside.'

'Bless you, child!' Kvist said. He looked sourly at Grette before dropping to his knees to scrub the floor.

On the wireless, Quisling announced a brave new day for the people of Norway.

'You should come with me when I travel back to Stavanger,' said Magnus. Grette handed him a tankard and smiled in what she believed to be an inviting fashion.

'I will think about it,' Silje replied, though she had already made her decision.

'You cannot stay here your whole life, Silje.'

'Why not? Mother did. You have only been gone for three months, and you have already forgotten how much she—'

Magnus suddenly bade her to be quiet.

'You cannot tell me what to do, Magnus Ohnstad!'

'The radio, Silje!'

The voice went on to deliver the most dreadful news.

Save for the sound of matches being struck and tankards being filled, the tavern remained silent until Lisbeth Fehn, the farrier's daughter, could contain herself no longer. 'Did none of you hear that? The King has fled! Haakon has fled and we all sit here!'

Jon Ohnstad said, 'No, he has escaped. There is a difference.'

'What difference is that, Jon?' Olaf cried. 'The King is gone and the government is in hiding. Quisling and Terboven are our new leaders, supported by that madman in Berlin.'

Silje looked about her, taking heed of the change in the air. Lisbeth seemed to have begun something of a revolt.

'May God smite them and the goats that sired them!' Kvist spat upon the floor and got to his feet to stand to attention, the cloth in his fist and his fist pressed against his chest. 'The King will not abandon us. You will see.'

'The King will be on the next boat out.'

Kvist whipped his head left and then right, his eyes narrow. 'Who said that? Show yourself for we shall have words, you and I!'

'It is the Jews I fear for.'

It took moments for Silje to realise it was her father who had spoken. His voice sounded tired and distant, as it had in the final weeks before her mother died.

'I have heard stories from the hat-maker in Bergen,' he said. 'He tells of atrocities the like of which I have not heard since the first Great War. Inhuman crimes against Jew and gypsy alike.'

'We must do something!'

'And what would you suggest, Lisbeth?' said Silje.

'A resistance!' Lisbeth's eyes were wild and streaming. 'We must mobilise ourselves in the government's absence.'

'We will do no such thing.'

As though they were a single pair of eyes, the tavern's encumbrance turned to Silje.

'We are a small village in the mountains,' she said. 'The Germans have no interest in us, and we should not give them cause to change that.'

'So, you are saying we should do nothing.' For the second time that night, Magnus looked at his sister as though he hardly knew her.

'I am saying we should protect the village.'

'By doing nothing,' said Lisbeth.

'What is to be gained by fighting the Germans?'

'Our freedom!'

'And how do you know we will not be free under them?'

'Because we have seen what they have done in Poland and France and—'

'We are not France and we are not Poland. We have no particular fondness for the Jews, so why should the Germans—'

'So we should welcome them then,' said Lisbeth. 'Or perhaps it is you who wishes to welcome them, Silje.'

'We are not made for this.' Silje turned imploring eyes to her father. 'You have fought before. Tell them.'

Jon Ohnstad stroked at his moustache. He stood and tried to look over a sea of expectant faces.

'I think,' he said finally, 'it is time I took my children home.'

Magnus protested that he was twenty-three years old and did not need taking anywhere.

'If you wish to have somewhere to live when you tire of being a priest then you will do as you are told.' Jon Ohnstad lit his pipe and blew small grey clouds towards the rafters. 'Well?'

Silje opened the door and stepped aside to allow her brother, seething, out into the night.

'I will pay you tomorrow, Grette,' Jon Ohnstad said.

Grette nodded, and told Kvist he must clean the floor again.

* * *

'You embarrassed me,' Magnus said, 'in front of all our friends.'

Jon Ohnstad puffed heartily on his pipe. Silje stopped to pick orchids that grew wild between the taverns and cottages.

'I am a priest!'

'Not yet you're not.'

'I am a priest and I think that should command a level of respect. Don't you?'

Jon Ohnstad called out to Silje, telling her to keep up. 'She is right, Magnus. You should not have left.'

'I could not stay and watch any longer.'

'I do not understand.'

'I could not stay and watch you both turning your lives and Fólkvangr into a shrine to Mother.'

Silje appeared alongside them and handed the orchids to her father. Jon Ohnstad smiled, a small thing he did so rarely.

'I thought they might inspire you,' she said proudly. 'Help you think of more colours.'

'That is most thoughtful of you, Daughter.'

'It is *unusually* thoughtful,' Magnus added.

'Are you saying I am selfish? I am not the one who left.'

'I went to find a life for myself. Is that so wrong?'

Their father sighed and walked on. He took a lamp from his bag as they approached the Monument. Silje was not surprised when he stopped at the circle of stones and peered at the orchids. Her father would notice such things; others would not.

'Who would dare?'

'It was Marit,' Silje said. 'She was here when I came down from the hills.'

Her father plucked the headless flower from the circle and closed his eyes. 'She did this?'

'They are only flowers, Father,' said Magnus.

'How can you say that? They are a memory of our mother! How can you be so unfeeling, Magnus? Is this the compassion they teach at the seminary?'

'I carry our mother in my heart, Silje, not in a stone circle.'

'And that is all you do to repay the love she bestowed on you, on all of us? Father has created a new flower for her and her alone. He has nurtured it and shaped it so it is a lasting monument to her. And I have—'

'And what have you done, Silje? What have you done that makes Mother smile down upon you and not me?'

'I do whatever I can for the village she loved.'

'Quiet, both of you.' Jon Ohnstad carefully placed the stem into his bag and wiped his hands on his knees. 'I remember that you both helped me build this memorial, fifteen years ago. I remember how you both swore you would not eat until it was finished. I remember you, Magnus, cutting and polishing each stone until it was a perfect fit. And you, Silje; you chose each flower. "That one," you would say, "because inside it is the colour of her lips", or "That one, because its petals are pale like her skin."' He licked his lips and relit his pipe. 'It seems you have both forgotten.' He carried on walking to the stone archway where Fólkvangr ended and the mountains began. 'I will replace the flower, Silje, but Magnus is right. We will not always be here to take care of the circle, and when we are gone the flowers will die and the stones will crumble. But your mother will endure in our hearts and in the hearts of your children, and the hearts of their children.' He opened his arms, and Magnus embraced him warmly. Silje, however, sidestepped his embrace and began the hill trek by herself.

'The stone circle will stay, and I will look after the flowers even if you tire of doing so, Father.'

'Silje, I simply meant that—'

'And as for you, Brother; you are a priest and so you will not be having any children.' She took off her shoes and turned to the east, looking for familiar trees shadowed in the twilight.

She stopped at a narrow outcropping that reached out over the pine forests, and there she waited for her father, who in turn waited for her brother.

'It is as black as tar out here,' Magnus said. 'How do you do it?'

'It isn't yet dark, Magnus, and if you'd spent time more time outside when we were children then you'd know how to find your way home at dusk.'

Jon Ohnstad looked beyond the forest and down to the base of the mountain holding Bergen in its cradle.

'I see fires,' he said.

Silje moved closer to the edge and followed his gaze. It was true; small pinpricks of light stood out in the harbour and in the main town. She could hear the sound of gunshots, carried on the mountain winds. She thought she could hear screaming...

'Tomorrow, I will travel to the town,' Jon Ohnstad announced. 'I have friends there; I would see that they are unharmed.'

'You will do no such thing,' said Silje.

'The hat-maker lives near the harbour. He has been a friend of this family for many years.'

'Father, he is Jewish. He is lost.'

Again, the look, she thought, and wondered why, this night, so many had gazed upon her as though the true Silje Ohnstad had been spirited away by trolls.

'I will help him if I can,' Jon Ohnstad said without taking a stern eye away from his daughter. 'He would do no less for me. He would do no less for the both of you.'

'At least wait a few days, until things have settled.'

'Silje—'

'She is right, Father.' Magnus looked solemnly at the fires burning in the town below. 'The Germans will be suspicious of anyone approaching the town now. You cannot help Mr Dorfmann if you are detained.'

Jon Ohnstad looked to his son, who stared back without blinking, and then to Silje who nodded her agreement. 'Then I will go two days from now,' he said. 'And I will travel alone.'

'No,' said Silje. 'We will all travel, together.'

5

I was thinking that I'd seen enough coach stations during my life to put together a small guide book: *The Fugitive's Guide to Bus Terminals*. I had a few of which I thought of fondly in a strange sort of way. Trondheim was cold but well lit; I could read there, and I remember an ice-cream vendor who'd given me a free mint fudge even though I'm sure he'd recognised Monica. Narvik was nice, but not nearly as clean as Holmestrand which lacked the homeliness of Drammen. I was trying to decide between Drammen and Narvik when Monica spoke to me for the first time in eight hours. Since we'd arrived at the terminus she'd sat next to me in a wounded silence, watching the black and white metal boxes shuttle in and depart. The first two fingers of her left hand crossed and uncrossed, searching the air for a cigarette.

I offered her one of mine. She took it without a word and waited for me to light it. She inhaled deeply and sighed.

Two more coaches departed and a group of young nuns walked past, giggling. Monica watched them, trying to decide if they were laughing at us.

'Okay, you're right, maybe. It was a long time ago, and my memory isn't as good as it used to be.'

Her memory was perfect. Always had been.

'So it's possible, yes. In a moment of desperation, I might have gone down on him a little bit.'

'Mother, for God's sake…'

'And if I did, and I'm not saying I did for sure, then I did it for you.'

'Excuse me?'

'Everything I have done, everything I will do, is to keep you safe, Brigit. And if you're leaving because you're ashamed of me then—'

'It's not why I'm going, and you know it.'

The night before had been the worst of our lives. She'd accused me of betrayal; I'd accused her of lying about that night in the farmer's cottage; she'd accused me of lying about what had happened at *The Echo.* She'd hung steadfast to her untruth and so I'd clung like a mad dog to mine.

She'd said I'd always been an ungrateful child, and I'd asked her – no – screamed at her if there was anything she wouldn't do to preserve this life of ours. *If I hadn't come back, how far would you have gone? Would I have found you in our bed, fucking him?*

And of course she'd hit me, again. I think she'd realised then that we'd been together like this for far too long.

She drew on her cigarette and stared at the advertising boarding ahead of us. It was telling us now was the time to think about a bank account. I wondered what it would be like, to be tethered to something else for the rest of my life.

'All I'm saying is that if I did—'

'Fine! It's fine! It's all fine! I believe you!'

I slid to the other end of the bench, folded my arms and crossed my legs away from her.

We sat looking in opposite directions until an old man, carrying a newspaper and a brown paper bag, sat between us. He smiled at us both then hunkered down into his over-sized coat to read the sports pages.

'And I would suck a mountain of cock,' Monica said, 'if that's what it takes to keep you safe.'

I tried to shoot her an enraged, nauseous look, but the old man was in my way. He swallowed and licked his lips.

'Well,' he said, smiling wretchedly, 'if that's not love then I don't know what is.'

I told him to mind his own business, but it was too late; the ice had been broken.

'I—I thought I recognised you both,' he said. 'You're his daughter, aren't you? The Traitor of Fólkvangr.'

I got to my feet and kicked my suitcase onto its wheels.

Monica followed me across the concourse. I could hear her laughing and saying she was sorry.

'This is a joke to you then, is it?'

'No, of course not.'

'Living like this is a comedy now?'

'Brigit, you have no—'

'Well here's a new plan: we can sell ourselves as a radio show. People can tune in, every Tuesday, and listen to the oh-so-hilarious adventures of Monica and Brigit as they walk, bus and train across the country, trying to escape from family history and Monica's enormous ego.'

I caught sight of the old man's reflection in the ticket-office glass. He'd folded up his paper and was talking to a handful of passers-by. He was excited; he was pointing at us. Some of his audience glanced at us, some stared, some whispered back to him. He seemed to swell in his seat, feeding on the attention. But no one came to spit at us, or swear at us. No one ran to find a policeman to arrest us for my father's crimes.

Monica drew level, and I told her we were better off apart.

'That isn't true. We're stronger and safer together.'

'They know us as two women. If we separate then we're different people. They'll leave us alone.'

'Look, just stop and think for a minute.'

The bus to Oslo pulled away from its bay and crawled slowly towards its pickup. The queue began to show signs of life, so I went to join them.

'You need me, Brigit,' she said, running to stay at my side. 'When have you ever been on your own? Do you even know what you're looking for in Oslo? Your father? Why do you think he's there?'

'I don't know where he is, but Oslo is a good place to start. They've gathered everything written about Fólkvangr at the Resistance Museum.'

She took hold of my arms, tightly, burying her nails into my skin. I pulled away. 'What the hell, Mother!'

'Yes, that's right. I'm your mother, and I'm just trying to make you understand that everything I've done, everything we've been through—'

'I do understand, but it doesn't matter. I'm leaving and I'm scared, and I would like you to hold me for a little while before I go. Do you think you could do that one small thing?'

Her jaw set and she turned away from me.

'Okay, well… I'm going anyway.'

Monica walked away without so much as a look. I bit into my lower lip to stop myself calling after her, clawed my toes inside my shoes to stop myself chasing her down.

'Are you coming or not?'

I looked up to see the bus driver giving me his most bored and impatient look.

The queue had stowed itself aboard and half of it was looking down at me in much the same way as the driver.

'We haven't got all day.'

I dragged the suitcase onto the bus and handed him my ticket. He ignored it, glanced at me and then looked again. He was about to say something but thought better of it.

I made my way to the back of the bus, looking for a shadow to hide in. The driver pulled away before I'd found a seat. I scanned the terminus for her, looking in the waiting rooms and the ticket hall. I couldn't see her. I guessed she'd already left the station. I had a vague memory of all this being my idea, but still couldn't escape the feeling I'd been abandoned, that it was *she* who'd left *me* at a terminus, and then made her way home without once looking back.

6

Silje arrived home one afternoon to find a truck laden with the dourest of young men waiting outside the Ohnstad cottage. Four of them she recognised: Benjamin Tofte, Sander Ronning and the Nore twins. The other three were unknown to her; they were smooth-skinned and their hands looked soft; town-dwellers, Silje decided, perhaps from Bergen or Laksevåg.

'Hello, Benjamin.'

'Silje.' Benjamin Tofte turned bright red as soon as she said his name. His right foot began to shake.

'Who are your friends?'

'Never you mind, young lady,' said the oldest of them, still not yet in his thirties.

The rest of them stared at the floor of the truck.

'And where are you all going?'

None replied, and Silje wondered if Fólkvangr was becoming a village of mutes. She scowled at Benjamin and went inside the cottage, where she found both Magnus and her father fuming at each other across the kitchen table. Magnus's haversack was packed and resting against his leg.

'Oh no, Magnus,' Silje said. 'You promised.'

'I promised nothing.'

'We were going to travel to Bergen together!'

'Tell him.' Her father's face was so red, Silje was afraid his heart would give way. 'Tell him he is being ridiculous.'

'Why?' she said. 'Magnus, what are you going to do?'

Both men were silent.

'No! Do not do this! Tell me what is going on.'

Magnus told her he was going away for a few days.

'No!'

'I promise I will come back soon. You will not even know I've gone.'

'I always know when you're gone!'

He hauled his belongings onto his back.

'Come, Silje,' Jon Ohnstad said. 'We will still travel to Bergen together.'

'Tell him, Father!'

'He has made up his mind.'

Magnus kissed her on the cheek as he left, and Silje thought that his skin seemed so cold – as though his soul had frozen through. He closed the door after him and a few moments later they heard the truck move away.

'They are the Resistance, aren't they?'

Jon Ohnstad nodded. 'I imagine they will be.'

'And you did not stop him?'

'I tried, Silje. though perhaps not as hard as I should have. Perhaps because if I were a younger man then I would be with them.'

'You cannot mean that.'

But the discussion was done. He walked out of the house and climbed into his truck, with a tearful Silje at his heels.

* * *

They travelled the road to Bergen in silence, save for Silje's petulant huffing. Jon Ohnstad drove slowly, his attention on the road.

'They have not set up checkpoints yet,' he said.

A number of buildings had been destroyed near the outskirts of the town, but everything seemed more or less as she remembered. She was relieved in a strange sort of way; she could not see why the Germans would be cruel without good reason.

Still, it worried her that the streets were almost deserted in the late afternoon. 'Where are all the people?' She looked at all the shops and houses as they rolled through the town, peering through any window without its curtains drawn or its netting down. German soldiers began to appear as they approached the harbour, their numbers increasing fivefold with every fifty yards they travelled.

'We should leave,' Silje said quietly.

'Not yet.'

There were more locals near the harbour, though still not as many as there should have been. They gazed at the truck, despair etched deep into their weathered faces.

'Father, please.'

Jon Ohnstad stopped the truck when a German soldier raised his hand.

The soldier walked to the cab and spoke in very precise Norwegian: 'You may not take your truck any further than this point.'

Jon Ohnstad said he understood.

'You are here for the speech?'

He looked puzzled, but Silje said yes, they were.

'Good. Good. You may leave your truck over there.'

Jon Ohnstad did as he was told. They climbed down and followed a slow-moving procession of townspeople to the harbour front, where a large podium had been erected, from mountain wood birch if Silje wasn't mistaken. She wondered how the Germans had managed to coerce the local craftsmen so quickly, and then realised she didn't want to think about it at all.

Behind the podium stood a golden eagle perched atop a swastika.

'Come,' Jon Ohnstad said, taking her hand. They slipped from the crowd and retraced their steps, making a turn to follow the shops that ran alongside Bergen's main jetty.

'Inside, hurry.'

They entered the establishment of Aaron Dorfmann, Bergen's most prestigious maker of ladies' hats.

Aaron, a round and elderly Jew with brown eyes and not a trace of hair on his head, greeted them and shut the door as soon as they'd stepped inside. The Jew and Jon Ohnstad embraced, and Silje was quite taken aback; the only other man she'd ever seen him take to his breast was Magnus. She decided her father was becoming quite strange, and that perhaps it was due to the strains of war.

'It is good to see you, my friend,' Mr Dorfmann said. 'And you also, young Silje.' He pinched her cheek. 'I am afraid that your father has not done you justice; you are far prettier than I imagined.' He saw she was looking at the yellow star pinned to his jacket. 'This?' he said. 'This is so I know who and what I am. The Germans are concerned I may forget.'

'Dear God, Aaron,' Jon Ohnstad shook his head, 'you make light of this?'

The shop was small and furnished in a dark wood that swallowed the light coming in through its tiny windows. The blinds were drawn and only two of the six lamps were lit. It was only on a second glance that Silje saw a thin, pale girl labouring in one corner. She folded and pinned a lining to the inside of a small white hat, while staring into space. Her dark hair was tied into two thick braids that fell to her waist.

Silje crept over on her toes and watched her work.

The girl sniffed loudly, her nimble fingers blurring inside and around the hat, adding stitching and silks and feathers. Such was her skill and assuredness that Silje wondered if she truly was blind, as her father had once told her.

'It is rude to just stand there,' the girl said, startling her.

Silje coughed and looked back to her father and Mr Dorfmann, both deep in conversation. 'How did you know?'

'I am not deaf,' the girl replied. 'I heard my father greet you when you came in. You are "young Silje", are you not, though you do not sound so young.'

'Compared to you, I am not, no. Though it is hard to tell how old you are; you speak like an adult but you have the body of a child.'

'I apologise that I lack…' The girl stopped to search for a word; Silje braced herself. 'The robustness of a farm girl.'

'I am not… *robust*.'

'I am sorry; you sound robust.'

'And how do you know I am from a farm?'

The girl turned her head away. 'I know of your father.'

Lying, thought Silje, *as plain as day*. 'Did I see you smell the air when I approached?'

'No.'

'Yes you did.'

'I did not!'

'You did! I heard you! I saw you!'

The girl shrank, trying to disappear from view. 'You live on a farm in the mountains,' she said quietly. 'The air from your home travels with you.'

Silje stood in silence, thinking of the myriad ways she disliked this child.

'It is the goats, most probably,' the blind girl continued, though there was little need. 'I understand that Fólkvangr has a lot of goats.'

'I have no idea why people think that,' Silje said hotly. 'We have a perfectly acceptable number of goats.'

The girl ran her fingers lightly around the hat's brim. It was the most beautiful hat Silje had ever seen, though now she did not feel inclined to say so.

The girl smiled somewhere into space. 'Do not worry; I am sure that no one else will notice.'

'Why thank you.' Silje could see the girl's arms were quite hirsute and took comfort in that. 'So,' she said, wiping her nose on her sleeve, 'have you been blind long?'

'Since I was a child,' the girl replied as though the question were asked of her at least once a day.

'Then you have no idea what you look like.'

'I know exactly what I look like.'

'And yet you have done nothing to remedy it.'

The girl placed the hat to one side and took a deep breath. 'I expect you are smiling now.'

'Yes,' said Silje. 'I expect I am.'

The girl picked up the beginnings of another hat. 'Perhaps you should go. I have much to do, and the smell is making it hard for me to concentrate.'

Silje would have loved dearly to reach over and slam the girl's head against the workbench. Instead, she snorted loudly and returned to the front of the shop.

'Where are you going?' her father asked.

'For a walk,' she snapped. 'I will be back soon.'

She left without saying goodbye to Mr Dorfmann, and took the longer path back to the podium. The crowd was large, colourless and surrounded by German troops. She smiled at one of the troopers, who moved aside to allow her to stand near the edge of the dais. The crowd fell silent as a loud scratching noise split the air, followed by the first strains of the German national anthem, and then a muted round of applause as a line of German officers took to the stage. They arranged themselves neatly according to rank and then stepped back. The man who was left at the podium was small, though handsome in a distinguished way. Although the men all wore similar uniforms, his seemed smarter, as though he'd been born wearing it and it had simply grown with him. He put on his spectacles, adjusted his tunic and placed his speech on the podium.

'Greetings, all of you.' His voice reached out across the crowd, even without a microphone. 'I am General Karl Gruetzmacher of the Third Reich, and you are now liberated.' He did not wait for applause, which Silje took as a sign of jaded realism. 'I am responsible for maintaining order and discipline in Bergen and the towns as far north as Hordvik and as far south as Osøyro.' He stopped and waited for his aide to turn the page. 'Whether I am successful in maintaining the rule of law will have surprisingly little to do with you.'

Silje noted that the aide was very young, barely out of his teens, yet his insignia indicated he was an officer of some sort.

'This will not be a war like the last,' the General continued. 'It will be over soon, and how you behave now, as subjects of the Fatherland, will dictate how you are treated when victory is ours. It is our intention to make this a very short war; do not incur our displeasure by embroiling yourselves in it.' Again he paused, this time to look out over the crowd, searching eyes and faces for signs of dissent.

He continued with a long and complex list of rules concerning curfew and the movement of the Jews, and indeed what defined a Jew, while Silje tried to catch the eye of his aide. Quite by mistake, she caught the eye of the General who smiled back without pausing in his speech. He spun neatly into the evils of the Jewish way of life and how it was draining the blood from the European continent. He likened the Jews to vampires, which he noted were perhaps not as mythical as people believed. After all, vampires were of Romany origin – a people that shared the traits of nomadism and night-wandering that were common amongst the Semites, and so perhaps the notion of these creatures stealing into the homes of decent people to drain the blood of their children was not so far-fetched after all.

'But we are not a cruel people,' he went on, not seeming to care whether he was believed or not. 'We understand that Judaism is an unfortunate accident of birth, and not a life any sane man would choose to make for himself. Yes we will do our sacred duty before God, by separating the Jew from the decent people of Norway. But that does not mean the Jew will be sold into slavery or hidden from the light of day.' He clicked his fingers. The aide stepped forward and handed him a pen which the General used to make a note on his speech.

The crowd waited patiently. Gruetzmacher cleared his throat and read out a list of orders for registration and transportation. He emphasised that this was a compulsory command with immediate effect and no process of appeal. He finished his speech with a paragraph detailing Scandinavia's new and glorious dawn under the leadership of Vidkun Quisling. Silje hardly noticed for she had, at last, caught the aide's eye, causing him to blush.

With his speech over, the General took a moment to study the reaction of his audience. Silje too turned to look; all she could see was the same sea of passive, defeated faces, stretching back as far as the clothes market. But Gruetzmacher saw something else; he sighed, shook his head and stepped down from the stage. He walked past Silje, accompanied by six stormtroopers in black uniforms. He stopped to speak to Mr Hoen, Bergen's mayor. Silje moved as close as she dared to hear their conversation.

'I see the beginnings of revolt in your townspeople,' Gruetzmacher was saying. 'See that it does not get out of hand.'

Without waiting for Mr Hoen's reply, the General climbed into his staff car and tapped his driver on the shoulder to move on.

Gruetzmacher's aide was still at the podium, gathering papers and ordering the soldiers to dismantle the stage. Silje watched him; his uniform was not a particularly good fit. In fact, his demeanour suggested that he didn't wear the mantle of 'warrior' particularly well. Still, he was diligent and his men seemed to respect him in spite of his shortcomings. Perhaps it is because he is a firm but fair hand to them, she thought. She believed the General shared the same trait.

The stage was taken apart in silence and with alarming efficiency; the German Standard was taken down last of all and placed reverently in the back of a truck. The soldiers climbed aboard while the aide answered the questions of the Jews who had been brave enough to step forward.

How long will we be gone?

'You will not return.'

But my home is here!

'Your new home will be in Poland.'

What of our belongings?

'They will be sent on after you leave.'

But you have not asked us to mark our possessions. How will you—?

'This will all be explained to you when you register.'

The truck driver sounded the horn.

'I must leave, but if you have any further questions then please contact the Reich Office.'

'And where is that?'

'We will be using Bergen's town hall for the duration of our stay.'

And how long will you be staying?

'Until this is over.'

The horn sounded again, and Silje saw her opportunity slipping away. She pushed her way through and took the aide by the hand.

'Follow me,' she said. 'You are in danger.'

The Jews looked about them, as if to say, *From whom?*

The aide looked at her, and Silje smiled in the way that she knew made her eyes shine; his hand seemed to melt into hers. She began to lead him away from the crowd.

'Where are we going, Fräulein?'

'Somewhere private,' Silje replied.

'I am afraid I cannot.'

The driver leaned out of the cab and said, 'Lieutenant, you do not have to reassure these scum! We must get back to—' He saw Silje, and a slow, leering grin split the lower part of his face. 'I apologise, Lieutenant. I did not realise you were speaking to a local.'

'I am not a local,' said Silje.

'Then I apologise to you, Fräulein.'

Silje could tell he did not mean it.

'I have to go,' the aide said, clearly on the verge of panic.

'No, you do not,' the driver said.

'Yes, I do!'

'I will wait for ten minutes, Lieutenant; not a moment more.'

A cheer of encouragement raised itself from the back of the truck.

Silje blushed.

And so did the Lieutenant.

'You heard what he said.' Silje took him by the hand. 'We have only ten minutes.' She led him back through the group of townspeople and towards a narrow passageway lined with wooden shop fronts and stone apartment buildings. A maze of winding alleyways took them to a dead end far from German and Norwegian eyes. Silje pushed the officer against the wall and placed her hand over his mouth. His eyes grew wide; he began fumbling for his pistol so she drove her fist into his elbow joint – something she'd seen Grette do to end fights at *The Mottled Goat*. The aide's scream burst silently against her hand, and his gun arm fell limp. Silje worked quickly, unfastening his breeches and reaching inside. His eyes rolled upward as she took hold of him, digging her nails into his flesh and quickly raising his erection with long firm strokes.

'What is your name?' She took her hand away from his mouth.

'Klein,' he croaked. 'Lieutenant Kl—'

'Your first name.'

'Gerbald.'

'Do you like this, Gerbald?'

'Yes.'

'How much do you like this?' She squeezed harder.

'I… I like it very much, Fräulein.'

'Good. I am glad that you like it. How old are you?'

'I am twenty.'

'You are young for an officer.'

His knees started to weaken; Silje pushed him back against the wall and held him there by his throat.

'I think you and I will be great friends, Gerbald.'

'I… hope so.'

'I hope so too. And I trust you, Gerbald. Do you trust me?'

'I don't know.'

She felt him stiffen further so she slowed her pace. 'I led you here, and you followed. So I think you trust me.'

'Yes… I suppose…'

'That is good, Gerbald. That is very good. I want to help you. I want to help you and the General. And we can help each other if we trust each other, yes?'

'Yes.'

He lacks experience, Silje thought, and stamina; *I must hurry.* 'You will tell me things, and I will tell you things, Gerbald.'

'I do not understand.'

'We will keep each other informed of things that concern us. You will use this knowledge to keep the peace; I will use this knowledge to keep my family and my village safe. The General will hold you in high regard when you bring him this information. Now, do you understand?'

He nodded, and with a cry that sounded as though he were being tortured, he was done.

'Good. That is very good, Gerbald.'

He sank to his haunches, sliding from Silje's grip, choking.

'Breathe, slowly.'

He fell to his hands and knees and tried to draw air from the ground.

'That was your first?'

He nodded again.

'You did very well, Gerbald. Now do you have a handkerchief or a scarf; something you won't need back.'

* * *

When Silje arrived back at Aaron Dorfmann's millinery, the proprietor and her father were waiting anxiously outside, Dorfmann gently restraining Jon Ohnstad with a hand upon his shoulder.

Her father shouted at her, something he rarely did. 'Where have you been, you stupid little girl?' Shaking himself free of the milliner's grip, he threw his arms around her and held so close she could not breathe. She closed her eyes. *No matter what may come,* she reminded herself, *my father will always love me.* And the thought made her dizzy with joy.

'He was going to kill every German he saw until he found you,' Dorfmann said, lighting his pipe. 'There is a cleverness about you, Silje Ohnstad; I told him that whatever trouble you found yourself in, you would get yourself out.'

Finally, Jon Ohnstad found the strength of will to let her go.

'I will take my daughter home now,' he said. 'I think that we have had enough of Bergen for today.'

Silje nodded happily and flexed her fingers; her hand ached from servicing the lieutenant. She wondered if she could persuade Erik to milk the goats for her that evening.

They said their goodbyes and set off for the truck. Silje looked back at the little shop and waved once more to Mr Dorfmann. She decided she liked the hat-maker, even if the devil himself was welcome to his daughter.

7

The bus driver proudly announced he'd gotten us into Oslo eight minutes early.

I'd endured the company of an elderly couple for most of the trip. They showed me pictures of their children and grandchildren and finished each other's sentences while they told me of the lives they'd led during the war. He'd been a Resistance fighter – a decorated one at that. She'd been a school mistress who'd refused to teach Quisling's brand of Nazism to the children in her care. As a reward for her defiance she, and ten of her colleagues, had been placed on a train bound for Belsen.

'And this brave, brave man,' she said, squeezing his trembling hand, the light of love still shining in her watery eyes, 'came to my rescue.'

'Couldn't let them take her,' he said. 'Best teacher in the district.'

They laughed though they'd heard him say it a thousand times before. When I told them I was going to visit the Resistance Museum they were puzzled.

'It isn't open yet, is it?'

I said I was going to ask to see their archives. 'I lost a member of my family; I hope they might have something that'll tell me what happened to him.'

He said, 'You seem young to have lost family during the war.'

I told him I'd lost everything during the war.

We said our goodbyes at the terminus, and I hurried to find a telephone. I'd told Monica that she should be at the public phone box outside our apartment; I'd call at six.

I tried the number for a good half-hour; she didn't pick up.

I wondered if something had happened to her; perhaps she'd been recognised, attacked. Perhaps she was lying in a hospital somewhere, or in a ditch after being cornered by the sons of a Survivor. I thought about going back, getting on the same bus returning to Trondheim; or I could get a taxi – I had enough money. This had been a mistake, a terrible mistake. I spun out the number again and waited, hope against hope. I still had time; the bus wouldn't leave for another ten minutes.

And then she answered.

'Brigit?'

I took a deep breath, forced myself to speak calmly. 'Where were you?' I said, both angry and relieved.

'I'm sorry,' she said flatly, and I knew; she'd been there all the time listening to the phone ringing.

'Why didn't you pick up?'

'I was angry and I didn't know why. And then I realised that you—'

'I miss you.' I shouted so loudly that a circle of drivers nearby turned to look at me. 'I'm coming back. I'll get the next bus back to Trondheim.'

She said nothing for a time, long enough for me to think she'd just gone and left the receiver hanging.

'You'll do no such thing. You're going to finish this because you're right. Because I should have done this myself. This has gone on for far too long.'

'But what if *you're* right. What if they hate us so much that—'

'Then we'll turn and face them, Brigit. We'll stand our ground. And if you find your father, he'll face them too. He owes us that.'

'Then come to Oslo. We can do this together.'

I heard her inhale sharply, all the way from Trondheim. It was the same breath she always took before shattering my dreams.

Get your things, Brigit; we're leaving.

No we can't live here... Because I say so!

Get your things together, Brigit; we have to leave... now!

I have talked with your father and he said he doesn't want to see us; it would be too 'difficult'. I am so sorry, Brigit.

Leave that, Brigit! We have to go!

'I can't do this with you, Brigit,' she said. 'I'm sorry.'

I bit into my lip and waited for her to explain. As always, nothing came; what is, is – as she was so fond of saying.

'I will be here at the same time every night,' she said. 'Just call me and we can talk for as long—'

'That's not enough. I want you here, now – with me.'

She sighed again. 'Brigit, I can't.'

So I hung up the telephone. I think I must've stood gazing at it for a while before I took myself to a café and sat down. I ordered a black coffee, and a bowl of ice cream, and I started to cry, and for the first time in my life Monica wasn't there to stop me.

* * *

'First time in Oslo?' the driver asked for the second time.

'No, I've passed through here before.'

'Can get cold.'

'Yes, who would have thought it in Norway?'

He stole another glance through his mirror; I could see lines of concentration scoring into his brow; he was desperately trying to place me.

'Business or pleasure?' he asked.

'Neither.'

He laughed and geared down, pointing the car in the direction of the military academy. 'So you're not here for business and you're not here for pleasure. That doesn't leave you much to do in Oslo.'

'Except for research,' I said.

'Well, I would have said that counted as business, but I suppose you could say—'

'I'm Brigit Brenna.'

The car came to a screeching halt. I slammed my hand into the headrest to stop myself being pitched over the passenger seat. The air filled with the sound of car horns while the taxi driver adjusted the mirror so he could take a good long look at me. He scratched his nose, restarted the engine and we were moving again. He stayed quiet while I felt strangely empowered; I'd spent my whole life hiding myself as best I could. And now, after only a few hours away from my mother, I was shouting our wretched name from the rooftops.

'So your father is—'

'Yes, he is.'

'The Traitor of Fólkvangr.'

People like to say it, even when they don't have to.

'Then can I ask you a question?'

'I don't imagine for a minute I can stop you.'

'What business could you possibly have at the Resistance Museum?'

'I'm looking for someone.'

'Who?'

'My father.'

'Oh.' He made a right turn and drove past the academy gardens.

'The museum seemed like the best place to start.'

'Right.'

'And I can't think of anywhere else to begin.'

'Well, you may have come to the right place,' he said, stopping the cab at the museum steps. 'Head straight for the basement; there's someone there who may be able to help you.'

'How do you know?'

'Most of Oslo knows; he's something of an exhibit himself.'

I thanked him and dragged my luggage up the four stairs to the museum entrance. On the other side of the glass doors, a security guard told me that the museum wasn't open to the public yet.

'You're looking for volunteers.'

He nodded. 'What can you do?'

'I can help.'

He rubbed his chin and then disappeared for a few minutes without saying a word. I waited, feeling the cold whip around my legs.

I was hopping from one foot to the other when he came back and opened the door. 'No one here to speak to you, I'm afraid, but the old fella saw you on the monitor.'

'The old fella?'

'Says he'd like to talk to you.' He moved aside so I could step past him. 'I need to take your case though.'

My chest tightened and my mouth went dry.

'Security,' the guard said crisply. 'There's no need to worry; we'll take good care of it.'

The further I walked from my old life, the more lost I became. I understood why Monica sometimes cried when we had to sell things so we could eat; everyone needs an anchor – her wedding band was hers, she was mine, and now all I had left of us was the suitcase.

A short and narrow flight of stairs led down to the basement, a large, dimly-lit floor space telling the story of Norway at war through a maze of picture-covered walls and glass cabinets filled with relics, sketches and photographs. One of the glass cases contained a model of the ship the Germans used to transport Norwegians to labour camps; another contained the striped tunics worn by the Norwegian Jews transported to their deaths. Every exhibit told a story of courage and sacrifice that left me numb. I should have felt more: anger, pride, sorrow; but it just seemed so far removed from me, or perhaps I believed that I'd already had been through my own share of suffering because of the war.

I wandered through history until I came across the shrine the curators had laid out for Fólkvangr. Unlike the rest of the floor, the Fólkvangr exhibit was lit to draw people to it. It was the penultimate exhibit you would see before leaving, a shining testament to those who were brave and true to Norway until the very end. Every name was there: Soren, Kolsberg, Von der Lippe, Staffe, Nilsen, Ohnstad…

My father's picture hung on the wall of traitors, a black space next to the toilets and the exit. They'd placed him next to Quisling, his portrait illuminated in demonic red. There were score marks near the frame and across his neck; the picture had been attacked even before the museum had opened, yet no one had thought to replace it.

I looked up to see an ancient face staring at me, reflected in the glass. His skin was milk-white where it wasn't mottled with liver spots. His eyes, dulled by misery, continued to stare at the back of my head as I moved away from my father's portrait. He wore a plain brown suit and a brown tie, and he stood tall, which made me think that he was ex-military and not as old as he first appeared. I turned and headed back the way I'd come. I stopped and pretended to look at the equipment exhibit.

'They used it for transporting secret messages.' The old man tapped on the glass, and I looked down to see what he was pointing at: a long thin metal cylinder, polished to a mirror shine, and rounded at both ends.

'Are you following me?'

'You seemed a little lost.' He smiled crookedly and turned his attention back to the exhibit. 'Actually, I think you may be looking for me. Brigit, isn't it?'

I nodded. 'And you are…?'

He sniffed and tapped on the glass again. 'Ingenious when you think about it.'

I looked at the cylinder. 'Hiding messages in cigar cases?'

'Where they hid the cigar cases, that's the ingenious part.'

'Oh.'

'There were places even the Nazis were loath to search. Follow me.' He limped away, one hand behind his back. I followed, strangely grateful for having someone to tell me what to do.

'You still haven't told me your name.'

'I wondered if you'd ever come here. I wondered if either of you would ever have the courage.' He stopped at a small wooden door that was almost hidden by a case containing the camp tunics. 'You should have come sooner.'

I wanted to say that I couldn't, that the place wasn't open yet, but before I could speak he opened the door and disappeared inside. I followed him, and found myself in another part of the basement that was easily as large as the one I'd just left. Bundles of paper were tied and stacked up to the ceiling; ancient artefacts ranging from pens to jackboots lay scattered around the floor. The old man walked unsteadily to his desk which lay at the centre of the chaos. He sat heavily in his chair. Several books lay open on the desk, along with a dismantled Luger pistol. 'I've been cataloguing this crap for five years,' he said. 'It just keeps coming in. You'd think the Nazis were here for centuries judging by the amount of shit they left behind.' He started wheezing and I realised that the room had a cloying, damp feel about it.

'I'm looking for my father.'

'Well, he's not here.'

'He left the country. He wasn't a clever man so I think someone helped him, maybe a sympathetic Norwegian, or maybe a German.'

The old man raised an eyebrow and made a show of dusting down his trousers. 'He may not be alive.'

'Oh, he's alive. He has to be.'

He scratched his chin and a flurry of dead skin snowed down onto his desk.

'I don't know anything about him,' I said, 'but I need to learn everything there is to know if I'm going to find him.'

He looked at me through dull, wet eyes. 'Would you like a cup of tea?'

I refused, through force of habit more than anything else.

He shrugged and produced a flask from somewhere by his feet. He placed it in front of him and switched on the table lamp, training the light on the disassembled Luger.

'Do you know what they say about sleeping dogs, Miss Fossen?'

I had no idea what he was talking about.

'So you want to change your life. And how will tracking down your father help with that?'

'I don't know. I just want to—'

'You just want to find him so that Norway will punish him instead of you.'

Perhaps his eyes weren't as clouded as they looked. 'Who are you?'

He looked down the barrel of the assembled Luger and pulled the trigger. The click echoed around the chamber and died away. 'I will not tell you.' He picked up a pen and began scribbling something on a notepad. 'But I have some things I keep at home which may help you.' He thrust the paper in my direction. 'Come tomorrow morning at ten o'clock. I will make you breakfast; you look like you need it.'

'Is this a joke?'

'Do I strike you as a joker?' He waved the paper.

Of course I didn't trust him. I couldn't, but he was an old man and there was nothing between me and the door.

And besides, I could always scream.

I took a tentative step forward, and then another. I snatched the note from his hand.

'Ten o'clock,' he said, amused and making no attempt to hide it. 'Do not be late.'

'I'll think about—'

'One other thing; it's probably best you do not ask anyone who I am.'

'Really. And why would that be?'

'Because if you knew my name, young lady, I'm not sure you'd come.'

* * *

There was an Astoria Hotel just a few miles north-east of the museum. It wasn't cheap but I still had plenty of money from blackmailing Strande, even after I'd given half of it to Monica.

I ate alone in the hotel's restaurant, just fish soup and a bread roll. I waited in the lobby until six and then tried to call her. She didn't pick up, and I didn't feel like trying again. I wandered into the bar, perched myself on the stool closest to the exit, and ordered a vodka and lime. The bar was empty except for a group of business types seated around a large coffee table. The men were trying too hard; the women smiled politely but looked bored. One of the older men caught me staring, a second of eye contact which his tiny mind translated into an invitation. He picked up his drink and slid across the room to stand next to me. I looked behind him, though I'm not sure why; I think I was expecting to see some sort of mucus trail.

'You seem to be on your own,' he said.

'I prefer it that way, thank you.'

'I don't think you do. Why don't you come and join us? We don't bite.'

'I'd rather not.'

He narrowed his eyes to get a better look at me. 'Wait a minute. I know you.'

'I don't think you—'

'Don't say anything. I'll have it in a second.' He massaged the bridge of his nose while he sieved through his memory. His lips moved, apparently outside his control.

'Look, I really should be leaving.'

'You're that Fossen woman, aren't you?'

There seemed little point in denying it. I nodded and stepped down from my seat.

'Then I insist! You really must come and join us.' He smiled, a little too inanely, and tried to take my hand.

'Come on. We've been stuck on a pipeline materials conference for almost a week. We don't know each other and quite frankly, aside from tubular steel, we have nothing in common. Please, come over and take us out of ourselves. We won't judge. I'm Tor, by the way. What shall I call you?'

'Brigit is fine.' I took him at his word and carried my drink to the other side of the bar, dangerously far from my only exit point. Monica would've spit rivets if she'd seen me.

'Everyone, you will never believe who this.'

One of the women, a tall, rather round lady squeezed into a grey business suit, shrieked and leapt to her feet. 'Oh my good God! You're her, aren't you?'

'Yes, I suppose I am.'

'Nicely done, Kirsten,' said Tor.

Kirsten hopped out of the way and offered me her spot on the sofa. 'I have never ever ever met an honest-to-god celebrity.'

'Is that what you think I am?'

The others looked at each other, reached a silent majority and then looked back at me, nodding enthusiastically.

'I can't imagine what it must be like for you,' said a young man with receding blonde hair, who was the only one not wearing a jacket. He smiled, or grimaced; I wasn't sure which.

Then came the questions.

Do you blame your father?

Where is your mother?

What happened to your father?

Don't you get tired of being hounded?

Are you actually being hounded though? I mean, we're not hounding you, are we?

The surprising thing was that we only talked about me for five minutes. The conversation quickly turned to them and the shipwrecks they'd made of their lives. They hated their careers, all of them. They hated steel, especially steel shaped into cylinders, steel that would be used to move oil from one end of Norway to the other. I listened without saying much. They paid for all my drinks, which I felt a little guilty about because I still had plenty of money.

Harriet was a dark-skinned English woman in her early thirties, and I barely understood anything she said. She told me she was rich, the illegitimate daughter of a well-heeled gangster, and that she had 'dropped out of Cambridge and wound up in pipes'. Every time I spoke she squeezed my knee and said, 'You're lovely, you are. Do you know how lovely you are?' At first I thought she was attracted to me, but as the evening wore painfully on I realised she was just being patronising.

The other man was a watcher. He was grey, slim, in his fifties; he drank heavily, said nothing, but hung onto the few words I uttered when Harriet gave me the chance. I tried smiling at him once; he raised his glass, drained it and went to order more drinks.

The bartender closed up at around eleven, and alcohol withdrawal set in an hour later.

Half an hour after that, I struggled to my feet.

'You're not going?' Kirsten was horrified. 'We can find another bar.'

'Thank you, but I can't. Really.'

'Oh come on! I thought that's what you Norwegians did,' said Harriet. 'Get lubricated at home, then go out.'

Tor grumbled about the price of alcohol in Oslo.

Harriet said, 'You like us, don't you?'

'Of course I like you.' I wasn't entirely sure.

'Then come on!'

'She can't.' It was the first thing the Watcher had said all evening.

'My God, it speaks,' said Tor.

The Watcher ignored him. 'It could be dangerous, in a bar I mean. Someone might recognise her and…' an appropriately delicate phrase eluded him at first '… take offence. Is that right, Brigit?'

I nodded. 'Sorry.'

The Watcher finished his sixth whisky sour. Kirsten coughed, and Tor made a face like he was trying to eat his own teeth.

'I'm going to call it a night. Thank you. Feels like years since I've spoken to anybody.'

Harriet tried one last time. 'Evening's still young.'

'It's past midnight.' The Watcher didn't like Harriet; I'd only just noticed it.

I said my goodbyes and shook hands. Harriet stood up to kiss me on the cheek.

I staggered from the bar, picked up my room key from reception and made my way to the elevator. I stared blankly at the 'call' button, unable to remember what floor I was on. Not that it mattered: I couldn't remember my room number either. While I fumbled in my skirt pocket for the room key, a hand with long, yellowed fingers reached over me to tap the 'call' button.

'Hello,' said the Watcher.

I smiled and tried to read the key fob in the dim light.

'As you can see, we hate pipework.'

'So you do.' I peered at the key as though it were being deliberately obtuse.

'It's not the life any of us would have chosen.'

I said, 'Amen to that,' and he laughed, stopping suddenly to say, 'Come back to my room. Sleep with me.'

It wasn't that I was surprised he'd asked me; I was just taken aback by his… terseness. He stood frozen with his finger on the button and his eyes closed; he'd clearly surprised himself.

'Thanks,' I said, 'but I'm not planning on being anyone's souvenir conquest. Not tonight.'

He opened his eyes. 'It's not like that.'

'No? So tomorrow morning you won't tell the others you fucked the Traitor's daughter.'

He looked mortified, which was to his credit. The lift arrived and I stepped in. He followed and thumbed for the third floor. I pressed the button for the fifth.

'I don't normally—'

'Do things like this. Yes, I know.' I stared straight ahead.

'I just wanted—'

'To get laid.'

'Company! I don't know why I asked you like that. I'm so sorry.' He drew his hands down his face. 'God, I don't even want to sleep with you.'

'Then what the fuck do you want?'

He shrugged his shoulders. 'Just a friendly ear for a few hours.'

'But you've said nothing all night.'

'I know,' he said. 'I don't like them, any of them. But I like you. Look, I've spent the last five years on the road, talking about metal pipes. I drove around Scandinavia while my wife was sleeping with my boss and my daughter was sleeping with everyone else. My boss is still my boss and my wife is now *his* wife. She's happier than I've ever seen her, and my girl has stopped sleeping around because he's a better father to her than I ever was.'

When the elevator doors opened he stumbled out, landing heavily against the door opposite. He made two or three half-hearted attempts to insert his key in the lock, then just pressed his head against the door. He said he was sorry and that he was a mess, and then he said he was sorry for being a mess and embarrassing us both.

I gave him a minute to get it out of his system, the same minute Monica sometimes gave me. I said, 'That's enough.' After five years running from whatever he was running from, he should have been tempered; he should have been as hard and unyielding as the metal cylinders he peddled across Norway.

I took the key from him and opened the door. He fell into the room, landing face down on the carpet; I had to step over him to reach the bathroom, and once inside I locked myself in. I removed the belt from my skirt and ran a fingernail along its seam until I found the hiding place for my protection: a razor blade wrapped in foil. Monica had given it to me for my thirteenth birthday.

If you're trapped, she'd said, *and there really is no other way out, then take this, hold it tight between your thumb and first finger. Slash down across the hand that's holding you; that should be enough. If they don't let go, try for the cheek, but never the throat and never the eyes. A judge won't be sympathetic; you're Erik Brenna's daughter.*

I think I'd asked for a tape recorder.

I splashed cold water over my face and ran my fingers through my hair; a small handful came away, stuck to my palm. I stared at it for while before dropping it in the bin. I wished I had a toothbrush.

When I left the bathroom I found him sitting on the edge of the bed. His hands were clasped behind his neck and he was staring at the carpet.

'I'll stay,' I said.

He nodded. 'Thank you.'

'We can talk, then we can fuck, then I'll go. Understand?'

He nodded again, but still wouldn't look at me.

The Friends of Fólkvangr

(12th April 1940)

Editorial

Dear friends.

As many all of you will know, our beloved land now finds itself caught in the midst of a most hateful war. The Allies prepare to abandon us and the Germans have already moved inland from the coast and the harbours. The Nazis are well-trained, well-armed and they are great in number with more arriving by the hour, and the question in all our hearts is what, as proud Norwegians, should we do? Should we not take up arms and defend our mountain, our homes? Should Fólkvangr not become a shining beacon of hope and resistance for all of Norway? Shouldn't we, as un-trained, un-armed and mostly infirm dwellers of a small village in the hills, take Bergen by force and drive the invaders from our shores?

Dear friends, I respectfully submit that we should do no such thing. We are, after all, a village - and a small one at that.

The Germans have no interest in us, and I think we owe it to ourselves to ensure they continue to have no interest in us. So when we ask ourselves what should we do, then I think the answer is plain: survive. We should survive this terrible war.

The Allies have abandoned us, the Germans are here, and this conflict is none of our concern.

Now, other news. During my errands in the village, I may have mentioned that my tireless investigations had solved the mystery of Kvist Gundersen's missing ladder. Unfortunately, the ladder I found in the possession of Jonas Kleppe did, in fact, belong to Jonas Kleppe – though Mr Kleppe himself told me he had found it. I have no idea why he would deny ownership of his own ladder, but regardless, shame on you, Mr Kleppe!

8

'I am sorry, Silje. I cannot print this. Not this time.' Junges Fehn handed back the bundled sheets and moved to close his front door.

Silje placed her hand against it. 'I do not understand. You have never refused me before.'

'This piece is different.'

'I am a journalist,' Silje announced grandly. 'I am bound to speak the truth.'

'You speak of appeasement.' Junges replied. 'You speak of bowing our heads while these filthy sons of dogs rape our homeland.'

Silje looked back to the gate where Erik stood obediently holding her bicycle and pretending not to hear.

'I do not like the Germans any more than you do, but they are here and they are dangerous. I do not think we should do anything to place the village in peril.'

Lisbeth, Junges' daughter, appeared briefly at the window; she frowned at Silje and disappeared.

'Did she tell you not to print the newsletter?'

Junges stroked his beard and coughed.

'Yours is the only printing press between here and Bergen. Where else can I go?'

'That is not my concern, Silje. The things you said in *The Mottled Goat*, the things you say in your newsletter... Lisbeth is right; this is cowardice and I cannot condone it.'

'She has put you up to this,' Silje said. 'I knew as much. She is jealous of me, you know. She is jealous because I take after my mother and she takes after hers.'

'Have a care, Silje. This is my family you're talking about.'

Erik rang the bicycle's bell as the leathered, sour face of Mrs Fehn appeared at an upstairs window. She opened it and thrust her head out into the crisp, dew-laden morning. 'You are not welcome here, Silje Ohnstad! And is that you lurking by our fence, Erik Brenna? Take your strumpet and leave.'

'Silje, I think we should go.' Erik smiled sheepishly at the passers-by who slowed their pace as they walked by the cottage.

'Good morning, Mrs Fehn,' Silje said. 'And how are you today?'

Mrs Fehn scowled and went back inside, slamming the window after her.

'What does she mean "strumpet"?' Silje asked hotly.

'What does she mean?' Junges took her by the arm and led her away from his front door. Erik dropped the bicycle to the ground and vaulted the gate.

'Erik, I think Mr Fehn would just like a private chat.'

Erik demanded to know what kind of 'private chat'.

'The kind that does not concern you. Please watch my bicycle; there is still a thief in the village.'

'One stolen ladder will not lead us to the pit,' Erik mumbled, but still did as he was told.

Silje wrestled her arm free and walked herself around to the side of the cottage, away from the prying eyes and Erik's ears.

'Why should she call me that?'

'Because she knows, Silje,' Junges whispered through his teeth. Silje caught his breath and realised he'd been drinking. He ran his fingers through his thin wisps of grey hair and then cracked all his knuckles, one after the other. 'Because she has always known. She has chosen to stay silent until now. When Lisbeth told us what you said about leaving the Jews to the mercies of the Germans—'

'I never said that!'

'Lisbeth says that you did.'

'Then she is lying!'

'It does not matter.'

'It matters to me!'

'The point is,' Junges said, the strain to his patience making a vein in his temple throb, 'she knows. She knows that we were intimate. She knows that I was weak, and she now knows you did it only because you needed that old printing press in my barn. She knows that I am a pathetic excuse of a man.' He stared at Silje, his eyes stained pink, waiting for her to say something.

And Silje, fearing the loss of her printing press, chose to say something she hoped would save it: 'Did you tell her we were only intimate once?'

* * *

Erik was busying himself straightening the spokes on Silje's bicycle when she appeared from behind the cottage and walked briskly towards him.

'We're leaving,' she said, taking the bicycle and setting it on the road.

'Where is Mr Fehn?'

'In his barn, crying.'

'Crying?' Erik looked anxiously back towards the cottage. 'Is he all right?'

'I'm sure he'll be fine. Are you coming or not?'

Erik nodded and followed her away from the cottage.

The village was uncommonly busy for the time of morning. Silje was used to having the streets to herself when she delivered her newsletter from the weekly print run, but now it seemed that the villagers turned out en masse, gathered in small huddles to discuss what had now become known as the 'German problem'.

We should fight!

We should do no such thing!

But the British are fighting them!

The British are fighting them in other peoples' countries. God forbid they should leave a mess on their own doorstep!

Are we to let these scum run roughshod over us then? Even the French are fighting them!

The snatches of conversation were as varied as they were passionate – passionate with an unmistakable undertone of resistance.

'I need another printing press,' Silje said, watching Tomas Lostrom, the baker, demonstrate how to incapacitate an enemy soldier. His audience, the dour group of ancient women who formed the Fólkvangr cake-making circle, seemed guardedly impressed.

'Listen to him. He plans to fight the invaders, armed with the contents of his kitchen drawer. This is madness.'

Erik said nothing, though his pace had measurably slowed. He shuffled his hands in and out of his pockets and seemed to be quite unlike himself.

'Erik, whatever is the matter? Are you still brooding over our last meeting?'

Erik shook his head, and then nodded. 'You did not call on me. We fight and it is always me who has to come crawling back to you.'

'I would not call it crawling—'

'Then what would you call it, Silje? What would you call it when a man is made to swallow his pride over and over again.'

'I have no idea what you're talking about.'

'You have been with him!' Erik shouted so suddenly and so loudly that he startled Fólkvangr's shepherds who were gathered in the shadow of *The Mottled Goat*.

'The farrier. I know about you and Junges.'

'Erik, whoever told you—'

'I am not a fool, Silje; please do not treat me as such.'

They walked on in a most terrible silence. Erik, she thought, had run out of patience while she herself had run out of lies.

'I needed the printing press. That is all. He was lonely and I needed the printing press.'

'For your newsletter.'

'Yes, for my newsletter.'

'And your newsletter was worth your virtue.'

Silje felt herself swallow. 'You were my first, Erik,' she said. 'You know that.' And to her shame, she realised she had not run out of lies after all.

They passed the monument to her mother, and she resisted the draw to spend a few moments tending it. She looked at Erik and saw that he was waiting for her to hurry away from him, to go to the orchids and turn the soil, or remove aphids, or uproot weeds.

She stayed with him as the cobbles became the dust track that led away from the village.

'Will you stay for breakfast?' she asked hopefully.

His reply was brisk and sharp. 'If I may.'

'Of course you may.'

'Then I accept. I would very much like to speak to your father.'

When it became clear he was not going to elaborate further, Silje asked him why. She put a lightness into her voice, anxious that Erik would not be left with the notion that she cared whether he spoke to her father or not.

'That is between myself and Mr Ohnstad.'

'If you insist, but he will tell me anyway.'

They carried on to the crossroads that could take them to the Ohnstad cottage, or Bergen, or to the hills and the chestnut tree where they had first made love.

'My home is that way,' said Silje.

Erik looked towards the hills, and perhaps by virtue of memory, Silje thought, the chestnut tree.

'I sometimes think you care little for me, Silje.'

'That is a terrible thing to say,' she replied, and was alarmed to find herself wondering if it were true. The sound of a poorly-maintained engine grew steadily from the east.

'Yes,' Erik said, 'indeed it is.' He scratched his head and turned to see a cloud of dust rattling towards them. A moment later, Jon Ohnstad's truck hove into view, and Silje couldn't remember when she was ever so grateful to see him. He came to a halt at the crossroads.

'Hello there, young Erik,' Jon Ohnstad said. He reached from the cab and shook Erik's hand. 'I haven't seen you at the cottage for a while. The smithing and your artistry keeping you busy, I suppose.'

'Yes sir, amongst other things.'

Silje wondered when, if ever, she would see the fruits of Erik's artistic labours.

'Or has my sister been keeping you at your wits' end?' Magnus reached over his father to cuff Erik's shoulder.

'She likes to keep me… alert. Sir, I wonder if I might come to the cottage later this evening so that we might—'

'I would enjoy nothing more, my boy; but tonight is not a good night.'

'That's right,' Magnus agreed. 'Perhaps some other time.'

And it was only then Silje noticed that both her father and brother appeared uncommonly anxious.

'Yes,' Jon Ohnstad said, 'another time.'

Erik looked hurt.

'We have errands to run,' said Magnus. 'Get in Silje; we may need your help.'

Silje asked, 'What's going on?'

'If it's help you need—'

Jon Ohnstad said, 'That's quite all right. Three is plenty.'

'More than enough,' said Magnus. 'Silje, get in the truck.'

Without taking her eyes from them, Silje walked around and opened the door. 'I will come and see you later,' she said to Erik.

'Don't feel you have to if—'

'I want to. So I *will* see you later this evening.' She climbed into the cab, and over Magnus to sit between him and her father.

'What about your bike?'

'Look after it for her,' Jon Ohnstad said. 'I'll come for it this evening. Mind how you go, young man.' He gunned the engine, leaving Erik cocooned in a cyclone of smoke and dust.

* * *

'I am sure that one of you will tell me what is going on.'

The truck rattled and lurched from one side of the road to the other. Her father was driving like a madman, which was very unlike him.

And then there was her brother, Magnus. His hair, dirty and unkempt, his chin unshaven, and an unsightly cut near his right eye.

'Where were you last night?' Silje asked. 'Where were you the night before that?'

'We received word from Bergen,' Jon Ohnstad said. 'It is almost over.'

'What are you talking about, Father? What is "almost over"?'

'The transportation,' Magnus replied. 'The Jews have been turned out of their homes, rounded up and taken to the docks, or shot in the street if they resist.'

'Ah, so we're to bring them all back; the three of us.'

'Do not be facetious, Daughter. It is most unbecoming.'

'Then someone had better tell me why we are going to Bergen.'

'We are going because I made a promise,' Jon Ohnstad said, 'and if I am anything then I am a man of my word.'

His mind was set; there was little point arguing further. Silje fumed and busied herself writing notes for her next editorial. She entitled it *Secrets within our Family* and began by saying Fólkvangr was a family and that families should have no secrets. Secrets, she wrote, bred mistrust which led to further secrets and further mistrust. She finished the note with a stern mention of the missing ladder.

The town of Bergen was greyer than she remembered, though it had been less than a month since she'd last travelled there. At first she thought it was just the unseasonably dark sky; or perhaps the sombre aspect was merely a reflection of the countless grey uniforms that stood in almost every doorway, at every corner, that could be seen riding on every tram, or in every car. If there are so many Germans here, Silje thought, then who is laying waste to the rest of Europe?

The townspeople swelled the numbers, though they moved more slowly than the invaders, and with their heads bowed. The shops and offices were still as pristine, except for the Jewish establishments that nestled between the marketplace and the law firms. Some of them had been destroyed by fire; the ones that remained had been daubed with the bright yellow stars of St David. The curtain-maker, a young man with bright blue eyes and a slow, measured smile, and whose name Silje could not recall, was lying on the ground outside his shop. There was blood on the wall above him, blood and a neat cross of bullet holes.

'He was caught trying to hide them,' Magnus said. 'They will leave him there for a day as a warning.'

Her father drove slowly, as though they were part of a funeral procession. He smiled politely at the soldiers manning the checkpoints and barricades.

Magnus, to Silje's surprise, appeared to be praying.

'We are going to see the hat-maker, aren't we? Mr Dorfmann and his blind daughter?'

'Mr Dorfmann is gone.' Jon Ohnstad drew in his lower lip and inhaled deeply.

'What? How? How do you know this?'

Ahead of them, a German staff sergeant raised his hand.

'Damn him,' Magnus said.

His father brought the truck to a halt. 'Calm yourself. We have done nothing wrong.'

'But we are about to, aren't we?' said Silje.

'That depends,' said Jon Ohnstad, 'on what you think is wrong.'

The sergeant approached and looked inside the cab, casting his eyes over everything inanimate and paying no attention to the occupants. 'Where are you coming from?'

'Fólkvangr,' they said as one voice.

'I have never heard of it.' The soldier reached inside and pressed his hand against the steering wheel, sounding the horn. He walked around the front, tapping at the metalwork with the stock of his rifle. 'And what is your business in Bergen?' Again he reached inside the cab, this time searching inside the compartment by Silje's knees.

'I am delivering flowers to my friend,' Jon Ohnstad said quickly. 'He owns a shop on the harbour front.'

Silje was relieved she remembered him. 'Mr Helsing. He sells clothing for the fishermen.'

But the soldier seemed uninterested. He walked to the back of the truck and threw open the tarpaulin. Silje felt her throat tighten.

He poked at the bundles of flowers, then he nodded to his colleague, who raised the gate.

'Orchids,' Silje called out. 'The finest orchids in all of Norway.'

'Silje!' Magnus hissed.

Jon Ohnstad eased the truck forward, slowly, barely touching the pedal until they were clear of the barricade. Silje realised she was holding her breath.

They made a left turn just shy of the harbour and then a shallow right. It was only when the truck stopped in an alley behind the hat-maker's shop that Silje let the air back into her lungs.

'I have never been so frightened,' she said, 'and I have no idea why.'

Magnus and her father jumped from the vehicle without a word. She followed and saw that the hat-maker's neighbour was waiting for them. Mr Helsing was an extraordinarily tall man who was so thin that Silje often wondered how he remained upright in the harbour breeze. He was older than her father, with strands of white hair below his crown and weathered skin that whispered of an old life spent at sea. He did not, Silje thought, look like the kind of man who enjoyed flowers.

'You came,' Mr Helsing said. 'Thank God. I do not think I could prevent them from ransacking the place any longer.'

He and Jon Ohnstad embraced, tears streaming from their eyes. Silje wondered what terrible things Mr Helsing had seen, and what things her father imagined. Mr Helsing stepped back and straightened his jacket. 'Follow me.'

He had the key to the hat-maker's shop. Silje followed her father and Mr Helsing inside, with Magnus as rear guard.

'What did you tell them?' Jon Ohnstad asked.

'I told them that I needed a few days to search the place. I told them the filthy Jew had stolen some of my stock and I would like to rip apart his home in case he had not sold it.'

'And they agreed?'

'They are looking for "a calm and orderly transition" so they are perhaps a little more accommodating than they were in Poland.' Mr Helsing took a handkerchief from the jacket of his suit and mopped his brow. 'They came for him, Jon; three days ago. They broke into his shop, beat him senseless, mutilated him, and took him away.'

'He knew they would.'

'And I just watched, from my window.'

'As we agreed *you* would, if it ever came to it.'

Silje asked what had become of Mr Dorfmann and his daughter; none of the three men answered her. Instead they formed a circle in the kitchen and began lifting away the floor tiles. Magnus, Jon Ohnstad and Mr Helsing worked quickly, without speaking; fearful, but without panic. Next came the layer of soil.

'For warmth,' Jon Ohnstad said. Magnus nodded.

Under the soil, more boards. Not floorboards, but old, rotten planks taken from ships.

'Your planks, I take it,' Jon Ohnstad said with a thin smile.

Mr Helsing smiled back. 'I still have many friends in wet places.'

Silje noticed the smell, familiar, like the barn back at the cottage, though much stronger. 'It smells like something died under there,' she said, wrinkling her nose.

Her father glanced at her; it was not a look she recognised, but suspected it was one of disappointment.

The last plank came free and then a large wooden sheet that Silje recognised as the door to Mr Dorfmann's storeroom.

And beneath the door, lay the milliner's daughter.

'Dear Lord.' Magnus crossed himself.

The young girl was folded around a small pile of empty pans and scraps of paper, in a space barely large enough to hold one of her father's hat boxes. She was in the same dress Silje had seen her wearing only a few weeks before, though it was almost unrecognisable, as was she: thinner, paler, and caked in her own filth.

Silje covered her mouth and turned away, catching her father's eye as she did so. He did not appear the least part surprised.

'Help me lift her out,' he said.

'Her limbs have set. Be careful.'

Freya offered no resistance as the three men hauled her from her hiding place. She did not move as they set her gently on the floor.

Magnus asked if she was alive.

Jon Ohnstad placed his ear to her chest. 'Yes, she lives, but we must hurry.'

'I will fetch some water,' Silje said, keen to escape the stench.

'There is no time,' said Magnus. 'Go to the front and keep watch. Signal us if the Germans come.'

'Signal you? How am I supposed to—'

'Silje!' her father said through pressed teeth. 'For once in your selfish little life, do as you are told!'

Silje turned and walked away, chased and stung by his words. She stepped outside the shop and wiped her eyes with her sleeve.

He had never said such a thing to her before. Never.

The store front faced a wide, cobbled street that led to Bergen's largest jetty. She understood why Mr Helsing had set himself up there; thick jerseys and waterproofs were always in demand by the men who worked the town's fishing vessels. But now she thought on it, why Aaron Dorfmann had chosen to open a ladies' hat shop near a harbour was something of a mystery.

'Miss Ohnstad!' A familiar voice cut through her thoughts, and it was with a profound horror she realised she had already failed in her duties as lookout; Lieutenant Klein hurried across the street, beaming uncontrollably. 'Miss Ohnstad!'

Silje hurried across the road to meet him, took him by the arm and led him away. 'Lieutenant,' she said crisply. 'I believe we had an agreement.'

'An agreement?'

'Yes, you would tell me everything your commander says, plans or does. Is that not what you promised?'

She spied an alleyway, between a café and a small tea room.

'Yes, I did, but—'

'And did you not think the mass transportation of Jews is something I should hear about?' The alley would suffice for just a few minutes, long enough for her to reinforce her hold over him. 'You should have told me. That is what we agreed.' She reached down and rapped her fist against his crotch. He shrieked, not unlike a small child. Strangely though, he was still smiling.

'It is not easy, Fräulein. I cannot just abandon my duties and travel to Fólkvangr to find you.'

'In future, you will find a—'

'Lieutenant!' Another voice. Silje wondered if her luck would continue to worsen as the day wore on.

Klein took a step away from her and snapped to attention. 'General!'

Gruetzmacher stepped from his staff car and strode across the street.

Silje licked her lips and looked for a direction in which to run.

'What do you think you are doing?' the General said quietly. 'And who is this?'

'This?' said Klein as though he were unsure. 'This is Fräulein Ohnstad.'

Gruetzmacher looked disdainfully at Silje.

'She is from Fólkvangr.'

'Where?'

'Fólkvangr.'

'I am not deaf, Lieutenant. I wanted you to tell me where Fólkvangr is.'

'My apologies, Gener—'

'It is a small village,' Silje said quietly, 'in the mountains about twenty miles north of here.' She decided she would say no more; Fólkvangr was of no interest to the Germans and it would stay so.

'Fólkvangr. I have not heard of this place.'

'It is a very insignificant little place,' she said, almost desperately. 'A few cottages, barns and taverns. And goats,' she rambled. 'Lots and lots of goats.'

The Lieutenant looked as fearful as she felt.

The General was clearly a man who believed he should know everything; Fólkvangr had escaped his eye and this was of some concern. He stared at her, trying to pierce her skull through sheer force of will. She would have withered beneath his eyes, but there was something else: the scent of alcohol – a weakness in him that gave her a small measure of strength.

'And what business do you have with my lieutenant?'

Klein started to speak, but Gruetzmacher waved him to silence.

'And did I not see you here a few weeks ago?'

'I do not think so, sir.'

'Yes, at my welcoming address. I thought I recognised you.' His eyes fell to the bundle of papers that Silje held crushed against her chest. 'And what are you carrying?'

'This, sir? Nothing.'

'Really?' He took the newsletters from her.

'Now, where are you taking my lieutenant?' he asked again and turned to the first page.

Her father's truck drew to a halt on the other side of the road. There was a commotion in the cab. Magnus was restraining him from getting out and running to her aid.

Please, Silje thought, stop him. 'I was taking him to the alleyway,' she said to the General. 'I merely wished to pleasure him.' The phrase had dropped into her head, the same words that Erik had muttered to her.

I sought to pleasure you, Silje...

Gruetzmacher looked up, an eyebrow raised.

'You are correct, sir. I was at your address. It is where I met the Lieutenant.' She took Klein's hand; he appeared to be in shock. 'I am sorry I was untruthful. I did not think the Lieutenant would wish it known that we are in love.'

Klein looked at her, his eyes the size of hens' eggs.

'I see,' The General glanced at Klein, and at Silje, and then over her shoulder at the alleyway. 'Right.' He read to the end of the page while an armoured car and messenger motorcycle veered around them.

'Perhaps we should step out of the street, General,' Klein said.

The General ignored him. 'Forgive my suspicion, Fräulein,' he said without looking up from the newsletter. 'It was your clothes.'

'My clothes?'

'Yes, that dress. It is little more than a sack if you don't mind me saying so.'

'No, of course...'

'It is probably unwise to walk the streets dressed like a Jewess.'

'Yes, I am sorry; I should have thought.'

'Just a friendly warning.'

'Thank you.'

'And as for you, Lieutenant...'

Klein, exhausted, slowly arranged his limbs into something akin to standing to attention. 'Sir.'

'I was young myself once; but there is a time for duty and there is a time for... other pursuits.' He treated Silje to a slow unpractised wink. 'And you are still on duty. Return to my car.'

Klein gratefully hurried away.

'And smile at the locals, Klein! It will be a short war; try to enjoy it!' Gruetzmacher turned to Silje and held up the newsletter. 'May I keep this.'

It wasn't a request; Silje nodded and looked over his shoulder. The struggle in the truck had attracted the attention of three soldiers who were speaking to Magnus and her father.

And in the back of the truck, something was stirring under the tarpaulin.

'May I go now, sir. I do not wish to keep my father waiting.'

'Yes of course, but another word of advice, Fräulein.'

'Sir?'

'We will not be here for very long, so make the most it. Klein should buy you some new clothes, perhaps nicer shoes.' He smiled in what he believed to be a fatherly way. 'And be mindful as to how you conduct yourself in public.'

'I will think on that, sir. Thank you.'

She hurried back to the truck, and almost wilted with relief when she heard Gruetzmacher bark at the soldiers, telling them to stop haranguing the locals.

The soldiers stepped away, giving her room to climb into the cab alongside Magnus.

'Well done, Daughter.' Jon Ohnstad put the truck into gear.

'Yes, I suppose,' said Silje, 'for someone as selfish as me. Now can we please leave this place? I think I'm going to be sick.'

* * *

And Silje was sick, twice, on the journey home. The first time they had barely left Bergen, the second was high in the hills on a blind curve that took them out of sight of the town below.

'Would you like me to hold your hair?'

'You are not funny, Magnus.'

'Son, do not tease your sister. She has done a very brave thing today.'

'How is she?' Magnus called out.

'I think she is dead,' Silje called back.

Both men jumped out of the cab and ran to the back of the truck, where Silje held up the tarpaulin and peered at the trembling form underneath.

'See?' she said. 'The Jew isn't moving.'

'She clearly is,' said her brother.

'Her name is Freya,' Jon Ohnstad said, his nostrils twitching at the stench, 'as you well know.'

'She is cold,' said Magnus. 'We should put her in the front; the heat from the engine will—'

'She is not sitting in the front with us,' said Silje. 'She is covered in her own mess!'

'Do not be unkind,' Jon Ohnstad told her.

'But the stench, Father! She smells worse than old Mr Ruud!'

'And now you exaggerate.'

'If you do not wish to sit with her,' said Magnus, 'then why don't you sit in the back of the truck?'

'I am not going in the back of the truck.'

The Jewess spoke, her voice cracked and dry. 'I am fine where I am.'

Jon Ohnstad was startled. 'You are not, my dear. You are cold.'

'I have been sealed under a floor for four days. A few hours in the back of your truck will matter little.' She inclined her head slightly, guiding an ear to where Magnus stood, clearly in awe of her, Silje thought, though he can barely see her for the filth she is covered in.

Freya said, 'I do not know your voice.'

'I... I am Magnus. Silje's brother.'

'I am Freya. I wish I could say I was pleased to meet you.' She appeared to lapse into unconsciousness.

'Magnus, help me carry her to the cab. Silje, you will ride in the back.'

'Father!'

'There is not room for three us!'

'Then why not Magnus?'

'Because you have already volunteered.'

'I did no such thing.'

'You said you wouldn't sit with her, which I take to mean you would rather sit in the back.' Again he'd made up his mind; the argument was lost, but Silje made her feelings clear by refusing to help move Freya into the cab. Her father started the engine. Silje climbed into the back and gingerly pushed away the tarpaulin with her foot.

9

'I think,' said Jon Ohnstad wretchedly, 'this is the longest time you have gone without speaking to me.'

Silje scrubbed angrily at the pots and renewed a silent vow to never utter a word to him ever again.

'Though there was the time I took Pollyanna to the market and returned without her. You cried for a day and a night and said that you would not speak to me again under pain of torture.'

And Magnus, she thought, Magnus who left them with the Jewess almost as soon as they arrived back in Fólkvangr. Magnus, whose latest calling, whatever that may be, meant he had to steal away, with people she neither knew or trusted, in the dead of night, instead of remaining at the cottage to help with the latest stray to whom their soft-headed father had opened the Ohnstad home. Yes, Magnus; she would never speak to him again either.

'Though if I remember rightly,' Jon Ohnstad said, 'I did not have to torture you.'

'Do not even think about it,' said Silje.

'You broke quite readily under pain of tickling.'

She raised a pan and held it in front of her. 'Do not come near me, old man. Do not think that I am not angry enough to use this.'

Jon Ohnstad raised his hands and backed away. He sat down next to his orchid pot. 'A truce then,' he said.

Silje dropped the pan into the sink and carried on scrubbing. 'I was not angry about Pollyanna. She was just a goat, and not a very nice goat at that. I was angry because you sold her without telling me. I am angry because you and Magnus hatched this ridiculous scheme and did not think to tell me about it. I live here too – which is more than I can say for Magnus.'

'He thought you would say no.'

'He is right! I would have! What are we to do with her? Do you plan on keeping her in Magnus's room until the war ends, or we are shot as sympathisers?'

'It will not come to that.'

'And you know this? How?'

He put on his microscope – a cumbersome, home-made contraption cobbled together from pieces of brass, iron and lenses he had procured over many years. 'Because we will keep her hidden away in Fólkvangr. The Germans have no reason to come here.'

'And after three days, she has not moved from that bed and has eaten little more than a mouthful. She has not washed herself since we found her in the pit under the shop floor!'

'She mourns the loss of her father. I would like to think you would be just as upset.'

'And the smell!'

'If I approach her she screams. Above all else, we cannot have her screaming.'

'Did Mr Dorfmann make you do this?'

'How could he make me do anything?' Her father moved a lever and a thick lense slid over his left eye. He peered into the column of the largest, most beautiful orchid. 'I agreed to save his daughter because it was the right thing to do. I would have saved him too, but he was known to them; they would have come looking and they would have found her. How could I refuse any man making such a sacrifice for his child?'

He opened the small box resting on the table. Inside was a single bee which flew on to his hand. He placed it on the lip of the orchid and watched intently as it went about its work. 'Your mother was very sick near the end of her life.'

'Father, please…'

'That… thing that grew from her; it made her…' He looked to the ceiling and squeezed his eyes shut. 'It made her want to hide away. She did not want you to see what she'd become. She wanted me to send you away until after the end. Do you remember this, Silje?'

'I remember that you did not ask me.'

'The Fehns looked after you for the last month of your mother's life. Mrs Fehn, your mother and me: we thought that was best for you.' Her father used a small wishbone lacquered with honey to take the bee from one orchid and place it on another. 'So you see, Daughter, there are a great many things I have not told or discussed with you. Sometimes they do not concern you, other times I seek to protect you.'

'And Magnus? Does he not require protection?'

Jon Ohnstad sighed and removed his microscope. 'He is my son. He will always be my son. But you, Silje – you are my child.'

Silje watched him replace his eyepieces and resume his strange vigil over bee and orchid. 'Fine,' she said, and stormed out through the back door.

The third-acre behind the Ohnstad cottage was home to three trees and a carpet of grass kept even by the family's four goats. They looked at her curiously, not used to seeing her behind the house so late in the evening. She tripped on a log on her way to the woodshed, where she found two metal bathtubs. The newest hadn't lost its sheen; the older one was dull with age and was now used to clean the goats and dip the sheep. She took the older tub and dragged it back into the cottage.

'Start boiling some water,' she told her father. 'I cannot prevent the Nazis from shooting us, but at least I can do something about the smell.'

* * *

Freya remained curled up on the small bed while Silje dragged cloths, oil-sheets and the bathtub to the centre of the room. She called downstairs for the first pot of hot water. The tub was half-filled after a few minutes. Silje told her father to fetch more.

When she closed the door, the tiny dark room closed in on her; the cloying warmth, the smell of old wood and human waste. She coughed, her eyes streaming.

'Get up,' she snapped. 'Take off your clothes.'

Freya did not stir.

'I would very much like to avoid touching you,' Silje said. 'I would very much like to not have to slap you.'

After a few moments it became clear the Jewess was not going to move. Silje approached the bed and reached for her, and in that instant Freya became a wild thing, clawing and snarling and blindly lashing out at the world she'd so come to despise. Silje weaved between her limbs and took hold of her wrists; they felt thin and brittle in her hands and she feared that if the child did not stop thrashing she would surely break.

'Stop it, Freya! You must stop!'

'Silje, is everything all right in there? Do you need—?'

'All is well, Father! And I told you to start boiling more water!'

Freya cried and spat and snarled, smearing her filth on Silje's dress and hands.

Silje herself marvelled at how such a slight girl could be so strong. 'I lost my mother!' she cried. 'She was taken from me when I was a child. And I wish I'd had someone to claw and scratch at. Well you are in good fortune, Freya.' Silje hit her, as hard as she could. 'Because you have *me*.'

Exhausted, she climbed from the bed and wiped her hands and her face with a dampened cloth. She swallowed, feeling an uncommon dryness about her mouth. 'Now, stand up and take off your clothes.'

Again, Jon Ohnstad's voice came from beyond the door. 'Silje?'

'Father, please – the water!'

She listened to him making his way down the staircase and turned to see that Freya was still trying to rise from the bed, the eruption of grief having drained the very last of her strength.

Foolish, Silje thought. *I should have made her eat something.*

'Come,' she said. 'Let me help you.'

The girl was almost unconscious, so Silje sat her upright and raised her arms so she could take off her dress. She was thinner than she'd imagined; her bones poked out at strange angles from beneath her milk-white flesh. Silje laid her down and covered her hands with a dry cloth to peel away her undergarments. The smell collided with her, making her cough and fight to draw breath. Fearing that at any moment she might lose consciousness herself, she carried Freya to the bath, kneeling to set her down gently in the warm water. Then she ran to the other side of the room and threw open a window to take in lungfuls of the outside air.

In her weakness, Freya was little more than a rag doll. She said nothing while Silje washed her hair and her neck, and cleaned her legs and her arms.

Jon Ohnstad knocked on the door and left more pots of hot water before retreating to the safety of the kitchen. Freya turned to listen, her lips forming words without sound.

'Speak up child; I cannot hear you,' Silje said, lifting her right arm and scrubbing furiously along its length.

'I said he is very kind.'

Silje stopped to look at her, watching her lifeless eyes searching for her face. 'Yes, he is.' She set about Freya's neck and shoulders with the brush.

'And you are kind too.'

'Think nothing of it.'

'I am sorry for hitting you.'

'You were upset. I understand.'

'And I am sorry about your mother.'

'You may stop talking now.'

'My father said you are pretty, so I think your mother was pretty too.'

'I do not like it when people talk about my mother, especially those who did not know her. Now lean forward.'

Freya leaned forward, and Silje poured hot water over her back.

'When they came for my father, I did nothing.'

'There was nothing you could do.' She lifted her hands from the water and began cleaning the soil from under Freya's fingernails.

'I stayed under the floor and tried not to make a sound. I heard them beat him, and I heard them ask where his daughter was. He said he had sent me away. They did not believe him. They said they would cut off his fingers one by one until he told them.'

'Please do not say anymore.'

'Eleven screams. I heard him scream eleven times.'

'Freya, please stop.'

'He begged them to kill him, but he did not give me to them. And so I hid under the floor like a frightened child while they cut pieces from my father and took him away.'

'That is enough for today. Stand up.'

With Silje's help, Freya got to her feet and stepped from the bath.

'Inside the camp, how will he live? How will he eat? Who will take care of him?'

'I do not know,' Silje said, thinking that poor Mr Dorfmann was very unlikely to reach the camp.

'And when he returns, how will he make his hats?' She began to weep, and Silje thought it odd that dead eyes could make living tears. She took a fresh cloth and knelt down, drying Freya's feet and her calves and her thighs. The girl stood with her eyes pointed towards the ceiling. Silje thought her skin felt softer, more delicate than her own, though her fingertips were as hard as stone. The girl's raven black hair and alabaster flesh imbued her with a beauty she found somewhat unearthly and cold – and yet still she was beset by envy.

Envious of an orphaned, blind Jewish girl. *Perhaps it is my nature to covet anything I do not have, even if I do not truly desire it.* She lost herself while staring at the hollow of Freya's stomach. 'I can say nothing to comfort you,' she said hurriedly. 'All I know is that your father gave himself to save you, and that if you die of grief then his gift will have been wasted. I will not see such a good man go to waste. Do you understand?'

Freya nodded. She reached out, her fingers lightly caressing Silje's chin, and with her bearings discovered she pressed her lips against Silje's cheek. 'You are kind. Why do you hide it?'

Silje cleared her throat. 'You seem much better now,' she said, wiping her cheek with the heel of her hand. 'I will bring you some soup.'

'Thank you.'

'Stop thanking me. It is only soup.'

'Not just for the soup. And thank your father for me. I do not know what I can do to ever—'

'When you have your strength then I expect you to help around the village and on the farm. There is always lots to do and that is the only payment we need.'

'Of course. I will help as much as I can.'

'Though I am not sure how much you can do if you cannot see.'

'I can sew and I can cook.'

'What the village needs is farmers and woodcutters.'

'I can cut wood.'

'Well, we shall see about that.' Silje realised she was staring again, at this frail creature trembling in front of her, all sharpened bones, marbled skin and a cascade of wild black hair.

And her eyebrows, she thought. *I wonder if the poor creature knows that she always seems to be scowling.* A fine layer of down covered the girl's forearms and her calves. It thickened to a dark forest below her stomach. General Gruetzmacher was wrong; if the Jews were demons of the night, then surely this one would take a form far more beguiling.

'I will find you some clothes before you die of a chill,' Silje said hoarsely.

'Thank you.'

'And please stop thanking me.'

* * *

Jon Ohnstad looked up from his orchids when he heard Silje on the stairs.

'Ah, the enraged stamping,' he said. 'Passed down from your mother and down from her mother before her.'

'She cannot stay here.' Silje threw open the back doors and looked outside. 'I tossed her bedding out of the window. Where is it?'

'I think I heard the goats take it.'

Silje slammed the door shut. 'She cannot stay here.'

'I believe you said that.'

'I am sorry; I did not think you heard me!'

'She is a blind, lonely, frightened girl.'

'I am not stupid, Father; I understand that. But she will bring the world down around us; I know it.'

'Nonsense. Only you, Magnus and me even know she is here.'

'The Germans know that Mr Dorfmann had a daughter. They will come looking for her.'

'And why should they look for her in Fólkvangr? And why do you keep wiping your cheek like that?'

'You are trying to change the subject.' Silje snatched her hand away from her face. 'She kissed me, if you must know. I think she may have had something on her lips. My skin itches.'

'She kissed you?' Jon Ohnstad raised both eyebrows and beamed. Silje couldn't remember the last time he'd smiled so freely. 'That is wonderful!'

'What is so wonderful about being kissed by a blind Jew?'

'It means she likes you! You have a new friend! And lower your voice; she will hear you.'

'I have plenty of friends; I do not need another one.'

'You have plenty of *male* friends, Silje.'

'What do you mean by that?' The itch quickly spread from Silje's cheek to her jaw, her forehead, behind her ears – until it seemed her entire face was burning.

'You're blushing; there is no need.' He beckoned for her to sit next to him.

'I am going to be honest with you, Silje.'

'Must you?'

'Women, in general, do not seem to like you very much.'

Silje remained silent for the space of a heartbeat. Her eyes narrowed and Jon Ohnstad shrank in his seat as though he'd heard the mountains suddenly breathe.

She tapped a fingernail on the table, a hollow sound that rang out like a gunshot. 'What did you say?'

'Not all of them,' he added hastily, 'but a few, especially those around the village, and perhaps some in Bergen, and maybe one or two in the outlying—'

'Father!'

His thumbs chased each other in tight circles. 'Anyway, women do not seem to like you very much.'

'That is a lie!' Silje cried, jumping to her feet. 'Everyone likes me!'

'I am afraid that is not entirely true.'

'Ask Erik or Benjamin or Simen or Nils or Mikker; they will all tell you that I—'

'All men, which is the point I am trying to make. Women do not seem to take you, and I think it is important that you have female friends. I am hoping that Freya will be the first of many.'

Silje exploded, sweeping away his instruments, books and honey jars on her way to the cottage door. Before slamming it behind her she turned to her father and said, 'It is not my fault I'm pretty!'

The cottage shook, and Jon Ohnstad was left alone to look sadly upon the only two things Silje had not sent crashing to the floor: the orchids.

He sighed and rose to his feet to search for the cottage broom.

10

'You have a Jew,' Erik said, 'in your cottage.'

Silje thought if his eyes opened any wider they would tumble from his face. 'Tell me you think it is madness.'

'Well…' He sneezed and sat upright.

'If the Germans find her then we will all be executed.'

'But your father made a promise.'

'He did, but I did not.'

'Silje,' said Erik solemnly, 'do not do anything stupid.'

'I will not betray her if that's what you're worried about.' She lay back in the hay and gazed at the barn ceiling. It occurred to her that she would know any barn in Fólkvangr simply by looking at the latticework that supported the roof, or the stacking of the hay bales, or by the smell of the animals that were kept there. Erik's barn stood next to the cottage where he lived, left in his care by his parents when they took his sisters and emigrated to the Australias. It had been a sorrowful parting; his mother had said that war was coming, and that they would be safer there. She had begged Erik to come with them, but he'd refused.

'*Not without you*,' he'd said to Silje, leaving her both humbled and guilty at once.

And so the Brennas had left without their son, and made him promise that Silje would not set foot in their home while they were gone.

He often invited her, and though she longed to see the artwork he kept in his attic room, she was proud enough not to cross any threshold where she was unwelcome. The cottage still belonged to his parents, after all…

In truth, Silje did not really mind; it was the barn she loved. It was where Erik laboured as an apprentice mechanic and farrier, under the stern tutelage of Junges Fehn. The barn smelled of machine oil and fresh winter pine. It smelled of him.

She said, 'I was not asked, or even told, that she was coming to stay with us. I live there too.'

'Perhaps there was no time. I understand the Transportation happened quickly.'

'Yes, I suppose.' She ran her fingers down his back. 'The General is a man of unfeeling efficiency. I fear for us all, should he turn his attentions to Fólkvangr.'

Erik kissed her on the cheek, the same place where Freya had kissed her a few hours earlier. The flesh there heated and tingled.

'He has no reason to come here,' Erik said.

'What if he finds out about her?' Silje wiped her face with the back of her hand.

'No one knows she is here.'

'You know, I know, my father knows, Magnus knows, poor Mr Dorfmann's neighbour knows…'

'Then perhaps,' Erik said, gently guiding her hand away from her cheek, 'we should resolve not to tell anyone else.'

'I didn't tell—'

'You told me.'

'Well, of course I told you. You are my—'

'I am your what?'

'You are my man,' she said, firmly, finally. 'You are my man, Erik Brenna, and if I cannot trust you with my heart and my secrets then I cannot trust anyone.'

Erik was overjoyed, so much so that he sprang upon her, sending them tumbling down into the bales of hay. Silje shrieked with delight as they rebounded from one stack and then the next, to land on the barn floor, covered in straw and sawdust.

'You have made me the happiest man alive!' Erik cried.

'Erik, our clothes!'

'We will climb up and find them,' he said, picking her up and casting her into a haystack. He threw himself down beside her and covered them both with loose hay. 'You do not know how long I've waited for you to say that.'

'They are only words, Erik.'

'They are words when they are said. Until they are said, they are a yearning, Silje – a painful yearning.'

'Erik, you have me.' She smiled and reached down between his thighs. 'Often.'

He pushed her hand away. 'That is not what I mean. I am talking about a commitment. I am talking about promising to spend our lives together, forsaking all others.'

There was something in the way he said 'forsaking' that chilled her to her marrow. She shivered and asked, 'How long have you felt like this?'

'Since we were children.'

'I am being serious.'

'So am I.'

'Then that is a very long time.'

'You are worth the wait.' He leaned over her. 'I have something to tell you. Well, something to ask you.'

Silje braced herself. Her stomach tightened and she heard her own breathing quicken. She touched her cheek, much kissed of late, and found herself thinking of her father and her brother and of Freya, and of the enemy that had landed on Norway's coast.

'Erik, the war…'

'Exactly, and that is why I need to ask you now.'

She closed her eyes, unsure of what she would say: *yes; no; perhaps; there have been many others.* 'Then if you must. Ask me.'

'I am joining the Resistance,' he announced grandly. 'Will you wait for me?'

Silje opened her eyes and blinked. 'What?'

'I am joining the Norwegian Resistance. Will you wait for me? I do not know how long I will be gone, but knowing that I have you to come back to will make the time—'

'No,' said Silje. 'No you will not. I forbid it.'

'But it is my duty. As a free man of Norway I must do what I can to repel the Nazis from—'

'You are a man of Fólkvangr! Your duty is to this village! Your duty is to me!'

'I am doing this for you! Do you want us to live our lives under Quisling's thumb? Under German rule?'

'I do not care!' She jumped to her feet and began climbing the bales. 'I do not care about anything else but you, my family, and this village!'

'You cannot save Fólkvangr while the rest of Norway goes to hell!'

'I do not know what has gotten into people of late! Stolen ladders, stray Jews… My father behaves like he has been gifted a second daughter, and Magnus… I have not seen Magnus for days. And I know he has not returned to the seminary; his bible is still at the cottage. And now… this… you!'

When Silje reached the top of the bales she searched for her clothes. She looked down at Erik and saw that he wouldn't look back; instead he turned away from her, scratching nervously at his chest.

'But you have seen him, haven't you? It is the Resistance. He's joined the Resistance and he has convinced you to go with him.'

'Would you marry a coward?'

'No sooner than I would marry a dead man,' she said, putting on her undergarments, 'which is what you will be, Erik Brenna!'

'You are being unreasonable.'

'And you are being stupid,' she replied, fighting her way into her dress. 'Do you think you are being any less brave by staying here, and looking after the village? Is it less courageous to help look after the people you are supposed to love?' She pushed her feet into her sandals and jumped down into the haystack, sliding down and through it to land on her feet. 'You will not do this, Erik Brenna. I will not allow—'

'Sshhh!'

'I will not!'

'There's someone coming.'

'If you think this will distract me, Erik, you are sorely—'

The barn was suddenly flooded with moonlight, and a small, stout figure stood in the doorway, a shadow painted onto the low moon.

'Silje?' the shadow said, running inside, its bare feet rustling on the layers of strewn hay.

'Lisbeth!' Erik scrambled further back into the haystack to hide his nakedness. 'What are you doing here?'

'Erik.' Lisbeth panted a curt greeting and turned her frantic attentions to Silje.

'If you have come all this way to insult me, Lisbeth, then you should know that I am no mood for your—'

'The Germans.' Lisbeth doubled over, clutching her knees. 'The Germans, they are at your house.'

* * *

Erik's cottage and his barn stood in a circular clearing about a quarter-mile west of the village. It lay beyond a ramshackle collection of bricks and mud that the villagers referred to, grandly, as the 'wall', and a nameless lake of sharp stones and volcanic rock where the trees refused to grow. It was in the lake of stones that Silje lost her sandal. She didn't stop to collect it; she continued to run, caring little for the trail of blood she left in her wake.

Erik and Lisbeth stayed close behind, flanking her.

Silje vaulted the wall with her heart in her mouth; she ran along Fólkvangr's only thoroughfare, past the bakery and the grocery, past the thin and crooked houses and cottages, past the monument to her mother where the villagers had lined both sides of the road, an honour guard of sombre faces and bright lanterns. Old Mr Kleppe took off his hat as she flew past him; he clutched it to his chest and shouted, 'God be with you, Silje!'

Silje thought, *He will not be with any of us this night.*

They left the village behind and ran into the hills, down into the gully and past the stone tablet that Magnus had carved as a child, a small obelisk that marked the southern boundary of the Ohnstad lands.

They slid to a stop and dipped low behind the felled trees at the edge of the copse.

'Christ,' Erik breathed. 'So many of them.'

There were twelve men stationed outside the cottage. An armoured troop carrier and two motorcycles with sidecar-mounted machine guns had been left near the hen houses. The soldiers seemed at ease, though they shivered in the mountain wind.

'What are we going to do?' Lisbeth asked nervously.

Silje recognised a third vehicle that had been left near the tractor barn: the General's staff car. It was being carefully inspected by Baldur, the family's oldest goat.

'You will do nothing,' Silje said firmly. 'I will go to the house and see what is going on.'

'You are not serious,' Erik blurted.

Lisbeth told him to keep his voice down.

'They will be expecting me; I live here.'

'Going in there will achieve nothing!'

'I do not know that until I try.'

She stood up. 'Stay here. I will come for you if I can.'

'No!'

'Erik, they will hear you!'

Silje threw away her other sandal and walked towards the cottage. The soldiers moved for their guns as she approached. They did not warn her to stay back or identify herself; they simply aimed pistols at her face.

Silje closed her eyes and told herself not to cry.

'I know her. She is the old man's daughter.'

She opened her eyes to see a broad, unshaven face doing its utmost to smile in a friendly, non-threatening manner. 'I am sorry,' Silje whispered. 'Have we met?'

The soldier looked hurt; he removed his helmet, licked his hand and tried to smooth down the thin curls about his head.

'A month ago,' he said. 'I was driving the truck.'

Silje looked puzzled, still.

The soldier glanced nervously at his companions. 'When you took the Lieutenant away for… privacy.'

Somewhere behind her, a soldier coughed.

'Ah,' said Silje. 'I have you now.'

The soldier looked oddly relieved. 'Please, go inside; the General is expecting you.'

Silje's legs almost gave way. 'Me?'

'Yes. Now, please.'

She walked on, pushed open the door, and as calmly as she could, entered the cottage.

Inside, Lieutenant Klein stood and snapped to attention.

At the kitchen table, sitting opposite her father, was the immaculate General Gruetzmacher. He sat with one leg crossed over the other, a mug of tea resting on his knee. A brown briefcase stood propped against the table leg nearest him. He turned to her and said, 'Fräulein. Come in, shut the door. You are causing something of a draught.'

Silje's father shot her a fearful look. Despite the cold breeze that had followed her into the cottage, he appeared to be sweating an abundance, and his skin was flushed a bright red. He clutched his cap in his hands and his right foot danced a jig of its own accord. 'What are you doing here?' he asked quietly. 'I thought you were spending the afternoon with—'

'I live here,' Silje said quickly. She closed the door and walked to the table, passing Lieutenant Klein as though he didn't exist. She sat next to her father and placed her hand on his leg to stop it moving. 'This is an unexpected pleasure, General.'

The General was clearly in a good mood; she could smell drink on him. And Freya was nowhere to be seen. Good signs, both.

The General picked a goat's hair from the knee of his breeches and placed his mug on the table. 'As I was telling your father, I have come to see you, my dear.'

Silje's heart sank. 'I am honoured.'

'You never told me that your father was a keen horticulturalist.' He reached out to one of the orchids, taking a petal between his fingers.

Jon Ohnstad's eyes moved rapidly between Silje and the General.

'I did not know you would be interested,' Silje replied.

'No, of course not. Why would you.'

She risked a glance at the Lieutenant, who was perspiring almost as much as her father. The General did not seem to notice the petrified demeanour of both men. She thought that perhaps he'd grown accustomed to seeing fear in the people he met.

'He breeds orchids,' the General went on, speaking to Silje as though Jon Ohnstad had left the room. 'A rare skill. I myself have bred a number of flowering plants, including an entirely new strain of rose.' He waited, for a round of applause it seemed. 'Perhaps you have heard of the Munich Ruby?'

Silje and her father solemnly shook their heads, and the General's face set as a mask of anger and disappointment.

'So you are a botanist, then.' Jon Ohnstad said quickly.

'Why, yes! I almost made a career of it. How in the world did you know?'

'You are clearly an intelligent man, General, but you also possess the hands of someone who works the soil.'

Gruetzmacher visibly swelled with pride, and Silje spared her father the faintest smile. She was aware she possessed a minor talent for manipulation, but had always assumed it had come from her mother.

'You are a clever and perceptive man, Herr Ohnstad.' Gruetzmacher sipped his tea. 'I always found the orchid a most obstinate plant to breed: the positioning of the ovaries; the fussiness with which they choose their partners. Tell me, how have you produced such beautiful blooms?' He plucked a petal from the closest orchid. Silje sat on her hands to stop herself lunging forward and slapping him.

'Bees,' said Jon Ohnstad, his right eye twitching.

'Bees?' The General examined the petal.

'Father has trained bees.' Silje looked at the silent Klein who stared fearfully ahead. Something is not right, she thought. *Why are they here?*

'You train bees,' Gruetzmacher said doubtfully.

'They are intelligent, as are you, General,' Jon Ohnstad replied. 'With the right encouragement and an enclosed environment they will happily—'

'What brings you to our home on such a bitterly cold night, General?' Silje asked.

The General smiled again and reached into his briefcase. Silje caught her breath, expecting him to lay pictures of Freya on the kitchen table. Instead, he placed a neatly folded bundle of papers in front of her.

'Your newsletter,' he said.

Silje tried not to swallow, but couldn't stop herself. Her heart pounded just below her throat.

'It is a childish pastime, General,' Jon Ohnstad said desperately. 'A hobby she refuses to grow out of.'

'Father!'

'I assure you, General, she means no harm.'

Gruetzmacher raised his hand, a half-salute that silenced them both. 'It is… entertaining. I enjoyed reading it. Perhaps it is a little parochial for the larger towns, but with some work we could – what was that?'

He stared at the kitchen ceiling which bowed slightly with a sudden mass pressed upon it from the floor above.

Silje and her father looked at each other.

'Is there someone upstairs?'

Lieutenant Klein unshouldered his machine gun, but the General patted the air with his free hand, telling him to calm himself.

'I had been moving furniture before you arrived,' Jon Ohnstad said. 'I may have left some of it poorly stacked.'

There was another loud thump from the floor above.

The General eyed them both. Jon Ohnstad and Silje looked passively back. The silence grew cloyingly thick.

'You were saying, General,' Silje said, 'something about larger towns?'

Again, the General glanced at the ceiling. 'Yes, indeed, Fräulein. This little venture of yours,' he tapped a finger on Silje's newsletter, 'may be the vehicle we need to bring an understanding between our two races.'

As far as Silje believed, Norwegians and Germans were both part of the *human* race; it appeared the Nazis thought otherwise.

'Your writing is simple, somewhat whimsical.'

Whimsical, Silje did not mind; she was not so sure about *simple*.

'What are you proposing, General?' her father asked.

Gruetzmacher chose to finish his tea before answering: 'I do not expect, or believe, that you are sympathetic to what we are trying to do here, but you do understand that it is in the best interest of the Norwegian people not to resist us. As I said before, this will be a short war; there is no reason why it must also be unpleasant. I see in her words that your daughter thinks the same.

'I have yet to seek the authority of my superiors, but I propose to greatly expand the production and distribution of your newsletter. It will include news and events for the districts under my supervision: Hordvik to the north; Kronstad to the south; Espeland to the east, and of course Bergen on the western coast.'

'I do not like to leave the village,' said Silje.

'You will not have to,' said Gruetzmacher. 'We have installed information centres in all the major towns and villages. They will send the contributions here for editing and collation.' He saved them time and discomfort by answering Silje's next question before she could speak. 'I will approve each issue before distribution, and on occasion I will ask that you include articles submitted by the *Reichskommissariat* and *Nasjonal Samling*.'

'Quisling's party.' Jon Ohnstad could not keep the venom from his voice, but if the General noticed he chose to ignore it.

'Aside from this small thing, your daughter will have complete editorial control.'

'And who will pay for all of this?' Silje asked.

'A joint effort, between the *Reichskommissariat* and *Nasjonal Samling*.' The General entreated Silje's father to a broad, cold smile.

'I am assuming that I have little choice in this,' Silje said.

'You assume correctly.'

Something crashed to the floor upstairs, and this time the General was on his feet with his pistol drawn. 'Perhaps we should secure your furniture this minute, Herr Ohnstad.'

'There is really no need!'

Gruetzmacher headed for the stairs, with Klein close behind. Silje stood and whispered to Klein as he walked past her. 'You have failed me,' she said, 'again.'

Klein swallowed and pushed her out of the way. Silje and her father exchanged glances and a silent prayer, and followed the officers to the stairs.

'As I said, General,' Jon Ohnstad cried desperately, 'there is no need to concern yourself.'

Silje tried to force her way past Klein, but he was having none of it. 'Help yourself and your father,' he said. 'Stay here.'

Silje ignored him and directed her plea to the General who was pointing his gun at the door to Magnus's room. 'General, please…'

Gruetzmacher kicked open the door and strode inside.

Jon Ohnstad turned to Silje and whispered, 'Child, we are undone.'

'What the hell is going on?' The General roared from inside the room. 'Who are you? What are you doing here? Quickly now! Explain yourselves!'

Silje and her father looked at each other.

Yourselves?

They both charged the stairs, past Lieutenant Klein, and into the bedroom.

Silje's jaw dropped.

Jon Ohnstad sighed with relief.

'Well?' The General stood with his arms folded, his gun still in his hand, but pointing, thankfully, towards the floor. He turned to Silje. 'Do you know these people?'

She nodded, and tried not to laugh. 'They are friends of mine.'

Lisbeth and Erik said nothing, but sank fearfully beneath the bed covers. Silje rolled her eyes from right to left, searching the room. There was no sign Freya had ever been there. The wardrobe, she thought. *Or perhaps under the bed; please god, not under the bed. That is the first place he will look!*

'This is my fault,' Jon Ohnstad said, without missing a beat. 'Their parents disapprove, you see, and they have nowhere else to go.'

Klein headed for the wardrobe and peered closely into the gap between the doors.

'You allow them to use your house like some brothel,' the General bellowed. 'Outrageous, Herr Ohnstad! Outrageous!'

Silje's eyes fell upon a long black hair, next to the General's left foot. She tried to signal her father, but Jon Ohnstad had problems of his own.

'You have encouraged their disobedience!'

'You are right, General. I am sorry.'

'Would you approve of your daughter lying with men behind your back?'

And it was at this moment that Jon Ohnstad chose to throw his daughter an oddly stern look. 'No, sir,' he said. 'I would not.'

'Then you would agree that it is not right to allow such wanton behaviour under your own roof!'

'Forgive me, General. I thought it poetic; I can see now that I was very wrong.'

The General turned his rage to the occupants of the bed. 'You two will get dressed and get out.'

Lisbeth and Erik nodded and threw back the bedcovers.

'Not now, you fools! When we have left!'

They restored the covers and cowered beneath them.

'And you will see no more of each other, do you understand?'

They nodded, a little too quickly for Silje's liking. She wondered if Erik would give up on her so easily.

'Speak!' the General snapped.

'Yes, General!' Erik cried.

Gruetzmacher set a final look of savage disapproval upon Jon Ohnstad, before turning to Silje. 'We will take our leave now. I will send instructions on how you are to proceed with your newsletter. I will return next week for your first copy. Klein! Come away from there! Are you not going to bid good evening to your young lady?'

Half-covered by the bedsheets, Erik's face froze.

'We are no longer together, General,' Klein said, firmly.

Gruetzmacher looked at them both and shook his head. 'I weep for the future.'

Klein hurried after the General without sparing Silje a glance. Her father followed them out of the room, apologising profusely. The General said nothing until they reached the kitchen where he continued to berate him.

They waited, Silje, Lisbeth and Erik, until they heard the door to the cottage open and slam shut. They remained frozen, listening to jackboots on shale, orders barked and, finally, vehicles departing. They waited until the sounds of the engines had faded into the mountains.

'Dear Christ,' said Erik. 'I thought we were dead.'

'Where is she?' Silje demanded.

'I am here,' Freya said weakly, from under the bed.

'That is the most stupid place to hide!'

'I am sorry.'

Erik was elated. 'I thought he was going to kill us!'

'How did you get in?' Silje asked.

'We crept through the woodland to the side of the cottage,' Erik said proudly. 'Then we climbed in through the window, put sheets on the bed, stripped and—'

'You made enough noise to wake the dead!'

'We were trying to help,' Lisbeth said flatly.

Jon Ohnstad appeared at the door, holding his favourite clay pipe, the one he smoked when he thought there was cause to celebrate. He smiled cheerfully but Silje could see his pipe hand was shaking.

'Well done, all of you.'

Freya hauled herself out from under the bed. 'It was my fault. I tried to hide in the wardrobe, but I could not find it. I panicked; I walked into the wall, and then the dresser. I am so sorry.'

'We heard her from the garden,' Erik said. 'We thought the Germans would too.'

Silje sniffed. 'Then my father is right. Good work, both of you.'

'Why thank you,' said Lisbeth, but Silje could tell she did not mean it.

Jon Ohnstad picked up their clothes from the floor and handed them to Erik so they could both dress beneath the covers. Silje watched them, suspiciously.

'We were acting, Silje,' Erik said. 'Nothing more.'

'Who do you think I am, Silje,' said Lisbeth, 'you?'

Silje looked at her father, shocked. 'She does not know what she's talking—'

'Now is not the time, Silje. Both of you, go. And not a word of this to anyone. Do you understand?'

They climbed from the bed, but as they left the room, Lisbeth whispered to Silje: 'Everything the General said about me, that is what the village says of you.'

Silje stared ahead, her fists clenched. It was clear her father had heard every word.

'I will fetch water,' he said, 'for the cuts to your foot.'

'Thank you, Father.' Silje could not look at him, and so was grateful when he took his leave.

Freya gazed at the stark wall as though it stood on the horizon, and Silje stared at Freya, pained to think that she was almost lost to them.

'I will leave,' the Jewess said finally. 'Someone can take me to the edge of the hills and I will make my way east.'

'You are being ridiculous. You cannot even find your way around a small room. The Germans will capture you in minutes.'

'Then perhaps that is best. I am a danger to you, your family, your entire village.'

'If you are captured, the Germans will want to know how a blind Jewish girl evaded them for weeks. They will torture you—'

'I will not tell them anything!'

'They will torture you, and you will tell them *everything*. Then they will come for me, my father, my brother – wherever he is – Erik, Lisbeth… No, you cannot leave now. It would be too dangerous for all of us.'

Her father returned with a large pitcher of water, a small basin and a jar of white vinegar. He smiled, filled the basin with water and lit his pipe.

'Not in here, Father.'

'Ah, right. I shall return shortly with more water.'

'Father, I think we need to talk.'

'I do not wish to speak of it now, Silje. Perhaps tomorrow, after we have all rested.'

He left the room, making solemn footfalls down to the kitchen.

'Sit,' Freya said.

'Why?'

'I will clean and dress your foot. Now sit.'

It was one of the rare occasions when Silje did as she was told. 'Are you sure that you are able?'

'I am more than able.' Freya knelt in front of her and felt for the basin and the bottle. She poured vinegar into her hands and into the water. Silje placed her foot in the basin. The water changed colour, and the room became hot and shrank away from her.

'What colour is it?'

'Sorry?'

'The water. Is it pink or red?'

'Pink, mostly.' Silje felt quite sick.

'Then the cut is not serious. It has probably dried.' Freya ran her fingers over the sole of Silje's foot, making the marrow of her thigh tingle. 'I have it. There is a small stone lodged in the cut.'

'Perhaps we should call my father.'

'Perhaps you should keep still.' Freya held the stone between her fingernails; Silje ground her teeth.

'I will count to five,' said Freya.

'This sounds like one of my father's tricks. You will count to three and then pull the stone when I am not expec—'

Freya twisted the stone and pulled it free.

Silje's whole body spasmed; she opened her mouth and began to pant rapidly; she squeezed her eyes shut and clamped her wrist against her teeth.

'That wasn't so very painful, was it?' said Freya. 'I need to dry your foot. Can you tell me where your father left the cloths?'

'He didn't bring them.' Silje wiped her eyes. 'They needed boiling after...'

'After cleaning me.'

'I am sorry, I did not mean for it to sound like that.' Silje cursed herself for her thoughtlessness, though she seldom cared so much for anything she said to anyone.

'It does not matter.' Freya pulled at the strings that kept her braid. Her hair fell free.

'What are you doing?'

'Making do.' She wrapped her tresses about her fist.

'You do not have to—'

'I want to.'

'There is no need.'

'You may stop talking any time you like.'

Her hair felt coarse, though not unpleasantly so. Less than a caress, Silje decided; an efficiency of care that reminded her of her mother's gentle ministrations, clearing her chest after she'd caught a chill. She swallowed and felt her stomach tighten. 'It feels nice.'

'I am glad.'

'Familiar.'

Freya tilted her head to one side. 'How so?'

'I am not entirely sure,' said Silje.

'Perhaps you have read of such a thing in your bible.'

'Yes, perhaps.' She looked at Freya's eyes and thought how easily – with a little work, weight and colour – she could be a thing desired by any man of the mountains.

11

Silje did not rise from her bed on the day that followed General Gruetzmacher's visit. When her father knocked on her door to see why the livestock had not been fed that morning, she moaned theatrically from under her bedcovers and complained of cold perspiration, a painful stomach, headaches, pins and needles, blurred vision and flatulence that was as mortifying as it was excessive.

'Temperament aside, you are no warmer than usual,' Jon Ohnstad said, placing his hand on her forehead. Nevertheless, he immediately fetched Dr Lomen, the village physician who also specialised in animal husbandry. The doctor was a stout man in his sixties who still possessed flame-red hair and a magnificent moustache of the same extraordinary colouring. He'd been widowed just once, during the birth of his fifth son, but had recently taken a second wife, a portly woman of thirty-two years from a neighbouring village. When she was fourteen, Silje had toyed with the idea of marrying him herself, but had quickly decided against it; Doctor Lomen always seemed to smell of horses.

He performed a thorough examination, during which he smiled congenially, made encouraging noises and regaled an unsettling blow-by-blow account of her birth. Silje often claimed that the doctor was the first face she could remember, and Magnus would laugh and say it wasn't true. After all, he was born a few moments after her, and he remembered nothing.

'Then perhaps all your brains left Mother's womb with me.'

That was usually enough to stop him laughing.

After ten minutes, Doctor Lomen announced he was done. 'Nothing to worry about,' he said cheerfully. He patted Silje on the head; she rolled her eyes and opened her mouth so he could place a lump of sugar on her tongue.

'Physically there is nothing wrong with her,' the doctor said to Jon Ohnstad, over a mug of ale and a plate of goats' cheese in the Ohnstad kitchen. His final diagnosis was 'emotional exhaustion' precipitated by the events of the previous evening.

Jon Ohnstad narrowed his eyes. 'What events?'

The good doctor finished his beer and wiped his mouth on his sleeve. 'Can I see her?'

Jon Ohnstad replied, 'See who?'

'The Jew,' said the doctor. 'Can I see the Jew?'

'Who told you we have a Jew?'

The doctor recoiled, seeing the alarm in Jon Ohnstad's eyes. 'I have told no one else,' he promised.

'I am more concerned with who told you! Was it Erik? Or Lisbeth perhaps.'

Doctor Lomen confessed that he'd heard the tale from Lisbeth's father. And during the conversation it became clear that most of the village already knew about the 'Jew in the goat shed'.

'We are not keeping her in the shed.' Jon Ohnstad groaned and put his head in his hands. 'My God, we are undone.'

'Nonsense! As your daughter is so fond of saying, Fólkvangr is a family. The Jew is as much our problem as yours. Now, can I see her?'

'Why?'

'I should examine her. In fact, after her ordeal, you should have brought her straight to me. She could have the chills, malnourishment. She could have dysentery or lice or measles. She may have contracted—'

'This way.' Jon rose from his seat and made his way to the stairs as though he bore Fólkvangr in its entirety on his shoulders.

* * *

'May I come in?'

Silje thought it odd that Freya didn't knock on doors; she arrived, announced herself, and waited – or simply walked in. 'You may.'

Freya entered, smiled in Silje's direction and then proceeded to take measured steps across the room. When she reached the window, she turned herself one quarter and measured the room's breadth in the same way.

'What are you doing?' Silje asked.

'I am finding my bearings. I may be here for some time so it is better that I know where everything is.' She bumped into Silje's old rocking horse. 'Doctor Lomen is a strange man.'

Silje said that Fólkvangr was full of strange men.

'He gave me a lump of sugar.'

'He does that for all his patients,' said Silje. 'How do you remember where everything is?'

'Without difficulty, thankfully.' Freya felt along the rocking horse's head, along its flank and then ran its tail through her fingers. 'Is this yours?'

'From when I was a child,' Silje answered guardedly.

'And you have kept it all this time?'

'I am not that old.'

'Though perhaps too old for a rocking horse.'

'Is there something else you wanted?'

'Well, I did think that perhaps there was something I could do for you.' Freya knocked an oak chair sideways. She found it and moved it back to the precise same spot.

Silje decided against hot soup, and asked instead for a mug of water. She thought the poor girl must spend her days tending bruises.

'I will return later.' Freya left the room, steering past the rocking horse and finding the door without a moment's hesitation.

And so for the rest the morning, Silje stayed wrapped in her bed-clothes. Her father went out to deliver his vegetables and orchids, but she could hear Freya moving about the cottage. The blind girl cleaned, cooked, tidied away bowls and utensils. Silje did not hear a single crash, or the sound of a table or chair in collision with a sightless Jew. Just after midday, the rear door opened and closed, leaving the cottage in silence.

A few moments later, Silje heard the sound of wood being split in the meadow behind the cottage. Alarmed, she threw back the bed-clothes and ran to the window.

Sure enough, Freya was chopping wood. It was a laborious process: a carefully selected log placed on the block, then a slow measure taken; a deep breath, a cry and the drop of an axe. The wood split first time.

Silje found herself consumed by admiration, but did not feel inclined to say so. Still, she thought it would be remiss of her not to say something, so she opened the window and called out, 'Be careful.'

'Thank you. I will.' Freya split another log and smiled up at her.

And such a pretty smile, Silje thought, and such good teeth.

She watched Freya from the window until nightfall, shouting instructions and guiding her to the blocks of wood that fell astray. Silje thought that there could perhaps be advantages in having no sight; the lack of sunlight didn't concern Freya; she could work just as well in darkness as she did during the day. Silje began planning a new farm routine that included midnight milkings for the goats. She wondered how Freya knew when it was time to go to sleep.

'When I'm tired,' Freya said, much later on, at the kitchen table, 'and when I can no longer hear the birds singing and when I can hear the mice in the grass and when I can feel the pull of the moon.'

'You must have the senses of a witch,' Silje said. She placed a steaming mug in Freya's hands and thought how sharp her words must sound.

Freya winced as she took hold of the mug. 'My father was in wonder of my hearing, and my sense of smell, and how I could discern the age of silk simply by touching it.' She sipped at the mug. 'He never called me a witch though.'

'I am sorry. I did not mean to say that you were—'

'I am teasing you,' Freya said. 'This drink you have made, what is it?'

'Melted chocolate, honey and goat's milk,' Silje replied, feeling oddly hurt. 'Do you like it?'

'Very much.' Freya placed the mug on the table, and rubbed at her palm with her thumb.

'Let me look.' Silje took her hands and peered closely at the joints where her fingers met her palms. 'Raw blisters,' she said. 'Welcome to the mountain. I will soak and clean them for you.'

'You do not have to do that. I am more than able to—'

'I know I do not have to,' said Silje. 'I want to.'

She filled a basin with water and added a splash of white vinegar and nettle oil. 'Tomorrow, I will take you into the village. It would be good for you to meet other people.'

'Are you sure that is wise?'

'Not really, but we have little choice. Erik will have stayed silent, but Lisbeth Fehn has a mouth as broad as her hips; she will tell her father and he will tell his bitch wife and she will tell the world.'

Freya giggled softly.

'I have no idea why you think this is funny. We must talk to the villagers and explain why it is important that knowledge of your presence goes no further than Fólkvangr.'

'Come sit beside me.'

Silje swallowed. 'Why.'

'Because I would know what you look like.'

Silje made her way back to the kitchen table and pulled a chair opposite Freya. She sat, slowly.

Freya reached out with both hands, searching the air until she found Silje's right cheek. She brought her hands together, starting at Silje's hairline, tracing her finger across her forehead and then down either side of her nose. Her fingertips felt hard and callused.

'Close your eyes.'

Silje did as she was told and Freya ran her thumbs over her eyelids.

'Colour?'

'What?'

'What colour are your eyes?'

'Blue,' Silje said, and then added, 'light-blue, like the sky – which of course you have not seen. Sorry, I am speaking nonsense.'

'I remember blue.' Freya's fingers pressed into Silje's cheeks. 'It smells like glacier water.' She moved to her jawline, feeling behind her ears and tracing forward to her chin. She leaned closer and breathed in.

'And your skin is less than white, but not quite pink.'

'I think you are teasing me again.'

'Your scent is not as dark as your father's; you are more like a butterfly orchid, which is not surprising.' She leaned back and declared, 'You are very beautiful, Silje Ohnstad.'

Silje blushed violently.

'And that is surprising for one with such a barbarous tongue.'

To tear a hole in someone with just a word, Silje thought. *So that is how that feels.*

Jon Ohnstad opened the door, and Silje lurched ungracefully from her chair. 'Father!' she cried. 'What are you doing here?'

'I live here,' he said, dropping a basket of vegetables and two fresh mountain hares on the table. 'Are you all right?'

Silje looked nervously at Freya, who stared at the door with a look of puzzlement on her face. 'We were just… That is to say, Freya was—'

'Seeing what you look like, I know. Hello there, young Freya.'

'Mr Ohnstad.'

'It is Jon, please.' Jon Ohnstad placed his palm on Silje's head. 'Odd, you are warmer than before. Perhaps you should still be in bed.'

'Did you remember the chocolate?' Silje said, moving her head from beneath his palm.

'You did not ask for chocolate.'

'In future, try to get chocolate. Freya likes it.'

Freya said, 'Please do not put yourselves to any trouble on my account.'

It is a little late for that, Silje thought, but surprised herself by not saying so out loud.

* * *

The following morning, as she had promised, Silje took Freya to meet the people of Fólkvangr. There was a spring chill in the air, and a light snow had fallen during the night. Silje fussed Freya into an extra coat and kissed her father goodbye before they set off from the cottage and walked down into the village.

'Do you think they will like me?' Freya asked.

'We are Norwegians,' Silje replied. 'We like everyone.'

'Except, perhaps, the Germans.'

'Yes, except the Germans.'

As they approached the road into Fólkvangr, young Ingrid Haug raced out on her bicycle to greet them.

'Is this the Jew?' she demanded, almost dizzy with excitement. Ingrid was a slim, dark-haired girl of nine years whose large green eyes now shone with feline curiosity. She rode her bicycle in tight circles around the two women while they walked. 'Oh Silje, she is so pretty!'

Silje looked at Freya and said, 'Is she?'

'You know she is! And she is blind?'

'As a bat,' said Freya.

Ingrid's jaw dropped. 'She can speak!'

Silje asked, 'Ingrid, do you know the difference between dumb and blind?'

'Yes,' Ingrid replied indignantly. 'I did not expect her to speak, that is all.' She peered closely at Freya on her next circuit, and on the one after that she stuck out her tongue. Freya stuck out her own in retaliation, and Ingrid almost toppled from her bicycle. She righted herself and rode quickly back towards the village. 'I will tell everyone that the Jew is on her way!'

'Thank you, Ingrid,' Silje called after her. 'And please stop shouting "Jew"!'

They walked on in silence, Silje feeling an apprehension most uncommon to her, as though she were about to introduce her betrothed to her family. She looked at Freya who was chewing nervously at her lower lip. 'They will like you.'

'How do you know?'

'Because I like you, and everyone in Fólkvangr knows I am a fine judge of character. It is one of my most often-forgotten qualities.'

'Along with modesty. We must not forget your modesty.'

'Well no, I never let anyone forget my modesty.'

A crowd had gathered at the end of the mountain path, under the arch. Silje counted at least three dozen, shouting and waving with worrying enthusiasm.

'Are there many people?' Freya asked anxiously.

'Not many, no.'

More arrived, pouring from the cottages and houses and on to the path. Silje took Freya's hand and said, 'It is probably best for me to do the talking.'

The villagers were boisterous, excited, yet gentle and friendly. The younger children wanted to touch her hair. While an alarmed Freya shook hands and thanked the villagers for their kindness, Silje called out instructions:

—She was to be referred to as Freya and only Freya – never 'the Jew' or 'the Jewess' or 'the hat-maker's daughter'.

—Her presence was not to be discussed with anyone outside the village (and Silje looked pointedly at Lisbeth Fehn when she said this).

'And if anyone asks who she is then her name is Freya Ohnstad and she is a distant cousin who has travelled from Sarpsborg to see us.'

The gathering looked to each other and agreed, some even calling suggestions of their own.

Perhaps your cousin should stay indoors during the day.

We could bring anything you need to the cottage.

We need volunteers to man the old hay store near the foot of the mountains!

They can warn us when the Germans are close by!

Yes! This will give us the time we need to hide the Jew!

Rolf, you idiot! What did Silje just tell you!

It is an excellent plan. Can we find radio equipment?

I have a contact in the Resistance. She will give us radios!

Silje was glad to see the villagers getting into the swing of things.

'I think that your cottage is not the best place for her,' said Junges Fehn. He smiled in Freya's direction and Silje saw him lick the corner of his mouth.

'And why is that, Mr Fehn?' she said, thinking how repulsive he was, and how she could have brought herself to do those things for him – even for the use of his printing press.

'You are situated on the north road, the only road from Bergen to Fólkvangr. If the Germans come then they will reach your home before they reach the village.'

The crowd nodded in agreement.

'My house, which is much larger than yours if I may say so, is located further to the west. There would be plenty of time to hide Freya.' He scratched his neck and smiled, somewhat unpleasantly. 'And then there is the small matter of the work you will be doing for the Nazis.'

This was news to many of those gathered. They began whispering amongst themselves, some looking at Silje with eyes she had not seen before and was not sure she cared for.

'What work? What does he mean, Silje?' asked Karoline Flom, the baker's sister.

'What I mean,' said Junges, 'is that Silje has been recruited by the enemy. Her newsletter will now carry propaganda written by General Gruetzmacher himself.'

'Oh, for shame, Silje Ohnstad!' a voice called out.

'That is a lie!' Silje cried. 'Where did you hear such nonsense?'

'From my own daughter.'

'You should bleach her hair,' said Lisbeth Fehn, keen to shift the subject of the morning back to Freya.

'And cut it short,' added Marit Ohnstad. Silje silently cursed the woman and her ungodly talent for materialising from nowhere. 'No self-respecting Norwegian woman would wear their hair so long.' And then she smiled and gave Silje a cool, penetrating look. 'Though a slut might.'

For her own safety, three of the villagers moved Freya to one side, as Silje set about Marit Ohnstad like a thing possessed. She screamed obscenities and lashed out with her fists and her feet. The old woman gave as well as she received, clawing for Silje's eyes and heaping curses upon Silje and her unborn descendants. It took four of the strongest men present to bring the altercation to an end. Silje shook herself free of them, gathered her dignity and took Freya by the hand, leading her through the gathering and past the memorial to her mother. Marit Ohnstad's taunts rang in her ears.

'What was that? What happened? Silje, were you fighting? Who was that woman?'

'Enough questions,' Silje said. 'And I think we have met enough people for today.'

'I would like to see more of the village.'

'You cannot *see* anything,' Silje snapped, and this time was determined to ignore the tightening inside her chest.

Freya pulled her hand away. 'If you do not wish me to stay with you, Silje, I will understand, but please stop saying these unkind things to me.'

It was a tone as strong and as sharp as any Silje had heard since her mother had passed away. 'I am sorry.'

Freya was so startled she hiccoughed, and then gave a sigh of surprise when Silje took her in her arms.

'You are not to leave us, and you are certainly not to leave us for the Fehns.' Silje stepped back and held her shoulders. 'You are safest with us. The Germans trust us. They will be visiting our cottage often, so it is the last place they would think of looking for an escaped Jew.'

She took Freya's hand, and wished that she could see she was smiling. 'I will take you to the baker's shop. I know he has chocolate.'

The rest of the morning remained cold, though Silje was untouched by it. The snow came again, lasting only a few moments. The villagers stopped to introduce themselves and say how happy they were to help in any way they could, the younger ones seeking to touch Freya's dress and her hair. Silje and Freya took a narrow lane to the southern corner of the village, and ran into Jonas Kleppe, the lamplighter.

'Freya, this is Mr Kleppe, the one I told you about; the one who lied about the ladder.'

Jonas Kleppe wrung his hat in his hands. 'You are not going to let me forget that, are you?'

'Not until I understand why you did it. Why say you had stolen Mr Gundersen's ladder when you had not? You made me look like a fool.'

Freya whispered that it was only a ladder.

'And I am sorry. And I am sorry that I do not know why I did it. That you will no longer accompany me on my rounds is punishment enough.'

'That is not the only reason, Mr Kleppe. My work on the newsletter will not allow me enough time to—'

'I will do it,' Freya said. 'I will accompany you.'

Mr Kleppe's face shone like daybreak. Silje was having none of it.

'Do not be silly. You cannot help light the lamps. You are... You know what you are.'

'And what better person to help light the lamps than someone who does not need them?'

Mr Kleppe started clapping, and was quickly silenced with a stern look from Silje.

'You said I should help around the village, Silje.'

'Yes, but I meant—'

'And I will get plenty of exercise and fresh air, which you tell me is the secret to your physical charm and flawless complexion.'

'I do not remember using myself as an example...'

'And I will learn to find my way around the village and I am sure Mr Kleppe will look after me.'

He nodded with a vigour Silje had not seen in him since she was a child. 'I swear I will guard her with my life, Silje. I will take good care of her.'

She was not at all sure Mr Kleppe could take care of himself. She looked to Freya, who tried to look imploringly back.

'I will ask my father,' she said.

Mr Kleppe and Freya screamed with joy.

'And if he agrees, I will bring her to your house every second evening, and you will return her to the cottage before ten.'

'I can find my own way, Silje.'

'I would feel better if you did not wander around the mountains at night.'

'I am not sure what difference the night would make,' Freya said glumly.

'You will do as you are told, Freya. Good morning, Mr Kleppe.'

They parted company, Mr Kleppe barely able to contain himself.

'He seems to have taken a shine to you,' Silje said.

'He would just like someone to talk to during his rounds.'

'There are a dozen people in the village who would be far more suitable.'

'And you would still be his first chosen. Do you know why he lied about the ladder?'

'No I do not, and neither do you.'

'He sought to make you happy.'

'You have no idea what you are talking about.'

'You have an extraordinary power over people, Silje Ohnstad. They love you without question or restraint, despite your many faults, and they hate to see you upset, or lonely, or disappointed. Mr Kleppe could not bear to sadden you, so he told you he had stolen the ladder. He said it to make you happy.'

Silje wondered if a blind girl could truly see so much. 'If what you say is true, it is nothing I do on purpose. I would not ask people to lie to me, or lie for me.'

'I am sure. But it is a rare gift you possess, to make people want you to love them as much as they love you.'

'Then I will use this gift to keep my village safe. And I will use it to keep you from harm's way, if you will let me. It is what your father would have wanted.'

Freya swallowed and turned her eyes to the ground. 'I have no answer when you say such things to me. "Thank you" never seems enough.'

'We are Norwegians,' said Silje. 'A "thank you" is all that is needed.'

Freya nodded and held out her hand. Silje hesitated, gazing at her slender fingers as though she'd been invited to grasp a naked flame.

'Take it,' said Freya. 'It won't bite you.'

Silje felt its inhuman warmth spread through her entire body. Demons, the General had said.

They walked to the baker's shop, hand in hand. Like sisters, Silje thought, realising how much she would have loved to have had a sister to share secrets with, to fight with. Of course she shared and fought with Magnus, but a sister would have been… different. They would be far more intimate with their deepest feelings; their sibling tensions would be far less—

She stopped suddenly, pulling Freya to a halt.

'What do you mean *despite my many faults*.'

12

I spent the night in his hotel room. We drank and we talked; he told me about his wife and his daughter. He said he missed them, especially his daughter who resented him for tying up the phone whenever he called. He said he was still in love with his wife, though he'd only spared her every third thought when they were married.

'So why do I want her so much now?'

'Because someone else is sleeping with her.' That came out wrong. What I meant to say was *now you understand what you've lost.* I knew it probably wasn't true, but I was too drunk to lie.

He didn't seem to notice. He looked at me, blinked and let the vodka bottle fall to the carpet. 'I guess we're done talking then.'

We took our clothes off without passion or urgency, and after a few minutes of dispirited fingering, I found myself staring at the ceiling while he guided his erection inside me.

He screwed me with short, workmanlike strokes, expending more energy than he needed to; I wondered why the light fittings in his room were different to mine.

He made a grunting sound in his throat and, somewhat impolitely, came inside me. To be honest I would have missed it if I hadn't been listening out for him.

We drank some more, talked some more, laughed self-consciously for a while, fucked some more.

He fell asleep before I did, and when I finally succumbed I dreamt we were still having sex; though this time, when I looked for the light fittings, I saw Monica standing over us. She took a razor blade from under her tongue and rested its edge between the salesman's heaving shoulder blades. I screamed without making a sound, while she scored a line down the centre of his back. His eyes glazed white and he split neatly in half.

I woke with my heart pounding inside my neck. I tried to swallow, couldn't; I turned over, half-expecting to find the salesman lying gutted beside to me.

I didn't find him at all.

There was a note left on the pillow. When I opened it out, a hundred Krona note dropped from the folds.

All it said was, *Your share of the bet.*

* * *

My head was thundering by the time I reached Reception. I settled the bill and turned to see Harriet walking away from the front desk. I called her name; she didn't stop so I called out again. I chased after her, yelling her name across the lobby. She had quite a start on me, but she was wearing a mini-skirt that she had to keep pulling down over her thighs, and four-inch platform shoes that rattled like machine guns as she hurried towards the exit. I broke into a run and caught her, grabbing her by the arm and spinning her so hard she almost fell.

'Did you know?' I screamed at her. 'Did you know what he was going to do?'

She looked desperately around the lobby, hoping an escape tunnel would appear from thin air.

'Well? Did you?'

A leper's circle opened up around us, the guests and staff giving us a wide berth.

'Come back to the bar,' she implored. 'We can talk there.'

'I'm not going anywhere with you. He left me a note – a fucking note!'

'It's what he does. He doesn't mean anything by it.'

'Oh, so it's nothing personal. I'm glad to hear it!'

Harriet took my hand and led me to a large faux-Roman architrave near the lobby entrance. 'Sit.'

I folded my arms to show her that I wasn't simply going to do as I was told, and then I sat. She took the seat next to me and gestured in the direction of the bar. 'He doesn't mean to do it,' she said, still looking over my shoulder and waving. 'He's had a rough couple of years.'

'Who hasn't.'

She looked at me and smiled as though it hurt to. 'Yes, I see what you mean. Look, he's not a bad person. He's just bitter, that's all. And when things get to him, he lashes out.'

'So what you're saying is that by sleeping with me, then leaving a note telling me he fucked me for a dare – that's just him "lashing out"?'

Her face gave no sign that she knew how ridiculous she sounded. 'You don't have to worry; there was no bet. He makes that part up just to—'

'Twist the knife?'

Harriet rubbed the back of her neck. 'He sometimes needs to hurt people.'

A waiter brought a pair of whiskey sours and placed them on the coffee table. He waited for Harriet to sign the chit and then quietly slipped away.

Harriet downed her sour in one; I pushed my glass to one side.

'How long have you been in love with him?'

She shrugged. 'I'm not in love with him, not yet. We just mess around.'

'When he's not lashing out.' There was a faint bruise just behind her jawline. She saw me staring so moved her head to hide it.

'One day though,' she said, brightening suddenly, 'if he can work it out of his system.'

It's rare that I run into someone whom I pity more than Monica and me. I stood up and tried to smile, but I think it came out as more of a grimace. 'Look, Harriet, you seem like a nice person,' I lied. 'But really, this has nothing to do with me. Go with him if you want to; be happy. You don't need my approval, or anyone else's.'

And that was a lie too; Harriet did need my approval. She needed the blessing of someone evil by virtue of their birth, someone connected by genes to the worst person imaginable, to tell her that her future life-partner – a man who used sex to hurt people and who, on at least one occasion, had attacked her – was really an okay person, or would be once he 'worked it out of his system'.

Harriet was a special kind of idiot.

She slid a business card across the coffee table. 'I travel a lot but call me once in a while; maybe we can hook up.'

Unbelievable.

* * *

The old man had promised me breakfast so I skipped my morning visit to the hotel's restaurant and took a walk and a ride to Pløens Gate. I took the wrong tram but I didn't mind; I got to see the cathedral and the National Theatre, and I figured the old man wasn't going anywhere.

I was about twenty minutes late when I arrived at an old tenement building nestled between a street café and an American diner. I rang the bell for his apartment, and he buzzed me straight in without asking who I was.

I took the stairs to the third floor and he opened his door before I had the chance to knock. He looked at me with his faded watery eyes and said, 'You're late.'

'But you're surprised I came at all, Mr Klein.'

His face fell and what little colour it had drained away.

'That's who you are, isn't it? Gerbald Klein, First Lieutenant in the Scandinavian Expeditionary Force.' A little too much drama perhaps; it wasn't exactly a secret. The museum security guard had told me. He'd even shown me a book where I could read all about Gerbald Klein – The Penitent.

'And you came anyway.' He stood to one side so I could enter the apartment. He followed me, keeping a respectful distance which I found strange; we were both pariahs after all.

The hallway opened out into a large living room with high ceilings and unpainted walls. The cornices were dark and spotted with mould. There was a musty smell that hung solidly in the air. And then there were the bookcases, dozens of them. Some found space against the walls, others stood free and out of place around the floor. There were a few tables of odd sizes and various eras which looked as if they'd been bought from second-hand shops, or culled from rubbish tips. There were three narrower passages; one led away to the kitchen – where he was cooking something that had my mouth watering; the others, I assumed, led to the bedrooms and the bathroom. Like the rest of the apartment, the hallways were stacked high with bundles of newspapers, magazines, and documents with the Nazi standard stamped on their covers.

And books – lots and lots of books.

Mr Klein's apartment was something of an archive in its own right.

'Shouldn't all of this be in the Resistance Museum?'

'Perhaps.' He handed me a mug of coffee that he'd had waiting. 'I'm still cataloguing most of it.'

I sipped at the lukewarm mug while he served breakfast: waffles, butter and syrup, scrambled eggs with cream cheese, salmon and dill. We ate in silence at the only table that wasn't laden with junk. I polished off the last of the grapefruit juice and he asked me if I wanted anything else.

I replied by saying, 'I don't know what I'm doing here.'

'Yes you do.' he said, his German accent growing momentarily thicker. I wondered if this was a trait he displayed when he found himself in the rare position of having the upper hand, or maybe he no longer felt the need to conceal it. 'You seek to uproot your family tree so you may plant anew. You believe you can do this by bringing your father to justice.' He chased a portion of salmon around his plate, then gave up. 'You seek this nation's forgiveness, as do I.'

'Is that why you never returned to Germany?'

He smiled. 'You read that?'

'The security guard told me.'

This made him chuckle; it wasn't meant to. He leaned back in his chair and looked at the ceiling. 'I was there,' he said, 'at Fólkvangr, on the day of the massacre. I didn't want to return to my homeland carrying such guilt.

'I could have escaped. I could have followed many of my fellow officers to South America. I chose not to. So when Germany surrendered, so did I. I was tried; I pleaded guilty. I was sentenced to death which, make no mistake, I deserved. I was held in solitary confinement for two years, awaiting execution, but in that time, Norway grew something of a social conscience. I suppose after the death and suffering they'd seen under the Nazis… They had no stomach for it, so my sentence was commuted to twenty years.'

He stopped talking and looked down at his plate, staring at it, as though he could see his future in the scraps.

I coughed, and when that didn't bring him back, I asked, 'What was it like? Prison, I mean.'

Again, he chuckled, and I nearly asked him what he found so amusing.

'Between the beatings and the rapes, not an experience I would recommend. I was moved constantly, but wherever I went, the guards and the other prisoners would eventually find out who I was and invent new and interesting ways to remind me what I'd done.' He lifted his shirt slightly and pointed to the edge of a colostomy bag, surrounded by puckered scarring. 'I took the punishment for those who escaped, the same as you.'

I swallowed my nausea and pressed on. 'You didn't return home after you were released.' And I really wanted to know why; I needed to know what had kept him living in a country that would despise him long after he was dead.

'A girl. Why else?' He rose unsteadily to his feet and hobbled to a large cabinet near the window. 'I have a picture.' He came back and placed a small booklet in front of me. It was old, dissolving prematurely – much like its keeper. He stood at my shoulder and carefully turned the pages, the smell of decay on his breath. 'There she is.'

I squinted hard, trying to piece together an image from the faded photograph. It looked like a beauty pageant. The date written underneath read 1938. The girls were dressed in traditional bunads, along with gloves and scarves to shield against the mountain cold. He pointed her out to me. She was blonde, unsurprisingly, with a very round and very pretty face. And she was tall with unusually broad shoulders. Her arms, folded against her large breasts to fend against the cold, were slim and muscular. In fact, *all* the women in the pageant had broad shoulders and unnervingly taut biceps.

'The women of the hills,' he said. 'Beautiful and strong. Warrior stock – like your own Valkyrie. The secret was in the vast quantity of goat's milk they consumed, or so the story went.' He massaged his throat and smiled. 'She won that year; the last year the contest was held. War came the year after, you see.'

'What was her—?'

'Silje. Silje Ohnstad. She was the daughter of a local farmer and she was the most beautiful creature I have ever laid eyes on.'

'Were you two – involved?'

He shook his head. 'God, no. Well… yes, but not really. For a short time, perhaps. I think.'

I had no idea whether they were involved or not.

'It took her only a few short minutes to destroy me, and though she cast me aside, I stayed. I stayed because I wanted to show her I had paid dearly for what I'd done.'

I closed the booklet and saw the cover for the first time. It carried the German standard and the flag of Norway, along with a title, *The Orchid.* Someone had pencilled in the Traitor's name above it so it read *The Quisling Orchid.*

'Silje was the magazine's editor,' Klein explained. 'A so-called collaboration between the invaders and the Norwegian people. It was quite common to find the booklet defaced and left on her doorstep.'

I would have liked to have read more, but I'm sure it would have fallen apart in my hands.

'She was engaged to your father, you know. At least, that's what he believed. In truth, Silje Ohnstad belonged to no man.' He caressed his throat and drifted away again. 'Your father married someone else, before he was unmasked as Fólkvangr's traitor, but it was Silje Ohnstad – she was the true love of his life.'

My mother had talked a lot about my father; she'd never mentioned this girl.

'Is she still alive?'

Klein shrugged. 'I wish I knew. At the end, many of the bodies could not be identified. I sometimes think I see her…' He shook his head, looking as sad as I'd ever seen him. 'No, she is gone, and that is the end to it.'

But it was too late; he'd already planted the seed. If she was still alive then perhaps my father remained in contact with her; perhaps they'd stayed in hiding to protect him. It was a wishful thought, but his trail was two decades cold; I needed somewhere to start, and I doubted the good lieutenant could tell me much more.

He sniffed and told me his shift at the museum would begin soon. 'You can stay and look through anything you want. Just be careful with the really old stuff.' He placed a spare key on top of the booklet. 'I hope something here helps you.'

'I hope so too.'

He picked up his raincoat and headed for the door.

I asked him: 'Did she love my father?'

'In her own way. Your father said she was very much like a rose: a thing of great beauty, though you had to watch for the thorns.'

'She doesn't sound like much of a catch to me.'

'Oh, she was,' he said. 'If you could endure the pain of holding on to her.'

13

It was no surprise to Silje that the villagers took to Freya as though she were born of the mountain. The Jewess would carry out her morning chores and then set off for the village where she would help out at the baker's shop, and spend the late morning with Mr Bergström, the grocer. He often complained how scarce produce had become since the Germans had invaded. Silje's father and the other farmers supplied what little they could, but it seemed that self-sufficiency was becoming the order of war.

In the afternoons Freya cleaned the village hall, and to hear Mrs Roys speak of her, one would think that she was the best domestic in all of Norway.

'Believe it or not, Silje Ohnstad,' Mrs Roys said during one of Silje's regular jaunts into the village, made to ensure Freya had not come to any harm. 'She is a godsend. You could eat from the floor once young Freya has had at it. Not a mote of dust or a single cobweb left anywhere, and all done so quickly!'

A similar tale, begrudgingly told, awaited her at the home of Mrs Tufte, the seamstress. 'The girl is a devil with needle and thread. Speed, accuracy and no blood left on the material... She will go far in this profession.'

On this particular day, less than a week since Fólkvangr had been made aware of the hidden Jew, Silje caught sight of Freya as she made her way back to the home of Mrs Tufte. She wore a white dress, laced with honey-coloured orchids that she had sewn herself. Her feet were bare and her long toes resembled fingers, feeling for the changes in the cobblestones that guided her. Her left hand traced along the walls of the cottages, seeking textures and doors, signs and symbols etched in the wood.

You must trust her, Silje told herself, she can take care of herself; you must stop following her. She wondered if she could. Freya was young and very alone, and so it was only right someone should take care of her, and as painful as it was to admit, there were times – the empty hours spent missing Magnus or crying for her mother – when she simply wanted to see her.

Occasionally Freya would stop and smell the air, and it was one such moment when she turned and said, 'Silje? Is that you?'

Silje's heart leapt into her mouth. 'I am sorry; I did not mean to spy. I came to tend my mother's flowers, and I needed to speak to Erik because I have not seen him in days and then I saw you and I wasn't staring, not that you would know, or care. I am sorry, that was unkind. It is just that sometimes I watch you and I find myself… How do you do it?'

Freya turned bright red.

'The whole world is a living, breathing thing inside you, and with your ears, your nose and your fingers you walk through it without hesitation or fear or—' Silje found herself seized by a sudden, most terrible thought. 'How did you know I was here, and if you say it is the smell I shall simply die on this very spot.'

Freya smiled and said, 'It is the smell.'

'It's the goats, isn't it? I wash myself straight after I have fed them, and still—'

'Orchids,' said Freya. 'Your family smells of orchids. I think it is why people like you so much.'

And it was Silje's turn to blush.

'Will you walk with me? I am going back to the seamstress's cottage.'

'No,' Silje said, more firmly than she had intended. 'I have much to do. I will see you back at home for supper. Be careful.'

'I am always careful.'

'Yes,' said Silje, 'I see that now.'

14

Fólkvangr was built within an open-sided funnel of ice and rock. The cold air from the mountain peaks was drawn down to the village, lending it an almost perpetual winter, while the shape of the mountains acted as a natural echo chamber, ensuring that approaching vehicles could be heard from many miles away.

And it was the sound of an approaching vehicle that evening which stirred Silje from her tapestry, and her father from his orchid breeding. Jon Ohnstad placed his wishbone tweezers on the table and raised his eyeglasses. 'A dispatch rider.'

Silje looked to the kitchen clock; it was a few minutes before ten. 'Mr Kleppe will be on his way with Freya.'

Her father jumped to his feet and reached for his coat and hat. 'I will meet them and take them back to *The Mottled Goat.*'

Silje was already tidying the kitchen, stowing away any signs that a second woman was living in the cottage. There were two dresses being dried above the stove that were clearly too small for her; she threw them into the pantry as her father left through the kitchen door.

'Hurry!' she shouted after him, and hid the bonnet that Freya had been making for Mrs Tufte.

The sound of the motorcycle drew closer.

There were three bowls in the sink, left over from supper. She added a fourth, thinking that an even number was less likely to arouse suspicion.

There were footsteps on the path, a knock at the door. Silje made one last sweep of the kitchen and took a deep breath before opening it.

Lieutenant Klein saluted. 'Fräulein Ohnstad.' He was carrying a typewriter under his arm. 'I have brought supplies for the newsletter, courtesy of General Gruetzmacher.' He entered the cottage without waiting for an invitation. He set down the typewriter and turned to face her. He opened his mouth to speak but seemed to think better of whatever it was he wanted to say. He strode awkwardly from the cottage and returned a moment later carrying boxes of scissors, craft knives and pots of glue. 'Take what you need and share the rest with the villagers if you like,' he said, and left the cottage again.

Silje began making hot chocolate and honey; the Lieutenant looked cold.

He came back inside carrying reams of paper and pencils. 'If you have trouble with the typewriter—'

'I shall be able to fix it,' she said.

'Of course, of course.' Klein wiped his hands on his breeches. He glanced around the kitchen as though looking for someone.

'I let you down, and I am sorry,' he said. 'If you give me another chance I swear I will not do so again.' He removed his helmet and stood straight. 'You are all I think about, Silje Ohnstad.'

Silje closed the cottage door and returned to the kitchen table to stand in front of him. She looked into his eyes and saw little more than his wretched longing, embers reflecting his desire for her and a hatred for himself.

'You are not going to tell me you love me, are you, Gerbald?'

He looked to the ceiling and squeezed his eyes shut. 'I do not know,' he said, and then he said, 'Yes.'

'Oh.' It occurred to Silje that she could obliterate him with a single word, cast her tongue to flay the flesh from his bones. The thought of it thrilled her. 'And how could I love one such as you?'

The Lieutenant implored her, 'Do not be unkind, Silje. I could not bear it.'

She knelt in front of him and began unfastening his breeches. 'I am never unkind, Gerbald, not to those who are loyal to me.'

'I swear on my life, Silje; I am loyal to you.'

'Then tell me, how fares the good General?'

Klein gripped the edge of the table and began to tremble. 'He is well, though he is… concerned.'

She drew a fingernail along his length, felt his blood pulse in the palm of her hand. 'And what concerns him?'

'Many things,' he gasped. 'Supply shortages, morale, the efforts of the Resistance, the effect the cold weather has on machinery and—'

'The Resistance?'

'Yes.' Klein's breathing shortened to sharp rapid bursts. 'They have attacked our ships docked at Bergen, Oslo and Trondheim. We have lost one vessel, though we killed at least half a dozen resistance fighters and— Ow!'

'Sorry, please go on.'

'The area commanders do not see a threat, but General Gruetzmacher can only see resistance to our cause growing. He is a good man, Silje, and a fine leader. His ability to see into the mind of our enemy encroaches on the supernatural.'

'Then perhaps it is his drinking that has brought him to this place.'

Klein fell silent.

'Answer me.'

'He has always struggled with his demons, his... desires, but Germany knows his worth. This post was not a punishment; he sought it. He wanted to come to Norway, and we gladly followed him.'

'And what plans does he have for the Resistance?'

'Why do you wish to know?'

'So that I can better use the newsletter to aid him. I have no wish to see my countrymen killed fighting you, Gerbald.' He needed more encouragement, so she drew his phallus deep into her mouth. His reaction surprised her; he began to struggle, tried to pull himself free. Silje pressed her weight against him, forcing him back against the table. She clawed her fingernails down his stomach and sank her teeth into his flesh.

He closed his eyes and whispered under his breath: 'He has sent for reinforcements and interrogators. He seeks to crush the Resistance before it can put down roots. He seeks to turn the common Norwegian away from them. Silje, you are torturing me!'

She nursed from him and bit into him until she felt him stiffen and burst against the roof of her mouth. Klein sank slowly to the floor.

Her jaw throbbed from her exertions and her legs felt weak, so much so that she had to use the table to support her journey to the sink. She could taste blood on her tongue. She swilled her mouth with cold water before returning to where the Lieutenant sat, crying softly to himself. She looked at him and felt strangely intoxicated. She raised his chin with a single finger, then struck him with her open palm. She raised her hand to strike him again, but stopped when he did not attempt to defend himself.

'That was not polite, Gerbald,' she said softly.

'I am sorry. I could not stop myself.'

There is a soft anger about him, Silje thought, *though he is more angry at himself than me.*

'God forgive you for what you have done to me.' He used a chair to haul himself to his feet and tried to smarten his tunic, forgetting that his breeches were still undone.

'I have educated you, Gerbald, that is all. There is no harm in it.'

'There is harm, Fräulein,' he said, 'when I betray myself for your affections.' He fastened his breeches, and after a performance of fidgets and coughs managed to regain a semblance of dignity. 'You promised me information,' he said sternly, 'in return for my cooperation. Well, I have cooperated, God help me, so now you must—'

'I have nothing for you,' Silje replied. 'We are a small village, unimportant in the scheme of all things, even before the invasion.' She knew men well enough; Gerbald would seek to expunge his guilt by taking something from her, some token of her betrayal to assuage his own. She knew men well enough to understand that guilt was a leash to hold them by, though not too tightly.

'You must have something!'

'I am sorry, Gerbald; I have nothing. If I had then I would tell you.'

He wiped his nose on his sleeve; he was on the verge of weeping. She tried hard not to smile. His breathing came in short, rough bursts, his skin reddened as his rage boiled to the surface. And when he opened his eyes and looked at her, Silje saw someone else in him; she saw the General's protege.

The Lieutenant's breathing slowed, and when he spoke, his words were calm, even, and measured: 'You could begin with the whereabouts of your brother.'

Silje felt herself swallow. 'What do you mean?'

'He was with you when you came to Bergen, but he was not here when the General and I came to see you, two weeks ago.'

'He was at the tavern.'

'I imagined as much,' Klein said plainly. 'He is a priest, yes?'

'Yes.'

'And yet he drinks in taverns.'

'He is still in training.' It was a wretched answer, one she felt sure would put her brother before the firing squad.

'Studying languages at the Mission School in Stavanger, yes?'

Silje nodded as though in a trance. 'How do you know this?'

'Do not be surprised, Fräulein. We know a great many things. We know your brother has not been seen at the school since German forces landed.'

'Come upstairs,' she said desperately, placing her hand against his groin. 'There is so much more I can teach you.'

He pushed her away, so savagely she fell to the floor.

'Perhaps another time,' he said, massaging his cheek. 'I must return; the General is expecting me.' He strapped his helmet to his head and walked to the door. 'Do not treat me like a fool, Silje Ohnstad. And it would be in your brother's best interest for him to return to this village and stay here for the duration of the war. I shall not warn you again.'

* * *

The cottage door creaked slowly open, and Jon Ohnstad poked his head into the kitchen. 'Silje?'

She looked up and said 'Father', but could not muster the strength to rise from the floor. Her father turned and called to Freya, telling her it was safe, and then went to his daughter's aid.

'Dear Lord, Silje, are you all right?' He cradled her in his arms. 'What happened?'

Freya appeared at the door and sniffed at the air. 'Klein,' she said.

Silje looked to the kitchen clock. Three hours had gone: three hours and she could not remember a single thought that had passed through her head in all that time. 'You have the nose of a dog.'

'Now is not the time to be unkind.' Jon Ohnstad held her more tightly.

She drew herself away from him. 'I was not being unkind.'

'Are you all right? Did he hurt you? Did he hit you?'

'And what would you do if he has hurt me, Father? What could anyone do?' She embraced herself and shivered.

'I will make soup.' Like Silje's own mother, Freya had come to believe that hot soup was the first and best remedy for an ailing soul.

'Stop fussing, both of you.' With her father's aid, Silje got up from the floor. 'I am fine. Really. Now, where is Magnus?'

She thought it odd that her father did not reply. Instead he looked to

Freya, who clattered pans and cursed at the stove, clearly trying to forget the question.

'I know you heard me, Freya,' Silje said. 'You hear everything.'

Freya stopped rattling the pans and stood motionless with her back to them both.

'So, you have told her what my brother is up to, but you have decided not to tell me.'

Jon Ohnstad licked his lips.

'You trust her more than you trust me.'

'Silje…'

'I am your daughter. She is not. She is a blind Jew we found under a floor.'

'That is enough, Silje.'

'It is all right, Mr Ohnstad,' said Freya.

'Yes, you are right, Father; it is enough.' Silje began making her way upstairs. 'Get a message to him. Tell him he must return to Fólkvangr as soon as he can. The Germans know he is with the Resistance.'

'Then he cannot come back here!' Freya cried.

'He will be safe. The Lieutenant has promised me, after a fashion.'

'How can you trust a German?'

'Get the message to him,' said Silje. 'I do not care which of you does it.'

The Orchid

(1st June 1940)

I bid you welcome!

Not just to you, my dear dear friends in Fólkvangr, but to all our new acquaintances in Bergen, Årstad, Nordnes, Sandviken, Hellen, Eidsvåg, and as far north as Trollbaken! I say to you all, welcome!

Now, those who have been reading this newsletter for some time will have noticed two important changes.

1) In celebration of our expanding readership, we have changed our name to 'The Orchid'. I chose this name in memory of my dear mother who held the orchid as her most favoured bloom.

2) I have a typewriter! In the past, many have complained that my handwriting is perhaps not as easy to read as it should be. I have refuted this, in the past, but having spent time with this wondrous device, I am prepared to entertain the possibility that those with failing eyesight may have found my penmanship something of a trial. Anyway, that is behind us now. We are pressing forward into the twentieth century with new sections covering recipes, local information, domestic hints for the busy homemaker, and news of the war from our friends, the Germans.

And this brings me to the third, less visible change, but one that is just as important. The Germans have kindly agreed to fund our expanded coverage and distribution. Understandably, many of you will find this news somewhat disturbing, but let me assure you that I have met with the regional commander and he promises me that the Orchid is to simply disseminate information; our neutrality in matters of war will be respected.

Now we have that out of the way, we shall start with a recipe for Rostbratwurst (I am reliably informed that this is a traditional German sausage) sent to us by Inge Krause, a staff sergeant stationed in Bergen.

Many thanks to you, Inge.

P.S.

And a personal note for the people of Fólkvangr. Mr Gundersen's ladder is still missing, and it grieves me greatly that it has not been returned.

15

'Hellish machine!'

Over the course of several days, Silje had come to the conclusion that the devil, in his efforts to confound and ultimately destroy mankind, had invented the typewriter. It wasn't just the tediously grating noise, or its constant need for oiling and maintenance; no, what annoyed Silje most about the typewriter was its insistence on stamping the incorrect letter on the page, though she had most assuredly hit the correct key. What was the purpose of this ridiculous arrangement? What was wrong with God's own alphabet?

She leaned back in her chair and finished her milk and honey. The taste was less sweet than she was used to. Her father often said that unhappy bees make for a bitter harvest. Silje wondered if the bees were upset about the war.

Or perhaps they simply disapprove of my service to the Germans.

Her room had become very much smaller of late, filled as it was with sheets of handwritten notes that had come flooding into the cottage a few days after the first issue of *The Orchid* was released. She had no idea how it reached so many in such a short space of time. An outrider – and she had been relieved that it wasn't Lieutenant Klein – had picked up her hastily prepared bundles on Monday, and the newsletter had been distributed across the north-east by Friday. In that time, her numerous typing errors had been corrected; pictures glued to paper, accompanied by hastily scribbled annotations, had been turned into attractive galleried layouts that filled her with a kind of begrudging pride. Pride because she still saw *The Orchid* as something that belonged entirely to her; begrudging because she suspected that more of Fólkvangr had read a single issue of *The Orchid* than had read the entire run of *The Friends of Fólkvangr*. It felt like a betrayal.

The door opened and Freya entered, her long toes feeling a path through the reams of paper littered across the floor. She moved past the columns that Silje had stacked, waist-high, without displacing a single sheet.

Silje often wondered if the girl was as blind as she made out to be. She would have chided her for entering her room without knocking, but that would have meant speaking to her.

'Your father says you are working too hard. You must rest.'

'My father should come here and tell me this himself.'

'He would like to, but you have not spoken to him for days.'

Silje sniffed and carried on typing, though she had nothing left to type.

Freya said, 'You have not spoken to *me* for days.'

'I am very busy, Freya. Is there something I can do for you.'

'You could tell me what I have done to offend you.'

Silje ceased her typing and said, 'You could stop trying to steal my father.'

'I am not trying to steal your—'

'It is not fair that you take mine because you have lost your own.'

'Silje, please…'

'You are a guest here, Freya; a welcome guest, but a guest nonetheless. You are not my sister and you are not his daughter.'

She heard Freya exhale. 'If I have caused you to dislike me any more than you already do, I am sorry.'

'I do not dislike you. I just think you should remember your place.'

'I know my place. Between you and the Germans, how could I forget?' Her voice was little more than a whisper, but her words pierced Silje as though they had been screamed into her ears. She returned to the typewriter, her fingers rattling over the unfamiliar keys. She looked down and saw she had been attempting to type a poem, something she remembered from her childhood though the title escaped her. She heard Freya leave the room, and began to miss her as soon as the door had closed, so much so that when the door opened a moment later, she was ready with an apology of her own.

'You must come!' Freya cried. 'You must come now!'

'Freya, whatever is the matter?'

But the silly girl had already gone; Silje could hear her running down the stairs. She rose to her feet and yawned, stretching out her limbs. Her back ached and she realised her father was right: she needed to rest.

Silje reached the kitchen and began with a tired, half-hearted admonishment: 'Freya, what have I said about running up and down the stairs. You will come to mischief one of these—'

'Hello, Sister.'

She looked up. She saw her father, his jaw slackened in disbelief. She saw Freya, almost delirious with joy. And finally she saw Magnus, and straight away she could see he was a different man: his eyes, hooded and darkened, his skin weathered, and much of his face hidden by a thick beard. But what struck her with sorrow was that he looked so much older. Her twin had grown into manhood and left her behind.

'Magnus!' She ran across the kitchen and threw her arms around him. 'Magnus! You are home!'

And he smelled terrible.

'Where have you been, for God's sake? And what happened to your face!'

Jon Ohnstad wiped tears from his eyes and shook his son firmly by the hand. 'My boy.'

Then he embraced them both. 'My children.'

Freya clapped her hands and announced, very excitedly, that she would warm some soup.

'Not soup, Freya, please,' said Magnus. 'I have lived on soup for the past month.'

'Then I shall make us a rabbit stew!'

Astonished, Magnus looked at Silje and mouthed the words, *Can she?*

'I am perfectly capable, Magnus; thank you for asking.'

Magnus's eyes widened still further.

Silje shrugged. 'Perhaps she heard your jowls move, Brother.'

He rapped her playfully on her shoulder.

'Ow! Father, tell him!'

Jon Ohnstad sighed. 'Magnus, you have just come home. Do not torment your sister.'

'It is so good that you have returned to us.' Freya struggled to move the huge pot closer to the oven.

'Freya, leave that. I shall help you in a moment.'

'But you must be hungry.'

'I can wait. Come and join us.' Magnus held out his hand.

'She can't see you, silly!'

'Silje, he has just come home. Do not torment your brother.'

'Join us, little sister,' Magnus said.

Freya jumped on the spot. 'What did you say?'

'I said, join us.'

'After that.'

Silje felt her whole body stiffen.

'I said "little sister", because that is what you are: my little sister, her little sister, his youngest daughter.'

Freya wrung her hands, unsure what she should do. 'You are all so very kind.'

'Child, this is the infamous Ohnstad Family Embrace,' Jon Ohnstad said. 'It could last for a moment, or it could last for days. Whichever, it is not to be missed.'

She smiled as though the sun had found its home in the Ohnstad cottage. She took a single step towards them and dissolved into a flood of tears.

'Fine.' Jon Ohnstad sighed. 'We shall come to you.'

* * *

They ate the stew and drank Jon Ohnstad's homemade mead – fabled throughout the mountains – until the small hours of the morning. And while they ate and drank, Magnus regaled exploits of daring carried out by the Norwegian Resistance against an invading force that was better-trained, better-equipped and far superior in numbers.

'But we have the most important thing in our favour,' he said, waving his mug while Silje attempted to fill it.

'What is that?' said Freya. She was trying to make eyes at him, but her excitement made it difficult for her to find his voice.

'We are Norwegians.'

'My God, yes!' Jon Ohnstad slammed his hand on the kitchen table, belched and quietly excused himself.

'Did you kill any Germans?' Freya demanded. Silje touched the blind girl's cheek, moving her head slightly so she could point her eyes at Magnus. 'Did you kill any Germans?' she asked again.

'Not many, if I am honest.'

Freya was on the verge of swooning. 'But you killed some, didn't you?'

'A few. Not as many as some, but more than others.'

'I think you are being modest, Magnus Ohnstad. I think you killed hundreds.'

'Definitely not hundreds.'

'I think you are very brave!'

Silje rolled her eyes in a wide arc, and at the arc's end she found her father's stern eyes looking back.

'Not as brave as some,' Magnus said sadly.

Silje said, 'Well, I think our "little sister" is quite exhausted.'

'I am not a child. I can tell you when I'm tired.'

'And from the tongue in her head I'd say she's had far too much to drink.'

Jon Ohnstad hiccoughed and mumbled his agreement.

Then came an altercation over where Freya should sleep. She insisted that Magnus, being a hero of the Resistance, should have his room; she would sleep downstairs.

'Why can she not share your bed?' Jon Ohnstad said to his daughter – his true daughter – while feeling his pockets for his pipe.

'Do not think you are smoking in the house,' warned Silje.

'There is Mother's old room,' said Magnus.

'She is not sleeping in Mother's bed.'

'Silje, it is time that we were allowed to use her room again.'

'I do not see why.'

'Are there not enough shrines to Mother around the village?'

'No,' Silje said without a whisper of irony. 'No, there are not.'

'I will be fine downstairs,' Freya said quietly.

'I think we should let her sleep in the other room,' said Jon Ohnstad. 'Magnus is right. It is time.'

'No.'

'Then she can sleep with you.'

'Really, I don't mind sleeping here,' said Freya, and then added hopefully, 'or I could sleep on the floor in Magnus's room.'

'You do not want to do that,' Silje said. 'He has the most frightening night wind.'

'I do not! Father, tell Silje to stop—'

Jon Ohnstad rose abruptly from his seat. He raised an eyebrow at Silje while lighting his pipe. 'The magic spun in our home is a source of fascination to me,' he said.

Silje and Magnus exchanged worried glances.

'What do you mean?' said Freya.

His father beckoned for them to come closer, his eyes shifting conspiratorially between them. 'There is magic,' he whispered, circling his pipe in the direction of the door. 'An ancient and terrible magic that encircles our threshold.'

Freya listened intently. 'What does it do?' she said, her voice held low, should the magic hear her and take offence.

'Why are you whispering?' said Silje.

Even Magnus appeared to be drawn into the tale of Scandinavian witchery.

'Whenever my children enter this house,' said Jon Ohnstad, 'the magic comes to life!'

Freya shrieked and jumped in her seat. 'Sorry.'

'Do not apologise, child. Indeed it is a thing to be feared. For whenever my children cross that step, the magic changes them, twists them, and without fire or smoke or the stench of brimstone, it turns them both into…' He swallowed, trembled, looked fearfully about the kitchen, and then, lowering his voice still further, he whispered '… six-year-olds' before straightening his back, smiling and scratching contentedly at his stomach.

Silje leaned back in her seat. 'I do not think that is very funny,' she said while her brother whooped with delight.

'I do not understand,' said Freya.

'Here is what we shall do,' Jon Ohnstad said. 'Magnus shall have his old room back. Freya will share Silje's bed until I clear the other room.'

'Father!'

'It is for the best, Silje. Thanks to your arrangement with the Area Commander, we have German riders treating our house like a miniature garrison. Only last week they asked if they could leave fuel inside the goat shed. Fuel! No, Freya must remain upstairs to avoid detection. She will sleep in your room for the time being. Now that is settled, I bid my children, all my children' – he ruffled Freya's hair, causing her to swell with pride and Silje to smoulder with rage – 'a restful night.'

* * *

Silje decided she would hold onto her anger until the morning, before forgiving Freya's intrusion into her father's heart. Then as she brushed her hair, Freya opened the door to her room and entered carrying a bowl of hot water and a towel.

'It has been some time since we tended to each other,' she said. 'I think it is because you have been angry with me. You are my friend, and I do not like it when you are angry with me.'

Silje eyed the bowl in much the same way she would eye a cooling Ring Cake. She would forgive the transgression, just this once. She sat down and rapped on the bedpost so that Freya would know where to find her.

Freya placed the bowl on the floor and knelt in front of her. 'Which first?'

'The left,' Silje replied. 'Always begin with the left.'

She watched her intently as the Jewess caressed and bathed her aching feet. Freya gently massaged her heels and ankles, and pulled lightly on each of her toes. After a while, Silje realised her eyes were watering; she'd forgotten to blink. Then Freya began drying her feet with a touch so light it made her stomach tighten at every stroke.

'Could you…?'

Freya stopped. 'Could I what?'

Silje coughed and leaned back on her elbows; suddenly she felt very tired. 'Your hair,' she said. 'I like it when you use your hair.' Even as she spoke, she wondered if she had crossed into some unseen borderland, though she'd never been one to concern herself with such boundaries before. 'I am sorry. I ask too much of you.'

Freya didn't reply, but a few moments later, Silje felt her soft braid against the soles of her feet. She closed her eyes, lost to the waves rippling out in soft circles from her abdomen. She tried to gather her thoughts, tried to reason with the sensation that had taken such a hold of her. The mead, she thought as the world fell away. *It is just the mead.*

After an eternity, the feeling ceased. She opened her eyes to see Freya sitting next to her, staring ahead and waving a hairbrush.

'Now me,' she said cheerfully.

'What?'

'I washed your feet, just how you like it. Now you must brush my hair, how I like it.'

Without a word, Silje took the hairbrush and kneeled behind her. She unfastened Freya's braid and spread her hair across her shoulders.

'We should cut it,' she said, brushing it through with long gentle strokes, watching the coarse threads pass through her fingers.

'I do not want to cut it. Don't you like my hair?'

'I think your hair is beautiful,' said Silje, surprising herself; the phrase sitting on her tongue was, *I think your hair is perfectly nice. Beautiful*, it seemed, had jostled past and forced itself from her lips. 'But if it were shorter then perhaps it would be more convenient.'

Freya giggled. 'I never thought Silje Ohnstad would be concerned with something so trivial as convenience.'

'Well then, there is much you do not know about me.'

Silje continued, slowly brushing her hair, silently praying that Freya wouldn't say *Enough*. Not yet, she hoped, not for a little while…

'Do you think Magnus likes my hair?'

She put down the brush. 'Enough. It is time for bed.'

'He is very brave,' Freya said, scratching her lip. 'Killing all those Germans.'

'I do not think he said how many Germans he killed.'

'I'm sure it is lots.'

'I'm sure it is a perfectly average amount for an inexperienced Resistance fighter.'

'He spoke of the bravery of his friends. He did not speak of himself at all.'

'That is what good men are like.'

'Do you know a lot about men?'

'Enough to keep most of them at an arm's length, yes.'

'So you do not like men.'

'If you ask too many questions you will not be able to sleep.'

'So if you do not like men then who do you like?'

'I like men, Freya.'

Freya hopped off the bed and began stripping off her clothes. Silje tried to look away but found she could not. *Does she think that because she cannot see others, others cannot see her?*

'Then I do not understand. You are quite old. Why are you not married? Erik Brenna likes you. He told me so. Why have you not married him?'

'I am not… old!' said Silje, pointlessly making a face.

'I am sorry. I did not mean to—'

'Men are like fruit: they grow, they ripen, they wither, they spoil. You pluck them too early and they are hard and bitter, pluck them too late and they are too soft and their richness has gone. There is a small space in time when they are just right, when you will gain the most enjoyment before the rot sets in.'

Freya stared glumly in her direction. 'So you are waiting for Erik to ripen.'

'In a manner of speaking, yes.'

'I think that is a sad way to look at things.'

'When you are older you will agree with me.'

'Do you think Magnus is ripe?'

'It would be improper of me to say so.'

Silje averted her eyes as Freya pulled back the covers and threw her thin, unclothed body onto the bed. She realised, with sudden and inexplicable alarm, that the Jewess slept naked.

'You suddenly care what is proper,' Freya said, drawing the covers to her chin.

Silje thought, *It is the mead talking. She will be herself again tomorrow.* 'If you had asked me a month ago, then I would have said no. But whatever he has done, whatever he has seen, it has changed him.'

'So he is ready for marriage!' Freya cried, her interest tediously reawakened.

Silje began removing her own clothes and folding them into a pile at the foot of the bed. 'I would say he's perhaps on the turn.'

'Now you are being unkind.'

'He is too old for you.' She slipped on her nightdress, and then struggled into a second one to compensate for Freya's lack of night attire.

'I am eighteen. I am more than old enough for him!'

She sighed and wondered if Freya would ever be sober again.

'And I assure you, Silje Ohnstad, I am perfectly ripe!'

'That does not apply to women. We are eternally at our best; remember that.' She climbed into the narrow bed and snatched some of the covers away from Freya.

'Silje.'

'What.'

'Being with a man – what is it like?'

'It depends on the mood and the man.'

'His mood?'

'Mine. Now go to sleep.'

'I have never kissed a man,' Freya said quietly.

I am sharing my bed with a night troll, Silje thought. *Why will she not sleep?* 'Indeed, Freya, that is a tragedy.'

'Silje.'

'What is it.'

'You will teach me to kiss men, yes?'

'No.'

'Oh. Why won't you—?'

'Freya, go to sleep or I will hit you with something.'

Freya turned over and snatched back the covers. 'You are very unkind, Silje Ohnstad.'

'No, I am very tired, and you are very drunk.'

Silje waited for a rejoinder, but none came. Instead she heard the soft purr of Freya's breathing; the child had exhausted herself and fallen into a deep sleep as soon as her head met the pillow. Silje decided her father's mead was perhaps not so bad after all.

And so she lay waiting for her own slumber. She stared at the ceiling, watching a large spider making its way towards the light that shone from the gap above her door. Freya rolled onto her back and Silje lost interest in the spider. She bit her lip and raised herself so she could better see Freya's face. *So plain*, she thought, *but one day she will be... less plain*. She watched the steady rise and fall of Freya's chest and felt her own heartbeat slow to fall in step with her breathing. 'But your hair *is* beautiful,' she whispered, and felt the first of a thousand tiny hot pins pierce her flesh. She swallowed. Her throat was dry, and she felt a furnace light beneath her skin. It wasn't just the second nightdress; it was Freya. Even asleep, the girl ran as hot as Junges Fehn's printing press.

Small wonder she sleeps unclothed. Silje cursed all her misfortunes, rolled from the bed and curled herself up on the floor.

16

'Freya! What have I told you about leaving the upstairs doors open! The goats will eat the furnishings!'

'She has already left for Fólkvangr.' It was Magnus calling back from the meadow behind the cottage. 'Glad to hear you are awake.'

'Where is Father?'

'He is here.'

And yet he had not said anything. Strange, Silje thought. She took a step towards the pile of clothes at the foot of the bed, and felt a soreness between her legs that gave her pause to stop and sit down.

'Christ,' she said through her teeth, and doubled over, realising that she had been very brutal with herself while she slept. She pressed her thighs together and tried to stand. Water, she thought, lots and lots of very cold water.

She cleaned her teeth and brushed her tongue which felt as though she'd licked the face of a goat, a feeling she knew because she'd tried it once as a child. She wondered if Baldur remembered.

She took off her night clothes and filled the sink with water; she scrubbed her flesh, as though punishing herself, and used a damp cloth to clean between her legs. She was sore to the touch, but the cold water helped. She thought of Freya lying asleep in the bed while she defiled herself on the floor. She left the cloth in the sink and got dressed. She passed Magnus's room on her way to the stairs, and remembering that her brother was outside and out of earshot, took three steps back. Without a second thought she pushed open the door and went inside. It was important, she told herself, that he did not leave anything incriminating inside the cottage, though this reason for invading his privacy only came to her while she was searching under his bed.

In spite of Magnus being twenty-three years old, his room always smelled of *boy*, a scent of young pine that all the men of Fólkvangr carried to varying degrees of pungency. Magnus was different though, due to his insistence on using something he called 'cologne'. Silje remembered that one of his lady friends from Bergen had given it to him on his seventeenth birthday, though she could not recall her name.

She turned her attentions to his wardrobe, sliding her hand around underneath it until her fingers came to rest on the old wooden box he kept against the wall. She tapped and swept at it until she could wrap three fingers around one of its corners and pull it towards her.

The box was locked, though the catch could be opened with little more than a few twists and turns of a hardened fingernail. It popped open, and in it Silje found Magnus's most private things: letters to past loves; applications to various seminaries; his bible – both Old and New Testaments; the pocket knife Erik had made for him while he watched in wonder; and at the very bottom of the box, under a pile of unused paper, his collected works of Parisian erotica.

She sat upright, leaning against the wardrobe door with the book in her lap. It was as at least as heavy as both testaments put together and just as intricately bound. Years of use had loosened many of the pages, though Magnus was always careful to place them back in the proper order, as was she. Silje often wondered where he'd gotten it from; she suspected it was the same woman who had brought him the gentleman's perfume, as he insisted on calling it.

'What was her name?' she mused. She rolled her dress to her thighs and slid her hand into her underwear, keeping a careful ear for her father or Magnus coming in through the kitchen door.

Most of the pictures were of women, sitting or squatting with their knees parted, displaying themselves for the artist or the camera, or lying with their legs splayed as though about to give birth. None of them were smiling; in fact, they all looked very serious. Silje supposed it was one of the intricacies of high art she would never understand.

There were very few pictures of men in the same poses, which she always thought something of a shame. She found comparisons interesting, if not entirely useful. Erik was not well-proportioned, but his care and attention to the minutiae of her pleasure was more than adequate compensation for this unfortunate shortcoming. On the other hand,

God had constructed Junges Fehn with the girth and rigidity of a stallion's fetlock; but in use, Junges would thrust and thrash it about like a whip over which he had no control. Silje believed that he was, in his heart, afraid of it.

She carried on turning the pages: women indoors, women outside, men with animals, women with animals, women with women, men with women, men with other men – there was no rhyme or pattern to the book, and Silje wished Magnus would spend a useful afternoon sorting the pages into sections. He was almost a man of letters now; surely such a minor clerical task wasn't beyond him.

She came across a picture that took an entire page. It depicted a French soldier – an officer, Silje believed, from the time of Napoleon – and a woman on a balcony overlooking a vast and beautiful park. She was leaning over the railing, gazing into the distance, with her chin resting in the palm of her hand and her skirts pushed up to her waist. The soldier looked out over the same parkland, smoking a pipe, lost in magnanimous thought with his breeches about his ankles, impaling her from behind.

Silje swallowed and pressed her back against the wardrobe to anchor herself. She clenched her teeth and stared at the picture, moving her fingers like pistons. Aside from being the largest picture in the book, it was fairly unremarkable; it wasn't even one of her most favoured, so it made little sense as to why it would affect her so on this most ordinary of days.

The woman in the picture wore a hat. It was dark, with a narrow brim and a profusion of coloured plumage set around its band. It sat at an angle on the woman's crown, and though it appeared to be pinned in place she used her free hand to hold it steady against the soldier's ministrations.

It was a very fine hat, and Silje felt sure that if she found the material and the feathers, Freya could make one just like it.

She closed her eyes and plunged her hand still deeper. *God in heaven*, she thought, *will I ever grow out of this?*

* * *

'Heh.' Jon Ohnstad tried to light his pipe in the ferocious morning cross-wind. 'Still worse for the mead, I see. You can barely walk.'

Silje leaned against the cottage. A hundred yards away, Magnus struggled to work a large double-handled saw across a felled oak tree. 'I had something of a difficult night.'

The wind blew out Jon Ohnstad's match. 'I am sorry, but it is for the best, and it is only for a short while. And I understand why you do not want me to put Freya in your mother's—'

'The sooner we move her there, the better.'

He struck another match. The wind blew it out. 'You have certainly changed your story since last night.'

'She is a young woman,' said Silje. 'She should have her own room.'

He struck another match and the wind blew it out. He dropped his pipe back in his pocket. 'That is very noble and understanding of you, Daughter.' He put his arms around her. His embrace was, as always, strong to the point of hurtful, yet still it made her feel cosseted and loved.

'When Freya leaves us, I will restore the room to exactly how it was.'

Magnus cursed loudly when the saw became trapped in the wood. He pulled and pushed, falling over as he tried to free it.

'What do you mean, when she leaves us?' said Silje.

Jon Ohnstad furrowed his brow as though he were not sure what he meant.

'Father, who else will look after her if not us?'

Magnus got to his feet and glared at his father. He took hold of the saw and slowly began to work it free of the oak.

'He is angry with me,' said Jon Ohnstad. 'I forbade him to return to the Resistance, and now he hates me.'

'He does not hate you. And who will look after Freya if we—'

'I tried to tell him that the Germans are watching us. He cannot keep slipping away to God knows where and expect that there will not be consequences.'

'I will talk to him,' said Silje. 'And what of Freya?'

'When the war ends, for better or for worse, Freya will have to leave us, Silje. Surely you can see that.'

'I see nothing of the sort.'

'And I have seen nothing that tells me she cannot look after herself.'

Silje glared at him.

'I have deliveries to make this morning. I will return soon. Speak to your brother; he will listen to you.'

He strolled past Magnus without so much as a word, and left through the side gate. Silje waited until she heard the truck drive away before approaching her brother, who was again sawing angrily at the wood stump. She took the other saw handle, and helped him work the blade back and forth. She said nothing, waiting until he began to smile.

'Stupid old fool,' Magnus said.

Still, she said nothing.

'Oh, so you agree with him do you? You think I should just stay in the village while others fight the invaders.'

'I never said that.'

'You don't have to say it.'

The blade caught for a second time so they changed direction, rocking the saw up and down. When it had worked itself free they continued, back and forth.

'So what do you think?' Magnus asked.

'I think that there are other ways to be a hero.'

'Would you care to share them?'

'You could save the lives of your family and Freya by not exposing us to the scrutiny of the Nazis.'

'I would never—'

'They know you did not return to your studies, Magnus.'

'I know, but—'

'The Lieutenant has given you – given us – a chance. One chance. Stay in the village. That is how you can become a hero. No one will remember you, no one will raise a glass to you, no one will write songs about you. You will be like the thousands of other heroes that will be forged in this war: nameless. But you will save us, Magnus. You will save all of us. That is the truth of it.' Exhausted, Silje stopped. She wiped her brow. 'Do not bring the enemy to our door, Brother.'

Magnus let go of the blade and picked up his tankard. 'But Sister, you have already done that.' He walked back to the cottage with Silje in his wake. 'Thanks to you and your damned newsletter, the Nazis are infesting our home like they infest Bergen. I did not bring them to our doorstep; it was you.'

'And what would you have me do? Refuse them?'

He stopped to look at her, and if it had been anyone else then Silje would have said it was a look of hatred. 'I would have had you do anything else, Silje. Anything other than write their anti-Semitic filth for them.'

'I do not write it!'

'Anything except try to convince our people to lie down and surrender.'

'Magnus, please—'

'Anything but fornicate with the enemy under our own roof!'

Silje caught her breath and pressed her mouth shut.

'I am sorry. I did not mean that.'

'I think you did.'

'No, I am just angry.'

'With me?'

'With everything.'

Silje pushed against the door and went inside. 'You would never have been so cruel before,' she said. 'Not to me.'

'And I said I was sorry.' Magnus sat at the table. He rested his head in his hands and seemed to shrink before her eyes.

'What is wrong, Magnus?'

He stared at a knot in the table, tapping gently with a gnawed fingernail. 'Freya thinks I am a hero.'

'It's one of the very few things she is right about. You are a hero.'

'No.'

'Why would you say such a thing?'

'Because I cry, Silje. Every time I kill one of them, I weep like a child.'

His shoulders fell and a sigh escaped his lips. 'And I have not killed many; I have killed one.'

'Magnus…'

'No, that is not true. I have shot one, but he lived. He lay in the mud, suffocating from the hole I made in his neck. One of the others slit his throat for me.'

'Cut his—?'

'Ammunition is scarce,' Magus said flatly. 'We cannot afford to waste it.'

Silje fetched him a tankard filled to the brim.

'We lost two men during that raid, and when we returned to the forest, I made some excuse about going to kill our meal. I walked for two miles, Silje – and I wept every step.'

She did not know what to say.

'The worst of it is that I did not shed a tear for Toril and Gunnar; I cried for myself. Dear God, I cried for the German.'

'You cried for the life taken, because you are a good man.' She sat next to him and put her arms around his broad shoulders. 'This war has already made us into things we are not, Magnus. You are not a killer, and I am not… I am not what people say I am.'

'I said I did not mean it.'

'It does not matter whether you meant it or not; you said it and you cannot take it back.'

He opened his mouth to protest, but Silje was having none of it. 'But you will stay, yes?'

He nodded. 'For a while at least.'

'And then you will go back to your Resistance because that is where you left your pride.'

'Now who is being cruel.'

'I am being honest.'

Magnus sniffed loudly and rose to his feet. 'The oak will not cut itself,' he said on his way to the door.

'Freya is very fond of you. She will be heartbroken if you leave us again.'

'It is you who she is fond of, Silje, even though you treat her badly.'

'That is not true.'

He left in silence, leaving Silje alone, wondering if it were the Nazis or the Resistance driving them apart.

She spent a fruitless hour tending to her chores: the stove cleaned, but not polished; the pantry cleared, but left unorganised; the goats fed, but not petted; everything done in half-measures and accompanied by the disquieting notion that her world was shifting beneath her feet. The day is broken, she decided, throwing down her aprons and cloths, so it will be the day I repair a ruined thing. She put on her sandals and her coat and set off for Fólkvangr.

It was uncomfortably warm for April, the last of the snow having melted from the earth. The sun rested on top of the mountain, sending white shafts of light to pierce the forests. Magnus's words still stung her, but when she pushed them aside, Freya replaced them, and along with Freya came fragments of a dream: Erik, Freya, herself, and the barn. Junges Fehn's barn if she was not mistaken, home to her many sins of falsehood and flesh.

One of the mountain's innumerable goats joined her for part of her journey, walking alongside her in the hope she was carrying food to the village.

'I have nothing,' she said to the goat, and was alarmed when it seemed to understand; it stopped, looked back, and trotted away. A strange day indeed.

Thoughts of Freya pressed against her until she reached Fólkvangr's arch. Her father had said that one day the Jewess would leave, and though she knew he was right, it was one of the many truths Silje lacked the courage to face, though Freya's silent haunting of the cottage – the child could walk on eggs without breaking their shells – and her refusal to work on one day of the week were incessant, gnawing frustrations.

She thought back to the movement of the world under her feet and found it was here again, with the villagers. Far from the solid mountain greeting she had come to expect from them, they regarded her coolly. Some stared through her as if she were made of glass; others simply averted their gaze; none came to engage her in conversation.

And the morning will worsen, she thought as she neared the monument to her mother. Marit waited near the circle of orchids, sitting on the stone seat inscribed with the poem Silje's father had written seven days after her mother had slipped into the afterlife.

'Are you waiting for me, Marit?'

Marit Ohnstad carried a copy of *The Orchid,* open and folded back. She smiled and waved the newsletter under Silje's nose. 'I have always said it; you are truly your mother's daughter.' She pushed the newsletter against Silje's chest.

'I do not have time for your hatred today, Marit. If you wish to punish me for my father not loving you then perhaps another time.' Silje noted, with a glow of satisfaction, that Marit's cheek twitched, and one of the gnarled veins in her neck bulged and throbbed.

'You are an evil child,' Marit whispered. 'And you are a whore, like your mother before you.' She struggled to her feet, every twist of her limbs causing her to catch her breath. She stood before Silje, their toes almost touching. Her breath reeked of sour wine and a lifetime's despair. 'But at least your mother only whored herself to Norwegians.'

Silje felt her words as keenly as she would feel a blow to her chest. A small crowd had begun to gather around them.

'Read your handiwork, Silje Ohnstad. Read it and ask yourself if your mother would be proud of what you have done.'

The fatal strike. Silje ground her teeth together to prevent herself from weeping. 'Leave me,' she said. 'I will have no more of you.'

Marit smiled, a twist at the corners of the mouth that conveyed satisfaction, if not victory. 'Read it,' she said and then made her way through the crowd.

The sea of grey faces looked solemnly at Silje, as though they expected more of her, more than she had already given.

'I do this for you,' she said loudly. 'I do this for Fólkvangr!'

The crowd exchanged glances, remaining silent until Alrek, the tanner's son, found his voice: 'It was not something we asked you to do, Silje.'

The crowd rumbled its agreement.

She drew herself up to her full height, and still wished she were taller. 'I will do it all the same, because you are my friends and you are family.'

She waited for their agreement. None came. 'I see. Well, I am sure you all have more important things to do than spite me.'

They looked at one another, and with the occasional shrug, slowly began to drift away.

As the last soul departed, Silje looked down to read the page Marit had left open for her, a single sheet embossed with the image of the *Reichsadler* and written in scissor-cut prose she felt sure belonged to General Gruetzmacher himself.

The page welcomed Germany's Norwegian allies to *The Orchid*, and promised recipes, stories of romance and heroism, household hints and news of the War For Scandinavia which was all but won. The General's tone was curt, fatherly, non-threatening – until he saw fit to mention the Resistance and the Jews. Anyone found helping a terrorist or a so-called 'child of Abraham' would be dealt with as a traitor to both Norway and the Fatherland. The punishment would be swift and final. He called the Jews demons and witches and things that were 'not of this earth.'

It was not the first time Silje had read the statement; indeed, she'd received a copy of the newsletter a day before the distribution. At the time her only thought was that the entry somewhat spoilt the carefree appeal she was trying to cultivate.

Now it seemed so different with Freya uppermost in her mind.

Freya, born of witchcraft and incest.

It simply wasn't true, and if that was a lie then how could she trust anything the General said? She could taste the alcohol in his every word. A weakness – ripe for exploitation.

'Is that you, Silje?'

The lilt of her voice made Silje's heart fold outwards in a fashion she found as alarming as it was sudden. She looked up from the newsletter and saw she had walked the breadth of Fólkvangr's main thoroughfare without realising it. 'Freya,' she said hoarsely.

Freya was cleaning the windows of Fredrik Bergström's grocery establishment, standing on the sill with her feet bare, holding the frame with one slender hand so she could reach the furthest corner of the glass with the other. Silje watched her, thinking that she could travel to Bergen with her father on his next flower delivery. There was a cotton importer near the docks; perhaps he would let her have some of his off-cuts in return for her favours. Then she could make Freya a new dress. The one she wore did so little for her.

'You are quiet today, Silje. That is most unlike you.' Freya strained to reach the edge of the pane and almost lost her footing. Silje's heart skipped again. She sighed to herself; the sensation was becoming tiresome.

'I was waiting for you to tell me how you knew I was here.'

'You know how.'

'Then I was waiting for you to tell me that it was the smell of the orchids that gave me away, and not the smell of the goats.'

Freya laughed and almost slipped again.

'Come down before you hurt yourself.' Silje was surprised when Freya did as she was asked.

'I am perfectly safe. You worry far too much about me, you know.'

'You are my responsibility, Freya, and I take my responsibilities very seriously.'

'Orchids,' Freya said, now standing close enough for Silje to inhale her. She did so, in spite of herself, and found that the Jewess carried no scent at all. If she closed her eyes she would not know if she was speaking to a young woman, or simply listening to a voice carried on the mountain breeze. 'You will always smell of orchids; now you have no need to ask me again.'

Though she knew she was being teased, Silje felt profoundly grateful.

'You called out my name last night,' said Freya. 'Four times. You called for me to come back, though I have no idea where you thought I was going.'

'It was a dream,' Silje said. 'I dream a lot. Especially at night.' *I am babbling*, she thought. *Why am I babbling?*

'Silje, it was more than a dream.' Freya reached out and ran the back of her hand across Silje's cheek. 'You are concerned for me because you love Fólkvangr. But fear not. I will not run away because I understand what will happen if I am captured.'

'Please do not say such things.'

'I will be tortured and I will break, and you will all pay dearly for the kindness you have shown me.' She stood on her toes and kissed Silje curtly on the mouth. 'I will not see that happen to you or Mr Ohnstad or Magnus or the villagers. So do not have nightmares about me; there is no need. I will stay hidden and keep you all from harm.'

Silje stood rooted to the ground, her lips tingling, her stomach burning. She opened her mouth and wanted to say a hundred different things all at once. Instead, she took a moment to cleanse her thoughts. 'When this is over – the war I mean… When it is over, where will you go?'

Freya raised an eyebrow. 'You wish me to leave.'

'No! That is not what I meant at all. I meant that if you want to, if you have nowhere else to go, then you can stay here, in Fólkvangr, with us. If you have somewhere else to go then you are still welcome to stay with us. We will clear out my mother's room and you will have space of your own for as long as you wish. I do not say this because I am kind, or because I wish to protect you, or protect the village; I say this because you are— Ah, you are crying. Please don't cry. I hate it when you cry.'

Freya sniffed loudly and said she was sorry. 'I cannot help it. You make little sense to me, Silje Ohnstad. I do not know what you will be like with me from the moment you wake to the moment you rest. I sometimes think you hate me more than anything else in the world, and then there are other times when you seem to care for me so much that I think… I do not know what I think.'

'Think that I worry about you. That is all.'

The two women stood motionless while the world breathed between them. Silje was grateful when Freya broke the maddening silence.

'Where are you going?' she asked, wiping her eyes.

'Erik,' Silje replied. 'I am going to see Erik, to settle things between us.'

'It is good that you set things right.'

Silje nodded.

'Silje?'

'Yes, I'm sorry; I sometimes forget.'

Freya parted her lips to speak, and the window she had been cleaning only minutes before shattered. Without thinking, Silje pulled her to the ground.

Fólkvangr changed in the same instant; a crowd of villagers appeared from beyond the square, running towards them, shouting. On the roof of the church, a hundred feet away and another thirty feet upward, young Jesper Bergström waved his catapult and pointed north – the direction from which the crowd was running.

'That was a foolish joke, Jesper,' cried Silje. 'You could have hurt Freya. I will have words with both your father and your mother!'

Jesper waved and pointed, more frantically than before. The villagers began to spread out, joining others in sudden conversations and performing a strange ballet of going-about-one's-everyday-business.

Freya inclined her head to one side and then the other, searching for vibrations carried on the breeze. 'Germans,' she said. 'They're almost upon us.'

Mr Bergström, a round, reddish man possessed with a shock of wiry grey hair, burst from his shop and took Freya roughly by the arm. 'Inside!' he shouted. 'And you too, Silje.'

'No, I will speak to them.'

Freya called to her, even as Mr Bergström pushed her inside the shop and slammed the door. A moment later he appeared again to make a show of examining his broken window.

A single staff car rumbled past the square, flanked by two riders and a small detachment of paratroopers on foot. The villagers swept back to the pavements and doorways to let them through. They removed their hats and bowed their heads as the car rolled to a halt in front of the grocery store.

Mr Bergström whispered to Silje, 'I do not know what I am supposed to do.' He was sweating. Silje hoped that Gruetzmacher would mistake him for a man scared for his life rather than a man with something to hide.

'Do nothing. I will talk. Just agree with everything I say. He is here for me, not you.'

Gruetzmacher stepped from the car. He smiled and saluted the villagers, who looked at one another, taking his affability as some sort of trap. He tousled the hair of Jesper Bergström who was running back to the store. A stern look from his father sent him scurrying back towards the square. The General appeared to be out for a morning stroll; he greeted the petrified villagers with a warm handshake and a cold, ill-rehearsed smile. He appeared calm, sober, and this worried Silje greatly.

'Come on,' Silje whispered through her teeth. 'The sooner we start this, the sooner you are gone.'

But Gruetzmacher was in no hurry; the soldiers took positions at every point where the cobbled streets met, and occupied empty doorways where they crouched down and shielded their eyes from the sun. Four men accompanied Gruetzmacher as he wandered from store to store, leaving frightened Norwegians in his wake. Each man, woman or child looked desperately to Silje as soon as he left them. What was worse, some of them looked anxiously towards the grocery store.

'We look as guilty as the devil,' Mr Bergström said.

Silje told him to be quiet. She looked across the street and was unfortunate enough to catch the General's eye. He feigned a look of pleasant surprise, though Silje believed he must have seen her as soon as his car rolled past the square. He walked across the road with his escort, his hands clasped behind his back.

'Fräulein,' he said, and shook her gently by the hand.

'General.'

'I must say I find your mountain air a little too crisp for my suburban constitution.'

'You will become accustomed to it, General,' said Silje, hoping that he would never feel the need to.

He pointed to the newsletter. 'You have a copy with you, I see.'

'Of course.'

This seemed to please him. 'I think you have done a marvellous job.'

'Thank you.'

Mr Bergström tried to shuffle sideways, away from the waves of terror that seemed radiate from the General's person.

'And who might you be?'

The grocer waited for Silje to answer for him. When she didn't, he uttered his name under his breath.

'Speak up,' the General said.

'Bergström, sir.'

'And are you the owner of this establishment?'

'I am, sir.'

'And what happened to the window?'

'We were just discussing that when you arrived,' said Silje.

Mr Bergström nodded, and continued to nod until Silje took his hand and gently squeezed it.

'Childish high spirits, perhaps,' said the General. 'It is a problem common across the region, I fear.'

'I'm sure that the young reprobates meant no harm, sir,' said Mr Bergström, the fear in his voice ever more pronounced.

'Of course, of course; but these high spirits can be counter-productive.' The General nodded towards the empty window pane. 'The energy of Norway's children must be tempered, moulded, harnessed, into more worthwhile pursuits.'

'Like the Youth Programme.'

'Indeed, Fräulein Ohnstad, like the Youth Programme. It has wrought wonders in Germany. I think that a similar initiative would do the same for Norway. What do you think?'

She glanced nervously at the grocer, who had nothing to offer. 'I think,' she started cautiously, 'that our respective youth are designed for different pursuits.'

The General smiled. 'Well, we shall see.'

Silje steered the conversation back towards the light. 'Lieutenant Klein is not with you?'

'Ah, I did wonder when you would ask. It is his duties that have kept you apart, so I feel somewhat responsible for the troubles in your relationship.'

Mr Bergström stared at Silje.

'But you will see him soon enough. He is at your home as we speak, talking to your brother.'

'My brother,' she said with all the wilful ignorance she could muster. 'Why on earth do you wish to speak to—?'

'Oh come now, Fräulein; I'm sure Klein has told you. Your brother's whereabouts were unknown for several weeks. He was registered as a student of languages and theology at Stavanger – and yet he has not been seen at the school for months.'

'I am sure he has an explanation,' Silje said desperately.

'I am sure he does. But a plausible one? That, dear Fräulein, is the question.' The General lit a cigarette and waited politely for Silje to stop shivering. He smiled and said, 'I was led to believe that you Norwegians were immune to the cold.'

'Sometimes the coldness of things surprises us.'

'Quite,' he said, and to Silje's dismay, looked back towards the grocer's shop. He asked Mr Bergström if he had any fruit.

'No,' Silje replied 'No one has.'

'Mmm. Pity. I would give the world for an orange.'

'Then it is a shame the world is not yours to give.'

He drew on his cigarette and looked at her as he might look upon an unruly child – one he would be more inclined to shoot through the head than put across his knee. 'I grant you certain freedoms, Fräulein Ohnstad, as a favour to my lieutenant. But please do not think my patience is endless.'

'Forgive me, sir. I speak out of—'

'You promised him information in return for those freedoms, and I expect you to fulfil your side of the agreement.'

He told him, Silje thought. Her hold on Klein was far more tenuous than she'd imagined. 'I understand, General.'

'No, I don't think you do, so I shall speak plainly. If you do not bring me something of value, then I will be forced to seek traitors a little closer to home. Now is that clear enough for you?'

Silje nodded, her legs shaking.

'Good, very good.' He signalled for his men to join him. 'Now, we will walk, yes? We have much to discuss.'

'I have nothing for you as yet, but I will—'

'I meant the newsletter.'

The troopers fell in step around them, seemingly guarding Silje along with the General. She began to walk quickly, distancing herself from them. They obediently kept up.

'I think it has been very well received,' the General said. 'Reports from the north of the region are encouraging, though the south has not taken to it, I fear. Still, for a first edition I think we have—'

'You asked people to betray the Jews.' Silje showed him the page, but he did not deign to read it. 'You told them to turn on the Resistance, and you did this in the pages of my newsletter.'

'You are misguided in your use of the phrase "betrayal". It is the Jews and the Resistance who are betraying Norway. I am merely seeking information helpful in securing their detention.'

'People will think I approve of this!'

'And you should! We are doing this for the good of your country. It is the Allies who invaded you, not us. And it is the Resistance that forces us to punish you.'

'Is it, or is it not, my newsletter?'

The paratroopers looked to the General, seemingly as curious as she was.

'It is and always will be yours, of course.' He dropped his cigarette and walked on without smothering it. 'You are vital to our work, as is all of Norway. That is why we seek to bring you all into the fold.'

'Then, General, perhaps there is more to be gained if you treat us as equals.'

'Dear lady, I did not say you were equals.'

The paratroopers laughed, and Silje felt more foolish than she had ever felt in her life. 'Then we are the vanquished.'

The General sighed. 'You are the liberated.' He glanced at his watch. 'We seem to have reached the border of your village,' he said, looking intently at the wall of trees and rocks and at the home of Junges Fehn. The Fehns peered out from an upstairs windows.

The staff car stopped next to them; his driver jumped out and snapped to attention. She looked at Silje and gave an almost imperceptible sniff.

'And may I introduce you to Staff Sergeant Krause. You included her recipe for—'

'The sausage,' Silje said glumly. 'I remember.'

'It is not a sausage,' said the Sergeant. 'It is Rostbratwurst. Did you try it?'

'I did,' Silje lied.

'And how did you find it?'

'It was delicious.' Turning to the General, she added, 'Please do not let me keep you from your duties. I am sure you have much to do.'

'Indeed.' He looked at his watch again. 'I have paperwork to attend to in Bergen. So very tedious. And what of you?'

'I will return to my home.'

'Most wise. May I offer you a lift?'

'That is very kind, General, but I would rather walk.'

'You wound me, Fräulein,' Gruetzmacher said. 'It would be ungentlemanly for me to allow you to walk such a distance.'

'It really is no distance at all.'

Sergeant Krause opened the door for her. She stared straight ahead, smiling, like the General, like the soldiers – all of them laughing behind Norway's back. Silje climbed into the Mercedes and sat down, wringing her hands in her lap.

It was the most hideous journey she could have imagined, travelling through the village of her birth, in the carriage of the enemy. The villagers stared as the convoy drove past; some whispered to one another; others shook their heads in disbelief. In her own mind Silje knew that any of it, all of it, she could live with. Perhaps she would cry, but in the scheme of all things, if she could protect the village, she would survive.

The convoy made a shallow right past the village hall and *The Mottled Goat*. The car had to swerve to avoid old Mr Kleppe – one of the rare times he was out of his home during daylight. He saw her as the villagers rushed into the street to help him to his feet. He took off his hat and crushed it to his chest; such was the disappointment in his eyes, Silje thought her heart would break.

'The old fool,' the General said, looking at his watch.

'Perhaps we should slow down,' she whispered.

'As I said Fräulein, paperwork waits for no man.' He seemed taken aback by his own words; he chuckled, excused himself, and produced a small notebook from his breast pocket. He mouthed the words as he wrote them down, and Silje found herself wondering if Magnus knew how to kill a man with his bare hands.

They had little to say on the road back. Silje found the silence almost deafening. The General hummed to himself. She hoped Freya had the good sense to stay hidden; the child was wilful and impulsive, and only now could she see those traits in herself.

The outriders overtook the convoy and disappeared into the forest ahead.

To break the silence, she asked the General where they were going.

'They're checking the road for a possible ambush.'

'You are quite safe in Fólkvangr.'

'Oh, of that I have no doubt, but one can never be too careful.' He leaned closer to her, as though he were about to share something personal to him. Instinctively, Silje leaned away. 'No one will try to kill me because I give them no reason to.'

'You are German, sir; surely that is reason enough.'

He took a moment to decide if he should be offended by this, and then he laughed. 'I see your point, Fräulein Ohnstad. But I say it to you again; we are not the aggressors.'

'If I may speak freely, sir.'

'I doubt I could stop you.'

'You were not invited to Norway.'

'Time was short. We could not wait for you to come to your senses.'

'An invasion in all but name, then.'

'Have a care, Fräulein.'

'Why is it so important we believe that you are here to help us? You invaded us; you conquered us; we cannot win if we fight you, so why do you care what we believe?'

The General sat back, scratching his chin. He said nothing for such a time that Silje began to believe he did not know the answer. Sergeant Klaus cleared her throat and announced that they would soon be at the cottage.

'When the Romans conquered nations, they adopted their gods. Did you know that?'

Silje said she did not.

'It made the transition of power much more fluid, the populace more compliant.'

'So that is what you seek: our complacency.'

'Whether you are complacent or not will make little difference to the final outcome. But there is little to be gained by the wholesale slaughter of the indigenous population. It is wasteful – for both sides.'

It was the first time Silje had heard him acknowledge that there were two sides to the invasion, that the Nazis were, perhaps, the enemy.

'There are two steps to a successful campaign: extinguish resistance and extinguish hope.'

The convoy stopped outside the Ohnstads' cottage, and the paratroopers spilled out of the armoured cars and swarmed across the garden and into the barns and outhouses. The General waited patiently, tapping his cane against the floor of the car.

Klaus returned and told him that the cottage was secure.

'After you.'

Silje stepped from the vehicle and hurried inside.

Magnus and Lieutenant Klein sat at the kitchen table, the Lieutenant standing to attention as soon as Gruetzmacher entered. Magnus looked as white as the mountain.

'Mr Ohnstad,' the General said and immediately lost interest in speaking to him. 'Has he accounted for his whereabouts?'

Klein flipped through his notes. 'He has, sir. It appears that he has not attended the school since before the invasion.'

Gruetzmacher threw the Lieutenant a stern eye.

'My apologies, General. Of course, I meant the liberation.'

Magnus looked to the floor.

'He was expelled from the school in January.'

'Really.'

'So it would it seem, sir.'

'And he did not tell anyone.'

'No, sir.'

Silje could not quite believe what she was hearing. 'Magnus? Is this true?'

Her brother kept his eyes to the floor.

'Then why did the abbots not inform us of his expulsion when we first approached them?'

'Ah,' said Klein, and scratched the back of his neck. He may have glanced at Silje; she wasn't sure. 'It would appear the school wanted to keep his expulsion a secret.'

'You are being obtuse, Lieutenant,' Gruetzmacher rumbled. 'You know I do not like that.'

'Again, my apologies, General. There appears to have been some scandal involving Mr Ohnstad here… and a nun.'

Silje's mouth fell open. 'Magnus!'

The General tensed his own mouth to stop himself from smiling. 'A nun.'

'Yes, sir. A nun. Sister…' Klein began searching through his notebook.

'I do not need to know her name, Lieutenant.'

'No, sir, of course not.'

'Then where have you been all this time, young man?'

Klein spoke before Magnus had a chance to reply. 'He has been working the docks around Hammerfest.'

Gruetzmacher turned his glare on the Lieutenant. 'I did not ask you,' he said, and then returned his attention to Magnus. 'Is this true?'

Magnus nodded.

The General straightened and rubbed his chin. 'And you have verified this with Hammerfest.'

'They confirm that he has worked there since January.' Klein swallowed so loudly that Silje was sure the General would have heard it.

Gruetzmacher eyed his lieutenant as if they'd only just, at that moment, met for the first time. 'And you are certain of this?'

'I am certain, General.' Klein stood to attention and thrust out his chest.

The General remained silent for a moment or two, long enough to see if anything in the cottage would break.

'Good work, Lieutenant,' he said finally, and put on his cap. 'We will bid you good morning, Fräulein.'

Silje smiled; it made her face hurt.

'As for you, Mr Ohnstad, my aides will be making frequent visits to Fólkvangr. I am not sure when they will come, and I am not sure how long they will stay, but know this; we expect you to be here, in this village, on each and every visit. Do I make myself clear?'

Magnus mumbled under his breath and nodded.

'Speak up, man!'

'Yes, General.'

'Good, very good. I see through you, Mr Ohnstad.'

For the first time since Silje had entered the cottage, Magnus raised his head. He met the General's eyes with an anger she'd not seen in him since the night their mother had passed. 'And what do you see, General?' he asked.

'A chained spirit.' Gruetzmacher pulled on his gloves.'This village was your prison long before you and I met. When you are ready to escape then speak to the Lieutenant and he will speak to me. The Reich can always use a man like you.'

'And what is "a man like me"?'

The General chose not to reply; he strode to the door with Klein at his heels. When he opened it he turned and said, 'A nun.'

'She was pretty,' said Magnus.

'I should hope so.'

Silje and Magnus listened to the convoy mounting to leave: the soldiers embarking armoured cars, the outriders starting engines, the General's staff car roaring into life. They listened for the sound of stones being churned under burdened wheels.

Silje dropped into a chair. Her chest felt tight and she realised she'd forgotten to draw breath for quite some time. 'What in the name of God was that about?'

'I don't know,' Magnus replied, his head in his hands.

'Does he know about the Resistance?'

'I don't know.'

'I think he knows, Magnus!'

'Then why are we still alive?'

'I don't know!'

'Then we are both in the dark, Sister.'

'He is toying with us.' She stood up and paced the kitchen, chewing rabidly on her little fingernail. 'What did Klein say to you?'

'He came in, he sat down, and told me I was a Resistance operative.'

'He said that.'

'Yes, he said that. I denied it of course, but he kept repeating it. It was as if he needed it to be true.'

'Christ…'

'He knew about the expulsion; he knew I'd been working at the docks. And he knew I left the docks in April – just after the Germans landed.'

'But he has no proof that you were fighting.'

'He doesn't need proof, Silje; all he needs is to whisper my name in the General's ear.'

'But he won't. Otherwise he would have done so by now.'

'So it would seem,' said Magnus. He looked at her, steeled himself.

To ask the question, Silje wondered, *or to hear the answer?*

'Silje,' he began, 'what are you doing to buy his silence?'

'Ask yourself honestly, Brother; do you really wish to know?'

He got to his feet and whispered that he needed to rest. They looked away from each other, and Silje wondered if he was ashamed of her, or he was ashamed of what she'd had to do to save him. He began to climb the stairs, the weight of their pudency born in every footfall.

'Do not tell Father,' said Silje.

She heard him stop on the third step – the step that had creaked since since they were children – and then carry on to his room, slamming the door behind him.

She busied herself by tidying the kitchen, though she had cleaned it thoroughly only hours before. She took all the pots from the cupboards and scrubbed them until they shone. She wiped the windows and polished the tables, deciding that they would look much better with a lacquer applied to their surface. Then the floors, then the inside of the pantry, which hadn't seen a firm hand and a clean cloth in many a month.

Silje was so engrossed in her labours that she only realised Magnus was in the kitchen when she heard the door click. She looked up from scrubbing the floor and saw him standing with his hand on the door lever and a rucksack on his back. She got to her feet and carried the bucket to the sink.

'I have to tell my companions that I can no longer aid them,' he said. 'I will return soon.'

Silje poured the black water away. 'See that you do.'

17

I stayed in Oslo for two months, and every day I wondered what Monica would say if she knew I was spending my time with someone like Mr Klein. It wasn't that I cared for his company; more the opposite – I found him a little odd. He worked for three days out of the seven; the other four he'd spend cataloguing the documents and artefacts filling his apartment.

And unless I was there to remind him, he almost never bathed.

There were some very unpleasant moments when I could hear him in the bathroom, wrestling with his colostomy bag: *'Come on, damn you!'* And then he would come out and say something like, 'I wouldn't have this problem if I were still in Germany.'

I guess there were times during his self-imposed penance when he wondered if he'd punished himself enough.

Sometimes he'd disappear for days, away at some underground auction looking for Nazi memorabilia. Most of the stuff he'd collected over the years was junk: historic medals eaten away by rust, and a lot of the papers rendered unreadable by time and the dry rot that crowned the ceilings of his apartment. I did point out, a number of times, that if he didn't take his collection to the museum then it would be lost forever.

'I will, I will,' he said. 'When I'm done with it.'

His path through the documents and guns, and knives and flags and deactivated land mines seemed random at first, but as I watched him flit from one pile to another I soon realised he was looking for something.

'Is it her?' I asked him one day over lunch. I was doing most of the cooking whenever I showed up at the apartment. In return for looking after him, he helped me with my reading.

'No.' He carried on examining an old copy of *The Orchid*.

'Then what are you looking for?'

He put down his magnifying glass and looked at me through eyes that were almost opaque. He opened his mouth to tell me but then thought better of it. He picked up his magnifying glass and carried on scouring the newsletter. I returned to the evening paper, sipping slowly at my mug of coffee which had grown cold some time ago. I looked at the clock; it was a quarter to six. I sipped and looked again: quarter to six, still.

'Is it time to call your mother?' he asked.

I said it was.

'And you are thinking whether you should even bother.'

'I've tried, for months. I've written to her, I've—'

'Has it occurred to you that something might have happened to her?'

'Yes, it has, thank you; that's why I check all the papers. She was married to Erik Brenna, remember? If something has happened to her then I would have heard about it.'

He mumbled something under his breath.

'I didn't catch that.'

'I said perhaps no one has discovered her yet.'

'Now you're trying to scare me.'

'No, I'm trying to get you to call your mother.'

I looked again at the clock: ten minutes before six. A phone call wouldn't do; she wouldn't answer for whatever reason. She might have had a seizure or choked on something. She might be lying in our apartment, being devoured by maggots.

And I was in Oslo, behaving like a five-year-old.

The phone rang and I almost screamed. Mr Klein took the handset from its cradle. 'Yes?'

The caller couldn't have said more than two words; whatever was said was enough to drain the colour from his skin. He leapt to his feet and began chewing nervously at the inside of his cheek. He covered the mouthpiece. 'One moment, Fräulein.'

I went to my room, thinking that he hadn't called me 'Fräulein' in weeks.

I could hear him speaking, in German, and at one point he was shouting. I started to pack my things. I was still something of a light traveller, though I'd been quite settled. I unscrewed the top of the old artillery shell that served as the doorstop to my bedroom, and removed all the cash I had in there, the remains of the blackmail money and the meagre earnings from the cleaning work I'd been given at the Resistance Museum.

When I came back into the lounge, he was in his chair, staring at the ceiling. He tapped on the armrests with his fingernails, his skin looked wet and pale, as though he'd just stepped from an ice pool. He said, 'I miss home sometimes.'

I said that I'd never had a home.

'Then in some ways you are very fortunate.' He wiped his forehead with his palm. 'You are leaving?'

'Just for a while. I'm going back to Trondheim.'

'Oh.'

'It was your idea, and I'm coming back.'

He nodded and smiled as though he knew I wasn't. 'We should have a meal together, before you go.'

'There's no need; I'll only be gone for a few days.'

'Then why have you packed all your things?'

I offered 'force of habit' as an explanation.

Mr Klein leaned forward and grinned, showing just five teeth which I didn't think had more than six months' use left in them. 'I think you should cook for me,' he said.

'Oh, so I'm cooking again, am I?'

He waved the newsletter. 'There's a recipe in here we should try.'

I picked my way through the debris he liked to call his filing system and took the pages from him. I tried to make out the drawings and text on the open page. 'It looks like a sausage.'

He nodded eagerly.

'You don't make sausages. You go to a market and you buy them.'

'The Rostbratwurst is no mere sausage, Fräulein,' he declared. 'It is the food of the gods. I will teach you how to make it.'

'I'm sure the supermarket will have—'

'The supermarket will not do.' He was trying not to shout. 'You will return to Trondheim and when you see your mother you will forget all about our quest. That is what will happen.'

'Fine.' I put on my coat. 'I'll get your sausage.'

'Child, you are heaven-sent.'

'You're making them though.'

'Of course.'

'And cooking them.'

'That is fair enough.' He gave me directions to the butcher shop; it wasn't far: three streets down and then a right onto Møllergata. Ten minutes there, ten minutes back, a couple of hours for cooking – I could still make the nine-fifteen coach.

'And no more sauerkraut,' I said.

'That too is fair enough.'

I opened the door and stepped out onto the landing, stopping to fasten my coat.

Mr Klein called out to me from the apartment. 'Goodbye, Fräulein.'

I felt something shift inside me, and closed the door.

I normally avoid elevators. *Don't use lifts,* Monica had said. There is nothing worse than being trapped inside a small space surrounded by club-wielding Fólkvangr fanatics. If she ever said it again, I'd have a reply ready for her. I'd say, *Yes there is: sauerkraut.*

Three flights of stairs, a hurried walk across the lobby, and I was out on the street. I moved quickly, anxious, as always, to be clear of the alley where the apartment entrance was located. I reached the main road and looked left and right. It was deserted, which was unusual for the time of evening. It was very cold though, even for Oslo, so I thought perhaps the commuters had merely hurried home to be away from the weather. I pulled my coat tight around my chest, and felt a blow to the base of my skull that made my teeth rattle. The air burst from my lungs and I fell to my knees. The Monica in me immediately took over. *Stay conscious! Get your razor blade! Scream and slash for all you're worth!*

I reached for my belt and a second blow sent me crashing to the snow. I heard something crack and saw blood spreading in the snow underneath me. I screamed for help – or at least I tried to – but the world was already shrinking away. Two pairs of arms hooked under my own and hoisted me from the street.

'I'm just his daughter,' I said. I could barely make out my own words. 'I haven't done anything!'

I half-stumbled, was half-dragged, to a waiting taxi; when I saw it I started to struggle. *If all else fails,* Monica had said, *then beg for your life.*

'I haven't seen him. I've never even met him. Please just leave me alone. I won't go to the police.'

'The police wouldn't help you.'

I couldn't tell which of them spoke.

The driver's skin was like leather; his head was clean-shaven. He was wearing dark glasses, even though it was dusk. His arm was draped casually over the headrest as though he were simply picking up a fare.

If you are taken then it will probably be a taxi, Monica had said. *They are inconspicuous, and two men can sit in the back to keep you still. No one would think twice about a taxi with three passengers.*

I gripped the door frame and locked my arms, shouting 'No!' as loudly as I could. One of my assailants brought his fist down on my right hand. My arms buckled and I was thrown into the back seat. He jumped in on my left, the other man on my right. A third got into the front passenger seat and said, 'Drive.'

'Please, don't do this.'

Keep begging, Monica had said, *though if I'm honest kid, if you've let things get to this point, you're already done.*

'Who are you?'

'Concerned citizens,' said the driver. The other three grinned and nodded.

'I told you; I've never met him. I don't know where he is. I don't even know if he's alive.'

'Do you recognise this?' The thug to my left, a swarthy, bearded man in his early thirties, showed me his hand. There was a tattoo between his thumb and index finger, a swastika with a dagger through it. I was in the gentle company of the Friends of Fólkvangr, a self-styled group of Nazi hunters that worship one Jesper Bergström.

Other mothers tell stories of trolls to keep their offspring in line.

Go to sleep, Brigit, or the trolls will come for you.

Monica didn't believe in trolls, and could see no reason why I should either. But she did believe in Jesper Bergström, so he became the fodder for my childhood nightmares.

Keep quiet, Brigit, or I will tell Cleaver on you. Monica believed that our lives might one day depend on her being able to silence me in a moment. No threat was too great, and so I lived my childhood in fear of Cleaver.

And tonight, I was going to meet him.

If you are going to die, kid, and there is nothing you can do to stop it, remember your dignity and carry it with you to your grave.

But I won't have a grave, Monica, I thought. I'll be cut into strips and thrown in a lake.

The Orchid

(16th February 1941)

Friends.

It is rare that I start this editorial with an admonishment, but recent events have left me with little choice. First, I would like to begin with the word that is whispered amongst Norwegians across our lands.

Resistance.

I do not speak of our young, brave and misguided men and women who have organised themselves into a force determined to oppose the German occupation (this is covered in an article written by General Gruetzmacher, beginning on page 9); no, I speak of the other Resistance: the ordinary folk; the men and the women and the children who move away from the troops when they board our trams; who refuse to reply when a German bids them good day or asks them the time; who ignore them when they demand service in our stores. I speak of the students in Oslo, who wear paperclips to symbolise that as Norwegians we are bound to each other and to God.

I inform you now, good people of Norway, that this disobedience has not gone unnoticed by our friends the Germans, nor will it go unpunished.

Under a new law ratified by Vidkun Quisling himself, it is now illegal to stand on a tram when there are seats available. This is the first step in educating us in the Reich's way of thinking.

So I implore you my friends, please be careful in your dealings with our allies, the Germans.

Now, it comes to all of us eventually; the family goat whom you have raised, loved and cared for, as though she were one of your own offspring, is no longer able to produce milk. What should one do? Well, the solution is given on Page 26, my friends! The war has brought scarcity, and Marit Ohnstad brings us her fabled recipe for goat stew. Thank you, Marit, for slipping your recipe under my door. You continually surprise me.

Good eating, my friends!

P.S.

It has come to my attention that copies of The Orchid are being defaced immediately after distribution. Please do not do this. It is not polite.

P.P.S

A personal message for the people of Fólkvangr. Whoever has taken Mr Gundersen's ladder, please return it. I shall not ask again.

18

'You will not get away with it,' Erik said.

Silje pulled her skirt down over her knees and began hunting for her undergarments. 'You know nothing.'

'The Germans will see through it, and our own people will think you are telling them to surrender.'

'No they won't.' She snatched up the reams of paper and used them to slap his hand away when he tried to take hers. 'I am rallying them to fight. They will see that.' She pushed the newsletter into her bag and set about looking for her sandals. When she found one she threw it at him.

'You are upset.' Erik leaned to one side to avoid it. 'And not about the newsletter, I think.'

'Of course I am upset!' More often than not, it was *she* who would expel *him* before he could ruin her in his excitement. For Erik to sigh and withdraw from her as though their coupling had suddenly become a chore… It was not a development Silje expected or cared for. 'You are never in the mood these days, Erik Brenna.'

'Silje, there is a war on.'

'What has that got to do with the infrequency with which we now make love?'

'A war in which I should be fighting.'

'We have talked about this.'

'*You* have talked about this. I simply agreed, as I always do.' He got to his feet, fastened his breeches, then stretched and yawned as though he had just awoken. Silje was mortified.

'Well, clearly you no longer desire me!'

'You are wrong,' he replied. 'I desire more of you. You are just not prepared to give it.'

'I give myself to you, Erik,' she said, buttoning her dress, 'often.' Her breasts did not feel hot or bruised; he had barely touched them.

'You think that is all I want?' Erik said. 'To fuck you every second Tuesday in a loft, or under a tree if the weather is fair?'

'Erik!'

He shook his head and jumped from the loft, landing in a stack of hay bales and sliding down to the ground.

'Erik, wait!' She jumped down after him.

It was plain to see he was angry, though Silje was unaware of any sin she'd committed of late. Since the Germans had taken over the printing and distribution of her newsletter, she had no need to pander to the perverse whims of Junges Fehn.

And the nascent spring had brought German soldiers to Fólkvangr where they admired the scenery and attempted, most often in vain, to engage with the locals. Silje had discovered that soldiers in search of a friendly word would often divulge more than they should to anyone willing to listen to them; therefore, she had no need to service Lieutenant Klein in return for information.

'Erik, tell me what I have done.'

The barn door swung open before Erik could reply.

'Lisbeth,' he said, exasperated, 'don't you ever knock?'

'It is Freya!' Lisbeth gasped. 'She cries for help! The villagers are—'

But Silje had already run past them and out into the night.

* * *

Most of Fólkvangr's residents had seen the first Great War; they were old and so moved very slowly. Still, Silje was grateful that the procession had brought torches, even though it was getting in her way. The street lamps were dark, and she remembered Freya had left the cottage a few hours before to help Mr Kleppe light them.

A small crowd had gathered in a circle near the monument to her mother.

Dear God, Silje thought, *if you must take someone then take someone else.*

She pushed her way to the centre of the circle, where the blind Jewess was on her knees, holding Mr Kleppe's head against her hip. His skull had been crushed inward near his right temple, and his blood had spilt out onto Freya's hands.

'Freya!'

Freya raised her head, her dead eyes searching for Silje's voice. 'Silje? Oh, Silje, I cannot wake him.'

'Has someone sent for Doctor Lomen?' Silje shouted. She knelt down and listened for sounds from the old man's chest.

'He is coming,' said Bengt, 'but I fear it is too late, child.'

Silje could hear nothing; the old man's skin had already turned grey, his eyes stared out into the void. Weeping, Freya reached out, searching for Silje's hand. 'You can wake him, can't you?' she said, nodding hopefully. Silje looked up; the gathering gazed helplessly back

'Silje, please wake him. The darkness has fallen; I can feel it. And we had only just begun; there are still so many lamps to light, so please wake him for me.'

Silje took her hand and held it against his chest. 'He was an old man, Freya. There is nothing I can do for him.'

'You have not tried!' Freya shook him and called out his name, shouting for him to wake up. The villagers did not stop her, not at first, hoping perhaps that the child's grief would be enough to restore him. Silje watched her, her own tears freezing against her cheeks. *Did I ask for this*, she wondered. *Did her god hear my prayer and take Jonas in her stead?*

It was the first time she'd thought of him as Jonas.

Two of the villagers decided Mr Kleppe should be afforded his dignity; they wrestled Freya away from him and she screamed and cried until her voice failed her and she collapsed into Bengt's arms.

'Take her home, Silje,' Mrs Heyerdahl said. 'There is nothing more you can do here.'

* * *

Freya and Silje arrived at the cottage just as Jon Ohnstad was leaving.

'Father, I have terrible news.'

'I have heard.' Jon Ohnstad turned his eyes to the moon before squeezing them shut. 'Poor Jonas.'

'I did not know his name was Jonas,' Freya sobbed. 'He did not sound like someone who was called Jonas.'

'You should take her inside,' said Jon Ohnstad.

Freya trembled violently, though four of the villagers had given her their coats.

'And you should be inside too.'

Silje asked her father where he was going.

'To see if there is anything I can do,' he said.

'Father, there is nothing you can—'

'He struck his head when he fell,' Freya whispered, 'on the Monument. There is blood, I think.'

'Then I will tend to it. Now go inside, both of you.' He strode to the front gate with his toolbox held tightly under his arm. 'And if you see your brother this night, tell him we will have words.'

'He has left again?'

'He has left, again.'

Silje took Freya into the cottage, setting her down in her father's chair near the kitchen fire. She stoked the flames and moved the soup pot to warm, and then she set about clearing the kitchen which her father had been using for siring orchids. 'You must be hungry,' Silje said. 'I am hungry. You never seem to get hungry, though you spend all day on your feet.'

'You work just as hard,' said Freya, a sob between every word.

'It is not the same. You are a baker, then you are a seamstress, then a moment later you are a lighter of street lamps and then…' She swallowed her tears and slammed the skillet down against the stove. 'You are not to go out at night!' she cried. 'Ever again. Do you understand me?'

'Then who will light the street lamps?'

'Someone else! I do not care who, but not you.'

'Do not shout at me, Silje.'

'I am not shouting! Why will you not do as you're told for once!'

'Because I will be nineteen soon, and you are not my mother! Mr Kleppe showed me what to do. He even let me light them on my own one night when he was too drunk to—'

'He did no such thing!'

'It is true! Lisbeth will tell you. She went with me that night!'

'Ah! Then you were not alone!'

'But I lit the lamps on my own! Why are you being like this?'

'I am trying to look after you, Freya. Why will you not allow me to—?'

'I do not need anyone to look after me. You are not even my real family!'

Silje gripped the handles of the soup pot so tightly her knuckles glowed red. She felt the skin around her mouth draw tight and could not tell if it was rage or the heat of the stove that set her flesh blistering.

'You unthankful little…' She would kill her this night; she was sure of it. She would kill her for her ungrateful words, for the havoc she'd brought to her family and Fólkvangr, and for not being blessed with the sight that would have saved Jonas Kleppe's life. She would end this little Jew for taking her heart and binding it in thorns. Silje breathed deeply and closed her eyes. 'I do not wish to fight with you, Freya. I simply want to do what is best for—'

The cottage door slammed, and Silje spun round so quickly she sent the soup spilling across the kitchen. 'Damn her.' She threw down the soup pot and followed her into the darkness.

* * *

The cedar wood that grew a few feet from the Ohnstad cottage was no place to wander at night. It covered only a few hundred feet in all directions, but even for a mountain wood the copse was extraordinarily dense. A few steps inside it and the traveller quickly lost the light of the moon, even if the traveller was as familiar with the hills as Silje Ohnstad.

She would have called out, but she was fearful of shouting out Freya's name when she could not be sure who would hear.

The branches cut into her arms and her legs, and the ground became treacherous. This must be what it is like, Silje thought, to live your life in eternal darkness. She wondered how Freya did not spend every waking moment screaming.

She pressed on, whispering Freya's name, hoping her words would carry softly on the wind. She stumbled, picked herself up and continued to walk with greater care. Perhaps the child had foolishly injured herself; the copse was home to four sudden and steep drops; three of them would result in broken bones, the fourth began fifty feet above an outcrop of razor-sharp rocks. The branches grew more dense, the cuts grew deeper. Silje wondered how a blind girl could move so quickly in the dead of night.

But you live in the dead of the night, don't you? It all suddenly seemed so very unfair. Silje cursed Freya's name just as her right foot stepped onto empty air.

She froze, feeling a new, harsher breeze caressing her skin. She moved her foot back and placed it on the ground, then made a half turn and took a step forward. Her foot searched uselessly for something solid. She tried to remember the shape of the ledge; the approach was narrow, very narrow, and then it grew from its stem into a platform that was over ten feet wide. She made another quarter turn and slowly sank to her knees, reaching out, searching for the stem. Had she turned again? Which direction was she facing? And now she cursed herself for not bringing a lamp. How quickly she lost her senses wherever that girl was concerned. She thought she should perhaps wait for daybreak, but realised she would not survive the cold for very long. She could shout for help, but her father was in the village and Magnus… She had no clue where Magnus would be at this hour. She felt the first ripple of panic seize her, the first thought that she would die out here and people would think it a very careless and silly way to lose her life.

'Take my hand.'

Silje could not remember being so overjoyed to hear a human voice. She forced down her pride in a single, painful swallow. 'Freya, I think I am lost.'

'Then I will lead you home.'

She said, 'I have been foolish,' as Freya's cold thin hand slipped into her own. She held her fingers tightly.

'You should pay more attention to the winds,' said Freya. 'The easterly winds sound more hollow than the winds of the west. The winds from the north are colder than those of the south.'

Silje felt herself being pulled along at an alarming speed; she dug in her heels, lest Freya lead them over the ledge.

'Trust me, it's this way.'

The child was strong and very assured for one who appeared so frail.

'I thought you were the one who needed to be looked after and protected,' said Silje. 'And you have saved me from a most undignified end. I am sorry, Freya.'

'You do not need to apologise, Silje; just know me better.'

'I will, I promise. You may light the street lamps if you wish.'

Freya laughed from somewhere in the darkness. 'I do not think you could have stopped me.'

'Perhaps you are right,' Silje said; she suspected there was no 'perhaps' about it, but saying it kept her humiliation from being absolute.

Freya walked quickly; Silje stumbled to keep up.

'You will not tell anyone about this, will you?'

'Of course not.'

'And you will teach me how to find my way around the mountain, blindfolded.'

'Why would you want to know how to do that?'

'So that I may know you better.'

Freya was silent, so Silje squeezed her hand to make sure she was still there.

'Then you will do something for me.'

'Anything,' said Silje.

'You will teach me to kiss boys.'

'Think of something else.'

'That is what I want,' Freya said firmly, 'and in return, I will teach you how to see the mountain as I do.'

The copse separated, revealing the lights of the cottage beyond.

'You can let go of my hand now,' said Freya.

'I'll keep it, if you don't mind.'

Once inside, Silje had to stop Freya from clearing up the soup spilt on the floor. She ordered her charge to bed and was most surprised when Freya climbed the stairs without a word of protest.

'You can teach me when you're finished down here, yes?'

'Yes,' said Silje wearily.

Freya smiled and hurried upstairs.

Silje cleaned the spill and washed the pot. She scrubbed the floor and then attended to her cuts. There was one behind her left knee that was deep and stung each time she flexed her leg. She chastised herself again for being so foolish, and made more work for herself by reorganising the pantry. She knew she was procrastinating though she didn't know why. She did not mind passing on her experience to others; she had taught Lisbeth Fehn how to kiss boys a few years before. Lisbeth was not a natural talent, as Silje recalled. Her lips were thin and rigid and her tongue unpleasantly wet, much like that of her father. Regardless, Silje had offered to her continue her instruction, and to her dismay the offer was spurned.

Because you bit me, Silje, Lisbeth had said, *and it hurt.*

Lies piled upon ingratitude...

Silje felt this was not the sort of thing she should be teaching an impressionable young Jewish girl. But a promise was a promise. Freya had saved her life after all.

And so an hour later, she went upstairs and knocked on Freya's door. She pushed it open and said, 'One kiss, that is all. And I advise you to take notes; we shall not be doing this again.'

In the darkness, she heard gentle snoring. Silje felt the skin of her cheeks warmed by a smile, though she had no idea what she had to smile about; perhaps it was because it was rare that someone would fall asleep while waiting for her. She shut the door and slid into the bed, too tired to undress. She whispered, 'Good night' and kissed the back of Freya's head, taking in the smell of her hair.

Orchids.

She'd had even taken the family scent.

Freya groaned, took her hand and held it tightly – so tightly that Silje felt the bones of her fingers pressed together.

'You can teach me another day,' she said, and fell back to her slumber.

'Yes, I think that would be best.' Silje closed her eyes and succumbed almost immediately.

She awoke and turned away from Freya before falling asleep once again. The cold night wore on, and Freya, as was her habit, became a small unclothed furnace.

Silje dreamed a dream familiar to her of late: making love to Erik in his barn while the Jewess searched blindly for a way out. There was a new player in her dream this night; General Gruetzmacher watched from the loft, laughing while reciting the evils of Judaism, sitting astride Silje's old rocking horse. As Erik climaxed, General Gruetzmacher, still laughing wildly, shot all three of them and scattered pages of *The Quisling Orchid* over their corpses…

She awoke once more, soaked in perspiration and her left hand in unbearable pain. She felt a familiar and unwelcome heat between her legs, and in horror remembered she was in Freya's bed.

Silje tried to slide out to the floor and her horror blossomed when she found her hand trapped, crushed tightly between Freya's thighs. She lay frozen, unsure what to do. The girl hadn't woken, or so it seemed. If she moved slowly then she could perhaps extricate herself and depart, and her crime against nature would remain undiscovered.

Freya was facing the window, her breathing deep and hoarse, her tiny frame shivering.

She was very much awake.

'Freya, I am so very sorry. I was dreaming, I think, and it was one of *those* dreams… My God, what must you think of me.' But when she tried to withdraw her hand – swearing wretchedly she would hack the cursed thing off – Freya seized her wrist and whispered, 'Don't.'

'I did not mean to.'

'I mean – don't leave.' Freya entwined her fingers through Silje's and pushed their hands deeper between her thighs. The girl was inhumanly strong, and it was a moment before Silje realised that Freya's quiet strength was only part of it, and that she herself was offering little resistance. Freya took Silje's other hand, and pressed it against her breast. Her heart pounded against Silje's palm; her skin felt slick to her touch, stretched tight over the sharp bones of her chest. She moved Silje's hand, forcing her swollen nipple between her fingers.

'Please stop this,' Silje whispered.

Freya squeezed her legs together and Silje sighed in pain, her fingers crushed and pushed deeper still. Freya's body tensed; she gasped and remained as still as a stone; she gasped again and the stillness escaped her.

The moment Freya's body softened, Silje snatched her hand away, causing Freya to catch her breath. She lay beside her, seemingly unable to draw air. There was a sweet, cloying smell that clung to them both. Silje wiped her hands on the sheets and then used the sheets to dry her eyes. Whatever Freya secreted made her eyes burn.

'I thought…' said Freya, still fighting to draw breath, 'I thought you were just going to teach me to kiss.'

Without another word, Silje threw back the covers and fled from the room.

19

Jesper Bergström was one of the very few who had survived the Fólkvangr massacre. He was the son of the local grocer. I don't know why I remember that; maybe because it's strange that the son of a grocer would grow into a butcher.

He'd been taken prisoner along with his family, and after a month of interrogation that had left his father without teeth or fingernails and his mother and sister near mute, they were transferred to Camp One at Beisfjord. His family died within two years of being sent there. Jesper was still a boy at the time, and how he survived is the stuff of nightmares.

I had learned a lot about Jesper Bergström since Monica had cast him as my very own monster under the bed.

Do as I say, Brigit, or he will come for you. In Monica's mind, any childhood trauma worth inflicting should be inflicted deep.

So I knew all about Cleaver: how he had been liberated from the camp at the end of the war; how he survived by his wits on the streets of Oslo until he was old enough to join the army; how he was discharged two years later for causing the death of a recruit; how he travelled the world for seven years, dispatching Nazis-in-hiding on behalf of the fledging Israeli state; how he returned to Norway and plied his trade here, butchering collaborators and those who'd supported Quisling's puppet government. It was the Israelis who called him Cleaver. It was a mark of respect. It was said that he could separate a man from his skeleton and leave him alive for close to eight minutes. It was said that

Cleaver would question his victims while snapping the bones from their ribcages.

When I thought about this in the back of the taxi, I wet myself.

The man next to me said, 'There's a cleaning charge for that.' No one laughed.

By the time Cleaver was caught, it was believed he'd killed eighty-six men and women in Norway alone, though only eighteen were proven beyond doubt. He still had a lot of support, especially from Fólkvangr survivors and their descendants. Offers had been made to fund his case being heard in an international court of law. Norway refused but it was too late; they already had a folk hero on their hands. Bargains were made, insanity pleas entered, pressure was exerted from Israel. Games of politics were played, and in the end Bergström was sent to a mental institution. Monica bought champagne on the day he was sentenced; it never occurred to me that she just as afraid of Cleaver as I was.

But I learned much more about Bergström while tied to a chair in a large, brightly lit room with a chequered floor, watching the man himself separate a cow's carcass into slivers of meat, bone and fat. Unless challenged, he was a quiet and methodical man, nimble-fingered and quick-tempered.

He took great pride in his work.

My pleading for my life annoyed him; my demands for a change of clothes annoyed him more.

I learned he was a certified sociopath, of which he was very proud.

I learned he had five sons and three daughters, each by a different woman who had written to him while he was in the hospital, and considered it her patriotic privilege to sire him a child who would continue his work.

He must have been thirty-five though he seemed much younger; nothing maintains youth like psychopathy it seemed. His skin was dark and weathered and his tall frame was powerfully built. He had a moustache that grew grey and thick beneath a thin red nose. He may have had a cold. Every time I breathed, my own nose made a faint whistling sound; I'd broken it when I hit the concrete, but that was the least of my problems.

Bergström's arms were tattooed. His right arm carried the mark of a swastika being cleaved in two with an axe. Six numbers had been scored into his left. The numbers were long, faint and distorted; there was an eight, a three and a nine. I couldn't make out the others.

Monica had shown me pictures of such tattoos during the hideous 'know your enemy' phase she went through during my teens.

Pay attention to the size of the tattoo, she'd said. *Look at how this one covers the whole forearm. This means it was applied when the victim was very young.*

Children of the camps, she'd said, *are the worst. They will hurt you the most because they are dead inside. They will kill you because they care for nothing. They will kill you because they can endure any consequence that would come of it.*

My heart sank to my stomach, and though I'd been given nothing to drink for three hours, my immediate problem was a desperate need to pee.

'Eight years old, to answer your question,' he said.

I said I didn't understand.

'You were looking at my mark.' He showed me his forearm. 'I was eight years old when I was taken to the camp. My parents and my sister died there. Only I survived.' He wiped his brow with his numbered arm and slammed another side of beef onto the table. He began to carve, slowly, skilfully – a show for my benefit. 'Do you know how I survived? Do you know how an orphaned child survived that final dreadful winter in a concentration camp?'

Someone standing behind me said, 'Have a care, Bergström.'

It was one of the men in the taxi; I recognised his voice. He'd been in the room with me for the whole three hours, and until then had not made a sound. In that moment he became my best chance of survival. 'Who else is here? Please, you've got to help me.'

There may have been others standing behind me, I wasn't sure.

Cleaver said: 'My father was a grocer, but his father was a butcher, a craftsman trusted by Fólkvangr's community. A fine man. A respected man. He taught my father his trade, though the boy that he was had no real stomach for it. But he learnt it well, and he taught me with knives stolen from the camp kitchens. He taught me in that last winter that took so many of us.'

A shadow shifted; someone had moved behind me. It took Cleaver's attention for a few seconds, and then he returned to the task at hand, his movements less fluid, his strikes against bone sending fragments and splinters flying into the air.

'While the Russians and the Serbs, the gypsies and the queers were dying around us, my family came to a decision, a decision they made without me. They decided that as the youngest I would survive.

Halfway through the winter of '44, my family took what little food they had left and gave it to me. My mother and my sister kissed me and held me. They felt like bones in my hands.' He pulled a rib and threw it away. 'Their skin was like paper, and I remember their eyes, so full of love, so empty of hope. My father sent me outside, into the cold. And when I returned, he had smothered them both.'

'God, not this again,' said the voice. 'Do we have to hear this?'

Whoever he was, he wasn't going to be any help at all.

'We dug a grave underneath our hut,' Bergström continued as though his companion hadn't spoken. 'He cut his own wrists as we began, and he made sure that he bled into the hole. We lined the grave with snow and ice and laid my sister and my mother inside. And then…' The butcher paused and placed the carving knife on the table. He stared at it, waiting for it to come to life. 'And then, before he succumbed, he taught his son the trade of his father.

'If you ask me how I survived, Miss Fossen, then I will tell you. I survived because as a boy I turned my back on God.' He began to carve again. His confession had exorcised him; the fluidity and flow returned to his movements.

'Bergström, enough.' Another voice.

'It is enough when I say so!' Cleaver roared so loudly that the knives hanging next to him rattled. He carried on separating bones from meat while we waited in silence. I would have been happy to let the silence sit because it was keeping me alive, but there was something I needed to know.

'Klein told you I was here in Oslo, didn't he?' I'd had time to think about it: the phone call that had drained him; the finality of his goodbyes. He'd sent me out and told them where to find me.

'He could not believe his good fortune when he saw you at the Resistance Museum. He knew that you would be worth much to me – eighteen months, perhaps more.'

I must've looked confused because Cleaver apologised and explained.

'Years ago, the Department of Correction made something of an administrative blunder.' He chuckled to himself and threw a handful of offal into a nearby bin. I was thankful that my sense of smell had left me. 'Some paperwork or other was misfiled, and Klein, suffering from pneumonia, was sent to the wrong hospital – my hospital.' He bared his teeth. 'And before the error was uncovered, Mr Klein and I had already met and come to something of an agreement, a pact if you will. A pact I sealed when I carved out his stomach.'

'Lev is right. Enough.' A third voice. This had turned out to be something of a gathering. Perhaps they were there as witnesses, or perhaps this was some sort of initiation. Perhaps they would all take their turn with the knives.

Bergström ignored them. 'For every Nazi soul, every collaborator he delivered to me, I would allow him time. Over the years he has delivered many, but the well has run dry and so his time has run out.'

'He sold me,' I said quietly, 'to save his own life.'

'For a short time, yes.'

'But it's not me you want, is it?'

He stopped working and looked first at me and then to his companions standing behind me.

'May I speak?' I said.

Again, he looked to the others before nodding. 'What is on your mind, Miss Fossen?'

'You can't carry on like this forever. You will be caught and you won't see the light of day again.' I waited for his reaction; he didn't say anything, but he didn't kill me. 'But before that happens you want the greatest prize after Quisling. You want the Traitor of Fólkvangr.'

He smiled, and put down the knives.

'And no matter how angry and how psychotic you want me to think you are, I don't think you will hurt me. You know I've done nothing wrong.'

'Then why are you here, Miss Fossen?'

'Because you want me good and scared so I will agree to betray my father.'

The others began to whisper and I think at least one of them sighed with relief.

Cleaver himself remained still. I began to think I'd passed some sort of test, that I would get out of this alive, then he took a fresh knife and walked around the table towards me.

One of the others shouted 'Bergström!' but no one made a move to stop him. I closed my eyes and held my breath.

Probably the throat, Monica had said. *If the Cleaver takes you, that's probably how he'll do it.*

I could feel the heat of his skin, and when I slowly opened my eyes, his face was only a few inches from mine, the tip of the knife pressed into the flesh just below my left eye.

'You said that I wouldn't kill you because you are innocent. Let me tell you how I see the world, Miss Fossen. It is very simple; you are guilty or you are not guilty. Anyone who refuses to aid me in my endeavour is guilty.'

His breath smelled like raw meat.

'Is that clear enough for you?'

I would have nodded, but if I did the knife would burst my eye. I swivelled my eyeballs to look down at it. He looked down at the knife too and moved it away.

'When you find him – if you find him – then you will bring him to me. Do you understand?'

I said I understood.

'It would be unwise to disappoint me, Miss Fossen.'

'I have no doubt of that.'

'If you disappoint me I will find you.'

I didn't doubt that either. He stood watching me for longer than I could hold my breath, examining every line, every imperfection, every bead of sweat. He was satisfied after a while, or just bored; I wasn't sure which. In any case, he returned to the table and carried on butchering the carcass.

The disciples came forward and hauled me to my feet. They looked as relieved as I felt.

* * *

Cleaver's men left me where they'd taken me, just outside the alley leading to Mr Klein's apartment building. There were still signs of a struggle, but a fresh layer of snow had covered the blood. Another snowfall would cover the vomit I left on the pavement as soon as his men had driven away. The good people of Oslo gave me a wide berth as I knelt there, weeping. One man did approach, but I held out my hand and told him to keep away.

I was still crying when I entered the building and took the stairs to Mr Klein's apartment. I stood outside for a few minutes and tried to compose myself. 'Enough now, Brigit' I said, speaking in Monica's voice. 'That's enough.' It seemed to work. I opened the door and stepped inside, ready to eviscerate him. I even planned my speech as I waded through the papers and notes littering the hallway.

How could you?

No, I couldn't start with that.

You treacherous fuck!

Not much better.

I wasn't particularly fond of Mr Klein, but I thought we had an understanding, a camaraderie in our solitude.

I pushed on the lounge door so hard I shattered a hinge. 'You lying piece of shit…'

Then I saw that Mr Klein had tidied the room. All the papers were neatly stacked with a small bound folder on top of each one. He had swept the floor and put away all his pens. He had moved his favourite armchair so it faced the window. Mr Klein had put on his only suit and brushed his hair, and then he'd sat in his favourite armchair and shot himself in the mouth.

20

In the days that followed, Silje's world shrank. No matter how far she roamed, her remorse was there, beating at her heels.

She avoided the village by day and took to spending the warmer spring evenings with Erik when she knew that Freya would be at home. She would return to the cottage late at night when she knew she would be asleep. She had listened at Freya's door on one such night and heard sobbing.

The day after, they chanced upon each other on the cross-roads between the village and the cottage. Silje saw her approaching using her hands to read the bushes and trees that would guide her home. She thought about hiding, then remembered the best way to avoid drawing Freya's senses was to remain perfectly still.

The slightest sound, she reminded herself. *That is all she needs.*

Freya was more than twenty feet away when she stopped and sniffed at the air.

Silje breathed a silent curse, realising she was downwind of her.

Freya inclined her head to the left, listening with her better ear. 'Silje? Is that you?'

Silje dared not turn her head.

For more years than she could remember, her father had used this path to ferry orchids to the village. He often dropped some, and over the years wild flowers had sprung to life along its course. Silje stood between pools of orchids to her left and to her right, their scent mingling with her own. It occurred to her that Freya may not be sure she was there. She wondered how often the girl stopped at this very spot and called her name.

'Silje, I know you are there.'

Clearly, she did not. Silje smiled and hated herself for doing so.

Freya waited and listened. She closed her eyes, which Silje had never seen her do before. Strangely, she had no memory of seeing Freya blink.

'If you are here, Silje, then please do not be cruel. I am sorry for what I did. It was sinful, and my own god will see me punished for it. But if you forgive me, Silje, I swear I will never—'

'Make a promise you cannot keep.'

Startled, Freya turned to face her.

'It has happened, Freya; it cannot be undone and it is as much my fault as it is yours. But I cannot live with it. I cannot live with you, not for the moment at least.' Silje breathed deeply, and Freya cried as though her words, as yet unspoken, were carried on the sigh.

'Do not send me away, Silje.'

'I will speak to Mrs Tufte. You can stay in the village with her. She adores you as much as I.'

'I do not want to live with Mrs Tufte! I want to live with you and Magnus and Mr Ohnstad!'

'It is only for a short while. I think we need time apart, to think and repent.'

'If you hate me so much, then why do you not just turn me over to the Germans?'

'Freya, I do not hate… That is a horrible thing to say!'

Freya gathered the hem of her skirt in her fist and stumbled and tripped her way to where Silje stood. To Silje, it seemed Freya's second sight deserted her in times of distress. She reached out and took her hand, but Freya pushed her away.

'I do not need your help!' she cried, then locked her hands about Silje's throat and pressed her mouth against hers.

Silje melted, the heat of Freya's body consuming her, turning her bones to ash, buckling her at the knees. She whispered 'Stop' even as her hands found Freya's breasts and her teeth sank into Freya's lip.

Freya pulled away, wiping blood from her mouth. She staggered back and stood with her chin thrust forward. 'I am blind, so tell me, Silje, have the heavens opened? Has the earth cracked under our feet? Has a flood washed away all mankind?'

'Freya, I am sorry! I did not mean—'

'Has God himself reached down and smote us for the sins we have committed under his sky? I am still breathing, Silje, so I think perhaps he has not. Or perhaps he has, and we are in Purgatory, awaiting his judgement. Please tell me, Silje, because I cannot see what is happening.' Freya pushed past her. 'At least the Germans would kill me quickly.'

'Freya!'

'And thank you, Silje. Thank you for everything!' She walked on, her feet perfectly in line, her assuredness restored.

Silje watched her until she disappeared from sight. She would have cried, but the sound would carry on the winds, and she did not want Freya to hear her weep.

* * *

Of course, Mrs Tufte was overjoyed when Silje asked her to take Freya for a time. She stood on her threshold and beamed, her hands clasped and her head bowed.

'Mrs Tufte?' Silje thought she might be praying.

'Child, I have longed for companionship for more years than I can remember. Alone in this cottage since Mr Tufte passed away…'

'Indeed,' said Silje, though Mr Tufte was in fact living somewhere near Fredrickstad with his new wife and nine children. Mrs Tufte knew this; the villagers knew this; Mrs Tufte knew the villagers knew this, and yet it was one of Fólkvangr's unwritten laws that the true fate of Mr Tufte was never to be spoken aloud.

'It is only for a short while,' Silje said, 'so please do not put yourself to—'

'I will make up a room straight away. And there must be a party. Yes, a birthday party! I will arrange it!'

Silje hadn't seen Mrs Tufte so animated in all the years she'd known her. 'A birthday party?' she echoed. 'It is her birthday?'

Mrs Tufte smiled broadly, pleased that she knew something that Silje did not; this was indeed a rare thing in the village of Fólkvangr. 'Yes, she will be nineteen years on the fifteenth of March.'

'Nineteen,' said Silje. 'Still so young.'

'I am surprised she did not tell you.' Mrs Tufte looked triumphant.

Silje would have lied but had already played her hand badly. 'No, she did not mention it.'

'A party then. You are invited, of course.'

'Of course.'

'Perhaps you can put an announcement in *The Quisling Orchid*?'

'That would be very unwise, Mrs Tufte. I think the Area Commander would have words if I were to announce a party for Fólkvangr's secret Jew. And the newsletter is called *The Orchid*.'

'Of course, you are right; forgive me.'

Silje was unsure if Mrs Tufte was apologising for the idea or the slur on her newsletter, though she was sure the sly old woman wasn't apologising for both. 'And perhaps it would be disrespectful to hold a birthday party so soon after Mr Kleppe's funeral.'

'On the contrary, young Silje, I think a birthday celebration is exactly what the village will need after such a solemn event. But you are correct; we must keep it a secret, which will be difficult since your efforts have brought us an infestation of Nazis on most weekends.' She tapped her lips thoughtfully. 'I will think of something.'

'Please remember, Mrs Tufte,' said Silje, clenching and unclenching her fists, 'that her living with you is a very temporary arrangement.'

'Let us see how things go, shall we?' And before Silje could answer she added, 'Now I really must get on. I have much to do. Please feel free to deliver her at your convenience.'

And then she closed the door.

* * *

Jon Ohnstad spared his daughter a sour look and continued to load Freya's meagre belongings into the back of his truck.

'There is no need to take her sewing machine! She is not going away forever.'

'I do not understand why she is going away at all.' He roped the sewing machine to the truck's bracings.

'I have explained,' Silje said, making sure her lies fell in formation. 'The Germans—'

'Yes, you've said. The Germans visit our house far too regularly, and whose fault is that?' A small suitcase followed, which Silje recognised as belonging to her late mother.

'Do you think I have a choice in this?'

'I just want to know the real reason, that is all.'

'So, you accuse me of lying?'

'I know you are lying. Have you fallen out? I do not understand. The villagers tell me how they often see the pair of you strolling through Fólkvangr, arm-in-arm, like an old married couple. This was not four days ago! And now you are sending her away.' He shook his head. 'I sometimes wish I could see the workings of your mind, Silje, and other times I am grateful I cannot.'

'I am trying to keep her safe.'

Magnus appeared from inside the cottage, carrying Freya's collection of pebbles and stones. He ignored his sister and stowed the small trunk next to the sewing machine. 'That is everything.'

'And you,' Silje said, her voice shaking. 'You are supposed to stay in the village! What if the Germans had—'

'The Germans come every fortnight. I will always return before they do.'

'Always? So you plan to disappear again.'

'I am not fighting, if that's what you are worried about. I am helping in other ways.' He rubbed the back of his neck. 'What have you done, Silje?'

'I am doing this for her!'

'You do nothing for other people, unless it is advantageous to you.'

'You are wasting your breath,' said her father, climbing into the truck's cabin. 'She will say nothing further.' He started the engine, throttled it and let it settle.

'I will fetch her,' said Magnus, heading back inside. 'She is in her room, crying.'

'That is Mother's room,' Silje called after him.

'He is right,' her father said, 'you do this for yourself.'

'Then stop me. It is your house.'

He looked at her, his jaw set, his eyes narrow and his hands clenched tightly about the steering wheel.

'Because whatever my reasons, you know I am right. She is safer away from here.'

Magnus reappeared, leading Freya by the hand. He was the only person from whom she would ever accept aid.

'Freya, I am sorry.'

Magnus helped her into the truck and then climbed in next to her.

'It is only for a short time, I promise you.'

Jon Ohnstad slammed the truck into gear and roared away in a cloud of dust.

And now she was alone, Silje found herself swallowed whole by a sadness more profound than anything she'd felt since her mother's passing.

You are being foolish, she thought, wiping her eyes. *She will be safe now. Safe from the Nazis. Safe from you.*

21

Without Freya as a distraction, Silje took to ravaging Erik Brenna whenever their paths crossed and time gave her the opportunity. He was, of course, delighted – and exhausted – after less than two days of her undivided attentions.

'We could do more of this,' she gasped and brought her full weight crashing down on his pelvis. 'We could do this much much more.'

Erik's eyes bulged. He ground his teeth and said, 'If I am honest, Silje, I don't think I can do much much more.'

'Of course you can.' She raised herself by pressing down on his chest with her hands. She smiled wickedly at him. 'Ready?'

Erik shook his head and Silje brought herself down on him again, squeezing her thighs together as she did so.

'Stop,' he pleaded. 'Please stop. I will ruin you and your father will kill me.'

'How will you ruin me, Erik Brenna?' Silje twisted her hips just to see his eyes roll into his skull.

'You know how! You will fall with child, and your father will throw me from the highest ledge of the mountain.'

'He would do no such thing if you were to marry me.'

'Do not tease me, Silje. I am in enough pain as it is.'

She leapt up and landed next to him in the bed of hay. Erik moaned, an odd sound that Silje guessed was both agony and frustration.

'I am not teasing you. I think we should be married.'

Erik winced, raised himself on one elbow and studied her eyes intently. 'This is a very cruel trick, Silje, even for you.'

'So you do not want to marry me,' she said innocently.

'I have wanted to marry you since I was eight years old. It is *you* who has cared little for the notion of marrying *me*. Why have you changed your mind?'

She did her utmost to look horrified. 'You think I am deceiving you?'

'Why have you changed your mind, Silje?' he asked wearily.

She lay back in the hay and wondered what she could say. Will it even matter? she thought. Whatever I say will be a lie. 'You are ready. Before you were not. Before you were just a boy. Then I asked you to stay in Fólkvangr, and you stayed. So – you are ready.'

Erik rolled his tongue around his mouth. 'So I am ready because I did what you said.'

'That is not what I meant.'

'Then what did you mean?'

'Do you not wish to marry me, Erik?'

Erik lay staring vacantly at the barn rafters while she sat up and stared at him in disbelief.

He's thinking about it!

'Do you know what I find most peculiar about you?' Erik said.

Silje folded her arms. This was not turning out to be the marriage proposal she'd had in mind.

'You bite people.'

'I most certainly do not.'

'Yes, you've done it since you were six years old. Do you remember when we first met in school? You walked up to me, pushed all my friends out of the way, and bit my arm. Then you said, "There! You are mine now."'

Silje tried to recall this, but could not.

'You bite things you want to possess.'

'That is so untrue…'

'And when we were older, I could always tell which boys you had been with—'

'Erik Brenna, I have never—!'

He raised his hand. 'I could always tell which boys you had been with because they each had a small scar on their lower lip. It's an affectation you have never grown out of, Silje. Even when you kiss, you like to bite: to stake your claim, to mark your territory.

'But since that time in the playground, in front of my friends, you have never staked your claim on me. And now I find myself thinking, Why is that?'

Silje chewed her own lower lip and shook her head.

'I think it's because you don't care enough about me to own me, Silje. I do not know who you are looking for in a husband, but I am not he.' Erik jumped to his feet and down from the loft. 'I will not marry you, Silje Ohnstad,' he called out. 'But I hope you find someone who will love you as I do, and I hope that he will give you the contentment that I cannot. But most of all I hope you will not bite him too har—Ow!' He stumbled back, holding his arm. 'What in the name of God did you do that for!'

Silje stood with her fists against her hips, her feet planted firmly in the hay. 'I love you, Erik Brenna. I love you easily as much as you love me! There have been others, but no more. We will belong to each other until everything we know is dust. This is not open to discussion or negotiation.'

Erik rubbed his arm, too stunned to speak.

'Tomorrow, you will come to the cottage and you will ask my father for my hand in marriage. He will say yes, and then you will ask me. Is that clear?'

He nodded, grinning as though he'd lost his wits.

'Is there any part of this you need me to repeat?'

He shook his head, grinning still.

'Are you sure?'

A nod.

'Good, then we should get dressed. We do not want to be late.'

They used the water pump behind the barn to wash each other, and handfuls of hay to dry themselves. Erik put on his father's grey suit that he'd cast off in the throes of his passion. Silje put on the smart blue dress she'd taken off, folded neatly and placed on a trestle.

'I see them,' said Erik, peering through a gap in the door.

'We should just put ourselves at the end,' said Silje.

'Agreed.'

She wondered if he'd ever stop smiling. She liked to think that he would not.

'Now.'

They ran from the barn, ducked around the corner of the farrier's stable and walked quickly to fall in at the rear of the funeral procession, alongside the Fehn family. They slowed their pace to match the sombre gait of the other mourners. Silje dug Erik in the ribs and told him to stop grinning. 'It is a funeral, Erik! Get a hold of yourself.'

Lisbeth Fehn shook her head. 'On this day, of all days, the pair of you choose to behave like rutting goats.'

Junges Fehn, walking at his daughter's side, gave Silje a nervous glance. His wife pounced upon it.

'And what are you looking at, Junges?'

'Nothing, my dearest!'

'Perhaps you would like to walk with the hussy?' She gave him a shove. 'Perhaps you'd like to slip away for a few moments. Would you like that?'

'Hello, Mrs Fehn,' Silje said glumly, and wondered if she should take Erik and move further on in the procession.

'Perhaps you'd both like to slip back to our home while I am not there!'

'Hold your tongue, woman!' Mr Fehn said loudly.

'Perhaps you'd like to have her in our bed, then in our kitchen, then in your workshop.'

Silje was mortified. 'It was just once!' She looked to Erik. 'Aren't you going to say something!'

'Yes,' said Erik, and chose that moment to burst. 'We're getting married!'

'Married,' Lisbeth echoed, her voice suddenly thick with grief.

'Erik!' Silje was twice mortified.

Mr Vanderfalk, walking in front of them with his wife and two sons, all wearing their finest clothes with such ease that Silje thought they must attend a funeral every day, turned and said, 'Married! Congratulations!'

'Thank you,' Silje said flatly.

A voice some way ahead of them said, 'Married? Who is getting married?'

Another voice replied, 'Silje and young Erik!'

'Bless my soul!' yelled a third. 'I never thought I'd live to see the day! Silje Ohnstad, tamed at last!'

'I have not been tamed!' Silje shouted. She asked Erik if he could see who'd said that.

The news continued to ripple to the front of the procession, causing the occasional cheer or the sound of muted applause to rise from the congregation.

Silje said, 'This is not what I had in mind at all.'

Some hundred feet away, the procession concertinaed, followed by a collective gasp. The coffin dipped and someone roared, 'For the love of God, Jon, keep your end up!'

Jon Ohnstad stepped out of the line and looked back. He gave Erik a grim thumbs-up and disappeared back into the congregation.

'I do not remember ever being so humiliated,' said Silje.

'I do not understand,' Lisbeth said. 'How could you do this?' She wiped her nose on the sleeve of her most precious black dress, which Silje thought made her look like a squat iron kettle.

'How could you do this to yourself?'

Erik looked confused. 'I'm afraid I—'

'Marry her? She does not love you. She doesn't love anyone save herself. She will be the ruin of you.' Lisbeth was crying freely. When her mother reached for her, she spurned her. 'She will only hurt you again and again, don't you see that?'

'Find your own man, Lisbeth,' Silje said, feeling the warm glow of victory, all the sweeter as she'd had no idea a battle was being fought.

'I can't,' Lisbeth cried. 'You have broken all the others and kept the whole one for yourself.' She raised a tiny fist and for a moment looked as though she might strike Silje, or Erik, or both. Instead, she sobbed, lowered her hand and walked away from the procession. She turned, walking backwards to gaze at Erik. 'You never even looked at me. Never. Not once.' And then she turned again and ran.

Her mother and father broke away to chase after her, calling her name. The aghast villagers could not think where to look: at Silje, at Erik, or at the rapidly departing Fehns.

'Well,' said Mrs Bergström, 'this is turning into quite an eventful funeral I must say.'

'And why should you look at her,' Silje squeezed Erik's arm, 'when you have me?'

'For once in your life, Silje,' he said, 'try not to take such joy in the suffering of others.'

* * *

Jonas Kleppe was buried in the tiny cemetery to the west of Fólkvangr. The sparse patch of hardened soil, close to a small forest and a mountain ledge, was marked by a circle of stones with no other sign to state its presence or purpose. It contained only thirty-four graves in all: elders of the village; heroes of war; and those whose passing had caused such sorrow that the villagers deemed burial appropriate, instead of the usual cremations that prevented the tiny graveyard from becoming overcrowded. The passing of Jonas Kleppe had caused such sorrow. He was laid to rest next to his daughters who had not survived their own births, and his wife who had thrown herself from the mountain many years before. Though he was not an ordained priest, Magnus Ohnstad presided over the burial. The villagers had decided not to send for a priest from Bergen, as they felt sure Jonas would prefer to have been seen on his way by someone he called a friend. When he was asked, Magnus said he would be honoured, and then wept for most of the night.

The snows fell as Jonas Kleppe was lowered into the ground. Four of the villagers, Silje's father included, delivered eulogies that told of a private man who had battled with a great sadness for most of his life. Erik squeezed Silje's hand when she began to sob.

Then Freya stood in front of the grave and spoke of the short time she'd spent with Jonas Kleppe, helping him light the lamps that kept Fólkvangr bright at night.

From the back of the congregation encircling the grave, Silje stared in astonishment. Though she was still, and always would be, appallingly thin, Freya's skin had gained radiance and colour, and her pale blue eyes possessed a new clarity, as though much of her grief had been spirited away. But it was her hair that shocked Silje the most. It had been cut neatly to her shoulders and had been bleached to a dark blonde. Freya spoke confidently and with an eloquence that Silje found spellbinding. She told of the long conversations she'd had with Mr Kleppe as they lit the lamps.

'He said he could not think of a better way to spend an evening in the mountains.' She wiped a tear from her eye. 'He said that in the narrow time between the light and the dark, his family would come and they would walk with us until we reached the end of the village. And there they would kiss him goodnight and walk on into the hills.'

The villagers looked at one another.

Silje whispered, 'Nonsense.'

Erik told her to be quiet.

'I could feel them, I think,' Freya said, 'or at least, I could feel the joy he felt in seeing them again.' She sat down, and then stood. 'That is why he lit the lamps,' she added, and then sat down again.

The congregation showered Mr Kleppe's coffin with white orchids before Jon Ohnstad and Grette, the barkeep from *The Mottled Goat*, turned him over to the soil.

The villagers mingled and discussed Jonas Kleppe with great fondness, though they were surprised how little they knew of him. Freya found herself the centre of attention as she seemed familiar with the deepest minutia of his lonely existence.

'I should help your father,' Erik said to Silje. 'I suspect there is much he wishes to say to me.'

Silje kissed his cheek, and he hurried away, picking up a spare shovel that was leaning against one of the graves.

'What do you think?' said Mrs Tufte, having stolen silently upon Silje, as was her wont.

Silje jumped on the spot. 'That is not polite, Mrs Tufte.'

'I feel little need to be polite at my age.'

'And what do I think about what?'

'Freya, of course. Doesn't she look much less… Jewish?'

Silje pretended she hadn't heard. 'I must speak with her.' She quickly made her way through the congregation, exchanging polite words of condolence as she went. She saw Magnus talking to a very tall man with dark hair and the look of trouble about him. He wasn't from the village, and his skin was too smooth for him to be a mountain-dweller. He was listening intently to whatever Magnus was saying, though Silje noticed his eyes sometimes drifted towards Freya.

Trouble indeed.

Freya inclined her head slightly as Silje approached. She excused herself from a small throng of elderly admirers and walked slowly to meet her.

Silje blushed without cause or reason and quickly charted a conversation in her head: *Hello Freya; you look well. Your hair! Let me think – lemon juice, vinegar and honey? Well, I know these things because I am clever (we will both laugh). Oh, I'm all right. Busy, as always. How is Mrs Tufte treating you? Well, I'm glad to hear it. Yes, I know she can be a little tiresome. You miss our little chats? As do I! Well, you are always welcome at the cottage whenever you like. Of course you can stay over! Your room is exactly as you left it.*

'Silje,' Freya said. 'I hope you are—'

'Come home. Please.'

Freya cast her eyes to the earth.

'Did you not hear me? I miss you.'

'You are to marry Erik, I hear,' said Freya, turning to walk away. 'It is rare you hear such joyous news at a funeral.'

Silje hurried after her. 'Yes, I am to marry. I think it is time.'

'I agree.' Freya stopped, unsure whether to go left or right. 'I think you will be very happy.'

Silje wondered if there was a reason she did not include Erik in this union of joy. 'What we did, Freya… what *I* did… It was unforgivable. And what makes it worse is that I punished you for it. I was wrong to do that. So please – come home.'

'There is no need. Mrs Tufte treats me very well, and she says that I am much safer in her cottage. She does not have Nazis stopping by every second week.'

'That is very unkind.'

'But it is true.'

A gust of wind set the trees rustling less than a few yards to their left. Freya turned and began walking towards them.

'Where are you going?'

'To find a quiet place where we can be alone,' Freya said.

'We can talk here. There is no one close.'

'I do not want to talk.' Freya's face was as cold and set as stone. 'I want to touch you, and I want you to touch me.'

'No. I cannot.'

Freya returned to where Silje stood trembling. She placed a hand against her cheek. 'You are cold.'

'I am frightened.'

'What are you frightened of?'

'Of you. Of me.' Silje felt as though she wanted to cry; she had done far too much weeping of late. 'You seem so different.'

'From a distance, yes.'

'It is your birthday next week and you did not tell me.'

Freya shrugged and ran a single finger along the neckline of Silje's dress. 'I was angry with you.'

'Then you must have been angry with me for some time.'

She found Silje's throat with her fingertips.

'Are you still angry?'

She shook her head, tracing a finger over Silje's breast. The teat swelled under her touch and Silje inhaled sharply through her nostrils.

'Freya! Silje!' Erik cried from somewhere near the cemetery circle.

Freya snatched her hand away and they both turned to greet him when he came running over, carrying a shovel over his shoulder. He'd managed to get much of the mud on his suit. She remained rigid as he kissed her cheek.

'We have seen so little of you since you moved out,' he said. 'You look beautiful. Doesn't she look beautiful, Silje?'

Silje nodded.

'And what you said about Jonas… wonderful. You almost brought a tear to my eye.'

'Thank you,' said Freya. 'I was just saying how pretty Silje's dress is.'

Erik planted the shovel. 'How do you know, if you don't mind me asking?'

Freya smiled. 'Like this.' She reached out and placed a hand on Silje's shoulder, running it down her arm and then across the line where the dress ended and her flesh began. Silje froze.

'Oh,' said Erik without really understanding.

'You feel the line of the material, how it rests against the skin, how it fits across the joints, under the breasts… What makes a dress pretty is how it is worn. That is why all Silje's dresses are pretty. Now you try.'

Erik looked unsure. 'Well, I'm not blind so I think this will be lost to me.'

'Then close your eyes. Do not be shy of her, Erik. You will be married soon, after all.'

Enough of this, thought Silje. 'I do not think this is a good—'

Erik closed his eyes and put a muddy hand on Silje's shoulder. He squeezed it and then moved down to her arm, and squeezed that too. 'Well, I can't tell you much about the dress, but I can tell you she is angry.' He opened his eyes to see Freya was already halfway back to the cemetery, and that Silje was standing with her arms folded, fuming.

'I do hope,' she said, 'that you will not be such an idiot throughout our entire marriage.'

* * *

Two of the Ohnstads were in inappropriately high spirits when the family returned to the cottage later that night. The funeral had ended with food, lemonade for the children, and gallons of ale and mead for the men and women. Jon Ohnstad and his son babbled excitedly about the upcoming wedding.

'My daughter!' Jon Ohnstad gushed, stumbling across the threshold. 'My very own daughter will be married!' He raised his hands to the kitchen ceiling.

'Do not say it, Father,' Silje said glumly. 'Not again.'

'At last!'

Magnus struggled to pick up the envelope that had been pushed under the door. He swayed dangerously back and forth as he tried to bend down. In the end, he chose to let his knees buckle to bring the floor closer to him. 'It is addressed to you.' He waved the letter at Silje.

She snatched it from him, and he fell on his face.

The envelope was so white it glowed in the darkness. It was sealed with the *Reichsadler* pressed into a circle of black wax. She took a knife from the table and cut into it. Her father staggered over to her and asked who it was from.

'General Gruetzmacher. He is inviting me to dinner.'

Jon Ohnstad was immediately and miraculously sober. 'What in the name of God…' He took the letter from her and read it. 'Not so much an invitation as a summons. He is sending his staff car for you, tomorrow afternoon.'

Below them, Magnus snored softly.

'What do you think he wants?'

'I have no idea,' Silje replied, 'but I will need Mother's other dress.'

Her father nodded. 'I will get it from the trunk.'

She kissed him on the cheek – a challenge as he was swaying from side to side – and then climbed the stairs to her room. She was at her door when her father called up to her.

'With the exception of myself and my son,' he said, 'no one will love you more than Erik Brenna.'

Silje replied, her voice barely a whisper. 'Yes, Father.'

Exhaustion claimed her as soon as she closed the door. She squeezed her eyes shut, and to banish thoughts of Freya from her head, turned her mind elsewhere: to the tall man she'd seen speaking to Magnus at the funeral; the man who could not tear his eyes away from Freya.

She thought of Mr Kleppe, and wondered if she could have been kinder to him when he was alive. She had not known about his family; she had never thought to ask. How he must have loved Freya to tell her of such an intimate sorrow.

And Mrs Tufte, Silje thought, *who commands her affections in your place.*

She climbed into bed and pushed her hand between her thighs. *And that is no one's fault but your own.*

22

Silje was still exhausted when she awoke the following morning. She inhaled sharply as she withdrew her hand from between her legs. Lust and rage was a painful blend, she decided, when the focus of those feelings were one and the same. She got out of bed and made another decision; the impasse between herself and Freya had gone on long enough. She would bring her home. She would *make* her come home. She brought water from the kitchen to wash and soothe herself before getting dressed and returning to make breakfast. She chewed slowly and without tasting anything. Moments after she'd finished, she could not remember what she'd eaten. She made a half-hearted task of cleaning the kitchen and went outside to feed the animals.

The morning had warmed the earth. Baldur and his harem were already basking in the spring grass. They seemed uninterested in the feed she put out for them, and by the state of the trough Silje could see they had already gorged themselves on corn and spoiled fruit. She heard the sound of laughter from the small barn next to the patch of orchids her father deemed 'experimental failures'. One of the voices belonged to Magnus; the other she did not recognise.

'Silje,' said Magnus as she stepped inside the orchid barn. His eyes darted between her and his companion, the tall man she'd seen at Mr Kleppe's funeral. Silje sniffed and waited for an introduction.

Before the silence could solidify any further, the stranger coughed into his fist and said his name was Gunther. 'And I am pleased to make your acquaintance.' He extended a hand at least as large as her father's.

Silje thought that he seemed handsome enough. He was young, perhaps a little older than Magnus and herself. His hair was blonde and fine and he carried an attractive scar on the left side of his face. His eyes were a solid grey in colour, and his nose seemed somewhat small for his broad skull. There were no lines around his mouth, so he did not smile very often, and if he did not smile very often then she wondered how he could possibly be a friend of Magnus.

'Your brother speaks kindly of you.'

'Does he.' Silje looked sternly at her brother, and her brother looked for somewhere to hide. 'This is most strange because he has never mentioned you. Did you both study at Stavanger?'

The two men looked at each other, each waiting for the other to reply.

'I shall take that as a "no", I think. Magnus, may I speak to you for a moment?' As she said this, she dug her fingernails into his arm and pulled him to the east corner of the barn.

'The Germans could appear and swarm over this village,' she said, 'in less time than it would take for you and your friend to think of a lie that would fool them.'

Magnus opened his mouth, but Silje placed her finger against his lips. 'I am going into the village to bring Freya home.' Beneath the pressure of her index finger, he curled his lips into a relieved smile. 'While I am gone, I suggest you practise what you will say, should the Nazis ever chance upon your friend and want to know who he is.'

Magnus nodded.

Silje released him and took her leave. She turned at the barn door and said, 'It was a pleasure to meet you, Gunther.'

'And you, Silje.'

'And you will try to think of a name more convincing than Gunther, won't you?'

The stranger looked puzzled. 'But Gunther is my name.'

Silje made a show of looking surprised. 'You do not look like a Gunther to me,' she said and closed the door behind her.

But instead of leaving, she walked in a tight circle, making light footsteps, and crept back to the barn. She put her ear to the door and listened.

'Your name is really Gunther?' Magnus was whispering.

'Yes! For the thousandth time! Why do all you people think this is not my name?'

His accent had changed. Silje's mind reeled. *He is English!*

'That is because she is right,' Magnus was saying. 'You do not look like a Gunther.'

* * *

The second unpleasant surprise of the day concerned Freya; she was nowhere to be found.

'I do not know where she is,' Mrs Tufte said, vigorously scrubbing an already spotless doorstep. 'I have not had any materials delivered in days, so I said she could have the morning to do as she pleases.'

Silje dug her nails into the palms of her hands. 'And you did not think to ask where she is going?'

'She is not a child, Silje. You know perfectly well that she can find her way about the hills as well as any of us. It is only you who treats her as though she is blind.'

'She *is* blind!'

'Yes, I sometimes forget. You should too.'

'If she returns then please tell her to come see me.'

Mrs Tufte stopped scrubbing and looked up, wiping her brow. 'I will ask her, Silje. That is all I can do.'

As the morning went on, Silje's anger deepened, but then at noon it vanished and was replaced by a fretful despair. No one had seen Freya and no one seemed to care.

'She could be in the hands of the Nazis,' she implored. 'We should search for her!'

'You worry too much, Silje,' Mr Bergström replied. He was sitting on the three-legged stool outside his shop, smoking the wooden pipe that had been carved for him by her father. 'She came to my shop looking for something to do. I had no work for her because I have no fruit and I have no vegetables.' He made a loud sucking sound and raised an eyebrow. 'Can you not do something about our situation?'

'I do not know what you mean.'

Mr Bergström scratched nervously at the side of his neck. 'Well, you seem to have the ear of the Germans, so I thought that perhaps you could intercede on the village's behalf.'

'Intercede.'

'Yes, we need supplies. We have no vegetables, no fruit, no raw goods with which we can trade…'

'I think you overestimate my influence, Mr Bergström. And the reason we have nothing is because the Resistance has destroyed the supply lines and blown up many of the harbours. Perhaps someone should "intercede" with them.'

The shop doorbell rang and young Jesper Bergström peered out from behind the frame.

Mr Bergström jumped to his feet and tried to shoo his son back inside. 'Go and help your sister!'

Jesper pressed his lips together and stared at Silje through narrow hate-filled eyes. 'The Resistance will free all of Norway! The Resistance will free the whole world! You will see!'

He was cuffed soundly about the head for his pains, and pushed back inside the shop. Mr Bergström slammed the door, making the glass rattle. The pane that had been broken weeks before slipped from its mount and shattered on the ground.

'Such a wilful child,' the grocer said nervously. 'He does not know what he is saying. Children just hear things and then shout them without understanding how these things could be misconstrued. It is a habit we are trying to break, but as I said, he is very headstrong, and when he hears fanciful stories about the Resistance—'

'I will not tell anyone, Mr Bergström.'

'Of course, of course. I did not mean to imply that—'

'You think that I am a Nazi spy who would betray your son to the enemy. He is a child, a child whom I have looked after more times than I can count!' She wiped her eyes. 'I am sorry. I did not mean to shout. I take it the whole of Fólkvangr thinks the same.'

Mr Bergström looked dumbly at the three-legged stool as though it held the answer.

'I see.'

Silje looked around her and saw the changes, gradual in their approach, now laid clearly before her. There was a greyness to things, a tangible aura of fear that pulsed from her in waves. The villagers glanced at her as they went about their business, but then looked quickly to the ground. Only one would fix eyes on her: Marit Ohnstad, sitting on a rocking chair outside her charms and trinkets stall. She spat a mouthful of tobacco into a basket, leaned back and closed her eyes.

'Excuse me, Mr Bergström,' said Silje.

He nodded anxiously, making no attempt to hide how pleased he was to see her leave.

Silje crossed the cobbles, causing a groups of whispering villagers to part hastily to allow her through.

'Is this your doing?'

Marit Ohnstad opened one watery eye. 'You are blocking what little sun I see in these mountains, child.'

Silje put her hands on her hips, blocking the light still further. 'Have you done this? Have you turned Fólkvangr against me?'

Marit rocked gently, but chose to say nothing.

'I thought we had begun a new journey, you and I,' said Silje. 'When you sent your piece to the newsletter, I thought it meant you were ready to—'

'Ready to what? Forgive the theft of my husband? To open my arms to his bastard children? The recipe was to help the village in times of need. I did not do it for you. Besides, you did not even thank me for it.'

'Then you did not read the newsletter.'

'You did not come to find me to thank me for it.'

'Dear God, Marit, if I had to personally thank everyone who sent a contribution then I would spend my whole life wandering the mountains.'

Marit Ohnstad snorted and closed her eye. 'I have said nothing. It is Mrs Tufte who is turning the village and the Jew girl against you.'

'I do not believe you.'

'Your name is my name, Silje Ohnstad,' she said. 'I would not poison it. And if you seek the Jew—'

'Please do not call her that.'

'If you seek Freya then you will find her in the hills where you whore yourself to Erik Brenna.' She smiled without looking at her. 'She asked me if I knew of somewhere she could be alone with her thoughts, and I said I knew the perfect place.'

'You are an evil woman, Marit.'

'Ohnstad,' Marit said. 'My name is Marit Ohnstad. I want you to say it, and I want you to thank me for teaching you how to make goat stew, and I want you to thank me for telling you where to find your Jew.'

Silje thrust a trembling finger under her nose. 'Now you listen to me, you bitter old—'

'And look,' Marit said, pushing the finger away. She nodded towards the sound of a truck rolling across the cobbles. 'More of your handiwork, I shouldn't wonder.'

Silje scowled at her and turned around.

The truck belonged to Mr Fehn, the farrier. He drove slowly, leaning on the horn to clear the villagers who looked on with eager curiosity. His wife sat next to him, occasionally dabbing her eyes with one of Mrs

Tufte's finely embroidered handkerchiefs. In the back of the truck, riding alongside her trunk and her cello case, was Lisbeth Fehn.

'We are not done here,' Silje said to Marit Ohnstad, and then ran across the street.

Lisbeth's parents did not answer when she asked where they were going with Lisbeth and all of her things.

'If you speak to her,' Mrs Fehn said loudly to her husband, 'then it is the end of us, do you understand?'

So Silje hurried to the back of the truck and climbed onboard. She poked out her tongue at Mrs Fehn who glowered at her through the rear window.

'Lisbeth, what is all this? Where are you going?'

Lisbeth picked up a book and started to read, raising it to her chin to hide herself away.

'I will stay here until you speak to me.' Silje perched on the tailgate and folded her arms. 'Come now, Lisbeth; we have been friends for—'

'We have never been friends, Silje,' Lisbeth said without showing her eyes. 'You are Erik's intended and I am Erik's friend. All we have in common is Erik. And now we no longer have that.'

'That is not true. We have been friends since we were children. You taught me to ride a bike, and I taught you to—'

'Kiss boys; yes, I remember.' She placed the book down at her side. Silje could not decide if her eyes spoke of longing or loathing. In the end she saw it was both; Lisbeth longed for her to never have been born. 'And why did I teach you to ride a bicycle, Silje?'

'So that I could ride quickly to my mother's monument. And I thank you for that.'

'And why did you teach me to kiss boys?'

Silje swallowed.

'Come now, Silje. It was many years ago, but I am sure you remember.' Lisbeth launched herself at her. Silje, thinking she was about to be pushed from the truck, held on tightly and squeezed her eyes shut. A moment later, finding she wasn't lying broken on Fólkvangr's cobbles, she cautiously opened one eye. Lisbeth was so close to her that their noses almost touched. 'Because I wanted to kiss Erik Brenna.'

'I do not know what you want me to say, Lisbeth. I cannot say I am sorry because I am not. I love Erik with all my heart, and the same heart wishes that you could be happy for us. Will you not stay?'

'So you would not have to travel far to gloat? I think not.'

'That is unkind.'

'It is *you*. So tell me, all those years ago when your lips were pressed against mine, were you thinking then that you would steal him from me?'

'Of course not!'

'Later then, when you were telling me that I should not be so eager, and that I had a tongue like a fat, wet snake. Was it then you decided you would take him simply because you could?'

Silje wanted to protest her innocence, but when she opened her mouth, no words came. The sudden truth, it seemed, had struck her dumb.

'Ah,' Lisbeth said, kneeling back on her haunches. 'So it was then.' She turned her head and called out to her father. 'Stop the truck. Silje is getting off.'

'I will write to you,' Silje said desperately.

'Don't be ridiculous.'

'At least tell me where you are going!'

'No,' Lisbeth replied. 'Now get off my truck.'

23

I didn't call the police, not straight away. I took the bundle of notes and papers he'd left for me and anything else I could carry. I moved to a hotel about two miles from the museum and then went into work. No one asked about Mr Klein; he often disappeared for weeks, chasing down a German uniform, or a medal, or a diary. I carried on as best I could, sorting artefacts, answering phone calls, pretending to ignore the sideways glances and whispers of the other staff.

It's her I tell you!

Don't be stupid; she wouldn't dare...

And all the time, I carried a picture of Klein in my head, sitting in his chair, rotting next to his favourite window.

'You talked to him a lot,' said Kirsten. She was Head of Merchandising and Personnel; that's what she told people. In fact she was the gift-shop manager – or would be when it opened. 'When was the last time you saw him?'

I scratched my elbow and shrugged. 'Six days ago, I think.'

She nodded and sat back in the chair that filled half of her tiny office. 'So you're probably the last person to see him here.'

'Probably.' My palms began to sweat.

Kirsten tapped her front teeth with a pen. 'Does he have a phone?'

I said I didn't know.

'I don't suppose you could pop round and make sure he's all right? He seemed quite fond of you.'

'I'll go after my shift.'

'Better go now, if that's okay. I'll get Daniel to cover you until you get back.'

'Right.'

'I just have this really bad feeling, you know what I mean?'

My life was a catalogue of bad feelings. 'I think so.'

We looked at each other for a moment; she raised an eyebrow.

'His address?' I said.

Kirsten made an odd little jumping motion in her chair. 'God, sorry! Of course!' She tried her drawer, then her rolodex, then her notebook. 'Are you enjoying it here? Not here in my office, obviously; I mean the museum. Do you enjoy working at the museum?'

I said I enjoyed it very much, and then I thanked her for giving me the job, handing over the mote of gratitude she'd been fishing for.

'Everyone said I was mad to take you on. "People still haven't forgiven her father; there'll be hell to pay if the public finds out!"

"Nonsense," I said. "She deserves a chance."' She peered at me over the top of her spectacles and smiled. 'In fact, I think you'll be a bit of a draw. "The Traitor's daughter" and all that. Anyway, I'm glad you're here.'

I wanted to hit her in the face, which was the feeling most people got after spending time in her company. The office reeked of cheap perfume and even cheaper cigarettes.

'And how is your mother doing?'

'Fine,' I said, wishing she'd just have the balls to admit she didn't know where Klein lived. 'Look, Kirsten, I'm sure I can find out from—'

'Here it is!' She waved a dog-eared note under my nose. 'Never doubt me, Brigit; I do have a system, believe it or not.' She was as surprised as I was.

I made a show of reading the address and then gave it back to her. She didn't say another word; she just steepled her fingers, smiled and nodded at the door.

I took a bus to Mr Klein's apartment. I knocked on the door and called his name, thinking I'd shit my own bodyweight if he replied.

'Mr Klein! It's Brigit! Are you in there?'

I had to shout eight more times before a suitable alibi popped out from her apartment, two doors down. 'He's not answering,' said Mrs Einhorn. 'I tried him yesterday. Nothing.'

'When did you last see him?'

She shrugged.

'Maybe we should call the police.'

She shrugged again and said, 'Up to you,' before shuffling back towards her apartment. There was a smell escaping from under Mr Klein's door.

'Can I use your phone?'

Mrs Einhorn turned and scowled. 'There's a public phone about two streets down. Just head towards the—'

'He could be ill, Mrs Einhorn.'

She was surprised to hear her own name, and I was stunned I'd made such a stupid mistake. She stared at me, and then came closer. 'I've seen you around before, haven't I.'

I swallowed and said that I'd come round to pick up some papers for the museum.

'Yes, I thought I recognised you.'

My mind flashed back to Kirsten's office, asking for Mr Klein's address, then raced forward to a police officer asking me why I needed the address if I'd been to his home before.

My fingerprints were all over the apartment. I should have just called the police the moment I found him. What the fuck was I thinking?

I'd been thinking like Monica. I'd been thinking of a pretend life on the run, the imagined need to cover my tracks. I cursed her and thrust my shoulder against the door.

Mrs Einhorn cried, 'What the hell are you doing?'

I threw myself at the door again; the wood split around the hinges.

'I'm going to call the police!'

'I very much wish you would, Mrs Einhorn.' Seemed the only way to go was forward.

On the fifth try, the door sprang free. I ran inside and screamed as loudly as I could. Mrs Einhorn followed me inside. 'Oh.'

'Get an ambulance!'

'I don't think that's going to help him, dear.'

I picked up the phone and made the call while Mrs Einhorn busied herself looking around the apartment. The woman on the line calmly took the details, stopping every other question to ask me if I was all right. When she asked me my name, I hesitated.

'I'm going to need your name,' she said emphatically.

'Brigit,' I said. 'Brigit Fossen.'

The line went silent. Behind me, Mrs Einhorn was taking large steps across the living room.

The officer came back on the line. 'I'm sorry but are you *the* Brigit Fossen?'

'I suppose.'

Mrs Einhorn said the apartment was bigger than her own.

'Would you stay on the line for me, Miss Fossen?'

I said I would, and imagined she was gathering a small choir to sing *Deutschland erwache* into the mouthpiece. Instead, a calm, almost kindly male voice came back.

'Miss Fossen?'

'Speaking.'

Another round of silence; I could hear voices in the background, so I assumed the choir had arrived. I was thinking like my mother, an expectation that I'd only ever see the worst in people. Funny that the longer we were apart, the more like her I became.

'Are you still there, Miss Fossen?'

'Yes.'

'We've been trying to trace you for quite some time.'

I gripped the handset tightly, closed my eyes. They couldn't know. If they'd known I was here then they'd know about Klein, and they wouldn't just leave him here. It was something else.

'We'll send a car for you,' the police officer said. 'I'm afraid it's your mother.'

24

By late morning, Silje felt so bruised and shaken by her encounters with Marit and Lisbeth she relinquished all notion of speaking to Freya that day. If the fates had turned Fólkvangr against her then she could not bear to think how Freya would answer her plea to come home.

And so, later that morning, Silje returned to the cottage, greeted Magnus and her father somewhat curtly, and then retired to her room. She lay on her bed, staring up at the ceiling and listening to the goats in the field and the sparrows chattering in the trees outside her window. It was more than an hour before a clear thought passed through her head, untarnished by images of war and memories of past misdeeds. Her thoughts turned to Freya so she pushed her hands under her pillow.

Magnus knocked on the door and entered at the same time. He smiled and placed a mug of honey and milk on her bedside stand.

'You do not have to tell me what is wrong,' he said. 'Just tell me if I can help.'

She smiled back and said all was well. 'I have had something of an unpleasant morning, that is all.'

'I have those,' he replied. 'Usually after an evening spent with Father in *The Mottled Goat*.' He waited for her to laugh, and when she did not, he shrugged and scratched at the whiskers on his neck.

'What of your friend, the Englander?'

Magnus gasped and then slammed the door to her room. He skipped over the bed and pulled the windows shut. 'How did you know?'

'Does it matter? I trust he will not return.'

'He will not! But you must not breathe a word of this to anyone.'

'Why does all the village think I am a collaborator? I would sooner cut out my tongue than betray you!'

Her brother's silence clawed at her soul.

'You are supposed to say "Yes, Silje, my dear sweet sister, I know that you would endure any torture the Nazis devised to protect Fólkvangr."'

'I know you would.'

'Then why did you not say it!'

Magnus had no reply. Or rather, his reply would make things a thousand times worse.

'It is Resistance business, Silje,' he said quietly. 'Not everything that goes on in this village is your concern.' He stroked her cheek, kissed her, and made his way to the door.

'Magnus.'

'Yes?'

'I think I'm in love with someone else.'

She barely had time to blink before he was sitting attentively on the edge of her bed. 'What? You mean someone other than Erik?'

'Obviously.'

'My God, Silje! Who?'

'Why is that important?'

'Is it Junges Fehn? Please God, not him! He is far too… married!'

'It is not Junges.'

'Then it is someone younger.' Magnus stroked at his beard and pursed his lips in concentration. 'But most of the younger men you have been with are fighting with the Resistance…'

'Magnus!'

'Olaf! It is Olaf, the miller's son!'

'Does it really matter who it is?'

'No,' he conceded. 'I suppose not. Have you told Erik?'

'I have only just realised this myself.'

'Then you must tell him; it would be a betrayal not to.'

Betrayal, Silje thought. *That word…* 'I will tell him. I will tell him as soon as I know how.'

'"How" does not matter, Silje. Any way you tell him will destroy him, so do it quickly. Make the cut clean.' He rose to his feet and shook his head. 'I sometimes wonder why Freya worships you the way she does.'

'Do you not think I feel bad enough?'

'I think you treat this village like your own personal doll house, and we are just mannequins that you shape and twist as you please.'

'You should leave now.'

'Tell him, Silje. Soon.'

'Just get out.'

* * *

Staff Sergeant Krause arrived at three that very same afternoon. She stopped the car at the cottage gate, climbed out and opened the rear door. She stood to attention and waited.

'She is here,' Jon Ohnstad said, peering through the window. 'Are you sure you do not want me to come with you?'

Silje slipped into her best footwear: the white dress shoes that had belonged to her mother. 'You were not invited.'

'Nevertheless, I am your father, so I am sure the General will have no objection if—'

Silje kissed him on the cheek. 'Stay here, do not smoke your pipe in the kitchen and keep Magnus out of trouble. I will be back soon. Now, how do I look?' She fanned the hem of her blue dress, and her father smiled.

'Like your mother.'

'You always say that.'

'Because you will always look like your mother. But you should be careful, Silje. This General Gruetzmacher is—'

'Nazi scum, but I think I have charmed him. Perhaps I remind him of his wife.'

'Yes,' said Jon Ohnstad, with the barest hint of irony in his voice. 'That must be it.'

She left the cottage, smiling at her father one last time before closing the door.

Sergeant Krause clicked her heels together. The last time Silje had seen her she was wearing the standard uniform of a Reich soldier. Today, she was dressed in a black skirt suit with a red armband. There were tiny silver skulls pinned to her lapels. 'Fräulein.' She swept her hand towards the back seat of the car. Silje climbed in and pulled the door shut before the Sergeant had the chance to do it for her.

It would be a long journey so as soon as they set off, Silje started counting trees: firs, pines, the rare and beautiful mountain oaks… The winter snows had gone and the mountains had reclaimed vibrant green as their colour. Silje wondered how Freya could stand not being able to see any of this. The sun hung low between the mountain peaks, bathing the forest with a gentle warmth. She would feel the warmth, Silje thought, but still…

'Are you enjoying the Rostbratwurst?'

'What?'

'The recipe I sent,' said the Sergeant. 'Have you tried it again since we last met?'

'Not as yet.' Silje vowed that she never would.

'You said that you enjoyed it before.'

She remember that she had. 'I have been very busy, and meat is very scarce.'

'Of course, yes. The Resistance makes life difficult for all of us.'

Silje fumed.

The Sergeant coughed and cleared her throat. 'You and Lieutenant Klein are no longer courting.'

'What did you say?'

'You and the Lieutenant. You have parted ways, yes?'

'Forgive me, Sergeant, but I do not think that is any of your business.'

'Forgive *me*, Fräulein. You are quite right.'

Silje scowled to herself and carried on counting the trees.

'It is just that the Lieutenant has not been himself of late, and I wondered if that was the reason. I thought that perhaps you and he had—'

'Are you fond of Lieutenant Klein, Sergeant?'

The back of Sergeant Krause's neck turned bright red.

'If you wish to make your feelings known to him then you have my blessing.'

'I do not wish to interfere if—'

'We are no longer together, Sergeant. I am to marry another.'

The Sergeant, uncharmingly, breathed a sigh of relief. 'Then I shall make myself known to him this very night. It is why I have worn my dress uniform.'

'It is very nice, very… dark.'

'I am older than he is. Do you think it matters?'

'No.'

'And I am not very pretty, and I do not have a good shape, and he is a lieutenant. Perhaps I should wait. I have applied for officer's training, but I do not know if I will be accepted.' She slowed down and leaned closer to the windscreen. 'How do you people find your way around without road signs?'

'We built this land,' Silje replied curtly. 'We know where everything is.'

'Of course. Sometimes I forget that I am the intruder here.'

It was the first time Silje had heard a German admit to that which the whole of Norway knew to be true: that this was not a rescue, or aid from a distant neighbour. It was an invasion, breathtaking in its size and brutal in its execution. She looked closely at the back of the Sergeant's neck. Her hair was pulled up and tied beneath her cap, but stray hairs fell across her collar, below which her flesh curiously changed hue.

'You have beautiful hair,' said Silje. She actually thought it rather coarse, even more so than Freya's.

The Sergeant blushed again. 'Thank you, Fräulein.'

'Why do you think that you will not be accepted into officer's training?'

'There are those who think that I would be unsuitable.'

'Because you are part-Jewish?'

Krause sighed. 'On my grandmother's side. Is it so obvious?'

'You seek to lighten the tone of your skin. It would seem a lot of trouble for a soldier to go to without good reason. It is unfortunate.'

'In many ways.' The Sergeant took one hand from the wheel to adjust her collar.

'Do you believe what your masters tell you about the Jews?'

Krause was silent for a moment. 'The alternative to not believing is too terrible to think about.'

'I would like to know what you think… I am sorry, I have never asked your name.'

'Ingeborge,' the Sergeant said. 'Though my friends call me Inge.' She tapped the steering wheel and looked at Silje through the mirror. 'That is not true; I have no friends. Everyone calls me Krause.'

'I would like to know what you really think of the Jews, Inge.'

Staff Sergeant Krause spoke slowly. 'I think they are people. I think they are a good people and they are a bad people, and they are a people who are both. But until one man said otherwise, they were Germans, just like me, or Norwegians, just like you. They worship differently, but how does this make them a plague?'

* * *

The staff car drew into Bergen's main square, and Silje witnessed the true extent of the General's desire to keep the peace: gallows erected from the finest Norwegian oak; gallows from which eight corpses hung and collided gently in the harbour breeze.

Five men, two women, and a boy who could not have been more than ten years old.

Silje demanded that Krause stop the car.

'Three Jews,' said the Sergeant. 'We found them hiding in one of the fishing boats. The fishermen were attempting to take them out to one of the British ships stationed just beyond our waters.'

'And the others?' whispered Silje.

'The fishermen, their wives and one of their sons.'

Three soldiers stood guard at the gallows, presumably, Silje thought, to prevent the corpses from being taken away.

'He murdered a child,' Silje said.

'He does what he must to maintain order.'

'And this sits well with you, does it?'

'Do not ask me any more questions, Fräu Ohnstad.'

And so they drove on in silence, through the grey streets where hardly a Norwegian could be seen. The town had become a garrison, Germans infesting its every square yard. Along the main thoroughfare that faced the harbour, where Mr Dorfmann once ran the finest millinery in all of Bergen, a series of wooden posts had been driven through the ground. The wall behind the post was crumbling under the weight of bullets.

'For the firing squad,' Krause said.

'I know what it's for.' Silje sat back and closed her eyes.

Another left turn brought the staff car to Bergen's centre, and the town hall which served as forward area command for the German forces. Their flags hung from its lateral poles, and the iron cross festooned every arch and every window. The invaders had erected barricades and posted a heavy machine gun at each corner, and when she looked up Silje could see the shadow cast by an anti-aircraft battery mounted on the roof.

A paratrooper raised the barrier, allowing the car into the main courtyard. Krause stopped the car near the steps, got out and opened Silje's door.

'I will return for you at six o'clock.'

Silje nodded and made her way up the staircase to the main doors. The guards either side snapped to attention; she almost leapt out of her own skin. She wondered if she should knock, and while she wondered, one of the guards reached over and rapped firmly on the oak door.

The door opened, and a man Silje recognised as the town hall curator stepped out. He looked as grey as the rest of Bergen; there were deep red circles below his eyes, and Silje imagined that he must spend all his nights in tears. She did not want to imagine the things he'd seen.

'Miss Ohnstad,' he said. 'General Gruetzmacher is expecting you. Please come inside.'

Silje did as she was told, following him along a wide hallway carpeted in blood red. The walls were lined with large portraits of the Nazi High Command, Hitler featuring most prominently. The pictures had been hung close to the high ceiling to prevent defacement. Lower down, and contained in much smaller frames, were portraits of Norway's *Nasjonal Samling.*

'Who is that?' Silje pointed to a larger portrait that hung at the same height as Hitler, though its subject did not appear to be wearing a uniform.

'Josef Terboven,' the curator replied without looking. 'Soon to be appointed *Reichskommissar* of Norway.'

Silje wasn't sure what the title meant, but it sounded grand, much more important than leader of the despised fascist party. 'Then Quisling is no longer our leader?'

'Quisling has failed to bend the Norwegian knee, and Hitler is displeased. As editor-in-chief of the Germans' most popular regional newsletter, I would have expected you to know this.'

'I pick the recipes and judge the contests,' Silje said. 'The politics and the war fall to the General's staff.'

'Our people call it *The Quisling Orchid.*'

'Yes, I know.'

'Perhaps it should be renamed *The Terboven Orchid,*' he turned his head and smiled thinly at her, 'to keep with the times.'

A long flight of stairs arced to the left and then levelled out to another hallway. Silje thought she was being taken to a huge pair of doors at the end of the hall; instead, the curator veered right.

'In here.' He opened the door and she followed him inside.

The General stood behind a chair placed at one end of a dining table dwarfed by the size and majesty of the room.

'Fräu Ohnstad.'

He'd chosen to leave the dining hall untouched; there were no German flags or portraits of high-ranking Nazis. The pale cream walls were decorated with fine tapestries, and the Norwegian flag hung from pikes mounted high at each corner. The floor was marble, darker than the walls and polished to a muted sheen that swallowed the light reflected from the chandeliers. Silje clamped her mouth shut when she realised it was hanging open. The General didn't seem to mind; indeed, he seemed pleased that she was so impressed.

He pulled out her chair. 'You must be hungry after your journey. Please, sit.'

Silje walked over, conscious of the scraping noise her mother's shoes were making on the marble floor. Her father was always telling her to lift her feet.

The General's eyes swivelled to the floor and he fixed a smile to his face. 'I hope you are prepared to have your palette educated this evening.'

Silje took her seat without saying a word. There was a moist sheen to his skin, and the smell of whiskey exuded from his pores.

'I have travelled much, thanks to my duties with the Reich, so I have been fortunate enough to sample—'

'Why am I here, General?'

His smile vanished, replaced by a flash of confusion, then rage, and then the smile was restored. 'Down to business I see. I like that.' He did not, clearly. 'Conversation, Fräu Ohnstad. That is all.'

He is quite, quite drunk, Silje thought, and wondered if this placed her in more danger, or less.

'I am sure you can find much more interesting dinner companions closer to Bergen.'

'I could indeed,' he said, 'but I wanted to speak to you specifically.'

A waiter arrived with the first course: a very thick soup and rolls of freshly-baked bread. The scent of herring and shellfish wafted from the bowl, making Silje's nose twitch.

The general swelled with satisfaction. 'I thought you would like it. I have a Norwegian chef in my employ.'

She doubted his use of the word 'employ'.

Gruetzmacher ate slowly, allowing each mouthful of soup to rest on his tongue before swallowing, and then after every fourth mouthful he dabbed effeminately at his lips with his napkin. Silje slowed her pace so she would not empty her bowl first. She was worried that the soup would grow cold before she finished it, which she decided would be a tragedy as it was the finest soup she'd ever tasted.

'How is your soup?' the General asked.

'Passable.' She tore a bread roll in two.

The General frowned. He tapped his spoon on the table while watching her with measured disdain. He dropped his spoon in the empty bowl, and the door behind him opened. A troop of waiters filed out and began clearing the table.

'I have some changes planned for *The Orchid*.'

'I thought you were happy with the newsletter.' Silje tried not to sound alarmed.

'Indeed I am, and High Command is also pleased with your efforts, but they are concerned that newsletter doesn't align with *our* efforts.'

'I'm afraid I do not understand, General.'

'Of course.' Gruetzmacher rose to his feet, and Silje was unsure if he meant *Of course; I have not explained myself well* or *Of course you do not understand; you are an ill-educated scion born of an inferior race.* When she looked up, the General was standing over her, holding out a single sheet of paper, immaculately typed. His breath, laced with whiskey, washed over her in shallow waves.

'My proposals,' he said, returning to his end of the table. 'You have time to read it before the second course.'

He wrote much as he spoke: directly, succinctly, with nothing spared for sentiment, his words not so much written as scratched out with a razor blade.

'You cannot do this,' she said.

'I can,' he replied. There was no anger, no air of superiority or entitlement; he was simply stating a fact.

'You are dropping the *Historical Norway* page.'

'We are simply changing the newsletter's focus. We believe that a history of Fascism in Norway is more in keeping with the times.'

'And this conundrums page?'

'Puzzles that will encourage young minds to think creatively.'

'These are questions about Hitler.'

'Indeed.'

'Why would our children know such things about Hitler?'

'Our children do.'

'And what is *Traitor's Gate*?'

'Ah, that is a new section where traitors to the Reich will be named prior to transportation or execution. Collaborators and Jew-lovers mainly, but we will expand our coverage as needs demand.'

Silje gripped the edge of the table to steady the room.

'We will also detail incentives and rewards for handing over Jews who are hiding from us. Would you like some water, Fräulein? You look a little pale.'

'I am fine, thank you, General. You think there are many Jews in hiding?'

'A great many. There always are. You would be amazed the lengths these people will go to avoid processing: living in attics and basements, like rats; in caves and woods; hiding in sewage pipes and privies like – I cannot begin to think what that is like.' He shook his head. 'They have no pride in themselves. They will survive and live without integrity or honour. They are cowards. They are worse than cowards. They are evil, by design of the devil himself.' He clapped his hands and the second course entered the room. The serving staff forced smiles at the General as they laid the dishes. None spared her so much as a glance. The plate that landed heavily in front of her was beautifully presented: a warm meat, delicately sliced and adorned with potatoes, and a swede and parsnip puree garnished with a thick mound of pickled cabbage. Silje's nose twitched again; the meat was very familiar.

'It is goat,' the General said as the serving staff departed. 'My deepest apologies. Our supplies are somewhat constrained due to the actions of the Resistance.'

'I understand.'

'They are but an annoyance, an inconvenience.' He began to eat, without waiting for her.

'You do not strike me as an emotional man, sir.' She tried a mouthful of the pickled cabbage and was forced to swallow it.

'Passionate, yes.' Gruetzmacher tried to smile, and Silje felt her skin trying to crawl away from her bones. 'Emotional, no. Emotion clouds the thinking. What is your point, Fräulein?'

'Your hatred of the Jews goes far beyond passion, General. Hatred is an emotion, and if I am not mistaken, you hate them very much.'

Gruetzmacher eyed her for a moment and then dabbed his mouth with his napkin before taking a sip of wine. 'Astute,' he said. 'I believe I have said that of you before. Yes, I hate them. I have reason to.' He put down the glass and loosened his collar.

Silje waited.

'Before I joined the Party, I thought as you Norwegians think. I thought the Jew was harmless. I thought the Jew was a person, like you or like me. I bore them no malice, I wished them no harm. I even welcomed the Jew into my home.' He sat back and crossed his legs, appearing to have lost his appetite. 'Two of them in fact, a woman and her daughter. The woman worked well enough, though perhaps she was prone to slacking when unobserved. And the daughter was a playmate for my children. My wife was a teacher, you see, and I often worked late at the ministry. Believe me, Fräulein, I would have done what I could for them once the transportations began. I would have pleaded their case, stated that they were vital to my household. I would have done these things and more, if not for...'

He stared at the wine glass.

'The daughter,' he said, speaking as though a block of stone had been lifted from his chest. 'The daughter was a witch. A Jew demon that turned me away from my wife and my family.'

'Perhaps you should not be telling me such things, General.'

Gruetzmacher waved a dismissive hand in her direction. 'Do not concern yourself, Fräulein. My fall from grace is common knowledge. Three years ago, I was the talk of Berlin. It almost ruined me. My wife left and I was branded a traitor, a Jew-lover.' He drained the wine glass and poured himself another. Then, as an afterthought, he got up and hurried over to Silje to charge her glass. 'Do you know who saved me?'

Silje said she could not begin to imagine.

'Hitler,' Gruetzmacher replied proudly. 'Adolf Hitler himself saved me, my career.' He sat on the edge of the table and Silje found herself leaning back to remove herself from his shadow. 'He came to me after a rally, after news of my bewitchment had reached the ears of the Party. I thought he would castigate me, berate and humiliate me in front those who were once my peers. He did not. Do you know what he did, Silje – may I call you Silje? We have known each other for some time now and I think we are beyond such formalities as "Fräulein".'

'If that is your wish, General.'

'But of course, you will still refer to me as "General".'

'I had not supposed otherwise.'

'Good. Good.' He looked at his wine glass; it was empty, and this seemed to disappoint him more than it should have. He filled it the brim and pressed on. 'Where was I? Yes! Hitler! He embraced me, Silje! He took me in his arms like the prodigal son. The other Party members were astounded. One had the audacity to whisper to him, "Mein Führer, do you know who this man is?" Of course he knew! And he told me that he knew the true reason for my downfall. He said that I had fallen foul of Jew magic.' Gruetzmacher leaned back and left his revelation festering above the dining table.

'Jew magic?' Silje echoed.

The General nodded with a maniacal vigour she found most disturbing. 'He took me under his tutelage; he showed me papers, documents, treatises and speeches he had yet to show to anyone else. Can you imagine the sense of honour, Silje? To share his knowledge of semitic witchcraft. He told me I had been seduced by a demon, a demon that had ripped everything away from me.' He drained his glass, and he glanced down at his breeches, scowling at whatever they contained. 'But under the Führer, I was reborn, restored.'

'Witchcraft,' Silje intoned. 'You said… witchcraft.'

'My beliefs surprise you, do they not?'

'I was raised to believe there is no such thing, sir.'

'And so was I. I am a man of learning. Indeed, during the months I travelled with him, the Führer found my lack of vision frustrating. He often had cause to thrash me until my eyes opened.' He leaned closer, and Silje found she could not move any further away. His breath was strong enough to intoxicate her.

'He told me there is a guile about the Jew, a cunning in its dealing with man and the devil. Science demands we examine the semite and learn how it communicates with the forces of darkness.'

She thought that perhaps it was a trick, that the General was playing games at her expense, but when she looked into his eyes, she saw only the truth – his truth.

'The Führer assembled Iscariot to examine Jew witchcraft and gave me unimpeachable control over it. I immediately ordered experiments on the mother and the child to see if this magic could be turned against the semite menace. Would you like some more wine?'

Silje placed her hand over the glass and shook her head. 'You dissected them?'

'Nothing so gauche,' he said with a smile. 'A Jewess so powerful that she could enslave an officer of the Reich. She was only seven years old, Silje. Can you imagine the power she would wield as a grown woman? I sought to harness it. You have known Jews, yes?'

'No! I have never—'

'Come now, there is no need to tell me lies. Norway was overrun with them. You must have known one or two. Perhaps a young man who caught your eye when you came into Bergen?' The General began to nod his head, very slowly, staring into her eyes. 'I am right, am I not.'

Slowly, fearfully, Silje began to nod herself. 'There was one,' she whispered.

The General shot to his feet, making her heart lurch inside her chest.

'Hah! I knew it! And did you feel drawn to him, in spite of yourself? Did your heart thunder whenever you heard his voice? Did he make you feel as though your soul was no longer your own?'

Silje said yes, and saw that he appeared to be weeping. He saw her staring back at him and turned away. He took a handkerchief from his pocket and blew his nose.

'Jew magic,' he said, his voice cracked and pitched higher. 'You were a victim of Jew magic, as was I.'

'Or perhaps,' Silje said, 'I was merely in love.'

'With a Jew? You do not strike me as the kind,' said Gruetzmacher. 'And neither was I.' He sniffed loudly and trembled. 'Jew sorcery. And I can tell you have been touched in the same way.' He turned back to her and inhaled deeply through his nostrils, swaying as though caught in a strong breeze. He held onto the table to steady himself; Silje feared if he let go he'd lose his grip on what little was left of his sanity.

'I appear to be quite exhausted,' he said. 'It has been a trying day. You must excuse me.'

'Of course, General. Are you unwell?'

'I think that perhaps I am.' He walked unsteadily towards the far door. 'The Sergeant will take you home. A great pity; you would have enjoyed dessert. And I think you will come to appreciate the changes I have proposed for the newsletter. Together we will defeat the Jewish witches… and warlocks, you shall see. We shall be heroes, you and I.'

25

Staff Sergeant Krause had little to say on the journey back to Fólkvangr. She stole glances at Silje through the mirror, and halfway between Bergen and the village, she asked how Silje had found the meal.

'It was very nice,' Silje replied. 'Though the General did not appear to be quite himself.' It occurred to her that perhaps Gruetzmacher was himself, and everything she'd seen of him up until tonight was a carefully staged performance.

'Do not judge him harshly,' Krause said.

'I shall try not to.'

'Something happened to him, years ago; it haunts him.'

'Do you know what he did? To the mother, her child?'

The Sergeant nodded and tried to push her hair further inside her cap. Silje imagined her shaven, her eyes sunk, and her frame stripped of its mass and its dignity.

'All this talk of secret projects and witchcraft. He is clearly insane.'

'He is not insane,' Krause shot back. 'He is troubled.'

'He drinks whiskey as you and I drink water.'

'Many of our senior officers drink. They bear a great and terrible responsibility. In spite of his many faults, Silje, he is still the finest man I have served under.'

'I am sorry, I did not mean to—'

'Perhaps it would be best, for both our sakes, if we did not discuss the General any further.'

Silje tried to catch her eye through the mirror, but the Sergeant remained steadfastly focussed on the road ahead. *She mistrusts me*, Silje thought. Perhaps Inge Krause was not the hapless weakling she first believed her to be.

'Did you speak to the Lieutenant?'

Krause nodded. 'He was very polite, very kind. He said that he was flattered, but he still hoped that you and he would one day be reconciled. He asked me to tell you this.'

'Then I do not think that was very kind.'

'No, he was being honest. I know unkindness when I see it.'

They were the last words spoken until Sergeant Krause brought the car to a halt outside the Ohnstad cottage.

'I have enjoyed your company this evening, Fräulein,' she said, 'and I sincerely hope you have enjoyed mine. Perhaps we can do something together in a less formal setting. You could show me your charming village, or we could see a film. I understand that Chaplin is very popular here, in spite of our attempts to ban it.'

'I do not think that—'

'I was not attempting a romantic overture, Silje.'

'Why would I think such a thing?' said Silje, though it was the first thing that came into her head.

'I find my solitary existence unbearable. Please say you will consider it.'

Silje lied and said that she would. And she could tell by the flash of disappointment in the Sergeant's eyes that she knew they would not be taking walks through the mountains, or watching Chaplin at the Bergen Picture House. But at the same time, Krause seemed grateful that someone would spare her feelings.

She is lonely, Silje thought, and this could perhaps be useful. She would have liked to have learned more of the General's life before Norway, more of this Iscariot and his plans to defeat Jewish sorcery.

The Sergeant smiled and put the car into gear. 'We shall probably meet again.'

Silje replied, 'Of that I have no doubt,' and wondered if she could bewitch Inge Krause in the same way Freya had bewitched her.

'Until next time then.'

Silje waited until the sound of the car's engine faded from the wind and then ran as fast as she could down the hill towards Fólkvangr.

* * *

She did not stop to speak to the group of women talking outside *The*

Mottled Goat; she didn't stop to exchange pleasantries with the gaggle of men smoking outside the village hall.

She did not stop to fix the orchids that surrounded the monument to her mother, or to chastise young Ingrid Haug for riding her bicycle across her path. Silje didn't stop running until she reached the door of Mrs Tufte. She was about to pound on it and demand to speak to Freya, but stayed her fist when she heard voices coming from inside. One belonged to Magnus, her brother; the other was English in origin and a voice she'd heard before. She withdrew from the door, and after making sure she was unseen, scaled the wall at the side of Mrs Tufte's cottage. She dropped heavily into a bracken patch, swore loudly, and then crept to the back door. Like most villagers, Mrs Tufte left the rear door unlocked for the free movement of livestock. Silje slipped inside and made her way through the kitchen, noting with a twinge of avarice how much bigger Mrs Tufte's cottage was than her own. Small wonder that Freya was reluctant to come home.

She slowly pushed open the door and peered into the front parlour.

Mrs Tufte held a full house. Freya was sewing furiously in one corner of the dark room while Mrs Tufte herself served tea and biscuits to the two men squeezed together on the parlour's twin seat: Magnus – and Gunther the English spy.

'You are too kind, Mrs Tufte,' Gunther was saying.

Mrs Tufte reddened and said something that sounded very much like 'Oh pish'.

Magnus laughed, and as he threw back his head he caught sight of Silje glaring at him. He shrieked and leapt to his feet. Gunther rolled from his seat and crouched on one knee, pointing a small pistol, conjured from nowhere, at Silje.

Silje screamed, and Freya, unable to see what was happening, screamed too.

Freya cried, 'What is going on?' She sniffed at the air. 'Silje? Is that you? What are you doing here?'

Gunther squinted at Silje in the poor light. 'Miss Ohnstad,' he said, and put his gun away. 'That is a fair question. What are you doing here?'

'Snooping, no doubt!' Mrs Tufte said. She looked down, and seemed very surprised to find the biscuits and the teapot lying on the floor. 'For her friends, the Germans!'

'Please, Mrs Tufte! She is not a spy.' Freya jumped up and ran to stand in front of Silje. 'She just came to see me! Isn't that right, Silje?'

Silje was too overjoyed to speak.

'Then she should have knocked – at the front door!'

'I think that perhaps we should calm ourselves,' Gunter said, unfolding his tall frame until he was standing upright. He had to stoop to prevent his head from pushing against the ceiling. 'Mrs Tufte, perhaps some more tea?'

Mrs Tufte opened her mouth to protest, but a stern look from Magnus sent her grumbling to the kitchen.

'Now then, Silje,' said Gunther. 'What are you doing here?'

'It is as Freya said. I have come to speak with her. I wish her to come home, but now…' Silje looked around the room. There was a map on the occasional table, held flat with two pistols and an ammunition clip. Next to Freya's chair, a sewing kit and a pile of tunics taken from German uniforms. 'Now I would very much like to know what is going on.'

Magnus and Gunther looked at each other.

Silje stepped past Freya so she could stand in front of the two men. 'Perhaps you, Gunther – or whatever your name is – would like to tell me.'

'My name actually *is* Gunth—'

'I do not care. Dear God, Magnus, you have brought the Resistance to the village, haven't you? And you have involved Freya? Have you lost your mind?'

'He did not involve me, Silje. I asked to be involved.'

Silje picked up one of the tunics; there was a needle and thread lodged near a hole in the breast pocket. She showed it to Magnus. 'An impressive shot.'

'It wasn't me,' he said glumly.

'You?'

Gunther shook his head.

'And it certainly wasn't Freya.'

'It might have been,' Freya mumbled.

'She is helping us with the captured uniforms,' Gunther said, adding that her skill with the needle was inhuman. He picked up another tunic lying on the floor. 'Two shots: one to the stomach, the other to the chest. Look. Not a mark. No blood, no signs of repair.'

Silje could almost hear Freya swelling with pride. 'She is very clever.'

'With these uniforms we will be able to—'

'Freya, you are coming home with me, this instant.'

Mrs Tufte, famous throughout the village for appearing at the worst possible moments, returned from the kitchen and placed the tray of tea and biscuits on top of the map.

'She is not going anywhere with you, traitor,' she said. 'And how was your dinner with the General, by the by?'

Magnus restrained his sister before she could move.

'I asked you to keep her safe, and what have you done? You have allowed the Resistance to use her!'

'No one is using me, Silje! I want to help!'

'Freya, be silent! I am trying to—'

'You are trying to control me!'

'Control you? My God, how can you say something so wicked!'

'Silje, please mind what you say now.'

'Magnus, shut up! Now you listen to me, Freya. You will go to your room, pack your things and—'

'She will do no such thing!' shouted Mrs Tufte.

'And you,' Silje seethed. 'You are trying to take her from me. You are as bad as Marit! Because your husband abandoned you for another, you cannot bear to see anyone live their life less bitterly than you!'

'I do not belong to you, Silje,' said Freya.

'My husband did not abandon me! He is dead, as you well know, Silje Ohnstad!'

'He is not dead! He is living in a big house on the edge of Fredrickstad with nine children! Nine!'

Gunther blinked and threw an enquiring look at Magnus who shrugged and said nothing.

'That is a wicked thing to say, Silje Ohnstad! Truly wicked! You will burn in hell for the lies you've told and the men you've ruined!'

Gunther's mouth fell open, but this time he found that Magnus refused to meet his eyes.

Freya reached out to find Silje's arm, holding onto her sleeve as tightly as she could.

'What are you doing?'

'Come with me,' said Freya. 'We're going outside. We will have words, you and I, and I do not wish anyone I care for to hear them.'

Mrs Tufte smiled triumphantly as Freya led Silje away through to the kitchen.

'I am just trying to do what is best for you, you silly child!'

'I understand that.'

Silje closed the kitchen door behind them, and allowed herself to be led through to Mrs Tufte's garden. 'Then why won't you *let me*?'

'Because as I keep trying to tell you, I am not a child!'

They reached the end of the garden and crossed a narrow log laid over the barren brook that ran the length of the village. The light was fading and as they carried on towards the trees, Silje realised that again she would have only Freya's affinity with the darkness to guide her.

'Where are we going?'

'Somewhere we can be alone.'

'Why?'

'You know why.'

Silje's stomach tightened; her mouth, inexplicably, filled with salt water. She swallowed and said, 'I am not sure that is wise.'

'I am very sure it is not, but it is all I have thought about since you cast me from your cottage.'

'I did not cast… You exaggerate, Freya, and it is a trait most unbecoming.'

'Then I shall add that to the scroll of the million other things you despise about me.'

'And you exaggerate still…'

They lost the moon as soon as they entered the trees. A few more yards and Silje found herself completely blind. 'You know I do not like it when you do this. You know I do not like the dark.'

'It is good for you to walk in my footsteps once in a while. Perhaps then you will understand that I do not need you to carry for me, or lead me, or look out for me. I will always be grateful to you and I will always love you, but my life is my own.'

'What did you say?'

'I said that my life is my own.'

'Before that!'

'I said I will always be grateful to you.'

'Are you playing with me?'

'No.' Freya let go of her hand and Silje walked into a tree. 'Now, I am playing with you.'

A litany of chastisements sat poised on Silje's tongue, but before she could utter a single one, Freya pressed herself against her back, pinning her to the pine tree. Silje dug her nails into the moist wood and squeezed her eyes shut. 'I did not cast you out.'

Freya reached inside Silje's dress and began twisting and kneading her breast, pushing down against her nipple with her thumb.

'I did not cast you out,' Silje repeated, her words expelled in sharp bursts. 'I sent you away for your own good.' The hem of her dress was drawn to her waist. Freya's free hand began struggling with her undergarments.

'You sent me away because the only thing that frightens you more than being unable to control people is being unable to control yourself.'

Silje moved her feet apart and planted them, sinking her fingernails still deeper into the pine tree. 'That is not true.'

'It is true, even if you won't admit it to yourself.'

'Here, let me…' Silje pushed her hand away and began undoing the fastenings of her underclothes.

'I can do it myself, Silje!' Freya said, slapping her hand. She went to work on the buttons again, this time releasing them with deft flicks of her index finger and thumb.

Silje asked why she was so angry. 'You were never like this when you lived with us.' Freya's hand slid into her undergarments, setting her senses aflame. The smell of the pine filled her nostrils; the cotton of her dress scratched and tore at her skin; the pounding of her heart was so strong she thought it would burst her ribcage.

'I am angry because you treat me like a child.'

Silje moistened and parted. She breathed the scent of the bark through her open mouth; Freya's fingers slipped inside her.

'What do you expect when you behave like one?' Silje breathed, locking her knees to prevent her legs from giving way.

'You see? This is what I mean. You speak to me like I am ten years old.'

Silje could smell cinnamon, and hear the sound of Erik's laughter – so clearly that if she were not lost to her desire she would have surely pushed Freya away. And then General Gruetzmacher whispered to her: m*agic, an evil magic born of the Semite. A magic with the power to seduce…* and to her shame she wondered if the General was so mad after all.

'How do you think I survived before I met you, Silje?'

'I think,' said Silje breathlessly, 'that it had much to do with your father.'

Freya fell silent. Her breath seared. Her fingers drove deeper and so harshly that Silje's whole body was pushed upward against the bark of the tree. It scratched her flesh, drew blood from her cheek. She reached behind her and ran her hand down Freya's stomach, slipping inside her dress and down further until she found the mound of coarse hair, and then further still, between her legs, feeling her moist flesh open and close around her fingers. Freya's heart pounded against Silje's back, and her teeth sank into her shoulder. Silje clamped her jaw shut to stop herself from crying out.

'I'm hurting you.'

'No.' Silje shook her head. 'No, go on.'

And so Freya turned her wrist again, easing her fingers deeper still. Silje held her breath and her release came, sending waves of pleasure from her groin to her neck, hardening her spine and snapping the air between her bones. She gasped and Freya withdrew from her, holding on to her as she slid to the ground. The stones were cold and sharp, like blades pressed against her skin. She fought back the urge to cry: for shame, for joy, she did not care which. She shivered, though she was not cold; she wanted nothing more than to sleep. She could not remember when she felt so free, as though she were as tall as the world was vast and the mountain was a stone she could hold in her hand.

The grass cracked like ice under Freya's feet. She was moving.

'Are you there?'

'I am here,' Freya said. She sounded out of breath; her voice rattled though she tried to hide it.

Silje leaned back against the tree, still feeling its bark between her teeth. The silence closed in again, for a lifetime, or so it seemed. She could hear Freya sighing, once after every sixth breath. The sounds of the animals had vanished, perhaps years ago; Silje was no longer sure of anything.

'I had dinner with Gruetzmacher,' she said quickly, fearing the silence as much as she feared the dark.

After a moment, Freya replied, 'I am sorry. I would never have wished that upon you.'

The silence returned, chilling her until Freya spoke again. 'What is he like?'

'He is weak,' Silje replied in a heartbeat. 'He did something terrible, years ago, and he lacks the courage to face it. He believes a Jew made him do it, that Jews are demons, that you are all in league with the devil, that you have magic that can turn a man in on himself. He believes you can steal souls.'

The tree shook, and Silje felt a wave of heat laced with cinnamon. Even though Freya was now sitting beside her, she still could not see her.

'And do you believe that, Silje? Do you think I am a demon?'

'I think you have stolen my soul.'

'Then perhaps I should take my own life, if it will show you that I am as human as you.'

'What you are, or what people say you are, does not matter to me. If you are a witch who captures souls then you have already taken mine. If you possess the power to make people fall in love with you then I am already lost, and if the spell cannot be broken then I no longer care.'

Freya's calloused fingertips caressed her cheek. Silje tilted her head into her hand and kissed her palm.

'It was while I dined with the General that I realised that he and I are not so different.'

'You are nothing like him, Silje. Do not say such things.'

'It is true. He hides behind lies because he cannot face the truth of what he did to that poor girl. And I am the same. I was cruel to you. I pushed you away because I feared my yearning for you. You are beautiful, Freya, but you are young. It does not feel right; it will never feel right, and God help me, I don't care.'

Freya rested her head against her chest. 'I am not so young as you think, Silje. I will be—'

'Nineteen next week.' Silje sighed, barely able to move her lungs. 'We should go back. They will begin to wonder why we spend so much time out on such a cold night.'

'I am not cold.'

'That is the fortitude of youth.'

Freya laughed. 'And you are not so old as you pretend to be, Silje Ohnstad.'

Her laugh was shrill and new, and Silje did suddenly feel very old.

'We can stay a while longer,' said Freya, kissing her mouth.

A light came on in the cottage, and Silje was not surprised to see she had been looking in the wrong direction. The light was put out, almost as quickly. *Magnus*, she thought. *He is worried.* But she knew he would not venture out; he would trust Freya to bring her back. Thinking of Magnus now felt strange: a series of images, a moving picture playing inside her head. She realised that she spent most of her waking hours consumed with Magnus, or her father, or the village, or the newsletter, or her dead mother.

But not now. Not this night. She wondered if she would ever feel so consumed again. Freya's hand slipped between her legs; Silje gasped and bowed her head. She inhaled deeply, filling her throat with the scent of her hair.

26

When Silje opened the rear door, Magnus, Gunther and Mrs Tufte were huddled together in one corner of the kitchen. It was the corner furthest from the window which was still misted over from having three faces pressed against it.

'We were worried,' said Magnus. 'What the hell were you talking about?' He craned his neck to get a better look at his sister. 'Your cheek is bleeding. Have you been fighting?'

Freya stepped inside and went to stand by the stove.

'So.' Mrs Tufte looked anxious. 'Have we reached an accord?'

'Freya will stay here for the time being,' said Silje. 'You are right, Mrs Tufte; the Germans visit our home so frequently now she would surely be discovered.' She could tell that Mrs Tufte was overjoyed, but at least she tried to hide it. This raised her slightly in Silje's eyes.

'And I will continue to help with the uniforms,' Freya added quickly.

Gunther cried, 'That is excellent news!'

'And I trust you, Gunther – if that is indeed your real name – will not endanger her further.'

'She will not be in any danger,' said Magnus.

'I was not asking you.' She stared pointedly at Gunther, who began to look as though someone was holding his hand over a naked flame. 'Well?'

'On my life, Miss Ohnstad.'

'Good.'

Gunther licked his lips, and with a sideways glance at Magnus, said, 'And perhaps, Silje, we can look to you for support.'

'We talked about this, Gunther,' said Magnus. 'The answer is no.'

'I think perhaps Silje should hear us out.'

Freya's eyes moved wildly around the room as though she'd suddenly lost sight of Silje. 'You can't involve her! You said you wouldn't!'

'I know what I said, but our need is great and Silje can turn—'

'I do not care! Do not ask. If you do then you can find someone else to fix your uniforms.'

Silje said, 'Freya, let him speak.'

Freya folded her arms and pursed her lips. Silje thought that in the same way Erik was most handsome when he was angry, Freya was more beautiful when she was sulking.

Gunther said, 'Thank you, Silje.' He cleared his throat. 'I will speak as plainly as I can.'

'I am not an idiot.'

'No, of course. Right, do you know what cryptography is?'

Silje cursed inside her head. She wondered if it was the study of crypts, but decided that such an activity would not serve the Effort and so was, in all likelihood, incorrect. Feeling somewhat foolish, she shook her head.

'That's fine,' Gunther said quickly, 'not many people have heard of it. It is the science of encoding messages so that they cannot be read by the enemy.' He reached into his breast pocket and pulled out what appeared to be a fat cigar case. 'We use different methods of hiding messages when transporting them between resistance cells: hollow shoe heels, fake books. This is my own personal favourite. It is rare that our fighters are caught carrying messages in one of these.'

Silje scratched her head. 'Where do you hide that?'

Gunther looked at Magnus, who picked at his fingernail while looking impassively unhelpful. 'She's all yours,' he said.

Gunther coughed. 'Internally.'

Freya giggled, Silje felt her ears redden, and Mrs Tufte decided it was time for her to return to the parlour. 'Come along, Freya. This conversation is not for ears as young as yours.'

'I am not a child.'

'Go with her,' said Silje, 'please.'

Freya reluctantly did what was asked of her, dragging her feet as she followed Mrs Tufte into the other room. When the door had closed,

Gunther continued. 'If the messages are discovered, many lives are lost, so they are encoded.'

'Unfortunately, the Germans are adept at code-breaking,' said Magnus, 'and this has cost us dearly.' His skin turned ashen. Silje wondered who he had lost, and marvelled at how great the distance between them had grown. Her twin was in mourning and she had not felt it.

'British Intelligence has sent me to instruct the Resistance in advanced cryptography,' Gunther said. 'We're going to make the Nazis work damn hard to break the codes, and so save the lives of your brave fighters. Do you understand so far?'

Silje said that she did. 'Though I do not understand why the British have sent us teachers instead of soldiers and guns.'

'Silje, please...'

Gunther raised his hand. 'No Magnus, it is a fair question. The Allied withdrawal was unfortunate, but necessary. The Germans took us by surprise, forcing us to regroup. There is politics in war, Silje, politics and scarcity. But know this: even if you believe the Allies care little for the Norwegian people, then you must believe that Norway and her waters are strategically vital to the European war effort. That is why we will do what we can to aid you.'

'Aside from sending soldiers and guns.'

'We will send guns.'

'Good. Then tell me what I must do to help.'

Gunther chanced a look at Magnus, who gave his permission with a slight nod of his head.

'From now on, messages transmitted by the Resistance will require a key to decode them.'

Silje realised that she must have looked puzzled because Gunther scratched at his whiskers and tried a different path. 'What is a map, Silje?'

'I beg your pardon?'

'Just tell me, what is a map?'

Silje answered without thinking. 'It is a picture of the land that tells you how to get from one place to another.'

'No,' said Gunther. 'It is a picture of the land, but it does not tell you how to get anywhere.'

'Yes, it does.'

'No, it doesn't.'

'It does,' said Silje, thinking Gunther had so far shown very few signs of 'British Intelligence'.

'It is the list of directions that tell you how to get from one place to another. Without directions, a map is just a picture of the landscape.'

Silje, begrudgingly, admitted she understood.

'And that is what we are planning to do with Resistance communications. We will send a map, that will require directions to interpret it.'

'Directions?'

'We call it a key.'

'A key?'

'Yes.'

Her brow furrowed. 'A map is sent with directions. If you send the directions along with the map then the Germans will know how to reach the destination if the map is captured.'

Gunther smiled. 'That is why we do not send the directions with the map.'

'Then how will the Resistance follow the… How will the Resistance translate the message?'

'Because the key to reading it will be broadcast freely and openly, right under the nose of our enemy.'

Silje's eyes grew wide. '*The Orchid.*'

'Silje, you do not have to do this,' Magnus said.

Gunther ignored him. 'We can embed the key in your editorial. It will change every fortnight, with each edition of the newsletter.'

'The Area Commander sometimes changes the editorial before *The Orchid* goes to press.'

'We shall give him no cause to. I shall write a section for you. The key will be hidden in the text.'

'This will never work,' said Magnus. 'And I told you, Gunther, it is far too dangerous.'

'And the Germans will not see the key when they read the editorial?' Silje asked.

'The less you know of the technical aspects, the better. It is for your own safety as well as ours.'

'You speak as though she has already agreed to this!'

Silje told Magnus to be silent. 'If I am to do this, then I wish to know everything.'

Magnus was finally left speechless, so Gunther hurried on: 'Within the text, the position of words will be used to generate a mathematical sequence that, in turn, will be used to generate a key for our decoding machines, but the key will only work until—'

'The next newsletter. And how will the decoders know which words to look for?'

Gunther beamed. 'You are more clever than you pretend to be, Silje Ohnstad.'

Silje swelled with pride, in spite of herself.

'Each message decoded will carry the words to look for in the next newsletter. There will be no reference as to where the words will be found; it will be completely safe.'

'Nothing is completely safe,' Magnus rumbled. 'Why are you doing this? This will not benefit you, or me or Father or the village. It will bring the Nazis down on our—'

'When do we start?'

'Silje!'

'As soon as we can,' said Gunther.

'One newsletter goes to press tomorrow, the next one is being edited by the Germans. It will have to be one after that.'

'Can we not submit a new editorial?'

'No, it will make them suspicious. If this is going to work then we must not give them cause to look too carefully.'

Gunther nodded.

'Silje, think about this,' said Magnus. 'When you are found out, there will be no mercy. You will be tortured, executed, and the village destroyed. And you will be found out, Silje. It is only a matter of time before the Germans discover what you are doing.'

'Then let us hope the war is over before they do,' she said, hoping she sounded much braver than she felt. 'There is something else, Gunther. I dined with the General this evening, and he mentioned something called Iscariot. Do you know what that is?'

'I have never heard of it.'

'It was some kind of plan to fight Jewish magic.'

'I beg your pardon?'

'That's what he said.'

Magnus laughed in a way Silje thought false and very unpleasant. 'I'm sure he said nothing of the sort.'

'He was quite drunk,' she said, doubting herself.

'I'll check with London,' said Gunther. 'Maybe they have—'

The door to the parlour sprang open; Freya burst through, her eyes red and streaming, Mrs Tufte holding her by both arms. 'You are mad,' she cried. Silje could not think when she'd ever seen her so angry. 'They will kill you.'

'I am sorry.' Mrs Tufte abandoned her struggle to restrain her. 'I do not know what came over the child.'

'It is all right, Mrs Tufte,' said Silje. 'Freya does not need to stand with her ear to the door to hear what is being said in the next room.'

'You cannot do this, Silje. They will kill you! Magnus, tell her!'

'Freya, I have tried.'

Freya snatched Silje's hand. 'I would speak with you.'

'Again?'

'Yes, again.'

She pulled Silje into the parlour and shut the door. 'Why would you do this? You risk yourself, your family, your village… You risk *me*.'

'Because I am a collaborator. I have helped the Germans further their cause in Norway, and unless I do this then I will be a collaborator until the day I die.'

'That is not true! You have saved the village. You have kept the Germans from—'

'No, I have saved myself,' Silje whispered, 'and unless I do otherwise I am not worthy of this village, or my family, or the memory of my mother. Until I do this, Freya, I am not worthy of you.'

27

The first time I saw her I cried, and when I tried to stop I couldn't.

From her hospital bed, Monica watched me for one minute and then said, 'If I could move, I'd slap you.'

The minute rule. Even now…

'Tissues on the window sill. No idea which moron left them there. How am I supposed to reach them? I'm not a fucking orang-utan.'

I took a handful and placed the box on the cabinet next to the bed.

She said, 'I don't need them now.'

We didn't speak for the first day. Her doctor – a rather stout lady in her early forties with large green spectacles and a fixed smile – told me I shouldn't do or say anything that might 'excite' her.

I said that would be difficult where my mother was concerned.

The doctor tightened her smile and said, 'Quite.' She explained everything to me as if I were an idiot, which I did appreciate. I only caught snatches, and my eyes stayed on my mother through the soundproof glass. Her hair was still thick, but showing grey at its roots. I realised she'd been colouring it and wondered how she'd done that without me knowing. Her eyes had sunken deep into her skull and her skin looked white and as thin as mist. The veins beneath her flesh glowed blue. Her lips were thin and dry.

I heard the words 'ovarian' and 'just in time' and looked back to the doctor who'd paused, waiting for me to catch up.

'As I was saying, she was found unconscious at a bus station near—'

'I know where it is.'

'Right.' The doctor pursed her lips for a moment; she'd already had enough of the Fossens for one lifetime. 'Anyway, it appears that she'd been ill for some time. I take it she didn't mention it to you.'

'No,' I said, 'she didn't.'

'And you didn't see any signs of stress, discomfort?'

'We've been separated.'

'I'm sorry. I'd read somewhere that you always travel together.'

'Not anymore.'

'Right, right.' She looked at her clipboard, just so she didn't have to look at me.

'Is she going to die?'

Her eyes returned to mine and she took another moment before she answered. 'Eventually, yes.'

I said I wasn't sure what that meant.

'Had she sought treatment sooner, then the prognosis would have been more in her favour. Unfortunately, we are already looking at secondaries in her liver and spine. We have drugs and treatments that will slow the progression, but I'm afraid that her—'

'How long?'

'Excuse me?'

'How long does she have?'

The doctor rested the clipboard against her hip and removed her spectacles. 'Are you always this blunt?'

'It's the way I was raised.'

She returned to the comfort of her clipboard before answering. 'A year, maybe eighteen months, that is if she sticks to the treatment regime like glue. If it reaches her brain then her time will be significantly reduced.'

'I'll make sure she stays on the drugs.'

The doctor's smile returned; it made her look as though she were in pain. Her eyes said, *I don't think you can.* I narrowed mine: *We'll fucking see about that.*

When I went back to her room, my mother appeared to be asleep. Her right eye was only half-closed and seemed to follow the shadows I made as I walked across the room. Remembering I wasn't supposed to upset her, I said nothing. She didn't say anything to me until the late afternoon.

'The police had a hell of a job finding you.'

'I was trying to stay out of sight, just like you taught me.'

'You think that reporting a dead body is staying out of sight?'

'I didn't have a choice. They would have found out I knew him. His neighbour had seen—'

'And you think hanging around a convicted Nazi is the best way to keep yourself safe?'

Exasperated, I asked her how she'd found out.

'The police told me. You see this is exactly what I said would happen if you tried to run on your own.'

'I was trying to *stop* running.'

She didn't hear me, or she wasn't listening. 'Did they question you about Klein? Did they want to know how long you'd known him?'

I shook my head. 'No, they just picked me up and brought me straight here.'

She stared furiously at the ceiling, searching for conspiracies that weren't there.

'I'm not a suspect, if that's what you're worried about.'

'Who else have you been speaking to?'

'No one,' I lied. I was not supposed to upset her. Telling her I'd been kidnapped by a man who'd made a career of butchering collaborators would definitely fall under 'upsetting'.

She looked at me sideways with one eyebrow raised.

'I'm not lying.' It wasn't getting easier and I wasn't getting any better at it.

I returned to the hospital the following day. There were a handful of reporters camped in the car park. They didn't even notice me as I went inside. Later I learned that the Minister for Education was having her appendix removed. She'd collapsed after a press conference. I didn't know her name; I didn't know Norway had a Minister for Education. There was a police officer stationed on the fifth floor. He was sitting in a chair a few doors down from Monica's room.

I asked him if he was here to protect my mother.

'Sort of,' he said. The hospital had put my mother and the Minister on the same floor so the police could watch both rooms. Apparently, the Minister wasn't very happy about it.

The day after that, I brought some of the notes I'd taken from Mr Klein's apartment. I sat in the chair at the end of Monica's bed, listening to the pumps and the monitors. Nothing changed after an hour, so I started to read. I'd barely reached the end of the first sentence when my mother asked, 'What have you got there?'

I told her, and she said, 'Let me see.'

'I don't think that's a very good idea.' I looked at the mound of bedding raised above her stomach, a frame keeping pressure from her abdomen. She saw me staring at it.

'Ovaries and womb,' she said, smiling. 'So I can kiss goodbye to my childbearing years, and I was so good at it. I'm lucky they let me keep my bladder, though that'll go soon.'

I hoped selfishly she wasn't always going to be like this. 'If you'd told me at the bus station, I would have stayed.'

'I didn't want you to stay.' She tried to sit up, winced and surrendered. 'You wanted to go, so I said "go".'

'That's not fair.'

'Then it's like life, isn't it?'

'So what was your plan? Just ignore it until you dropped dead?'

The fires lit, bringing her eyes back to life; she lurched forward, pulling the drip feeds from her arms and the oxygen tube from her nostrils. The frame crashed to the floor, taking a jug of water and a vase of flowers with it.

Her medics were through the door so quickly I would have sworn they were standing outside waiting for me to screw up. They pushed me out of the way and tried to calm her down. Her doctor, the woman I'd met days before, finished restoring her apparatus, pushing tubes into her nose and needles into her arms. A patch of blood appeared on the bedclothes just below Monica's stomach. It quickly spread.

'Shit,' the doctor said. 'She's pulled her stitches.' Then she turned to me. 'I think you'd better leave.'

'I'll just stay over there. I won't get in your way.'

'Wait outside. I'll come speak to you in a minute.'

She came out of the room about half an hour later. Before the door closed I snatched sight of the nurses feeding my mother. One of them was tying back her hair, while a third was holding her hand. My mother was crying. I wondered how long for.

'She's having a hard time processing,' the doctor said.

It occurred to me that I didn't know her name. I squinted at her ID badge.

'Just call me Dagrun.'

I thanked her and sat down. I thought it would be okay to cry now, and so let the tears run freely. Dagrun sat down and put her arms around me. My arms reached around her, pulling her close and holding her so tightly she gasped. When I finally let her go, she was bright red. She fixed her hair and fiddled with her name badge. She cleared her throat and told me I was very thin. I ignored the urge to tell her she was quite fat.

'You haven't been eating properly, that much is clear. How old are you?'

I had to think about it. 'Twenty-three.'

'You look much older, if you don't mind me saying so.'

'Actually, I think I do.'

'And what happened to your nose? Did someone punch you?'

'Look, do you really have to—?'

I'm sorry, I don't mean to be rude. What I'm trying to say is that whatever lifestyle you and your mother have chosen for yourselves, it isn't agreeing with you any more. You are malnourished; your fingernails clearly demonstrate a lack of vitamins in your diet; you have the most dreadful halitosis; you look ten years older than you are. Where are you staying?'

'A hotel,' I said, 'about ten minutes from here.' I wondered what halitosis was and if it was serious.

'And you don't have a shower in your room?'

'Yes, I do.' I said icily. 'I haven't had time to—'

'Halitosis is foul breath,' she said. 'And yours is particularly bad. Not the worst I have ever come across by a long way, but certainly enough to cause me concern for your general health.'

I cupped my hand over my mouth and huffed into my palm.

'I've shocked you. That's good, because polite explanations don't seem to carry much weight with your family.'

I couldn't smell anything, but I didn't doubt her; she wouldn't lie about something like that. I mean, why would she?

'Your mother has ovarian cancer, and she's lucky to have survived it this far. So now, I'm worried about you.'

'I feel fine,' I said, breathing into my palm again.

'You are fine for now. I want to admit you, get you thoroughly checked over. It'll only take a day at most.'

'You think I have cancer?'

'I think it would be foolish not to give you a full once-over while you're here. I take it you're planning to stay.'

I said I didn't know. 'She thinks I abandoned her; I'm not sure she wants me here.'

'Well, she has a lot to deal with right now, but at the moment, we're talking about you.'

Me. She was worried about me. I'd only ever thought in terms of *us.* Monica and I, alone against the world.

'We'll have a look at you, and then we'll talk about options.'

'Options? What options?'

She took a breath and adjusted her lapel, making sure her badge was showing. 'If we could look back through your family history, we will probably find a high incidence of cancer-related deaths, particularly ovarian. We can talk about ways to mitigate your risk going forward.'

I was barely keeping up. 'What are you saying?'

'Well, we could look at screening to begin with, and if that shows any anomalies then we can talk about preventative surgery.'

And just like that, my creeping affection for her vanished. 'You want to cut me open.'

'Well, no, of course not, but if it turns out you are at risk then I think we should consider—'

I was still hearing myself saying 'cut me open' when I stood up and walked away. Dagrun didn't try to stop me.

I went back to the hotel and spent the night with Mr Klein's notes, beginning with Silje Ohnstad.

Klein had drawn me a family tree that went back more than a hundred years. Silje Ohnstad and I were related, cousins, which shouldn't have surprised me given the size of Fólkvangr. Klein wrote at length about her. In places he seemed infatuated, in others, angry enough to have killed her. He wrote how sorry he was to have such thoughts, and then wrote out loud that he would kill himself.

So he'd always had it in him.

I wondered if he was angry enough to have betrayed the village to take his revenge on her.

Maybe that's why he'd stayed in Norway, enduring a lifetime of misery instead of returning to Germany. Maybe that was the guilty secret that had driven him, eventually, to take his own life. For such a thought to even enter my head I'd had to abandon almost two decades of history and hearsay. But now the idea had planted itself, I knew I'd never let it go.

* * *

'No.' Monica shook her head. 'It's not possible. It doesn't even make sense.' She pushed the notes off her bed, onto the floor.

'Would you just think about it for a minute.' I gathered the papers, reams of them, carefully ordered and annotated over four nights, and now scattered across the tiles. 'What if Klein found out about the Jew?'

'Your father confessed! Are you saying that he did that to protect a Nazi?'

'Or maybe he confessed to protect someone else.' I was flailing, grasping at anything, no matter how thin and fragile it was. 'Silje Ohnstad. He loved her. If she betrayed the village wouldn't he give up his own life to protect her?'

'Silje Ohnstad,' my mother said. 'You're going to accuse Silje Ohnstad of betraying Fólkvangr. Good God, Brigit, the woman's a national hero! And why? Why would she do that? You've read the books; you know what the village meant to her. Why would she—'

'Okay, not her. I get it.' I pushed the bundle of papers into my rucksack and dropped into the chair.

Monica struggled and growled until she was lying where she could see me. 'Did you have the check-up?'

I said I had. 'You should have warned me about smear tests.'

'It never came up.' She replied promptly, seeming to have had the answer ready for years.

She took a mouthful of water straight from the jug and then settled back into her pillows, staring at the ceiling. 'One day, this will all be nothing to me. Everything I've seen or heard or touched will just vanish.' She swivelled her eyes towards me. 'That's the way I see it. The world is ending, not me.'

'And am I ending too?'

She tried to roll over so she wouldn't have to look at me. She was in too much pain so she just settled for closing her eyes. 'Not you,' she said. 'You and me will outlive everything else.' She wiped her eyes with the back of her hand and asked me if I'd had the results back.

'Dagrun spoke to me,' I said.

'Who?'

'Dagrun, your doctor?'

'Oh, you mean Doctor Nese?'

'Probably. Anyway, I have "abnormal cells" according to her.'

'And?'

'And I have nothing to worry about yet, but I should worry nonetheless.'

'Oh,' said Monica. 'I'm sorry, Brigit; really I am.'

'It's not your fault.'

'Bad genes,' she said.

'More like bad luck.'

'What are you going to do?'

'Well, first of all, I'm going to have my wisdom teeth out.'

Monica blinked at me.

'Two of them are rotten, the other's impacted. The last one never came through. You never told me I had bad breath.'

'It never came up.'

'This isn't funny, Mother.'

'It must be recent,' she said. 'I never noticed it. I would have told you.'

'Like you told me about the smear test.'

'Oh for God's sake, Brigit.'

'I'm not talking about mine; I'm talking about yours. The one you had a year ago. The one you did nothing about.'

She stared at my shoulder, wringing a corner of her sheet in her hands. 'We had to run. If we'd stopped then they would have found us.'

'So that was the plan, was it? Just keep running until you were just a big fleeing tumour.'

'Yes, that's exactly what I did. And I did it for you.'

'That's just it! I wouldn't have wanted you to do that! I would have wanted you to go to a hospital and get well!'

'Well, what's done is done, and if it would save you then I'd do the same again.'

'No,' I said. 'This isn't mine. This big mound of guilt you're trying to push is yours and yours alone. No one is chasing us, Mother. They've forgotten Dad, they've forgotten us. The only person keeping the hatred alive is you. I just haven't figured out why.'

I shouldn't have said it. I thought she would fly into one of her rages, tell me what she'd sacrificed to keep me safe from Fólkvangr's ghosts. She didn't, and I think in some ways that was much worse.

'I think maybe you'd better go.'

'I'll come back tomorrow,' I picked up my bag, 'when we've both had some rest.'

'I think perhaps…'

'Perhaps what?' I said, though I already knew.

'I think you're right; neither of us can do this anymore.'

'That's what I've been saying. We don't have to. When you're better, we can get another apartment. We can go back to school, maybe think about university.' There were tears running into my mouth; I was lying to myself. I knew what she meant, but I thought if I could lay out my dream for her, instead of us both chasing across Norway, living hers, then we could connect again.

But Monica is Monica, and the only dreams worth pursuing are those that keep us running. 'I meant that we shouldn't be together anymore.'

I waited to see if she would say something else, or take it back. 'So, are we talking about forever?' I chose the last word carefully; I wanted her to understand what she was saying.

She looked away, shrugged her thin shoulders. 'I don't know; maybe. Yes.'

'Okay,' I said. 'Right.'

'You want your own life, and I don't blame you. It takes a quiet, constant courage to survive against the—'

'Oh, don't you do this.'

'You're a different generation, Brigit. More ambitious, perhaps not as strong. I understand why you would want something more for yourself. But this is the life chosen for us, and we have to make the best of it. You think I enjoy this? You think that I didn't want a normal life, with a house and a husband and brothers and sisters for you? I wanted all of those things when I was your age, but your father denied them to me.' She sniffed loudly and tugged at her chemo line. 'At least you don't have children; be thankful for that.'

* * *

Dagrun was waiting outside the room when I came walking briskly out. She asked me where I was going.

'Home,' I said. 'I'm going home.'

She hurried after me. 'She's not thinking straight, Brigit.'

'Were you listening?'

'Yes,' she said without an ounce of shame. 'She's going to die; that's hard to take in, even for someone like her.'

'She's not my problem anymore, Doctor Nese; she's yours.'

'You don't mean that.'

'I've been out there. For the first time in my life, I've been out in the world, without her paranoia screaming in my head. And you know what I found? Aside from the occasional knife-wielding maniac, Norway doesn't hate us. They don't even care. So now I ask myself, what are we running from? Or are we just running because that's all she knows how to do.'

I thumbed the elevator button while Dagrun played with her name badge, trying to think of a few words that would fix everything.

'She does love you' was the best she could come up with. I told her that I never doubted it. The emotional approach wasn't working, so she returned to familiar ground: medical reasoning. 'She's damaged, psychologically. I suspect you both are.'

'But only one of us wants to get well.'

'And while she's here, we can make her better.'

'This is the only life she knows. She doesn't want to live any differently. Maybe she's right; maybe I'm not as strong as her. It doesn't really matter. I've just had enough.'

The elevator doors opened. Dagrun slid past me to stand inside and place a finger on the *hold* button. 'You will come back though, won't you.'

I promised I would be back tomorrow and she seemed happy with that.

* * *

I returned the following day for more tests and another talk with Dagrun. She said I should consider a hysterectomy as a 'precautionary measure'.

I flat out refused.

'Were you planning on children?' she asked.

I said I wasn't planning on anything, but even then that was a lie. In the few weeks I'd been on my own, strange dreams of a different life had taken hold.

I could change my name.

I could leave Norway.

I could start again.

I could marry.

I *could* have children of my own.

I'd never thought of any of this, not while running in Monica's shadow, but now – God forgive me – now that I thought I'd soon be free of her, I could see a future far less grey.

I stayed for a few more weeks. I had three fillings, two wisdom teeth removed, and lunch with Doctor Nese, who sat on the side of my bed and fed me cold soup.

'That's going to hurt for a bit,' she told me, 'but it should fix the halitosis.'

'Don't you have other patients?' I asked sharply. My whole head hurt, and I really wasn't in the mood for her peculiar kind of bedside manner.

'No,' she said flatly and fed me another spoon. 'It's my day off.'

'And you want to spend it in the hospital?'

'No family.' She pushed the spoon into my mouth before I could ask her any more questions. 'Besides,' she said, looking around my room, 'I really like it here.' When she looked back to me her eyes were shining, like she'd seen magic in the walls.

'Really?'

'Yes. The place is a great cure for self-pity. I see people come here and fade away. Sometimes it takes a few days, sometimes more than a year, and in that time, no one comes to see them. Not family, not friends.'

'Perhaps they don't have any.'

She put the spoon down in the bowl and rubbed at her name badge with her finger. 'Your mother's talking about discharging herself. She thinks the hospital isn't safe.'

'She's determined to die on the run then.'

'Don't say that.'

'It's true. And she knew you'd tell me.'

Another spoonful of soup and a change of subject: 'What will you do? When you get out of here, I mean.'

I shrugged, and it made my jaw ache. 'I was thinking of going to Fólkvangr.'

The spoon stopped about an inch away from my mouth. Dagrun looked at me as though I'd lost my mind. 'You are joking.'

'My family has avoided the place like trolls avoid daylight,' I said. 'I think it's time one us went there and said sorry, don't you?'

'I don't think that's very wise,' she said, 'and I think it would look...'

'Disrespectful?'

'Well... yes. There are still people living in the mountains, you know.'

'Yes, I know.'

'And if they recognise you...'

'Now you sound like my mother.'

She chewed nervously at her lower lip, and then put the spoon in my mouth. 'When are you going?'

'As soon as my face stops hurting.'

'That could be a few weeks then.'

'In that case, tomorrow.'

'That's far too soon. We still need to talk about your treatment.'

'You said yourself, I'm not sick yet.'

'And we can stop you getting sick.'

I told her no. 'I'll come back, I promise, but I have to do this first.'

'Fólkvangr,' she said.

'Yes, Fólkvangr.'

The Quisling Orchid

(8th March 1941)

My fellow Norwegians.

Is it March already? I can hardly believe it! Soon we can expect brighter weather and clearer skies. Although we Norwegians can thrive in all conditions, our German friends are especially looking forward to the less inclement weather the Scandinavian spring will provide.
So what can we expect in the March newsletter? Well, to begin with, more recipes from the ever-popular Mrs Ohnstad! (no relation). I am taken aback at the number of letters asking that I dedicate a permanent corner to Marit's household tips. Mrs Ohnstad is indeed a fathomless pool of wisdom in these matters, which is astonishing when you consider that, to the best of my knowledge, she does not even own a house!
By the next newsletter I will have decided whether or not Marit will have her own column, so keep your eyes fixed on The Orchid!
Now, on to other news.
Our friends the Germans are pleased to report the discovery of more than thirty Jews hiding in the forests near Jotunheimen. Those that survived the encounter were transported to Bandeklosteret for processing and transportation.
More information concerning this glorious effort can be found on page 6, along with information on bounties offered for information leading to the capture of Jews.

28

The children's love for Freya rivalled Silje's own. They would play games with her senses, demanding she name flowers from scent alone, or speaking in ever-fading whispers until their voices were lost to her.

'You have the ears of a mountain goat!' Jesper Bergström said.

Ingrid Haud, riding her bicycle in tight circles around them, nodded her agreement.

'I should hope not,' Freya said, pulling Jesper to one side to avoid her.

'Why not?' said Ingrid, 'You do not know what a goat looks like.'

'But I do know what a goat looks like.'

'Then you are very brave.' Jesper said. 'I would never run my hands over the face of a goat, even one I knew very well.'

'Do not be silly, Jesper,' said Ingrid, 'Freya is far too pretty and clever to ever do something like that.'

Freya blushed. 'Do you think I'm pretty?'

'You are *very* pretty.' replied Jesper, and Ingrid cuffed his shoulder on her way past. 'Though you are not as pretty as Ingrid.'

'Well, how could I be?'

'Ingrid is the prettiest thing in all Fólkvangr.'

She rode past him again with her fist raised.

'If not the whole world!' he added desperately.

Silje watched them from her seat in front of the village hall, and took deep breaths to calm her heart.

'Hello, Silje.'

'Hello Freya, children.'

Ingrid treated Silje to a musical good morning she composed on the spot. Jesper, however, said nothing.

'The weather is turning at last,' said Freya. 'I am looking forward to a little more warmth.' She sat down and brushed Silje's arm with her smallest finger; Silje thought her heart would burst.

'You will not feel much warmer, I'm afraid, but there will be more sunlight.'

'Which means little to me.'

'Of course. Forgive me.'

'I will,' Freya said, 'always.'

The children looked at them both with bemused eyes.

'Jesper, Ingrid, I'm afraid I must steal Freya away from you for a short while.'

'Why?' said Jesper, throwing the question from behind a churlish pout.

'Village matters, young man,' Silje replied. 'Nothing for your small ears.' Though she thought Jesper's ears were in fact quite large.

'No,' he said.

Ingrid cried, 'Do not be rude, Jesper!'

'I am not being rude. I will not let Freya go anywhere with her.'

Freya's mouth fell open, and Silje herself was too stunned to speak.

'She is a traitor. Everyone says so. She helps the Germans collect the Jews and kill them. That is what everyone says, isn't it, Ingrid?'

'I cannot lie to you, Silje.' Ingrid turned her eyes to the ground. 'It is what they say.'

'I think you should both go,' Freya said softly.

'I won't leave you, not with her.'

'Then will you please say you're sorry?'

'It is all right, Freya. He does not have to.' Silje brushed down her dress and said she would go home; there was much to be done at the cottage.

'I will come to see you.'

'Perhaps tomorrow,' and while Jesper watched her for signs of treachery, she kissed Freya lightly on the cheek. 'I think today is not a good day.'

* * *

At the cottage, Jon Ohnstad was loading bundles of orchids onto his truck, his melancholy reflecting her own.

'Why are you sad?' Silje said to him. 'When people finally see the beauty in what you grow.'

'It is for funerals,' he replied. 'For the Norwegians who fall to free us, and the Jews murdered for the way they choose to worship.' He gazed at his field where the orchids grew. 'I sometimes wonder if I will have enough left for my own son.'

'Father, nothing is going to happen to Magnus, do you hear me?'

He nodded sadly and climbed into his truck. 'I envy you. Would that I could walk through life and remain untouched by it.'

He hadn't meant to be cruel, but it was cruel all the same. He started the engine and waved, smiling in a way that said his daughter alone would not be enough.

Silje went inside and sat by the fire. *The day is hollow because the newsletter has arrived*, she reminded herself, *that is all. It is why the village shuns you and Jesper despises you, no matter what you meant to him before.* She remained there for more than an hour, motionless and on the edge of tears, until the kitchen door slowly creaked open.

Freya sniffed at the air then ran to embrace her. 'I have missed you,' she said.

Silje tried to pull away. 'Freya, I told you – tomorrow.'

'I wanted to see you today.' She tightened her hold until Silje could barely breathe. 'You should not care so much what people say.'

'Of course I care. This is my home. The people are part of me. When they hate me, how can I feel anything but hatred for myself?'

'Then why do you not tell them what you're doing for the Resistance? Tell them about the newsletter.'

'I cannot tell them! If the secret falls into German hands—'

'Fólkvangr knows about me and I have not fallen into German hands. Do you not trust the villagers?'

'I trust them, but any of them would break under German inquisition. I have heard stories: prisoners throwing themselves from the windows of Victoria Terrasse, even before their interrogation has begun. Do you think the Fehns could withstand such torture? Or Mrs Tufte? Or Mr Bergström? Or young Jesper?'

Freya snatched Silje's hand and held it against her chest. 'Please, do not say such things.' Silje felt a heart pounding and was unsure if it was Freya's or her own.

'We shall go upstairs,' said Freya. 'It will make us both feel better.'

'I am exhausted and I am not in the mood.'

'Please!' Freya leaned closer to whisper into her ear, though there really was no need, not to Silje's mind at least. 'We can try those things again, from Magnus's book. I promise I won't make any noise this time.'

Silje nodded as though she'd been asked to clean out the goats' pen, and it was such an ungracious gesture she was glad Freya could not see it. 'Just for an hour, no more. We both have much to—'

Freya shrieked with delight and ran for the stairs, pulling a tired and startled Silje behind her.

* * *

There were times, if they had been apart for an hour, or a day, when they would seek out one another and run to find a stable or an outhouse where they could be alone. There they would explore every part of their joined flesh; their need for intimacy would drive them beneath each other's skin, leaving them spent and aching. And afterward, Freya would wonder aloud where they could travel to spend their lives together. Silje would wonder, in silence, how she could be so cruel to Erik, and to Freya's bewilderment she would often weep.

Then there were other times, when Silje would lie next to her with the book taken from beneath Magnus's wardrobe. She would read stories and poetry to her, delighting Freya with her portrayals of salacious queens and their submissive maids. And afterward Silje would treat their lovemaking as a kind of nature experiment, labouring between Freya's legs with great diligence while referring to the more instructive chapters of the book.

'Do you like it if I do… this?'

'Yes… yes, I think so.'

'And what about this?'

'Again, yes. I will like whatever you do, so I see little point in—'

'And this?'

'What are you…? Silje… wait… no… just… stop… Silje, stop it! I'm not a pregnant goat!'

Silje, being Silje, preferred to be adventurous on her own terms. She would describe the book's pictures and illustrations in great detail, responding to Freya's inquisitive lust with 'Yes, we can try that' or 'No, because it sounds disgusting' or 'Yes, I'm sure they do it in Oslo, but we are not in Oslo; we're in Fólkvangr.'

It was most frustrating, and Freya, being Freya, was at her most unpredictable when frustrated.

And so it was, during the hour together which would leave them bitten, scratched, exhausted and estranged, Freya slid over Silje's back and snaked an arm under her breasts. She kissed her and whispered into her ear. 'If you do not like it then tell me.'

Silje closed her eyes, feeling her lover's heart pounding between her shoulders. She turned her head to plant kisses along her arm. 'If I do not like what?'

But Freya had already lost herself to a passion that burned with the heat and ferocity of a fever. She drew her tongue along Silje's neck, tasting the blood orchids in her perspiration, her hand delving softly between her haunches.

'What are you doing?'

Freya kissed the side of her throat, breathing in the scent where her hair met her skin. She whispered again, 'Hush' and eased her thumb gently into Silje's bowel.

It was a part of herself Silje had surrendered only once before – to Junges Fehn.

But now it was different; now there was no coercion or pain; instead, she felt only hunger, an embrace of the forbidden, delight in a torment that served only to excite her more.

She squeezed her eyes shut and tried to arch her spine, but with Freya's weight pressing on her, found she could not. She melted against the sheets and cried out, clenching the covers in her fists.

'Do you like this? Do you want me to stop?'

She pressed her fingernails into Freya's arm and whispered, 'I don't know.'

'Silje, do you want me to—?'

She reached her climax, raising a cry that left its echo burning in Freya's ears. Her body rattled for moments longer until she was at last spent. Freya folded her arms around her, caring nothing for her own repletion, and held her until the tremors ceased. Then she kissed her shoulder and whispered to her: 'Don't ever leave me. I won't ask you to make me promises you cannot keep, or say that you will never love another, or that I will always be your most favoured. Just never leave me.'

Without a word, Silje jumped to her feet and slipped into her dress.

'Silje?' Freya swept the sheets with her hand, becoming frantic when she realised she was no longer there. 'Silje, what's wrong? What have I done?'

Silje ran from the room, shrouded in a thundercloud of her own making – and it was six days before she spoke to Freya again.

29

On the morning of Freya Dorfmann's nineteenth birthday, Magnus Ohnstad was nowhere to be found. In the early hours, Silje had crept into his room to replace the book he kept hidden under his wardrobe.

Since they were children, Magnus had set small, invisible traps that would tell him if she'd ventured into his private space: a piece of paper placed on the dresser so it would fall in the draft of a door being opened; a single hair placed carefully between the same door and the frame; fingernail clippings that would scatter as she walked across the floor. Of course, Magnus did not set his 'whisperers' when he retired for the night, and as fate would have it, he possessed the determination of a corpse when it came to not being woken. And so, as Silje had discovered early in their lives, the best time to sneak into Magnus's room was when he was in it.

But in the early hours on the morning of Freya's birthday, Magnus was not in his bed. These days, he often did not emerge until midday. She looked around the room. The bed was made, the floor spotlessly clean. He'd become strangely house-proud since he began his assignations with the Resistance. Silje wondered if Gunther Braithwaite had stolen away from Mrs Tufte's home in a similarly furtive manner. Magnus was enamoured with him; it is almost love, she thought, though a very different love than that she shared with Freya. Magnus simply wanted to *be* Gunther Braithwaite: an officer, a spy, a trained killer. Silje considered Freya and herself equals, as long as she did not account for her own wisdom, beauty and fair complexion.

Though Silje was forced to confess that under Mrs Tufte's bothersome care, Freya had indeed transformed. Her hair was blonde and her skin had darkened under the mountain sun. Her thin, girlish frame had blossomed, thanks to a diet rich with goats' milk, cheese and freshly baked bread (though Freya often complained that the staple of Fólkvangr was wreaking havoc with her digestion). Her deceptively strong musculature grew stronger still, as she was, like all the villagers, cursed to spend at least half her waking hours walking up hill.

But even before, when Freya had been the blind slip of a child they had rescued from under the floorboards of a milliner's shop, Silje knew; she knew that Freya would take her heart from her chest, hold it to her own and never return it.

She would love her forever, and this, more than anything, terrified her. Her skin broke into pins and needles, and her legs threatened to give way.

All this, even when I just think about her...

She pushed the book under the wardrobe as far as it would go. Then she got to her feet and looked through the window for the sun; dawn had broken. She decided she would spend the morning looking for Gunther. Wherever he was, Magnus would be close by.

* * *

Mrs Tufte had awoken to find Freya bounding about the cottage in a state of childish excitement, and her occasional guest, the erstwhile and unlikely-christened Gunther Braithwaite, grimly packing his haversack to leave. He seemed agitated.

'What is the matter, Mr Braithwaite?'

Gunther checked his pistol and pushed it inside the haversack. He followed it with four clips of ammunition and a grenade, which she had told him before to keep in the outdoor privy, not inside the cottage. She would have said something, shaken a stern finger at him, taken time to restate the cottage rules that neither he nor Freya seemed to pay any mind to. But Gunther was in haste and did not appear to be in the mood for reprimands. For the first time since they'd met, he carried the bearing of the British Intelligence officer he claimed to be. She took his arm, finding the sinews in his bicep and gently pressing her fingers into them until he was forced to stop and listen.

'Where are you going? You will miss Freya's celebration.'

Freya was busy making a terrible noise with the pots and pans in the kitchen. She had threatened to bake something.

'Bergen,' Gunther said.

'And what is there for you in Bergen, on today of all days?'

'Even if I knew for sure, I would not tell you.'

Mrs Tufte had done her best to look hurt, and in some small way had succeeded.

Gunther sighed. 'I have received word from London concerning your countrymen.'

'Treachery?'

'Far worse: stupidity.'

'So London is spying on us, as it spies on the Nazis.'

'It is war, Mrs Tufte; we spy on everyone.'

'Are you going to kill our countrymen, Gunther?' She had hoped the bullets were destined for the head and chest of General Gruetzmacher.

'No.'

'Then you must tell me what is going on.' It was only then she realised that his shadow was missing. When some Resistance operation was afoot, he and the Ohnstad boy would stand in this very room, blackening their faces, checking their ammunition, grinning at each other as though this were all a schoolboy's game.

'Where is Magnus?'

Gunther threw his bag across his back. 'I must go. Tell Freya I am sorry. I will return before darkness falls.'

'We are in the mountains,' Mrs Tufte said grimly. 'Who knows when the night will come.'

Gunther smiled and told her again he was sorry. As he walked to the door, Mrs Tufte called out to him, though she was sure she did not mean to. 'I expect to see you back at this cottage, young man, before the night is over. Do you understand me?'

He stopped for a moment, and she prayed he would not turn around; there were tears in her eyes, and she disliked showing anyone her heart.

Thankfully, he mumbled 'goodbye' and left without sparing her another glance.

She took a moment to compose herself and then went to see what had befallen her kitchen.

* * *

'You have lost your mind, Eva,' said Mrs Munsen, who had been Eva Tufte's best friend since they were children, and who was the only person in the village permitted to speak of the true whereabouts of Mr

Tufte. 'The Germans are not stupid. Such a gathering will attract attention and put the child, and us, at risk.'

Mrs Tufte eased herself back in her rocking chair and drew on a long clay pipe, the only personal effect her husband had left when he'd vanished into the night all those years ago. Mrs Munsen, a thin, weather-beaten woman with thick grey hair and whiskers to match, lit her own pipe and raised it to a group of men trying to erect a stall in front of the candlemaker's.

'They will suspect nothing,' said Mrs Tufte, 'as long as these fools remember that this is not a celebration; it is simply a barterer's market, with more cake stalls than are perhaps necessary.'

'Hmph,' Mrs Munsen said.

Mrs Tufte scrutinised the square to see if there was anything she had missed. The bunting was in place, and every window box was laden with flowers: roses, tulips and orchids of every hue, creating an orchestra of sight and scent. Jon Ohnstad had outdone himself. She looked to the line of tables laden with plates of homemade biscuits, small cakes, and juices crushed from vegetables and the very few fruits that Jon Ohnstad had managed to trade during his travels to Bergen. He had also supplied several kegs of his honeyed mead, which Grette, *The Mottled Goat*'s barkeep, was carrying three barrels at a time across her broad shoulders. The tiny village post office had pulled out its awning for the first time in years, and was selling paper and bottles of ink. There was a banner attached to the table, written out and painstakingly coloured so as to be an artwork in itself. It read, *When did you last write to your sweetheart?*

Mrs Munsen sniffed and said, 'Freya is not your family.'

Mrs Tufte puffed stiffly on her pipe, but did not reply.

'I am just saying, Eva, she will not always be here.'

'She has no other family; where else is she to go? Fólkvangr is her home now, and I daresay after the war she will choose to stay with me.' Mrs Tufte swallowed. 'Us – I meant stay with us, in Fólkvangr.'

Mrs Munsen thought that perhaps now was not the time for painful truths, so she took a different path, one that she hoped would burst the cloud she'd placed over her friend. 'I saw that young man of yours leaving the village this morning.'

'And which young man is that?'

'You know who I mean, Eva. Do not be coy.'

'Do not be disgusting,' Mrs Tufte said, blushing. 'He is young enough to be my grandson. And while we are about the subject, there is far too much carrying-on in this village for my liking. When people make a commitment, they should stick to it. I have mine, though my husband chose not to.'

Mrs Munsen shrugged. 'If the gravy is good for goose, it is good for the goat.'

'I have never understood what you mean by that.'

'Gunther! That is his name! I knew I would remember it. He left on that infernal motorcycle of his, racing from the village as though his short life no longer mattered to him.'

'An errand,' Mrs Tufte said flatly, 'for me. And what business have you being awake at such an ungodly hour?'

'I was making cakes,' Mrs Munsen said, waving her pipe at the cake stall. 'And like yourself, I was too excited to sleep. It seems so long since we had a birthday.'

'Hush!'

'A celebration then. For so long, we have bowed our heads at memorials.' She patted Mrs Tufte's thigh. 'On second thought, a fine idea, Eva; a very fine idea.' Mrs Munsen groaned, creaked up from her rocking chair and announced she was going to direct the menfolk in setting up the candle stall. 'They will either injure themselves or burn the village to ash unless someone takes charge.' She limped away, and as soon as she'd gone, Freya appeared in the doorway of Mrs Tufte's cottage. Mrs Tufte wondered how much she'd heard.

Freya squeezed her shoulder and leaned over to kiss her on the cheek. Nothing more was said. She listened for the trucks and carthorses before making her way across the cobbles towards the candle stall.

'Be careful,' Mrs Tufte called.

Freya called back that she was always careful.

'And you look very beautiful, young Freya.'

The girl had made the most striking dress for the celebration that wasn't. It pinched her small waist and flowed down to cover her knees; a patchwork of rough diamond shapes hastily sewn together; a confusion of magical colours that could only have been cast by a girl who could not see. Mrs Tufte wondered if her own daughters would have been as gifted as Freya, had she been blessed with them.

Freya half-turned and curtsied before continuing on her way. She joined Mrs Munsen at the stall, where the menfolk patted her on the back and watched in awe as she sniffed the candles and identified the precise ingredients of each one.

Mrs Tufte rocked gently in her chair. Of all Freya's parlour tricks, this was her most favourite. But when Freya took a cigar from Rolf Soren's mouth and attempted to light a candle, Mrs Tufte leapt from her seat. Fortunately, Mrs Munsen was as quick as she was vigilant. She snatched the candle from Freya's hands while the menfolk roared with laughter. Shaking a finger under Freya's nose, she reminded her, in a needlessly loud voice, that silly blind girls and naked flames were kept apart for very good reasons.

Freya apologised and tried her best not to smile.

Satisfied that the danger had passed, Mrs Tufte took her seat again. She decided there and then that daughters, while a blessing, would have been the death of her. She did not understand how Jon Ohnstad had not simply wasted away through worry.

* * *

As the sun climbed above the mountain peak and the morning wore on, Fólkvangr turned out in its entirety. They exchanged goods and talked at great length about the invasion, the Resistance, and Norway's place in the world when the war was over.

Some expressed fear there would be little left of Norway for its place in the world to matter.

And though Mrs Tufte had strictly forbidden it, the villagers were wishing Freya a happy birthday and furtively pressing coins and small gifts into her hands.

'Are you crying, Doctor Lomen?' asked Freya.

The Doctor coughed gruffly and smoothed the teardrops from his magnificent moustache. 'No, child. Why would you say such a thing?'

'Your voice,' said Freya. 'I must be mistaken.'

'Indeed you are,' said the doctor and coughed again.

'But if you were crying,' she said, 'what would you be crying about?'

'Well, if I were crying – and it is important you understand that I am not – then I would be crying for you, my child.'

'Oh.'

'Yes.' The doctor looked about him nervously. 'Fólkvangr was a grey place before you came to us. Since your arrival, I have noted a marked decline in rheumatism, bad backs, unpleasant and unexplained inflammations… When you came you brought us colour, young Freya, and something to care for beyond ourselves. And if I were crying Freya – which I am not – then it would be because you cannot see the joy you have wrought in our small corner of the mountain. Ah! Now who is crying!' He took a handkerchief from his jacket and dabbed gently around Freya's eyes. 'I have something for you,' he said, pressing five coins into her hands and closing her fingers around them. 'Don't tell Mrs Tufte.'

'I think she already knows.'

Doctor Lomen looked to where Mrs Tufte sat, glaring at him. 'Ah.'

'But thank you.'

To his surprise, Freya threw arms about his neck and embraced him with a strength he wouldn't have believed possible in one so pale and slight. He returned the gesture, gently pressing his fingers against the glands in her neck to check for any signs of swelling.

'I am well, Doctor Lomen!'

'Can never be too careful,' said the doctor. 'Fólkvangr is a martyr to spring flu.' He tapped her on the nose, and Freya opened her mouth so he could place a lump of sugar on her tongue.

'Good girl,' he said. 'And remember, plenty of water and fish whenever you find it.'

'I will, Doctor Lomen.'

Before he left he said, 'I have children, you know.'

'I don't think I knew that.'

'Sons, five of them. Stout of leg, good hearts. They're fighting in the Resistance near Trondheim.'

'You should never tell me such things, sir. What if I am taken?'

'You will not be taken,' he said firmly. 'Fólkvangr will not permit it.'

'Then I wish your sons well, and I thank them, for they are also fighting for me.'

'Yes, yes, I suppose they are.' He turned and walked back towards a stand trading in clay pots. 'I have no daughter though,' he said, 'which I must speak to Mrs Lomen about.'

He faded from Freya's awareness and she suddenly found herself weeping. Each time she tried to seize control of herself, the tears came more forcefully than before.

'You cry such a lot, don't you?'

Freya sniffed and forced herself to stand up straight. 'Well… so do you,' she replied with as much indignation as she could muster. 'I miss my father, that is all.'

Silje took her hand and gently closed her fingers around the stalk of a single flower. 'It's an orchid.'

'I know what it is,' Freya replied, her indignation melting faster than she could tighten herself around it. 'I don't know what I did to make you leave like that but I'm sorry. I have missed you so much. If I ever do something that hurts you or offends you or would make you love me less, then please tell me! Don't just run from me! I was afraid you would leave the village and I would never see you again. Perhaps not leave the village then, but you would avoid me and treat me as you did when I first came here. And I thought you wouldn't come today. I thought I would not see you on my birthday! Have I told you how much I adore you? Of course I have, but I will tell you again because I think sometimes you forget: I love you, Silje Ohnstad, today and forever. What are you wearing? Is it your mother's best dress? It doesn't smell like your mother's best dress, which always smells wonderful by the way. I can't stop talking. Please say something because I need to breathe.'

Silje glanced about and saw that Fólkvangr was paying them little heed, though Mrs Tufte was watching them with the severity of a vulture. Silje brushed her fingers across Freya's hand. 'It wasn't you.'

'There were just two of us in your bed. Of course it was me.'

'There are three of us,' said Silje. 'There have always been three of us.'

'Erik,' Freya said.

'Yes, Erik.'

She took a step closer, close enough for the scent of cinnamon to weaken Silje at the knees.

'When I said I did not care if I were one of two or one of many, I meant it.'

'And when you say such things,' Silje said plainly, 'you make me feel like a common whore.'

'I did not mean—'

'It is not you. Please stop thinking it is you. I feel like a streetwalker when in truth I am far worse. I treat the people I care for like pieces of jewellery, picking them up and wearing them as I see fit. Today, I will put on Erik because he is utilitarian. Tomorrow I will adorn myself with you because you match my eyes. Next week I will wear Junges Fehn because… God, I do not even like Junges Fehn.'

'Do not end us, Silje.'

'I am not ending us. I am ending everything else. I will tell Erik this very night. I will tell him everything, and we will no longer be a secret. I am tired of secrets.'

Freya ground her bare heel against the cobbles.

'I thought this would please you.'

'It is what I want more than anything; you know this. But… Erik. It will destroy him.'

'For a while.'

'I do not wish to see him hurt.'

'And you think that is what I want?'

'I like him.'

'And I love him… just not enough. Not the way I love you.' Silje glanced at Mrs Tufte who was looking at them with fresh, open eyes.

'And the villagers?' asked Freya.

'It is nothing they have not seen before, especially during times of war. We are not as unworldly as we seem.'

'Though you are not Oslo.'

Silje smiled. 'No, we will never be Oslo.'

'I thought it was the thing I did, the last time we were together.'

'No, it was not that.'

'So… you did like it?' Freya asked coyly.

'I did not say that.' Silje felt her neck becoming uncomfortably hot. 'But I do not like surprises, so warn me the next time you are taken by a desire to poke about in unseemly places.'

'I think I did warn you,'

'You did not.'

'I said that you should tell me if you did not like it.'

'But you did not tell me what I might not like before you did it.'

'So you did not like it.'

'I did not say that either, God help me. What I am saying, Freya, is that I do not like surpr—'

'Erik! How wonderful of you to come!' Freya gushed. 'Look, Silje! Erik is here!'

Erik ambled over to them and kissed Freya on the cheek, and Silje on the mouth. He looked at her oddly when she passively accepted his greeting.

'How is that no one can hide from you, Freya?'

'It is your boots,' Freya said, sounding almost desperate. 'Your boots on stones; there is no sound like it.'

Erik looked doubtful. 'I'm sure there is.'

'Not to me!'

'Of course, of course. Forgive me.' He scratched his chin, drawing Silje's eyes to his freshly grown whiskers. 'This is a wonderful party.'

'It is not a party,' Silje said stiffly.

Erik placed a finger on his lips. 'Yes, of course! I am so sorry. What I meant to say is that it is a glorious day for an impromptu market.'

Silje rolled her eyes. Freya narrowed hers and nudged her, as though she'd heard Silje's eyes turn in their sockets.

'You are being cruel to Erik, Silje,' she said firmly, 'and there is no need for it.'

She is right, Silje thought. *He stands between us and I am starting to hate him for it.*

Erik raised a hand. 'That's quite all right, Freya. It is just Silje being Silje. She doesn't mean it. But I wonder if I might steal her away from you.'

'Is everything all right, Erik? You seem rather… strange.' Silje hoped Freya would not see her words as cruel.

'I am in good spirits, Silje, and if you accompany me to my home, then I will show you why.'

'Your home?' echoed Silje. 'But we never go to your home.'

'That will change from this day. Come.'

Silje hesitated. His manner, his deportment: he displayed no outward sign that he knew of the love she hid for another. Still, it was an odd, masterful change in him which she found strangely appealing.

When she did not move, Erik took her hand. 'I shall return her to you before the afternoon is done,' he called to Freya. Freya waved half-heartedly as he stole Silje away. She did not move from her spot on the cobbles, looking as if she would remain there until Silje returned, be it an hour from now or a hundred years.

And Erik looked so very happy, so assured – something Silje was never sure he'd be, not while he was with her. They walked past Mrs Tufte's cottage, past the old fountain that had stopped working years ago, and took the pavement that bulged out onto the street to accommodate the Fehns' cottage.

'I have heard from Helga Bratvold. Lisbeth is staying with her in Lillehammer.'

'Good,' said Silje. 'They can hate me together.'

Erik laughed. 'Poor, poor Silje.'

'Are you making fun of me now?'

'No. Are you trying to be angry with me?'

'No!'

'Then we are happy, are we not?'

Silje chose not to reply.

'We have not seen much of each other of late.'

'Yes. I am sorry, and I will tell you why.'

'I already know why.' His voice shone.

No, Silje thought. *No, you do not.*

'The truth is I have been avoiding you,' he said.

'Avoiding me?' This was most unexpected. 'Why?'

'Because I have kept something from you, in much the same way as you have been keeping something from me.'

'Erik, I swear I have kept nothing—'

'I know about the others, Silje. I know about Mr Fehn; I know about the men in Bergen; I know about the German officer.'

When he did not give Freya's name, Silje felt her heart lift. 'I am sorry, Erik,' she said. 'There is no excuse for what I have done.'

Erik said nothing further, scratching his neck and reciting his continuation under his breath.

'If you wish to call off the wedding,' said Silje hopefully, 'then I will understand.'

'You mean the wedding for which we have yet to set a date?'

Silje narrowed her eyes. 'That would be the one, yes.'

'We will not be calling off the wedding. Today is our day of truth. All our secrets shall be laid open, and we shall have our new beginning. As you have been keeping things from me – or so you thought – I have been keeping a secret from you. It has weighed heavily on me, Silje, so heavily that I have been avoiding you, lest you see my crime in my eyes when we are together.' He walked the four steps to his front door.

Though she'd known Erik her whole life, she could count on one hand the times she'd seen the inside of the Brenna cottage. He'd always been reluctant to bring her here, and since she knew that his mother and father had never warmed to her, she had accepted his reticence without question or complaint. Before emigrating to the underside of the world with his father and sisters, his mother had made him promise that 'the Ohnstad hussy' would never set foot across their threshold, and Erik had kept his promise as best he could, spending days paralysed with guilt whenever the promise was broken.

Though not today, Silje thought. *Today he is different.*

The cottage shared the same map and furnishings as the Ohnstad homestead, except that it faced the west. It had a smaller kitchen and a larger drawing room which was never used.

Silje noted that in the three years since her last visit, Erik had changed the kitchen so that it resembled her own.

'I had planned for us to live here after we're married,' he said, taking off his coat. 'But if you would live somewhere else then I will sell it and build us a home wherever you want.'

He made for the stairs, and Silje swore that if he sought intimacy with her then she would spurn him and tell him why.

'Come,' he said. 'I wish to show you something.'

She followed him up the stairs, surprised – and somewhat hurt – when they continued past his bedroom to the end of the landing. There, Erik reached up and pulled down the ingenious folding steps he'd designed himself. He disappeared into the loft space and then reached down to help Silje.

It was dark inside the cottage roof, but as soon as Erik lit an oil lamp, the loft became a place of wonder.

'Oh, Erik,' Silje whispered.

He had often told her that he liked to draw, but his modesty in this was as breathtaking as his work. There were pictures of her, of course, and then there were landscapes of the mountains and the village. There were sculptures in metal and stone, and sketches of her, clothed and undressed, certainly drawn from memory because he had never asked her to sit for him – though she would gladly have done so.

'These are beautiful, Erik. They should not be hidden away in your roof.' She touched a metal figurine, which by shape alone she could tell was a forging of herself. 'I do not know what to say.'

'Say you will forgive me.'

'Forgive you for what? These are wonderful. Why did you never tell me?'

Erik waited for her eyes to fall on the picture in the loft's darkest corner, a painting, rendered in oils, of a ladder floating high in the skies above Fólkvangr. The ladder shone with an inner light and its frame was adorned with silver orchids. And next to the painting, leaning against the attic wall, the ladder Erik had used as his muse.

Silje's face turned to stone. 'Is that…?'

Erik turned away from her in shame and said, yes, it was.

'You took it.'

'I am sorry.'

'It was you.'

'Yes.'

'Why?'

Erik shrugged. 'I needed it for the painting.'

'So you just took it, without asking Mr Gundersen.'

'I'd asked you to marry me, and you'd refused – again. I was angry. I was of a mind to pour my anger into a painting, and then I saw this ladder… I would have returned it, but you and your newsletter turned a minor theft into the fall of Norwegian civilisation.'

'And even when Mr Kleppe confessed, you said nothing.'

'I am telling you now.'

Silje wanted to sit down but couldn't see a chair. 'So you are angry with me, and you paint a ladder in the sky. I am not sure how it helps, but then perhaps I am too simple to appreciate it.'

'It is you, Silje. The painting is of you. Everything you see here is you or is inspired by you.'

'All I see is a ladder in the sky. It is a beautiful ladder, I grant you, but it does not touch the ground and it cannot reach the stars. What is the point of a ladder that goes nowhere?'

Erik looked to the floor, and Silje, seeing him so overcome with remorse, looked at the picture again.

'Oh,' she said. 'I see.'

'I was angry with you,' Erik mumbled.

'So this is how you see me, is it, Erik Brenna.'

'But I am not angry now.'

'Oh Erik, how could you.'

'Silje, listen to me. I felt terrible, even while I was painting it.'

'And yet you did not simply stop. You finished it, and then showed it to me.'

Erik paused to choose his next words carefully. 'It is my finest work,' he said finally. 'I could not stop.'

Silje regarded him coolly and thought, *There is a way from this, for all of us. If I can rein my vanity I can cut him free, cleanly, with little pain and his pride left whole.*

She told him to destroy it.

'I cannot.'

'It's that… thing, or me, Erik. Make your choice.' She folded her arms and waited.

'It is just a painting.'

'It is an insult, is what it is.'

'You would really tear us apart over a painting?'

'No, I would tear us apart because you think I am beautiful but my existence in this world somewhat pointless.'

Erik looked at her, looked through her, trying to pierce her flesh and look beneath her skin for the very first time. He shook his head. 'Why is it me who has to spend his life proving himself to you?' He walked over to the workbench and rummaged around in his toolbox.

Silje watched him curiously, beset by feelings of dread and excitement.

When he came back to her he was carrying a large craft knife. He looked at it, and then at the painting.

'Just this once,' he said, 'you will have to prove yourself to me.' He put the knife in her hand and closed her fingers around the hilt. 'Now you know how much my work means to me, destroy it.'

Silje looked at the painting. It was truly his finest work.

'Go on,' he said. 'Score the canvas with the knife; cut it and slash it, and I promise I won't paint another. I couldn't if I wanted to. So have at it, Silje.'

She stared at the knife, suddenly unsure how it came to be in her hand.

'What are you waiting for?' he said. 'You hate it, and you are Silje Ohnstad. So why don't you just get rid of it, if it offends you so much. Why would you be so cruel to make me destroy something that means so much to me? The picture is you, the good and the bad, the beautiful and the ugly, the kindness and the rage. It is you, and there is no part of you that I would change because if I cut away the things I hate then I would taint the thing I love. So have at it, Silje; use the knife and destroy it if that is your wish.'

The sound of the knife hitting the floor startled her. She looked down to see it lodged in the boards between her feet.

Though he tried, Erik could not hide his relief. 'Thank you,' he said, taking her by the hand.

'I am a horrible, terrible human being,' Silje whispered. 'I should be alone. People deserve better than me.'

Erik drew her to him and held her against his chest. 'You are not so terrible, Silje. You are just not perfect. None of us are.'

Silje sniffed and nodded. 'I am sorry, Erik.'

'Do you understand why I told you?'

'Yes, I think so.'

'And is there anything that you would—'

'No.'

'Then Silje Ohnstad, on the fifteenth of next month, I would very much like you to become my wife.'

Silje nodded and whispered 'Yes', even as every tendril of her soul raised itself to bind her.

Erik finally exhaled, with such force Silje wondered if he'd drawn breath since entering the loft. 'That does not give us long to prepare.'

'I have nothing to wear. My mother's wedding dress is completely unsuitable.'

'Freya can change it for you. Mrs Tufte says she can work miracles with a needle and thread, and I'm sure all you need do is… Are you all right, Silje? You're shaking.'

A horn sounded from the street outside, and then sounded again, and again.

'It is my father!' Silje pushed herself free and ran downstairs, thinking perhaps fate disapproved of any attempt she made to be a human being. Someone had told her father where she was. Marit Ohnstad most likely, or perhaps Mrs Tufte.

She pulled open the front door and ran towards her father's truck with a cascade of lies poised on the end of her tongue. 'Father, it is not what you think!'

Her father looked at her, his face ashen. The door on the truck's far side opened, and a tall, stooped figure uncoiled itself from the passenger seat.

Gunther, his face carrying the same gravity as her father's.

Silje stopped in the middle of the street.

Magnus.

'Where is Magnus!'

Gunther walked towards her, and Silje, in spite of herself, backed away. 'No.'

Erik arrived at her side and demanded to know who this man was.

'He has been taken,' Gunther said. 'The Germans have him.'

'Where?'

'Bergen. Along with scores of others.'

'Silje, again, who is this man?' Erik peered up at him. 'I have seen you before, around the village. You were at the gathering today.'

'Then we must go to him.'

'That would be very unwise.'

'I will go,' Jon Ohnstad called out. 'Everyone else will stay here.'

Silje was halfway to the truck before either Gunther or Erik could stop her. 'You will do no such thing. I will go. I can talk to the General. I will make him—'

'You cannot make him do anything!' her father shouted. 'You are his pet, Silje, his plaything!' He started the engine. 'It is your damned newsletter that has brought this down on us.'

'Father!'

'You have done his bidding against your people and your country, and this is your reward. Christ knows what he is waiting for; I wish he'd just fuck you and leave us in peace!'

He slammed the truck into gear and roared away, sounding the horn to clear the villagers from his path.

Silje stood in the street, unable to blink. She felt nothing, empty; her bones, her heart, scored clean of her flesh.

'He did not mean it,' Erik and Gunther said. They looked warily at one another.

'Instead of going first to his son, he drove this way to spit on me,' said Silje. 'He meant it.' She turned to Gunther. 'Do you have transport?'

'I have a motorcycle.'

'That will have to do.'

'I can find us a car, Silje,' Erik said desperately. 'I will only need a few—'

'There is no time.' She cupped his chin in her hand. 'Find Freya, tell her what has happened, and whatever else make sure she does not try to follow us.'

'She would not be so stupid. I will find a car and follow as soon as I can.'

'No, Erik. Take care of Freya; that is all I ask.'

30

In the spring, the snows melted from the mountain and ran in white streams through the rocks and trees, only to freeze again as darkness fell and the post-winter chill spread across the hills. It made the road from Fólkvangr to Bergen passable by day, hazardous at dusk and the taker of many a careless life at night.

Gunther Braithwaite fought to keep the motorcycle on both wheels as he careened down the mountain track with a terrified Silje clinging onto him.

Jon Ohnstad was more than a mile ahead of them.

'If you try to catch him,' Silje yelled over the roar of the engine, 'you'll kill us both and we're no use to Magnus if we're dead.'

Gunther did not reply but he did throttle back. Still, Silje reeled off the numbers of people killed on the mountain road every year since 1925. She reached 1939 before Gunther politely shouted, if one could indeed do such a thing, for her to shut up.

'I am sorry,' she said. 'When I am frightened I talk.'

'You seem to talk whatever mood you're in.'

'Do not speak to me like that; I said I was sorry.'

Their journey continued in silence, Silje seeing the terrible things Magnus would endure at the hand of the General, while her father's words pressed their way into her thoughts, in spite of her best efforts to smother them: *I wish he'd just fuck you and leave us in peace.*

'What is Magnus doing in Bergen?' she asked, more to drown the whispering inside her head than anything else.

Gunther said he did not know. Silje said that he did and after much cajoling he confessed. 'You must not breathe a word of this to anyone.'

'I am writing coded messages to the Resistance in a newsletter run by the Nazis. And you still think I cannot keep your secrets?'

'I mean it, Silje; this must go no further. Do you understand?'

Silje thought, *If I cannot even gain the trust of a spy…* 'Just tell me!'

'Very well,' he said reluctantly. 'I received a message from my office in London, which in turn had received a note from our spies in the Resistance. There is to be an attack in Bergen today: an attempt to assassinate General Gruetzmacher.'

'You are spying on the Resistance?'

'We spy on everyone. It is our nature.'

'But we are your allies.'

'Especially our allies.'

'And it seems to me that killing Gruetzmacher would serve both our countries.'

'This plan has not been sanctioned. It is ill-conceived, doomed to fail and will, most likely, severely damage operations already in play.'

'Dear Christ. Is that what Magnus is doing in Bergen?'

'I think so, yes.'

'And you did nothing to stop him.'

'I only found out this morning. Do you think I would let him throw his life away on something like this?'

'Who is with him?'

'I do not know. The message said there are ten men involved, perhaps more.'

'You must ride faster,' Silje said.

'But you just told me to—'

'I do not care what I just told you; now I am telling you to ride as fast as you can.'

She could not see tyre tracks ahead; her father must have taken the left-hand road at the fork. It was safer for trucks though far slower. They might meet with him before reaching Bergen.

'You said that killing Gruetzmacher would interfere with other plans. What did you mean?'

Gunther hesitated.

'Tell me,' she growled, 'or I will pitch you from this infernal machine and ride it to Bergen myself.'

'Hah! You do not know how to ride a motorbike.'

This was of course true. 'I can ride a horse without saddle, reins or stirrups,' Silje said indignantly. 'It cannot be harder than that.'

'And I imagine you are stubborn and conceited enough to try.' Gunther sighed. 'There is a plan,' he said, 'a plan that will end the war in Norway before the Germans can gain a foothold.'

Silje wanted to say it was far too late for that, but for once she held her tongue.

'We are going to kill Vidkun Quisling.'

And still she held her tongue because now she wasn't sure what she'd just heard.

'Did you hear what I said?'

'I think so.'

'And you, of all people, have nothing to say.'

'You are going to kill the First Minister.'

'Yes.'

'Hitler's chosen traitor.'

'That is the plan.'

'And you say my brother is foolhardy.'

'It will work, Silje. His popularity within his own party and the Norwegian people is at its lowest ebb so he will be touring the provinces to bolster support.'

'To bolster his support, I would have thought he would need some to begin with.'

'Quite.'

'So when is this plan to be put into action?'

'Soon. A few months from now.'

'Where?'

He throttled the engine and rode high up on the rocks which Silje saw as an attempt to distract her.

'Fólkvangr,' she breathed. 'He's coming to Fólkvangr.'

'Yes,' said Gunther, 'and he's coming to see you.'

'*The Quisling Orchid*. He's coming because of the newsletter!' Silje almost fell from the pillion. Gunther slammed his boot against the frozen ground and steered the bike into the skid. He had the motorcycle under control without even the lightest touch on the brake.

He is good at this, Silje thought, her heart in her throat. 'I cannot meet him. Not Quisling. When were you planning to tell me all of this?'

'When it was too late for you to refuse.'

'You cannot assassinate him in the village. The Nazis will slaughter us in retaliation.'

'He will not be in the village. You have my word.'

'Then where? In the town hall? On the streets of Bergen? On this very road?' She liked Gunther, perhaps more than she should. She'd watched him laugh and joke and drink ale from the same tankard as men who had not cleaned their teeth in weeks. But she had the notion he wasn't making acquaintances so much as moving pieces on a chess board, and chess, she remembered, is a game of sacrifice. She wondered how much of Scandinavia Gunther would sacrifice in service to his King.

'I looked into Iscariot for you,' Gunther said.

'Yes...?'

'Well, for days after I was the laughing stock of Special Operations. Iscariot is something of a joke in intelligence circles. The name crops up from time to time, and is then filed away under "delusion".'

'So tell me; what is it?'

'Hitler believes he can turn the Jews against one another by using his own brand of honest Nazi witchcraft.'

'So Iscariot is an experiment in sorcery?'

'I believe so. To be honest, we have not devoted any effort to investigating further. We could easily fill Parliament with what we hear of Hitler's crackpot schemes.'

'Don't they worry you?'

'Of course not. The more time he wastes on this sort of idiocy the quicker we will win.'

'Hmm.'

Gunther tried to turn his head. 'Do you believe in this nonsense?'

'I just think you would be better served by taking everything he does seriously.'

'We do take him seriously.'

'If that were true, Gunther, then the world would not be at war.'

'I feel you're trying to make a point.'

'I would like you to think on this: you spy on him; he spies on you. You send coded messages, perhaps he does the same. Perhaps all this talk of witchcraft is simply code for something else. Is there a better way to hide your true plans than disguising them as a "delusion"?'

They carried on, picking up speed as the frozen track became a road. They encountered trucks heading away from the town, back towards the mountains.

'Something has happened,' Gunther said. 'We are too late.'

'It is not too late,' said Silje. 'I would know if we were too late.'

The number of vehicles increased as they approached the town, clustering near the first checkpoint. As soon as Gunther was forced to stop, Silje jumped off the motorcycle and brushed the dust and snow from her dress. Gunther took hold of her arm as she tried to set off in the direction of the town hall.

'Where do you think you are going?'

'To get my brother. That is what we came here to do, isn't it?'

'We should stay together.'

She shook her arm free. 'We stand a better chance if I go alone. Your accent is good and your mastery of our language is the best I've heard from any foreigner except Gruetzmacher himself. But if you make a mistake—'

'I will not make a mistake.'

'If you make a mistake and are taken, then Magnus, my father and myself will be lost.'

'Silje—'

'I have the General's ear. I can do this on my own. You should find my father and make sure he dos not do anything foolish.'

She made her way through the trapped vehicles and swelling crowds. She had not seen so many soldiers on the streets since the early days of the invasion. They numbered in the hundreds, more than enough to keep the angry and desperate Norwegians pressed behind the barricades. There were people weeping in the streets, and despite her words to Gunther, Silje suddenly feared the very worst.

A soldier stepped forward to challenge her, and then just as quickly stepped to one side as soon as he recognised her. He patted his machine gun and told her that he very much enjoyed reading *The Quisling Orchid*. 'All the men do,' he added, 'though we miss the recipes. Perhaps there will be room for them when all the Jews have been rounded up.'

Silje said she would ask the General and hurried on her way.

As she approached the town square she heard a sound like the wind drifting in from the sea. It grew louder as she walked on, becoming almost solid when the town hall came into view. It was not the wind; it was the sound made by a thousand Norwegians crowded outside the German HQ. It was the sound of anguish, a thousand Norwegians weeping in the cold. Silje pushed through them. They were in a daze, a trance, as though the horror they'd endured for so long had only now touched them. The soldiers, tasked with keeping them back from the fencing, looked bewildered, almost afraid.

Silje reached the barricade and looked to where thousands of other eyes looked also: to the courtyard beyond the iron gates and the barbed wire, where five posts stood with a bullet-riddled corpse tied to each one.

She commanded her feet to move, one weak and unsteady step at a time. The smell of cordite hung in the air, the same sharp tang that made her nose twitch after her father had used his shotgun. She peered closely at the corpses. They had been shot so many times they were barely recognisable as human, just slabs of meat hung out under the cold sun. One could have been Magnus…

'You cannot go any further, Fräulein.' An officer hurried over with his hand raised and his pistol drawn.

'It is me, Gerbald. Where is my brother?'

'Silje! You should not be here. It is not safe.'

'What have you done here?'

Lieutenant Klein looked to the ground in shame but did not cast his eyes to the wooden posts. For that Silje would be grateful for all her days.

'He is inside, being questioned.' When he looked to her again she saw his eyes were red and swollen. He'd been crying. *The General*, she thought. If Magnus had succeeded then there was nothing she could do for him except beg the Germans for his swift and merciful execution.

'Questioned? For what?'

Klein shook his head and said she should go home.

'Not without my brother. Let me through. I wish to speak to General Gruetzmacher.'

'There was an attack,' Klein said. 'An attempt was made on the General's life. He is in the infirmary.'

Silje felt her mouth run dry. He was alive at least. 'Still, I must speak with him.'

'I cannot just allow you—'

Silje hitched her dress and began climbing the barricades.

'Silje!'

She tore the dress, and the skin from her calf, and became trapped. Klein rushed forward to help her and two of his men followed, cutting away the barbed wire and moving the wooden stakes to make an opening in the barricade. The crowd looked on, puzzlement replacing grief which in turn was replaced by anger.

'As I am here you can take me to him.'

Klein said, 'You are the most infuriating woman I have ever known.'

'I am the only woman you have ever known.' Silje replied.

Nevertheless he took her hand and led her towards the steps of the town hall.

Exactly halfway between the barricade and the steps, the General's staff car lay, its front crushed against a stone pillar. The windshield had been shattered and the seats were covered in blood.

'A single shot,' Klein said, without looking at the car. 'The General saw your brother fighting those men for possession of a gun. Fortune was with him; he ducked down as the shot was fired. His injuries are minor.'

It occurred to Silje that there was too much gore for such a small injury.

'Staff Sergeant Krause… Inge… was not so fortunate.' His eyes reddened further and he angrily drew his sleeve across the bridge of his nose.

'I am sorry, Gerbald.'

'It is Klein, Lieutenant Klein.'

'Yes, of course. I am sorry.'

'She had an affection for me,' he said. 'She told me so once.'

'Yes, I know. She was very fond of you.'

'I spurned her, and I was unkind when I did it.'

'I'm sure you did not mean to—'

'I was cruel to her because she was not you. I was cruel to her because after you rejected me, you sent her to me as some sort of consolation. You were just as cruel to her, Silje, and she deserved better from both of us.'

They climbed the steps in silence. Two gun emplacements had been erected either side of the huge oak doors. Though not so much guns as cannons, Silje thought. To her left, one of the soldiers manning the gun eyed her and the Lieutenant as they walked past. He whispered something to his comrade who grinned and then turned his eye back to the gun sight trained on the crowd.

'You should wait here,' said Klein. 'I will ask if he will see you.'

'And why should I not wish to see her, Lieutenant?'

Klein snapped to attention so quickly Silje thought she heard his spine crack.

'My General!'

'You may stand at ease.'

Silje turned and curtsied slightly. The General spared them both the slightest of nods. There was a field dressing taped to his left cheek, and a bandage bound tightly about his left hand. He was flanked by two soldiers, each half as wide as they were tall.

'It is good to see you again, Fräulein Ohnstad, though I wish it were under less dire circumstances. Walk with me. Klein, stay here.' He strode back inside without waiting for her. Silje hurried after him. She hesitated when he entered a room just several yards beyond the hall entrance, but slipped inside as he began to close the door. The room was much the same as the others she'd seen in the town hall: ornate with a dizzyingly high ceiling. The shutters were closed and the only light came from a single lamp at the corner of a hand-carved writing bureau. The room hadn't been plundered for its artworks so Silje assumed it was one of the General's private offices.

'My brother, General. You have him here.'

He opened the door to a side office and held it for her. Silje stepped through. Gruetzmacher beckoned her to take a seat before opening a box and taking out a wooden pipe.

'I would rather stand if it's all the same to you, General.'

'As you wish.'

'My brother—'

'Do you remember my driver?'

'I—'

'A simple question, Fräulein. My driver, Sergeant Krause.'

'Yes, Gerbald… Lieutenant Klein told me that—'

'The shot went through the windshield and shattered her right eye.'

'I am truly sorry for your loss, General.'

'She died moments later. I could do nothing for her.'

'General—'

'I could not even bring myself to touch her.'

Silje decided to wait, to allow him to say what he needed to say. He tapped his finger on the brandy decanter, staring at it as though he could see a tiny Jew inside it. 'She was Semite, you know. Partly, at least. On her father's side… No, her mother's. She did not attempt to hide this flaw and she did not seek to gain dispensation for it. I admired her because she accepted her inferiority and yet strove to become the best she could be. She was, and I dare to say it, a true German.' He removed the glass stopper from the decanter, and laid it gently on the writing desk. 'And yet, I could not bring myself to touch her. She lay dying before my eyes, and I could not comfort her because all I could see in front of me was a Jew.' He poured himself a glass, looked at it and then poured the contents slowly on the floor, watching the stream until it was spent. Then he upended the glass and slammed it against the desk. 'But she was a Jew in a German uniform, Fräulein, and the uniform alone means she was worth a thousand of your countrymen.'

'General, please. My brother—'

'Was seen by myself and my men struggling with the scum I have nailed to posts outside my headquarters.'

'He was not part of this, I swear.'

The General stoked his pipe and lit it. 'It happened very quickly, Fräulein. So quickly that I could not tell if the five men were wrestling the gun away from your brother or he was attempting to take the gun from them.' He opened his mouth to allow a plume of blue smoke to cascade out. 'Which left me with something of a dilemma.'

He is trying to explain himself, Silje thought. *Dear God, what has he done?* 'Your actions seem decisive enough, General. You did not know who was innocent and who was guilty and you executed them all the same.'

'But not your brother.' His face split into a thin, humourless smile. 'Your brother I have spared.'

'Then take me to him!'

'In good time, Fräulein Ohnstad. Whether he was attempting to save my life or take it, he knew of the attempt. And so I have to ask myself, what else does he know?'

'He knows nothing! He just saw the gun as it was drawn and threw himself in harm's way to save you.'

This amused the General, and he rewarded her with a smile more terrifying than any he'd attempted before. 'But I have spared him,' he said. 'And I did this for you.'

'Then I thank you for your kindness, General.'

'I did not do it for nothing.' His smile did not change, and Silje wondered if it was a hideous reflex or if it required an act of will to keep it fixed in place.

But here we are, she thought, *at last.*

She walked to the centre of the room and unfastened her dress. She let it fall to her waist and clasped onto it tightly so that it would fall no further.

'For the life of my brother,' she said, 'I am yours.' She breathed in to lift her breasts.

General Gruetzmacher swallowed, such a sound that it echoed around the room. He came to stand over her. Silje looked to the floor and felt his breath on the back of her neck. He placed a hand on her shoulder. She closed her eyes and rooted her feet firmly to the floor, her heart pounding in terror. She felt his hand on her breast, his fingers squeezing and releasing in short bursts. He exhaled and took her nipple between his thumb and forefinger, pulling and twisting until Silje found herself gritting her teeth from the pain. He started to use his thumbnail, and as she tried to pull away, he increased the pressure on her shoulder, holding her fast. He told her to look up so he could see her face, and when she did not he stopped to raise her chin before quickly resuming his attentions: twisting and grinding while staring at her eyes – not into them, Silje marvelled, just at them.

'Just take me,' she murmured, remembering the words of her father, 'and leave Fólkvangr in peace.'

And then he stopped, slowly taking his hands from her, shifting his gaze elsewhere. 'Cover yourself, Fräulein.' His breathing laboured. 'You embarrass us both.'

He took the pipe from his mouth and looked at it, disappointed. He tried to light it again while he walked back to his desk. 'Your brother did not respond favourably to questioning.'

'You mean torture, I think.' Silje refastened her dress and did not feel any less naked.

'I will return him to you,' the General said evenly, 'and in return for my generosity, you will talk to him, find out whatever he knows.'

'If he knows anything, he will not tell me.'

'Pray that he does, soon, or I will have him brought back here.' He sat down and began searching the bureau drawers. 'I am showing you a kindness, Fräulein Ohnstad. Perhaps we would kill him before he broke, perhaps not; it makes no difference to me. This way we may both benefit.'

'Have I not done enough for you?'

He picked up a fountain pen, tapped it on the desk and then waved it towards the door. 'You may leave now. I have much to do.'

He took the second sheet from a pile and began to write. Silje waited for him to say something else. A few moments later she realised she'd slipped from his world and no longer existed.

* * *

They escorted her to the town hall's side exit and left her there. The door slammed shut, leaving her cold, defiled, and still without her brother. She made her way out of the courtyard, keeping her head low to avoid the inquiring looks of her fellow Norwegians.

Darkness had fallen and the crowd had yet to disperse. A thousand people, perhaps more, stood at the barricades, neither advancing or falling back. It was the sombre inaction that made the Germans wary, fearful – a passive violence to which they could not respond.

Silje decided to walk to the entrance and try to speak with Lieutenant Klein again. She was sure he would not see her but had to try all the same.

As she turned and began to walk back, dim headlights flashed from a narrow passageway close to the barricades. She stopped and peered at the shadow beyond the crowd. If it was a signal then whoever sent it would not dare do so again. She turned her eyes without moving her head; the German soldiers did not appear to have noticed.

The crowd had begun to stamp its feet to keep warm, but after a time the stamping fell into a rhythm. Ten by ten they fell in step until a thousand Norwegians marched on the spot, staring defiantly at their oppressors. The Germans looked to one another and brought their weapons to bear. An officer raised his hand and yelled for the crowd to stop.

Silje could not remember ever feeling so proud.

'You would be best to wait for the crowd to disperse, Fräulein,' one of the soldiers said to her. 'There is no telling what they may do.'

'I am Norwegian,' she said.

'Fräulein, if you—'

'They may hate me for what I have done, but I will stand with them, always.'

She walked to the barricade, and refused any soldier who offered her aid. Four Norwegians came forward and began tearing at the barbed wire with their bare hands, ignoring German calls for them to desist. They hoisted Silje across the threshold and placed her amongst the crowd.

The lights from the alleyway flashed again; she knew they would not signal a third time.

She thanked her countrymen for their manners and generosity and then made her way through the gathering. Once out of sight she slipped into the alleyway and approached her father's truck. He sat grimly in the front seat, staring ahead.

'Get in the back,' he said. 'Help Gunther with your brother.'

Gunther's motorcycle was secured to the side of the truck, and in the back Gunther held Magnus in his arms.

'He needs help but he would not let us leave without you.'

'You should have, you silly boy,' she said, wiping her eyes. Magnus had been beaten almost beyond recognition. His head had been shaved, his fingers broken, and they had tried to carve a swastika into his face. He was swathed in blankets; the blood soaking them had already begun to dry.

'Dear Christ.'

And his right eye had been gouged out.

Their father started the truck and pulled out of the alleyway. 'We must get him to Doctor Lomen.'

'Father, no. We must find a doctor in Bergen.'

Magnus shook his head.

'We must go back to Fólkvangr, to Doctor Lomen,' Gunther said quietly. 'He can treat Magnus and we can tell him.'

'Tell him? Tell him what?'

But Gunther and her father remained silent.

'Tell him what?'

'Did you not see them, woman?' her father cried. 'Butchered and shot in front of their countrymen?'

Silje looked back to the town hall, shrinking away in the darkness, the five executed men already lost from view.

'Doctor Lomen's sons,' Gunther whispered. 'All of them.'

31

I was almost out of money. There was some left from the Strande extortion and some from the work at the museum. The museum job didn't pay much, but I'd had no luck anywhere else. There are these tests they like you to do, even for cleaning work, and since school had passed me by, I always did badly at the tests. And of course, there was my family history.

You're lovely, Brigit, not what I was expecting at all, but we can't hire you. One of our delivery drivers/cooks/waitresses – his/her grandfather/uncle/brother died at Fólkvangr. It just wouldn't be fair…

Sometimes they took one look at me and asked me to leave. One woman, a manager of something or the other, was halfway through a question when she finally remembered where she'd heard my name before. She stopped talking and just started to cry. I got up to leave and she started throwing things: pens, her typewriter, ledgers, and a hefty personnel management text book. It was the paperweight that did the most damage; I needed four stitches just behind my hairline.

While she was sewing my head shut, Doctor Nese wondered aloud if it might be a good idea to change my name.

But most of the time I was turned down because I could barely read. I'd lost interest in being a journalist by then, imagining that all chief editors were going to turn out like Oscar Strande.

Doctor Nese came through for me in the end; she found me some admin work at the hospital. Nothing too taxing: errands, filing – lots of menial work that wouldn't result in someone dying if I misread a label or put notes in the wrong folder. She arranged to have me tested for dyslexia, and I think we were both disappointed when the results came back; I wasn't dyslexic, just uneducated.

'Well,' she said airily, 'that's actually good news. All we need to do is get you into an adult literacy programme.' And the following day she enrolled me in one.

She offered me a place to sleep for a few weeks. Her apartment was a five-minute walk from the hospital. It had a single bedroom and huge lounge-diner, part of which she'd converted into a library for her text books. While I was there I tried to read every spine on her bookshelves. The last shelf, closest to the kitchen door, was reserved for the six or seven books she'd written herself. Cookery books, which was something of a surprise, and a book on learning the harp, which for some reason wasn't.

She lived alone, had no children, few friends, and didn't like asparagus; that's pretty much all I learned about her during the month I slept on her couch. There was a harp in her bedroom which she never played, and a cooker in the kitchen that had enough buttons and dials to launch a rocket. She did enjoy cooking, and I ravenously consumed everything she laid in front of me. I often had to stop myself from licking the plate.

She could answer any geography question on any quiz show and she liked to read books on the apartment balcony, even when the outside temperature hit zero.

She made sure I visited Monica at least three times a week, and she would fuss with the tubes and drips while Monica and me stared glumly at one another.

She cried when Monica discharged herself.

I didn't.

Sometimes she would tap my shoulder and tell me to breathe in her face. Mortified, I'd do as I was told and she would say, 'Good, much better. Keep it up.' She believed all the world's ills could be cured by good dental hygiene.

She helped me make sense of Mr Klein's notes. She said she'd had student doctors who couldn't write a thesis as well as he could. And according to her, that's what he'd been doing – writing a thesis.

'On one General Gruetzmacher,' she said, 'who, according to this, served as a high-ranking officer even though he was a known paedophile.'

I had to tell her that I didn't know what that was. When she told me I thought she was making it up.

Klein had been obsessed with this General Gruetzmacher since he'd been released from prison. He'd traced the General's life and career from his days as a trainee botanist, up until his death at the hands of Jesper Bergström.

When she said Bergström's name I swallowed and turned to look behind me, expecting to see him standing over us holding a carving knife, reminding me of my obligation, telling me he owned me. I broke down, and it took the rest of the evening to explain why.

Over the next few days Doctor Nese became obsessed with Klein's notes, so much so that I actually began to feel a little jealous.

'This is amazing, Brigit, it really is.' She turned the page and popped an olive into my mouth. 'Watch for the stone,' she said, and turned the page again. She could take in a sheet full of words faster than I could take in a photograph. She carried on reading while slicing artichokes and dropping them into a pan of boiling water. I followed her around the kitchen, trying to remember everything she was doing. 'It says here that he was a friend of Adolf Hitler. After his fall from grace, the good Führer made him his personal assistant, promoted him, put him back on track.' She turned the page, then turned it back. 'Mmm. Seems the General's life was a blank page under Hitler's tutelage, except for this.' She showed me the page. Klein had written a single word on it.

'Iscariot,' I said promptly. She liked to test me. 'Question mark.'

She seemed pleased. 'Very good.'

'I *can* read, you know. I'm just not very good at it.'

'Do know who Judas Iscariot was?'

I shrugged – something she hated. 'A friend of Jesus, wasn't he?'

'Not exactly.' She put the notes down on the kitchen table. 'And after Iscariot – whatever that is – Gruetzmacher requested a transfer back to combat duty. He specifically requested Norway, which seems a little odd.'

I bit into an apple and asked what was so odd about it.

'Well, he distinguishes himself during the invasion of Poland, falls from grace, is saved by Hitler himself, and when he's given the chance of a high-ranking position in the Nazi party, he takes command of his old unit and brings them to Norway. Thousands of battle-hardened troops – for Norway.'

'I think we put up a pretty good fight.'

'Yes, but the Germans weren't expecting one when they invaded. He wanted to be stationed here, far from the frontline, far from Berlin. Why?'

I shrugged again. 'Skiing?'

Doctor Nese didn't really have a sense of humour. She stayed with Klein's notes for the rest of the night. I spent the evening watching quiz shows.

Doctor Nese – Dagrun – had a number tattooed on her arm. I saw it when I ran into her as she was leaving the bathroom. It was stretched and horribly distorted; it had been scored into her when she was young. She let me stare at it for a moment and then pulled on the sleeve of her robe to cover it. I opened my mouth to say something, I can't remember what, and she simply said 'No' and disappeared into her bedroom.

We never talked about it, and for days after that I sometimes heard her screaming in the night.

'I think I need you to leave, Brigit,' she announced suddenly over breakfast. It was a week after the tattoo incident and neither of us had had a full night's sleep since. 'I am sorry.'

I said that I understood while feeling like I'd been kicked in the stomach.

'I have loved having you here.' She meant it; she wiped her eyes with one of the napkins she always put out at mealtimes. 'I wish you could stay. I want you to stay.'

I realised she was a stationary version of my mother, or perhaps I was just being cruel because she had taken me in and then snapped me in two. 'I should be going anyway,' I said, which was true enough. As much as I wanted it to be otherwise, there was nothing to keep me here. Monica had vanished and there had been a plan, several lifetimes ago, to see Fólkvangr for myself.

Doctor Nese – Dagrun – slid a palm full of coins across the table and withdrew her hand. 'I want you to call me,' she said. 'Every day, if you can.'

'I won't be able to pay you back,' I said flatly. I wanted her to feel this as badly as I did.

'It's not a loan.'

'I won't be able to pay you back.'

She gave up and sat back in her chair. 'Can I call you?'

'I don't know where I'm going.'

'I need some time. Having you here, it made me think of things. Things long past. I thought I'd forgotten them; I really did. I need to speak to someone. I will call you. I promise.'

I said I didn't see how. 'I'll go get my things.'

'You don't have to go right now!'

'Yes, I do.'

She followed me around the apartment which now seemed suffocatingly small. I gathered the scraps of my life and pushed them into my rucksack while she desperately tried to explain. She whispered something about Camp Belsen, but the words swelled in her throat until she looked like she was choking. I folded Klein's notes and wrapped them in tin foil to keep them dry.

'I'll have to leave some things here if that's okay.' My stomach felt tight; I leaned against the cooker, feeling my knees start to give way. I didn't want to leave. 'I'll come back for them, or I'll have Mr Bergström pick them up if that works better for you.'

'Of course it wouldn't!' Dagrun closed her eyes. 'Brigit, listen—'

'Is it because you want something more from me?' It sounded arrogant and desperate, even as I was saying it. 'If you want… I mean I don't know, but I guess it's something we could try.'

She looked at me as though I were pointing a knife at her.

'You invite me into your home; you make me feel like I'm part of something safe. You don't ask me for anything, you don't tell me anything. And now you're telling me to fuck off out of your life. I don't know how these things work so… is it me you want?'

Her silence left me hoping – hoping that in exchange for something far from disagreeable she'd let me stay. She closed her eyes and I thought that I should do something: touch her face, kiss her, maybe.

'I'm going to work now,' she said. 'Please don't be here when I get back.'

She walked away without looking at me, picking up her briefcase and coat on her way out. She slammed the door and I was alone.

I finished packing my rucksack and then I cried solidly for a whole hour – something I'd never done before.

I cleaned myself up, brushed my teeth for the second time that morning, stole all the cash I could find, and then completely wrecked her apartment before walking out the front door, leaving it wide open.

32

I could have flown from Trondheim to Bergen in about an hour; instead I took the train. Four hundred miles in half a day, through forested mountains and plains of trees and rock. I'd crossed this country about six times and I think this was the first time I'd ever seen it; Monica and me mostly run at night.

I arrived in Bergen at around eight o'clock and got something to eat at a small café a few feet from the edge of the quay. There were a half-dozen tall ships anchored in the harbour, streams of tiny lights wrapped around their masts. The harbour was crowded, noisy; people were singing, celebrating. It all felt distant, as if I was watching it from behind glass. I wasn't enjoying it so I left a few of Dagrun's coins on the table and headed back towards the train station, making a detour into a supermarket for hair-dye and toothpaste.

There were three hotels and a youth hostel behind the station. I picked the youth hostel as I figured it would be much cheaper and the clientele a lot less likely to recognise me.

'You're lucky,' said the jaundiced stick-thin man behind the counter. 'We've had a party of six who haven't shown up. Take your pick.'

I chose a room facing away from the trains, and asked about tours to Fólkvangr. He gave me an oddly sour look. Bergen sees the Fólkvangr Massacre as its own intimate tragedy. The townspeople aren't keen on gawkers coming to see what's left of it.

'There's not much there,' he said. 'Just a house and rubble, more or less.'

I asked him again for tour information, and seeing that I'd made up my mind he slid three folded pamphlets across the counter.

'If you go early then you can get back and have the rest of your afternoon.'

I thanked him and headed up to my room.

'When you go,' he called after me, 'think about what happened there. I mean, really think.'

The room was large enough to hold about eight people and their rucksacks. I picked the bed closest to the window, another of Monica's ingrained habits that I couldn't shake. I checked the distance down to the street below; yes, I could make the jump if I had to. I ate a chocolate bar and started the slow process of dying my hair. I'd picked out a dull red colour, sort of hiding in broad daylight; that was my thinking anyway. The stench made my eyes water. The phone in the hallway started ringing and then stopped after three bells.

I wrapped my head in a towel and lay on the bed with one of Mr Klein's notebooks. In it he talked about his admiration for his commanding officer, even after the man developed an alcohol problem, which apparently got worse after he met Silje Ohnstad.

The phone in the hallway rang again.

Over the next few pages Klein described the dichotomy of the General's convictions: a scientist who believed in Jewish witchcraft. But did he really believe that Jewish women were witches, or was that simply a way for him to excuse his own lack of self-control? I'd already made up my mind by the time I reached the end of the page.

The phone in the hallway rang again.

I was the only one staying on this floor, so I thought perhaps it was Dagrun, that she'd somehow tracked me down. I ran from my room and snatched the receiver from the wall.

'Hello, Doctor Nese?' I thought about apologising for smashing up her home, except I wasn't sorry and she knew me well enough to realise that.

'It's not, I'm afraid.'

Jesper Bergström. I almost wet myself.

'How are you, Miss Fossen?'

I looked out of the hall window, down into the street. It was crowded with people making their way to and from the station. Heads down, collars pulled up against the harbour chill. I don't know what I was expecting: to see him standing under a lamppost, wearing a trench coat and picking dirt from his fingernails with a kitchen knife. He wasn't there. Of course he wasn't; he didn't need to be. 'How did you get this number?'

'That's not important,' he said. 'I was just calling to see how you're getting on.'

When I didn't say anything, he asked, 'So… how're you getting on?'

'Fine. What do you want?'

'I want what we both want: to find your father. I was very sorry to hear about your mother by the way. How is she? Ah! Forgive me. You don't know how she is, do you?'

He was trying to scare me, to show me that he had eyes everywhere. It was working.

'You stopped moving. I became concerned.'

'I was staying with someone.'

'I know.'

'Have you hurt her?'

The line went silent; he appeared to be thinking about it.

'She's quite safe,' he said finally. 'But it is you I am concerned about. I fear that your dedication to our cause – to finding your father – is beginning to falter.'

'I'll find him. I just needed some time to get my head straight, that's all.'

'And your head; is it straight now?'

'Yes.'

'Good! Excellent! So there'll be no more delays.'

'No.'

'Then why are you in Bergen? He is unlikely to be twenty miles away from the scene of the crime.'

'I'm heading for Fólkvangr. There are people still living in the mountains. They may be able to tell me something.'

'About your father's whereabouts?'

'Yes.'

He sighed, very theatrically. 'Why don't you tell me what you are really doing in Bergen, Miss Fossen? It would be so much easier than me travelling there to ask you in person.'

I didn't want that. 'Look, I've been reading a lot about him, about the village.'

'Go on.'

'Well… I'm not sure he did it. What they say he did; I don't think it was him.'

He stayed silent, weighing what I just said against what he knew, what he'd assumed his entire life. Or maybe he was sharpening knives and looking at the bus times to Bergen.

'There were almost two hundred people living in Fólkvangr at the time; any one of them could have been the traitor.'

'True,' he said, choosing to indulge me for a minute, 'but out of the two hundred, he was the only one who confessed.'

Minute over.

'I will call you again tomorrow, Miss Fossen. I expect to hear that you are working towards fulfilling your side of the bargain.'

I guessed his side of the bargain was to let me live. He hung up the phone, and I stood by the window, trembling. I went back to the room and dragged the bed around so I could see the door; then I climbed in and pulled the covers up to my chin. I didn't sleep at all that night.

* * *

The following morning I hid myself behind a pair of large sunglasses and took a bus to Fólkvangr. It was the cheapest tour I could find, and I didn't even have to book a seat. I could stay in the village for as long as I liked, and just jump on a return bus when I wanted to head back to Bergen.

I took a seat right at the back, and wedged myself into a corner. The bus filled quickly and I found myself trapped between the window and a large middle-aged woman who was wearing just a t-shirt, slacks and a large straw hat. I wondered what country she thought she was in. She smiled and nodded; I smiled back and shrank into my corner, putting my head down.

She fanned herself, even though it was around minus one outside, and gave me a gentle nudge. 'Canadian,' she said, as if it was an instruction. I nodded and answered: 'Norwegian.'

She whooped so loudly that it made my ears hurt. Everyone on the bus looked around, and I thought about getting off and waiting for the next one. Too late now; the engine had started, and with a few indifferent pushes on the horn, the driver got us under way.

I enjoyed the silence for just a few minutes and then as soon as we cleared the town limits, the tour guide sprang from her seat. She was around my age, perhaps older, with blonde hair she'd painstakingly styled to appear much thicker than it was. She was wearing a cap announcing she was a Friend of Fólkvangr.

I tried to make myself even smaller.

She wielded the microphone like a weapon, demanding that a few unlucky people near her tell the whole bus where they'd come from.

'Welcome to you all,' she bubbled. 'My name is Liv, and your driver for today is Tobias.'

Tobias raised his hand and the bus chorused an enthusiastic 'Hello.'

Without waiting for the greeting to fade, Liv pressed on with the house rules: do not distract Tobias (Tobias raised his hand again, expecting us to have forgotten him); do not leave litter on the coach; do not make rude gestures to other road users; and most importantly do not take anything from Fólkvangr that you didn't find in a gift shop.

All clear enough so there were no questions. Liv nodded and continued with a well-rehearsed history of Fólkvangr, starting with its founding in 1793, and ending with its destruction in the autumn of 1941. Along the way, she rolled through population statistics, and named a number of its more famous occupants, including Silje Ohnstad, whom she described as 'misunderstood.'

She said Fólkvangr was famous for its orchids, which I didn't know.

And of course she spoke at great length about my father.

'Erik Brenna,' she said, shaking her head. 'What can I say about Erik Brenna that you have not already heard?'

'Everything,' shrieked the woman next to me. 'I've never heard of the guy!'

This rated a muted laugh from the rest of the coach. She nudged me playfully. 'Canadian.'

'I know. You said.'

'Only took this tour because the concierge recommended it.'

I wanted to say the concierge probably got some kind of kickback from the operator. In the end I just smiled and huddled in my corner.

'Well, for the benefit of our guests from overseas, let me tell you about Erik Brenna, the coward of Fólkvangr.'

And she spent the next ten minutes describing a hideous cross between Goebbels and a mountain troll; I hardly recognised it as human. When she was done she took a deep breath and Tobias handed her a handkerchief. 'I am sorry,' she said. 'My family was also touched by this tragedy.'

She said her mother used to live in Fólkvangr. When she was very young, her family moved to Bergen so her father could work at the harbour. They returned to the village every year before the Germans invaded, to see old friends.

'Had my father not moved us away,' she said, 'then I would not be standing before you now.'

The bus cooed in sympathy. To be honest, I'd heard better survivor stories.

There was a thriving trade in Fólkvangr tours; we passed about six buses along the way, not to mention twenty or thirty cars. I counted them, facing the window to prevent an outbreak of conversation. My travelling companion took the hint and spent the whole trip reading a two-page brochure.

Tobias pulled into Fólkvangr about half an hour later. There was a level area near an old cottage sitting conspicuously next to a gift shop and a public convenience. We disembarked and Liv repeated that nothing was to be taken from this most sacred of places, then she pointed out the small gift shop.

'Is that the cottage?' I asked her.

She nodded. 'The Ohnstads' home, yes.'

'It's larger than I thought.' From the stories I'd heard, it sounded as though they'd lived in a potting shed.

'Everyone says that,' Liv replied. 'My father used to say the villagers were an odd lot; they took a sort of quiet pride in their poverty. Making do was all the rage here apparently.'

Aside from the cottage there wasn't much else to see. Liv said there was a monument less than a mile along the orchid paths, and a small museum about three hundred yards beyond that.

'The museum's well worth a visit,' she said. 'Lots of souvenirs.'

I took the orchid path down to the village where scores of people wandered back and forth trying to feel a sense of tragedy.

What remains of Fólkvangr is an oddly serene place. Even without the devotion of old Mr Ohnstad, the orchids have flourished.

Near an archway of pine trees there's a monument left by the village's first family. It's little more than a turret of stones with an inscription carved around its base. The orchids have grown in the monument since before the war, and left untended they spilled out onto the ruined cobblestones. Years later, Fólkvangr's high street was a sea of orchids over which the mountain dwellers have laid wooden paths. It's an unspoken rule that no one steps on the orchids. Even the fastidious Liv didn't see the point in mentioning it.

The tour guide said the monument was built by Jon Ohnstad in memory of his second wife who is now known – according to the guide book – to have died of a rare form of skin cancer.

I felt myself shudder.

There were framed photographs resting against the stone circle. Some showed the monument as it would have been during the war, set in a busy street with the locals walking, running or driving carts around it. Some of the figures shown were German soldiers. A shadow crossed the picture and I felt someone breathing at my neck.

'So, you made it.'

My first instinct was to run; it was what he expected so he took hold of my arm, pressing his finger and thumb into the elbow joint. I could feel the bones separating.

'You're not going to leave, are you.'

It wasn't a question but I shook my head all the same. Bergström slowly released my arm.

'What do you think of the monument?'

'What am I supposed to think.'

'Many believe it's a work of art despite its rural simplicity. I didn't think much of it myself when I was a child.'

I thought about screaming for help.

'Old Mr Ohnstad could turn his hand to anything, much like your father.'

'Are you watching me?'

'I prefer to think of it as looking out for you.'

'Really.'

He smiled, as an indulgence. 'You should walk around a little; take it all in.'

'There isn't that much to see.'

'There's a sense of history, of tragedy. Stay a few hours.'

'I thought you wanted me to find my father. He's not going to be here.'

'Take your time, Miss Fossen. It'll help you to understand why you're doing this.'

'I understand why I'm doing this,' I said, and knelt down to look closely at one of the photographs. There was nothing special about it except that it had a brand-new frame, and I recognised the name on the small plaque set into it. 'I'm doing this so you don't kill me.'

'A pity,' Bergström said. 'I was hoping you were doing it because it is the right thing to do.'

The photograph had been donated recently by Mr Klein. Probably something he'd dug up during his research for the Resistance Museum. It was the same monument, though you could see little of it due to the crowd gathered around it. The plaque said the picture was taken after the sudden death of Mr Josef Kleppe, the village lamp-lighter. I could make out a pair of boots on the ground, toes pointing to the sky; the rest of the body was hidden by the people standing over him or kneeling at his side.

And there she was again, the ever-present Silje Ohnstad. She was comforting someone, a young girl by the looks of it.

I stood up and asked, 'Where did you live?'

The question seemed to throw him; I swear I heard him swallow and when he finally spoke his voice lacked the threat of intent it had carried since we'd first met.

'Why do you want to know?'

'You said I should try to feel a sense of history. You're part of the history here, so show me.'

'Follow the main path to the farrier's,' Bergström said. 'There's a sign there that will tell you where the grocery store used to be.'

'You're not coming with me?'

He shook his head and mumbled 'I can't' under his breath.

So I went on my own, along the path, just like he said. When I turned to see if he'd change his mind, he'd already gone.

* * *

The tablet read, *The home and grocery of Fredrick Bergström who was taken, along with his wife Bente, his daughter Karin and his son Jesper, to Beisfjord Concentration Camp. All but Jesper perished there.*

There was nothing left of their cottage except a picture on the tablet. There were more plaques, left and right, that stretched to the edge of the village perimeter.

I read every last one: every tablet and engraving, every picture and framed newspaper cutting. I walked the orchid paths, stirring ghosts that would haunt me until my last breath. Some of the memorials mentioned my father by name, cursing him on behalf of the lost.

He couldn't have done it.

But I didn't really know him. I just knew that I couldn't share blood with anyone who'd caused this.

I ran back to the Ohnstad Monument, leaving the path when people got in my way and ignoring the gasps of outrage as I trod the orchids under foot. There was something about the stones. Something that, through my anger, had edged its way into focus. When I reached the stone circle, someone was waiting there for me: short, bow-legged with sand-coloured hair that had faded to white at the temples. He had a rather large red nose, burned and peeling from the mountain sun. His stomach spilled over his belt and his teeth protruded slightly from between his lips. I didn't recognise him at first because I'd only seen him from the back.

Tobias, the coach driver.

'I can't stay long,' he said. 'I was due back in Bergen a half hour ago. Where the hell have you been?' He glanced at his watch and took a stuffed envelope from his pocket. He said he'd lost track of me when he'd gone to use the toilet.

'You've been following me?'

'Keeping an eye on you; Mr Bergström's orders.' He handed me the envelope. 'He figures you'll have run out of money by now. There's enough there to keep you going for a while. Now, is there anything else you need?'

'A camera,' I said.

He looked doubtful.

'Do you have one?'

'I've got my own in the bus.'

'That'll do. Can I have it?'

'Er… no.'

I told him Mr Bergström would want me to have anything I needed. 'So go get me the camera.'

Tobias frowned, then dragged his feet back to the bus.

I returned to the monument, looking at each of the stones around the edge, examining each photograph carefully. It was the one showing Jonas Kleppe's final moments that intrigued me, though not so much the picture as the people in it: black-and-white, lost and faded into history.

Silje Ohnstad – I'd read a lot about her, and I'd drawn my own conclusion that she was a caring, much-loved, manipulative bitch.

Caring.

Yes.

In the picture she held the dark-haired girl as if she were her own child.

'One camera,' said Tobias, placing it on top of the monument. 'I'd like to think I'll get it back someday.'

'I'm sure Bergström will replace it.'

'I'm sure,' he grumbled.

I picked it up; it was large and heavy, and I had no idea how to operate it.

'You have used a box camera before, haven't you?'

I tried not to look too sheepish.

Tobias rolled his eyes and took the camera from me. 'Tell me what you want photographed and I'll do it for you.'

We used a whole roll of film on the monument, mostly closeups of the photographs that featured Silje Ohnstad.

'Get closer,' I told him. 'Make sure you get the front of her dress. I think that's blood.'

Tobias adjusted the lens and moved closer to the photograph. 'It *is* blood. When old Mr Kleppe had his heart attack he hit his head on the monument, round about…' He stood up and pointed to a slightly misshapen stone just above the photograph. 'There. If the heart attack hadn't killed him, the head injury would have done. Sad story. His wife killed herself, you know.'

I told him I didn't know.

'Tell you what. Let's go to the museum. They run films and they've got models of what the village used to be like.'

'I thought you had to get back to Bergen.'

'Fuck it,' he said. 'They'll forgive me just this once.'

And so we went to the Fólkvangr Museum where we watched a history of the village and the mountains and listened to potted biographies of some of the people who'd lived there. There was a whole wall devoted to Jesper Bergström, praising him as a hero and at the same time acknowledging him as a mass murderer. Fólkvangr was about genocide on both sides, it seemed.

A whole wing of the museum had been devoted to my father.

Erik Brenna was good with his hands; he could make anything from anything else. He was an accomplished painter and a poet, and he loved Silje Ohnstad more than life itself.

But not one sculpture, painting, faded news article or photo caption could tell me why he did it.

'I have no idea,' Tobias said over a mug of coffee. We'd made our way to the Ohnstad cottage, which was a mile north of the village itself and the only structure the Germans had left standing. 'No one does. Anyone who says they know is a liar. Remember that.'

'If he loved Silje so much then why would he betray the entire village? He would have known that would destroy her.'

Tobias stopped stirring his coffee so he could shrug. 'Maybe he wanted to destroy her. Maybe she did something that hurt him so badly he couldn't think straight.'

It seemed unlikely, or perhaps I just wanted it to seem that way.

The coffee shop was little more than six tables and chairs arranged in front of a large green tent. We were the only customers, though there were half a dozen people across the path, peering in through the windows of the Ohnstad cottage. There were two security guards posted front and back. Anyone attempting to gain entry was politely and firmly discouraged.

'It was her,' I said firmly. 'I know it was her.'

'Silje Ohnstad? Have a care, young lady; she's a national hero.'

'Do you think as a national pariah I don't know that?'

He glumly buttoned his mouth and looked down into his coffee.

'Why are you working for a man like Bergström anyway?'

He sipped at his mug so he could think a while. 'I'm not sure anymore. Our families are tied by blood; his grandfather was a cousin to my grandfather. We've helped him whenever we can. Sort of like a legacy from birth, I suppose.'

'You know Bergström threatened to kill me?'

'Yes,' Tobias said as though I'd told him Bergström had stepped on my foot. 'If you deliver Erik Brenna to him then you'll never hear from him again.'

'And what if my father is innocent?'

'Erik Brenna is not innocent. He confessed.'

It always came back to the confession.

'Look,' said Tobias. 'I can't imagine the kind of life you've had, but think about this: if your father answers for his crimes then you and your mother will have a chance to breathe again.'

'And by "answering for his crimes" you mean being murdered by your psychotic cousin? That's not justice, not as far as I can see.' I sat back in my seat, suddenly feeling very tired. 'Besides, I think our chance to breathe has long gone.'

For a moment Tobias looked as if he cared something for what I was feeling. Then he remembered he was here to do the bidding of my jailer. He nodded and drained his mug. 'We should be getting back.'

33

A coach party of English students arrived at the hostel so I decided to go. I don't like sharing my space with anyone except my mother. When I said I was leaving, the man behind the desk looked slightly relieved.

The hotel I chose was little more than two hundred yards away, an austere grey guest house that went by the unlikely name of *The Sunshine Inn*. I think it was meant to be ironic.

The woman behind the desk, who would have been a young girl during the war, didn't look up as she handed me the key to my room. She did look up when I pushed a palmful of cash across the desk. She counted it and told me that breakfast was served between seven and nine.

The room was like the rest of the hotel: spartan and small. I didn't really care though; to be honest I don't like large rooms. They carry the echo of people, lots of people, and years on the run have left me with an aversion to echoes.

I spread my things out on the floor and made a space on the desk for Klein's notes. I counted the money that Bergström had given me, trying not to think that I'd taken blood money to betray my own family.

No.

I was going to use Bergström's money to prove Erik Brenna innocent.

Even though there was still the confession.

I lay on the bed and tried to think of the reasons someone would confess to something they hadn't done.

Madness? It seems to run in the family so it was certainly a possibility.

Money: someone paid him to confess. I couldn't imagine anyone being paid enough to confess to being a traitor. Besides, if it was money then where was it? My mother had never seen it.

No, he didn't do it for money. I picked up a notepad and started drawing absently on the first page.

There was always love.

What if someone he loved had betrayed Fólkvangr? What if he'd confessed to protect them? I didn't have to think long to come up with a name, someone he'd lay down his life for without hesitation or regret; someone for whom he'd sacrifice his future and his family. I looked at the pad. There was an outline of a swastika drawn on the centre of the page. I blinked at it, unsure if I'd drawn it, or it had always been there. As I tore out the sheet and ripped it to shreds, the phone rang.

'Settling in?'

I wasn't even surprised. 'What do you want?'

'I'm calling to see if there's anything you need.'

'I'm fine. Thank you.'

'Tobias seems to think you're straying from the path, as it were.'

I said nothing. This was his conversation; he only needed me to agree.

'Are you straying from the path, Miss Fossen?'

'No.'

'Good. That's very good. Now, is there anything else we can do for you?'

'I need information,' I said. 'I need to know everything you remember about the people of Fólkvangr.'

'There are libraries in Bergen,' he replied.

'I need to know what *you* remember. You were there; you knew them better than anyone else alive today.'

'And you need to know this because...?'

'If I understand the people better, I can work out who knew him; who would be most likely to help him. He didn't escape Norway on his own, and I think the same person is helping him stay hidden now.'

I could almost hear him thinking.

'Fine,' he said. 'I'll start with the Ohnstad family and work outwards.'

I folded my legs underneath me and waited eagerly with pencil poised.

Bergström was less self-assured when talking about his past. Most of the people he only half-remembered, a previous life he'd swept away so he could become the man he needed to be: a judge, a killer. He talked breathlessly and without inflection, without any sense of nostalgia or sorrow. Fólkvangr no longer existed; that was all there was to it.

The only time he came to life was when he talked about Silje Ohnstad. He described her from the knees upwards, oddly enough.

'Sturdy,' he said. 'Sound mountain stock.'

He made her sound like an alpaca, and he coughed constantly while he described the newsletter she ran with the blessing of the Nazis.

'We called it *The Quisling Orchid*,' he said. 'We didn't know any better. She was a magnificent woman, one of a kind.'

'She collaborated with the Germans.'

'She had little choice; I see that now. But as a child I was cruel to her, very cruel.'

I could imagine Bergström meeting her for the first time, running his bicycle into her, gazing at her face while she berated him for not looking where he was going. A small boy meeting his very own Norse goddess. How disappointed he would have been, how utterly destroyed, when he discovered she was writing a newsletter with the blessing of the local area commander.

'Then there was the girl of course,' he said, relieved to leave Silje in the past. 'The Jew. Her name was Freya. Don't remember her second name.' He sighed as though he were in pain. The effort of being the child again was taking its toll.

'Dorfmann,' I said. 'Freya Dorfmann.' Soon after Fólkvangr had fallen, it transpired the villagers had been hiding a young Jewish girl from the invaders. There was little written about her (the people of Fólkvangr were fastidious about keeping her existence to themselves), though it was known that she was dark-haired, truculent and quite blind.

'Yes, that sounds right.' Bergström said, and then did the oddest thing; he took two deep breaths in, as if inhaling from a scent bottle. 'Inseparable, the pair of them. If they weren't together it meant they were fighting, and then the village just stayed out of their way until they'd made up. My father said they were like an old married couple, only more so.' He tried to laugh, found he'd forgotten how. 'Walking hand in hand one day and then ignoring each other in the street the very next. They put the fear of women in me.'

'They held hands?'

'Not on purpose,' he said. 'They were close you see, like sisters. Their hands would just find each other.'

I gave him a few moments to catch up.

'Hah! I see what you are thinking. No, it was a different time then; women often held hands! So did men. They were sisters, Miss Fossen, in all but blood.'

I was with him in Fólkvangr now, so I couldn't stray too far from the orchid path.

'Let's just say for one moment,' I began, 'that Silje and this girl were… involved.'

He sniffed loudly. 'If you will.' He'd almost rediscovered his childhood only to have a softer part of it taken away. I wondered which of the women he'd harboured a longing for: Silje or Freya. I would have guessed Freya; her blindness would have lent her an attractive vulnerability, especially to a seven-year-old boy.

'If that is the case then well done, Miss Fossen,' he said. 'You have found something that historians have failed to uncover for almost thirty years.'

I told him I didn't understand.

'Your father's motive: betrayal.'

34

He was overjoyed, if there was such a thing for someone like him. There had been speculation of course. Survivors, psychologists, historians, psychics and other assorted liars – all had weighed in on my father's reasons for betraying the village. Mental illness, many believed, brought about by being separated from his parents at an impressionable age. One psychiatrist claimed that he may have suffered from an MPD – a multiple personality disorder – and may not have been aware of what he was doing. One woman claimed that his stars were out of balance at the time of the betrayal and if he'd seen an astrologer then more than two hundred souls could have been saved.

The survivors were the most heart-breaking. They appeared on television on each anniversary and wept, saying they didn't understand; they'd known Erik Brenna since he was a child.

And now, thanks to me, Norway had his motive: Silje Ohnstad, the love of his life, loved another.

I lay on the bed staring up at the light. Even I had to admit that it was the most poetic and most likely explanation. Jealousy, plain and simple. Case closed. He'd been betrayed so he betrayed everyone else, including his wife and his unborn daughter.

I stayed awake for most of the night, running through the notes again. There were gaps; I didn't know very much about General Gruetzmacher, except that during his service in Norway he became a hopeless drunk.

Freya Dorfmann was very much a mystery to me.

Jon Ohnstad was a nice man even if he was a bigamist. Bergström said that was very common back then and that I shouldn't judge yesterday by today's values. He said this even though he clearly disliked the idea of homosexuality, or perhaps he didn't enjoy his childhood memories turning round and scorning him.

Klein had underlined the word *Iscariot* in his notes related to Gruetzmacher but had written nothing further about it.

Iscariot, then Norway, then alcohol – that was the last thing I read before I finally fell asleep, only to be awoken twenty minutes later by a knock at the door. Ignoring everything Monica had ever taught me about knocks on doors, I opened it without checking the spy hole first.

'Oh,' I said, yawning. 'It's you.'

'Good morning to you too.' Tobias stepped inside without being asked.

'So you're the permanent go-between now, are you?'

He shrugged. 'He prefers the shadows. I think it's a thing he picked when he worked for MOSSAD. Have you got any coffee?'

I told him no and then asked if there was anything else.

'Not from our side. Is there anything else you need?'

'I don't think so. I've already proved my father did it so maybe I should just quit while I'm ahead.'

'You can't, not until you've found him.'

'Look, if Bergström's so friendly with the Israeli secret service then why the fuck does he need me?'

'What makes you think he tells me anything?' Tobias picked up the kettle and went through to the bathroom. 'He's always been the "need to know" sort and that's to your benefit as well as his. If you're caught then you can't tell them anything. If he's caught then you can deny knowing anything about it.'

If that was supposed to reassure me then it did exactly the opposite. What was I getting into that meant I should worry about getting caught? Tobias came back and plugged in the kettle. 'I don't suppose you have any lemon tea?'

I told him I'd already drunk all the lemon tea. He settled for a camomile. 'What's really bothering you, Brigit?'

'I'm running errands for a mass murderer, and you have to ask.'

'He kills Nazis, no one else.'

'He wants to kill my father, and he's not a Nazi.'

'He's a traitor, and that's a hundred times worse.'

'He didn't do it.'

'He confessed.'

'He confessed to protect someone.'

He stopped drinking his tea and raised both eyebrows. 'Now, this is a new twist. Who?' But he didn't need an answer. 'You need to leave Silje Ohnstad out of this. She's a fucking hero, and you're... well, you're you.'

'I want to speak to Bergström.'

'You can speak to him as much as you like after I'm gone.' He reached into his jacket and took out a large white envelope. 'Your pictures from Fólkvangr. Let him know if you find anything useful. Thanks for the tea.'

After he'd left I opened the envelope and spread the photographs across the bureau. There was a magnifying glass inside; I wasn't sure if Bergström was trying to be helpful or sarcastic. I sat down and began examining each picture, without having much of an idea what I was looking for. Silje Ohnstad was in almost every one; it was as if she'd snapped her fingers one day and a whole village sprang from nowhere to give her life an attractive backdrop. I discarded most of the photographs quickly, but kept coming back to the last moments of Josef Kleppe.

I looked closely at Silje embracing her lover, both their dresses stained with the old man's blood. Even without the magnifying glass I could see where Kleppe's head had struck the stone monument as he fell. One of the stones had been dislodged and his blood had stained its lower edge. I guessed that the stone had come free and someone had replaced it upside down, though it seemed a strange thing to do while someone lay dying in the street. I looked again at Silje Ohnstad and decided that perhaps it wasn't so strange. Everything I've read about her said she loved the monument as much as she loved her mother. But if she was so callous as to fix the stones while Josef Kleppe expired on the ground then surely she would have made a better job of it. I realised that Tobias was right about being focussed. I had documents, notebooks, photographs and God knows what else, but not a clue what to do with any of it. Most of the stuff didn't make any sense to me, and even while I was trying to understand it there was a little voice inside my head repeating the single inescapable truth:

He confessed.

And that was all that mattered.

I thought about calling Bergström, telling him he might as well kill me now. Erik Brenna was as guilty as they come, but I wasn't going to deliver my father to a serial killer. I picked up the phone and it rang in my hand. The receptionist connected me, and an unwelcome voice ruined my morning.

'Miss Fossen.'

I hated it when he called me that. 'Well, this is a surprise. Your delivery boy only left an hour ago.'

'Yes, he called me. He said that you perhaps needed an incentive.'

'What I need is for you to leave me alone.'

'Fortunately, I foresaw this weakening in your resolve so I have taken steps.'

I could hear things in the background: bottles rattling, people talking, wheels creaking under dead weight. At first I thought he was in a bar, but then I heard someone say *anthracycline*. I felt my heart sink to my stomach. I asked him where he was, even though I already knew.

'Someone would like to speak to you.' The line crackled as he handed the phone to someone else.

'Brigit?' Her voice was quiet, frightened.

'Doctor Nese. Are you all right? Has he—'

'He hasn't done anything.'

'Is he alone?'

'There are five people with him. One of them is carrying flowers, which is a lovely touch, don't you think?'

Someone told her to be careful with her answers.

'Thank you for remodelling my apartment by the way.'

I said I was sorry. 'I was angry. I thought—'

'I'm the one who should be sorry. Wish you hadn't knocked holes in the walls though. The plasterer was curious; what did you use?'

'Claw hammer.'

'I didn't even know I had one of those. How did you find it?'

I wiped my eyes. 'I was looking for money.'

'Right. Well, water under the bridge.' I could hear it wasn't.

'Brigit, they want me to tell you that your mother is here.'

The world slowed to a halt.

'Mr Bergström found her living on the streets, not too far from the hospital. He and his associates brought her back.'

'Kicking and screaming.'

'Well, she thought he was going to kill her.'

'Can I speak to her?'

Someone whispered in her ear.

'No,' she said. 'Sorry, not yet.'

Bergström took the phone from her, and spoke quietly. 'As you can see, I have done you something of a service. I am hoping you will return the favour.'

'I want to speak to her.'

'All in good time.'

'I want to speak to her now.'

'Oh, it's not me; it's her. She doesn't want to speak to you.'

'You're lying.'

'Perhaps she thinks you betrayed her to me. After all, you are helping me exact justice from her husband.'

'Is that what you told her? Put her on the phone!'

'As I said, all in good time. Now, how are you progressing?'

I answered promptly. 'You need to find someone else.'

'There is no one else. There was; now there's only you.'

'I've never done this before; I have no idea where to begin.'

'You have already begun. You have gathered information. The answer to his whereabouts is somewhere on that desk.'

He was still watching me. The curtains were drawn, so there was a camera somewhere in the room.

'I have some advice for you,' he said. 'The key to any investigation is to look at the information and find what doesn't fit. You say your father didn't do it? Then the first thing that doesn't fit is his confession. The answer is in the things that don't make sense.'

He hung up the phone, thinking he'd helped me.

I cried for one minute and then twisted a pinch of skin on my arm because Monica wasn't there to do it for me. I had a shower, called room service and ordered a round of sandwiches and four bottles of water.

Then I started reading the notes again, from the very beginning.

35

Look for things that don't fit.

I stayed up for the rest of the night, slowly reading everything Klein had left me. I wrote things down, thought about them, crossed them off and wrote something else.

Things that didn't fit.

Gruetzmacher was top of my list. He was anointed by Hitler himself; after Iscariot – whatever that was – he could have gone anywhere under the shadow of the Reich. He could have had his pick of commands but he chose a small harbour town in Norway. That didn't fit.

And according to Klein's notes his real decline into madness and alcoholism began soon after meeting Silje Ohnstad. He was in love with her, obviously. And his love for her destroyed him. But that didn't make sense. He had a family, he was renowned as a formidable tactician and an exemplary leader of men. On the other hand he was a scientist who believed in witchcraft – and a paedophile.

Yes, Gruetzmacher was top of my list of things that didn't fit.

The next misfit was a little closer to home: Bergström. He had resources, access to money and manpower. He was still working for MOSSAD so why did he need me? With the Israeli Secret Service at his back he could have dispatched my father years ago; he hadn't. Why?

I rolled this over in my head while I showered, brushed my teeth and checked the holes where my wisdom teeth used to be. I thought about calling the hospital and talking to Doctor Nese. I sat down at the desk and munched my way slowly through three packets of biscuits.

Bergström hadn't killed Erik Brenna because he knew he was innocent.

Ridiculous.

But unlike everything else, it seemed to fit.

I called Dagrun to make sure she was all right, and to put things right. She answered straight away, almost as if the phone was already next to her ear.

'Brigit?'

'I'm sorry about your apartment. It was stupid and selfish and I shouldn't have done it. I wish I hadn't. You're the only person who has ever been kind to me.'

'Oh Brigit, I'm sure that's not true.'

'Don't patronise me. It *is* true. You're my only friend and I don't want you to stop being that, so I'm sorry. I'll get a job and I'll pay for the damage.'

'Twenty thousand Krone?'

Shit. That's a lot. 'I don't know; I'll find the money.'

'You don't have to.'

'I want to. If we're going to be friends then I have to—'

'We can't be friends, and it's not about the apartment. It wouldn't be right. I'm your mother's doctor and—'

'Then fuck you.'

'Excuse me?'

It's funny how you can hear yourself saying things that you think are hurting other people when you know, deep down, you're just gutting yourself. 'You heard me.'

She hung up; I would have too.

I wanted to hit my head against the desk. In the end I punished myself with a cold shower which I took with my clothes on.

I gave her another hour to forgive me and then I tried calling her again. She didn't pick up so I tried once more and gave up. I didn't know what I was going to say anyway. Instead I called Bergström.

'Yes?'

'I need something.'

'Go on.'

'I need you to find Iscariot for me.'

He was silent for a few moments, then he said, 'Iscariot?'

'Yes. There's nothing in here about it. All it says is that Gruetzmacher came to Norway from Iscariot. You asked me to look for things that didn't fit. Gruetzmacher was a career soldier used to fighting on the front lines. He was a glory hound so why would he settle for Norway?'

'You make it sound as though Norway was a pushover. I can assure you, Miss Fossen, that—'

'The Germans didn't expect us to give them a bloody nose. So if Gruetzmacher thought Norway would fall into line, then why would he waste his time coming here?'

'Unless?'

'Unless he came here for some other reason aside from the war. He was looking for something. If I trace back through his life then maybe I can figure out what it was and why he came here to get it.'

'It sounds like a waste of time.'

'I don't think it is and I don't think you think so either, because here's something else that doesn't make sense, Mr Bergström: you.'

He didn't say anything; he just waited for me to make an even bigger fool of myself. 'You could have found my father yourself, years ago. You didn't and I know why.'

'Surprise me, Miss Fossen.'

'Because you don't think he did this either.'

Again the silence; I waited for him to tell me what my life would be like now that I'd confronted him, disappointed him, laid out the truth as I saw it or how I wanted it to be. He could hound me across Norway. He could crush me. He could kill me.

I don't think I'd ever felt more alive.

'I will find you the information on Iscariot,' he said, and then he was gone without another word. I exhaled and almost passed out. I'd looked inside Jesper Bergström and I wasn't sure if that made me very brave or extraordinarily stupid.

36

That night I dreamed of Nazis and orchids and saw my father hanging from an oak tree. I woke at eight, exhausted and drenched in my own sweat.

I got dressed and went downstairs for breakfast. I managed a coffee, which I barely tasted, and left the rest untouched. The dining room started to shrink away from me, and I could feel a vein in my neck pulsing so hard it hurt.

I had to get back to Trondheim.

I needed to fix things with my mother and Dagrun. I needed to see them and make sure they were both okay.

I went back upstairs, packed all my things, and returned to settle the bill.

Outside the hotel, Jesper Bergström was waiting for me.

He was alone as far as I could tell, a huge man who curved his spine to tower over me. His eyes pierced me like needles; his stature, his presence – honed to make me believe he could kill me with a whisper.

'Your mother is fine,' he said, and then as an afterthought, he tried a smile.

It made my blood freeze.

'You didn't have to do that. You didn't have to threaten them.'

'You needed an incentive.' The smile didn't fade; I wished it would. He cast his eye over my rucksack, but didn't ask me where I was going. 'She's back at the hospital now, instead of dying in a gutter somewhere. In many ways I've done you both a favour.'

He said it without a trace of irony. If I hadn't been so terrified I would have laughed.

'A favour? She'll think I betrayed her, betrayed my father.'

'Then once this is over you can go back and tell her how wrong she is.'

And there was the irony.

When I was very young, Monica told me that Cleaver was a dwarf troll, that he could make himself as big as a house, that he didn't need to sleep and that he would materialise as soon as a child disobeyed its mother.

I wondered how he'd travelled here so fast.

'I have something for you.' He handed me a small envelope and quickly put his hand back in his pocket. Was he armed? I didn't know. Probably.

'What is this?' I said. 'I asked for stuff about Iscariot.'

'You did.' His cheek twitched; the smile was wearing him out.

'This can't be all of it.'

'It isn't,' he said. 'It's none of it, in fact.'

I tore open the envelope and pulled out a small long booklet stuffed with slips of thin paper. I must've looked confused because he sighed loudly.

'It's a plane ticket. No one in the Norwegian government will talk to us about Iscariot, so I had to contact friends further afield.'

'Where am I going?' I said.

'Germany. Dresden to be precise. There's a man there who will tell you all about it if you ask him nicely. You do know how to ask nicely don't you, Miss Fossen?'

'I can't,' I said. 'I can't go to Germany, not right now. Just give me a few days in Trondheim, then I'll go anywhere you—'

His smile vanished, and I was oddly grateful it had.

So, Germany then.

The Quisling Orchid

(9th September 1941)

My fellow Norwegians.
I have no doubt many of you feel that certain rules are curtailing the personal freedoms we were promised when the military first invaded landed. It is unfortunate that the activities of the Resistance makes these measures necessary for the safety of law-abiding Norwegians everywhere.

The German High Command are still seeking traitors for the attack on Bergen headquarters on the night of March 15th. This cowardly incursion resulted in the deaths of nine German soldiers including the Area Commander's driver. As you will remember, General Gruetzmacher ordered the immediate detention of three hundred Norwegian men between the ages of sixteen and forty as part of a measured response to this atrocity. Many were released within days but those who could not (or would not) account for their whereabouts at the time of the attack were transported to detentions centres in Poland and Germany.

Our friends the Germans reiterate that substantial rewards will be offered for information leading to the capture or killing of any member of the Norwegian Resistance. In addition to this, a separate reward fund has been initiated specifically for the capture of any Resistance member who proves capable of breaking encoded messages, especially those messages used to plan the March 15th attack.

So before I begin with our regular editorial, I have been asked to remind you of the governance laws that our friends the Germans have put in place for our own protection:

1.
The curfew rules must be respected, no excuses. Any Norwegian found on the streets after 8pm will be subject to summary execution.

2.
Congregations are illegal. A congregation, under German law, is a gathering of three or more people. Any Norwegians found contravening this law will be subject to punishment, including possible execution.

3.
I should not have to remind you again, but it is illegal to stand on public transport when there are seats available, which brings me to:

4.
Non-fraternization with German military personnel is illegal and contravening this law may result in punitive measures up to and including execution. If a member of the German peace-keeping force engages in conversation then you must respond in a polite and friendly manner.

I regret to inform you that once again our regular recipe and domestic hints section has been cancelled to make way for news regarding the capture and transportation of Jews.

However, friends, it does bring me great delight to deliver the most exciting news in the history of this humble newsletter. Our illustrious First Minister, Vidkun Quisling, will be staying in Bergen during his tour of the region in the coming weeks. The exact dates will be posted to all the towns in the next day or two, and our German friends expect everyone to take to the streets to greet him. Keep your diaries open!

Now, before I leave you, I would like to thank all the well-wishers from Fólkvangr and beyond who have prayed for my brother's rapid recovery. Thank you, friends, for your thoughts and kind words, and I offer the same to the many others who have fallen ill in a similar fashion since the events of March 15th.

37

When Jesper Bergström kicked open the door to Jon Ohnstad's barn, he found Silje Ohnstad had not throttled the life from Freya Dorfmann as his young imagination had led him to believe. Instead, he discovered Silje standing inside, gazing up into the rafters, one hand holding her dress at her waist, the other laced tightly through Freya's hair. Freya knelt in front of her, holding her firm by her wide, white hips.

Jesper froze on the spot, unable to comprehend this new, terrible form of Nazi humiliation Freya was being forced to endure. His eyes searched the twilight for a tool he could use as a weapon…

'Jesper Bergström!' Silje screamed. She stumbled back, crushing her father's prize flowers, trying to pull her dress down over her knees. 'What do you think you are doing?'

Freya cried out in surprise and jumped to her feet. 'It is very ungentlemanly to spy on people, Jesper,' she said, trying to keep her voice soft. She wiped the heel of her hand back and forth across her mouth, much as she does, Jesper thought, after we share an orange. Her actions on this occasion seemed more frantic, somewhat shamed… He thought perhaps the traitor had given her the orange and Freya had chosen to share it with her, instead of him.

This betrayal – from the woman whom he fully intended to marry when he reached the weathered age of twelve – was almost too much to bear. He swallowed, tears in his eyes. 'I thought she would do you harm so I came to save you.'

'My God, this again! How many times—' Silje tried frantically to fasten the buttons on her dress. Her hands were trembling.

'Silje, please.' Freya turned to face the sound of Jesper's breathing. 'I have said this to you before, Jesper. Silje is my friend, my very best friend, and she would never—'

'You said I was your best friend.'

'Did I?'

'Yes,' Silje said sourly, 'did you?'

'On your birthday you put your hands on my face because you said I was your best friend and you wanted to remember what all your friends looked like.'

'Oh.'

'She is not your best friend.' He pointed a small thin finger at Silje. 'She has betrayed Fólkvangr. She will betray you.'

'Jesper, that is a horrible thing to say.'

'I do not care! It is true!'

'I will tell your father, Jesper!' Silje said, shaking her own finger in his face. 'I shall tell him what a mean and hateful little man you have become. I shall tell him that you should join Quisling's youth movement because that is where spiteful little men belong.'

'Silje, he's just a boy.'

'I am not a boy!'

'Why are you defending him? He follows us everywhere we go, spying on us.'

'Because he is…' Freya hunted desperately for the right word, 'young!'

'Junges Fehn was young once.' Silje folded her arms and glared at Jesper. 'And look how he turned out.'

Jesper stood next to Freya for safety's sake and announced again that he wasn't afraid. 'The others may fear you, Silje, but I do not.'

'Others? What others?'

Freya put her arm around Jesper and pleaded for calm, but young Jesper was having none of it. 'The other boys. They know what you do to men in the village. We have seen you drag them into grain stores and barns, and when they emerge they look as though they have been mauled by mountain trolls! You are a witch and you leach the will from men as soon as they come of age! Mr Fehn told me and he would not lie!'

If Silje could have done so without Freya knowing she would have struck him. Her rage grew, making her skin burn and setting needles in the soles of her feet. She let forth a barrage of profanities that would have made the most hardened men of the mountain blush. Jesper Bergström closed his eyes tightly to hide from the maelstrom, and despite what he whispered to himself he was very much afraid.

Freya stood in front of him, shielding him, lest the love of her life should lose herself completely.

Silje finished her tirade with a flourish. '... So fuck the Germans, fuck the men of Fólkvangr, and most of all fuck you and all your hateful little friends, Jesper Bergström!' And finally she was spent and left gasping as her anger subsided.

Jesper saw his chance; he pushed Freya away and ran from the barn.

'That was cruel, Silje!' Freya said. 'It was cruel and spiteful! How could you say such things to a small child? Did you not see how frightened he was?' She turned her back on her and Silje realised she could no longer taste cinnamon in the air.

'And now you hate me.'

'It is not that,' Freya replied. 'There are just sides of you I care not to know.' She sniffed the air and found the entrance to the barn. She took three steps and then hesitated.

'Go after him,' said Silje, her heart scalded by Freya's words, as it often was of late. 'Tell him I'm sorry.'

'We should tell him together.'

'No, I must see to Magnus. He has been alone for too long.'

'We stand a better chance of finding him if we go together.'

Silje found her undergarments buried in the hay. She stared at them and wondered what she was doing with Freya – this blind Jewish girl whom she'd taken in as a sister.

What is this thing that you think you are doing?

'You do not need me to find one small boy, Freya; we both know that,' she said, and left her alone in the orchid barn.

* * *

Silje walked the two-hundred-and-fifty steps back to the cottage, a distance she'd measured frequently since she was a child. Still two-hundred-and-fifty steps; perhaps the distance had lengthened over the years to keep pace with her stride.

There was a time not so very long ago when the merest thought of Freya would parch her throat, set the blood pounding in her head. There was a time, not so very long ago, when they would make room in the barn so they could plunder each other to exhaustion and then lie still, dazed by the scent of orchids and cinnamon exuding from their skin.

And now our love seems almost like a stage play, she thought, *as mechanical as ploughing a meadow*. She still enjoyed Freya, but the greyness of the war had spread to them, turned them to stone.

She pushed open the cottage door and went to the pot on the stove. The pot was still full, which meant her father had not been home that day. Silje ladled four large spoonfuls into a bowl and tore two strips of bread from the roll. She carried them upstairs on a tray and knocked on Magnus's door. After a few moments she knocked again and said his name gently.

'Wait, I am not ready!' He sounded alarmed, anxious, which surprised her; she had grown accustomed to not hearing him speak at all.

'Do not be silly, Magnus.'

'Just wait, damn you!'

Silje stepped away from the door and put the tray on the floor. 'Are you all right?'

'I'm not ready!'

She could hear him turning over his room. *He's lost it again*, she thought. She promised herself she would get Freya to make him two more.

She waited, worrying that the soup would grow cold. 'I'm coming in, Magnus.'

'No! Not yet!'

She opened the door and dipped her head to avoid a vase thrown from the other side of the room. It sailed out into the hallway and shattered against the wall.

'I told you to stay out!'

Magnus stood in front of her, naked, covering his face with both his hands, his thin, grey body crossed through with scars and burns. When she looked at his hands, at the scarred and puckered remains of his right thumb, her heart broke.

'I will help you find it,' she said. 'Just stay there.'

'No! Get out!'

He would have thrown something else, his chamber pot perhaps, but he would need to remove his hands from his face to do so. She got down on her knees and ran her hand under the bed. On her fourth sweep she felt a thin leather strap beneath her little finger. 'Ah! I have it!' She got to her feet and offered the eyepatch to him. 'Here, take it.'

'Just leave it on the bed and get out.'

'No. You must take it from me.'

'Do you not have better things to do than torment me? There must be a man in this village you have not whored yourself out to. Why not hunt him down and leave me in peace?'

He was cruel these days, without pattern or reason. His self-loathing cast outward, engulfing all those he had once loved.

'Take it from me.'

'I hate you.'

'I know. Now take it from me.'

He snarled and lurched towards her, reaching for the eyepatch with his fingers clawed. Silje grabbed his wrist and pulled his mutilated hand away from his face. He fought, but his weakened limbs were no match for her.

'Is this what you want to see, dear sister?' he said.

Silje breathed deeply and swallowed back her revulsion. *It is still with me*, she thought, *and it is so long since he was returned to us.*

His single eye swivelled wildly in its socket. Silje forced herself to stare into the scarred hole where his other eye had been. It had been been a paler blue, she remembered; an aberration – much like her own.

His face, like his body, was sectioned by scars cut deep with the point of a combat knife, a smaller, broken Doctor Lomen had said. He had treated many such injuries since Magnus had been taken outside the Nazi HQ in Bergen. The Resistance stung and bit the invaders like hornets, picking their targets and then escaping into the night. Casualties mounted, the doctor had said; fathers and sons lost, and the invaders venting their anger on the people of Norway.

While she stared, Magnus snatched his eyepatch from her and slipped it into place. 'Why must you do that?' he asked. 'It serves neither of us.' He used his first and second finger where he would have used his thumb. He becomes more adept, Silje thought, though he tries not to.

'If you were stronger,' she said, 'then you could take your things from me without such a fuss.'

He sniffed and turned away from her to look at the field outside his window.

'I will leave the soup and the bread here; please eat it. If not for yourself then for me.' Magnus remained frozen on the spot, his hands clasped and trembling behind his back, his soul shrouded in despair.

'Who is that?' he snapped. Silje listened but heard nothing.

Magnus reached under his pillow, and when Silje turned to face him again he was holding a Luger in his hand.

There was a creak on the staircase and a voice, quiet and fearful, said, 'It is just me, Magnus. I have come to see you.'

'Go away, Freya; I wish to see no one.' As he said this he looked sternly at Silje. 'No one.'

The staircase creaked again and Magnus roared, 'Just fuck off! Both of you!'

Silje chewed her lip and looked at the pistol. He could fire it, she thought. Between the weakness in his limbs and his missing thumb, the shot could go anywhere; even if he did not mean to hit Freya, he could. She hurried from the room, closing the door behind her. She met Freya in the hallway and took her by the elbow to lead her downstairs.

Freya protested. 'I want to see him!'

'He does not wish to see you and we will do as he wishes.' Silje sat her down at the kitchen table. She ladled soup into two bowls, and placed a spoon in Freya's left hand and a strip of bread in the right.

'I'm not hungry.'

'Yes you are. Eat your soup.' Silje swallowed a spoonful and chewed slowly on the bread. They ate in the kind of silence she hated: the absence of words born not of fatigue or anger, but of a slow, creeping resentment. After a such short time together they had run dry of things to say. *It is the war*, Silje told herself; *it is just the war*.

'Did you find Jesper?'

Freya nodded. 'He had not gone far. He was waiting at the copse near the foot of the path.'

'And how was he?'

'Upset.'

'I will apologise.'

'I think you should.'

And then silence fell upon them again. Silje ladled more soup into Freya's bowl just to hear the spoon rattle. 'Did he see us?'

'Did he see us what?' Freya asked plainly.

'You know what I mean.'

'Yes, we both know what you mean, and still you cannot bring yourself to say it, can you?'

'Why is it you are so set on hearing it all the time?'

'Because you never say it at all.'

Silje looked to the stairs. She wondered if the door to Magnus's room had opened and that perhaps she had missed it.

'You are looking for Magnus, aren't you?' Freya said. 'You are afraid he will hear us.'

'I am not afraid of anything.'

'We both know that is not true.'

And now Silje found herself longing for the silence.

'I shall say it for you, shall I? You want to know if Jesper saw us making love in your father's barn.'

Silje chewed savagely at her lower lip and nodded.

'If you nod or shake your head I will not know what you are saying.'

'Yes! For God's sake! Did he see us?'

Freya pushed her bowl to the centre of the table. 'He did. He thought you were torturing me.'

'What did you tell him?'

She hesitated.

'Well?'

'I told him you had a rash and you'd asked me to examine it.'

'You told him…'

'I said it was a rash.'

'What kind of rash?'

'I did not say. Is it important?'

'Did he believe you?'

'I think he wanted to.'

Silje decided that there were worse lies she could have told, though the idea of the village thinking she'd contracted some sort of skin disease… Yes, there were worse lies but also some that would have been far, far better. Perhaps Freya had meant to punish her. 'Are you angry with me?'

'No.'

Then she is, Silje thought. She pushed her own bowl aside and took Freya's hands in hers. 'If there is something I have done that makes you hate me then tell me and I will make amends. If there is a part of me that you dislike then tell me and I will change. And please don't tell me that it is Jesper or the war. I am not the war and neither are you.'

Freya drew her hand away. 'When will you tell Erik?'

An angry sigh escaped Silje's lips in spite of her best effort to prevent it.

'He still believes that you and he are to be married.'

'Yes, he does, I know. And I will tell him when the time is right. And do not ask me when that will be because I do not know.'

Freya stared over Silje's left shoulder with tears in her pale eyes, and in a moment of yearning Silje wondered why God would grant her such beautiful eyes and then steal from her the blessing of sight.

'I promised I would never ask,' Freya said quietly.

'But you still want to know.'

She nodded. 'So that I know that one day we can be together.'

'We are together.'

'You are hiding behind clever words.'

'I am not.'

'You are.'

She will not be swayed. 'Soon, Freya; very soon. I should have told him on your birthday but since then I have had so much to think about: looking after Magnus, the newsletter…'

'Yes, always the damned newsletter.'

'It is important, Freya. Gunther says it is vital to the Resistance effort.'

'I am sure,' Freya said plainly.

'Do not be like this.' Silje reached across the table and tried again to take her hand. 'It is still warm outside. We can go back to the orchid barn.'

'Why?' Freya snatched her hand away. 'So you can fuck me in darkness where you cannot see me?'

'Freya!'

'Do you look at me, Silje? When you put your tongue in my mouth and your hand between my legs? Do you look at me or do you close your eyes so you do not have to bear witness to our sin?'

Though she opened her mouth to speak Silje took far too long to reply.

'Yes, that is what I thought.' Freya stood up. 'I said I would love you, even if you put Erik and others—'

'Why do you keep saying "others"? There are no others!'

'—even if you put Erik and others before me. I meant it, Silje; I will always love you, but if you are ashamed of what we do, of what we are, then that is something I cannot bear.'

'I will tell Magnus this very night if that is what you want.'

Freya closed her eyes. 'My father,' she began. 'My father did not give me away. They tortured him. They cut his fingers from him one by one, and still he did not betray me while I lay snivelling a few inches below his feet.'

'He loved you,' said Silje, 'as I love you.'

'They kept shouting at him. "Do you know if there are any other

Jews? Tell us and we will kill you quickly! Where will we find more of your filth. That is what you are: a filthy Jew. Say it! Say that you are a filthy Jew."

'But he did not, Silje. He did not give me up and he would not dishonour himself before our God. There are thousands, millions, of us who will be called to stand proudly before the Star of David before we are cut down. Do you understand?'

Silje nodded, cursed herself and said yes, she understood. When she looked again Freya was opening the door. 'I will wait my place, behind Erik, but I will not live in shame; I will not hide away. I am going home, Silje. Do not come after me.'

'I will not.'

Freya smiled in a way that seemed cold and pitying to Silje; she did not care for it, or the feeling of shame and helplessness it brought with it.

Freya closed the door, and Silje heard herself whisper, 'You are home.'

38

At night, Magnus Ohnstad screamed.

His torment had begun on the evening of Freya's birthday, the same night they'd brought him home to the care of Doctor Lomen.

Doctor Lomen who tended Magnus's ruined eye and broken fingers, while Magnus wept and told him that his sons had been killed during an attempt to assassinate a Nazi area commander.

Doctor Lomen who salved his burns, saved his left thumb and treated the remains of his right.

Doctor Lomen who set his shattered bones and wept as he repaired his torn flesh.

Doctor Lomen who sent his wife back to her family and shut his door on the world.

Doctor Lomen who could do nothing to restore Magnus's shattered mind, much less his own.

And so at night, Magnus Ohnstad screamed, while Silje sat in her room making copious, tear-stained notes.

'He said nothing.' She slid the notepad across the table. 'The same as last night, and the same as the night before.'

Gunther smiled at Grette who watched them intently from behind the bar. 'This is not me,' he said. 'It is London.'

'They think my brother is a traitor.'

'They think no such thing. We just need to know if he—'

'Broke?' Silje said without taking her eyes from his.

'No one would blame him, Silje, but we need to know what he told them.'

'And Gruetzmacher wonders what he knows about you. How special he must feel.' She tapped a fingernail on the stack of papers. 'It is all there: every cry of agony; every plea for mercy. He endured, Gunther. He did not betray you or the Resistance. Do you think you we would be sitting here if he had?'

Gunther ducked his head as though a pistol had been fired. He looked around the tavern; it was empty save for a woman and two men playing cards in the far corner, and Grette at the bar, pretending she did not hear.

'Silje, please. Lower your voice!'

'He did not betray you, Gunther, so it is time to decide.' She said nothing more, unwilling to push him one way or the other. She watched Grette set two jars of ale on the table and then quickly return to the bar, keen to escape the cloud of misfortune that followed the Ohnstad name.

'And you are sure,' Gunther said.

'I am sure.'

'Then we should go ahead?'

'Are you asking me?'

'No, I suppose I'm not.' He drained his mug and wiped his mouth. 'I shall contact London and recommend we continue.' He took a notepad from his bag and began scribbling. 'I shall need you to use this paragraph in the next editorial. I do not suppose you can convince the General to release *The Orchid* before next week.'

'I cannot convince him to do anything these days.'

Gunther stopped writing and looked up at her. He placed his pencil gently on the table. 'Does he still… hurt you?'

Silje shrugged. 'He tries, but it is not me he seeks to hurt, which is a small comfort I suppose.'

'What do you mean?'

'While he does these things he pretends I am someone else. I see it in his eyes; they look at someone far away, much further away than Bergen.'

'Berlin, perhaps.' Gunther tapped his teeth.

'Perhaps.'

'Is it his wife he hates?'

'No.' Silje pushed her ale towards him, her thirst having left her. 'There was a Jewish girl. He forced himself upon her. I think it is the child. I think I remind him of the child.' When she looked up, Gunther had already finished the second jar. A second jar of Norway's finest courage, she thought, and wondered what terrible sacrifice he was about to ask of her.

He stared at a small stained ring on the table. 'We need to know as much as we can about Quisling's movements when he is here. If you can get the General to talk while he is... while he...'

'While he touches me,' Silje said mildly.

Gunther nodded, his head bowed.

'I will do what I can.' She rose from the table and took Gunther's notebook. He reached out and squeezed her hand. 'England thanks you, Silje, for your sacrifice. And Norway will remember you for your courage.'

'Oh I have no doubt Norway will remember me,' she said, 'but not for this.'

'You will be a hero; you'll see.'

She took her hand from him. 'There is something you can do for me.'

'Name it.'

'Gruetzmacher intends to follow Quisling like a lapdog while he is in the region. When you kill Quisling it is likely that the General will be close by.'

Gunther smiled. It was the same humourless smile she often saw Gruetzmacher wearing, but she liked it better on the spy.

'I'm sure we can spare a second bullet,' he said.

'I don't want you to kill him,' Silje said. 'I want him to live. I want him disgraced in front of his men and his emperor.'

'If that is what you want.'

'That is all I want.'

39

Since Magnus had been returned, silenced and broken, a small detachment of German soldiers had been stationed permanently in the village. They had arrived the day after the attempt on Gruetzmacher's life.

The soldiers had presented their orders to the village elders and then quickly commandeered two of the farm outbuildings belonging to Junges Fehn.

'I am sure they are not supposed to do this,' Fehn had complained. The soldiers wandered freely in and out of his kitchen at all hours of the day and night, helping themselves to his milk and his ale.

The General had told Silje that the soldiers, never more than five, never less than two, were there for her protection.

'If they tried to kill me as an officer of the Reich,' he'd said, 'then they may come for you.'

Silje was sure that if this were true then the soldiers would be stationed at the Ohnstad cottage, not on the other side of the village.

The detachment brought a staff car with them, smaller than Gruetzmacher's replacement and without a roof to keep out the cold – or bulletproofing to stave off an ambush. Every Tuesday morning, one of the soldiers would drive Silje to Reich HQ in Bergen which was now a fortress that rivalled anything the Axis had built in Berlin. There, Silje would be treated to a sumptuous breakfast after which she and the General would discuss the upcoming issue of *The Quisling Orchid.* There would be a light lunch followed by a walk around the gardens. Gruetzmacher would tell her what life would be like once the Reich ruled all and the Semite menace had been expunged from existence.

'All will be as it should be,' he'd say, picking a single flower from one of the boxes underneath the windows. He would take the flower and stand it in a glass of water on his writing desk. Sometimes he would pick a rose; sometimes he would choose one of the orchids grown from the stock gifted by her father. Silje could tell his mood by the flower he'd chosen, and this, in turn, would speak of her suffering that afternoon: a rose, and she would be given a basket of fruit and bread and sent back to Fólkvangr; but sometimes the General picked an orchid.

How she hated his orchid days.

'Face the wall and raise your dress, if you please.'

On some of the orchid days she refused, and he would become angry; she could hear his teeth grinding behind his smile. He would shout, he would bellow, but he would never lay a hand upon her. On these days she was something delicate, something despised.

On the other days her defiance seemed to please him. His smile would be thin and weak. He would say 'As you wish,' and he would send her on her way without her basket of fruit.

But on some of the orchid days Silje would acquiesce. She would remove her undergarments, hold her skirt about her waist and place her free hand against the wall.

'Part your feet, Fräulein.'

She would close her eyes and listen while he slipped his hand inside a glove. She would whisper 'For the Resistance, for Norway' again and again inside her head, feeling his hand upon her shoulder and the chill of his breath against her skin.

His fingers were cold, like serpents, penetrating, searching…

He would press her head to the wall and whisper into her hair: express his gratitude for her compliance, tell her she was perfection itself.

And Silje would cast her eyes downward, see the pearls of her emission falling between her feet; she would think her body had betrayed her – had betrayed all of Norway.

When he was done, the General would return to his desk and write his notes in a journal stamped with Silje's name. She would wait, with her fist against the wall, for the sound of rustling pages and the scratch of lead on paper. If she turned too quickly their eyes would meet and the General would feel compelled to explain himself.

'It is research,' he would say, 'just research, for the good of both our races.'

And his eyes would implore her to believe him.

Silje endured this because on the orchid days Gruetzmacher's defences were at their weakest and he would often reveal the secrets he kept closest to his soul.

'When Quisling comes,' the General said on one particularly brutal day, 'he would like to meet you.' He stripped off his glove and threw it into the box labelled *medizinische Abfälle*.

Silje allowed herself to breathe. She opened her eyes and stood straight, thinking, as she often did, that if Gruetzmacher's experiments were sanctioned then the box would be adorned with the *Reichsadler*.

Instead he had labelled the box himself, in charcoal.

She dressed quickly, though she wanted to bathe, to wash away the stench of him.

The General settled into an armchair and mopped his brow with a handkerchief. 'The *Quisling Orchid* has drawn favour with the *Nasjonal Samling*, and so naturally, the idiot Quisling wishes to be more closely associated with our endeavours.'

'I thought the Reich supported him.'

The General lit a cigarette. 'Oh we do. Though in many respects he has failed in his promise.' He picked out a notebook, one of many, twenty in all.

'And what promise was that?'

'To deliver Norway to us without fuss, without all this mess.' He inhaled and tapped the cigarette on the side of the armchair. 'We thought allowing one of your own countrymen to govern would facilitate the transition.'

'It has not?'

'No,' the General said. 'It has not. You Norwegians fight against insurmountable odds, and with a tenacity I have not encountered in any other theatre of combat.'

Silje asked if she could sit in the chair across from him. Gruetzmacher nodded, watching her as she sat on the edge of the seat with her knees turned away.

'The Resistance has become a hindrance to our efforts here, and nothing he says in his broadcasts or his speeches has any notable effect on public opinion. In fact, Fräulein,' he said, 'it is my belief that most Norwegians hate him more than they hate us.'

She wondered if this were true.

'It does not matter.' He leaned back in his armchair and tried again to smile. 'This country will break one way or another. The only question is, should the Reich continue to squander resources on this fool.'

He stared at her with steady, unblinking eyes. Silje realised he was waiting for her to answer him. With little time to think, the best she could manage was, 'I am sure the Reich knows best.'

The General shrugged. 'I am not sure we do anymore. The Norway situation is... perplexing. For the moment, Quisling fills a vacuum until someone more effective emerges from the fouled pool of the *Nasjonal Samling.*' He chuckled to himself; Silje had no idea why. 'In the meantime, what is, is.' He leaned forward suddenly, causing her to lurch back.

'I have a proposal,' he said, 'a plan that will end the bloodshed between our peoples, and you are part of it.' He patted the notebook. 'The work we have done together, in this room, have revealed something quite startling.'

The notebook belonged to someone named *Isla W*. The first pages contained notes about her age and her education, and pictures of her standing naked with her palms against the same wall.

She is young, Silje thought, *so horribly young*. She could not remember the General taking pictures of her. She looked to the wall behind his wine cabinet – a hidden camera perhaps. Gunther had told her of such things.

'You are almost as perfect as our Germanic female,' Gruetzmacher said. 'and compatible with the Aryan male who stands above all races in terms of strength, stamina and intelligence.' His breathing became short and hoarse, as it did when he examined her. 'When Quisling comes I will present him with my proposal: a eugenics programme, cross-breeding Norwegian females with our finest men to produce a new, perfect Norwegian race.' He sat back in his seat and threw the notebook on the table. 'I have selected twelve women to be progenitors. After we have discussed plans for expanding *The Quisling Orchid* newsletter across Norway, I will ask – no – I will demand an audience with the Party. Think of it, Fräulein Ohnstad – living symbols of the link between our two races. A bond that will only strengthen with time. What do you think?'

Realising he intended to make a breeding sow of her, Silje chose to say nothing.

Gruetzmacher forced a laugh through his teeth. 'You are a conundrum, Fräulein. In spite of your cleverness I often find myself disappointed by your lack of vision.'

'Then I am sorry for that, General.'

He waved his hand dismissively as if to say *You will see – and if you do not, it matters not.*

'And if it is all the same to you, General, I do not wish to be a part of this. I am soon to be married and I do not think—'

'Have you been eating the fruit?' the General asked.

'The fruit?'

'The fruit I have been giving you; have you been eating it?'

Silje thought long before replying, suspecting a snare of some kind.

'Some of it, yes. Though I give most of it away to my family and my friends.'

'Most generous,' Gruetzmacher said, unimpressed. 'But it was meant for you and you alone.'

'It seemed such a lot for one person, sir. I felt sure you meant for me to share your gift.'

To Silje's surprise the General beamed at her, as far as he knew how. 'The fruit basket is not for sharing. You must eat all of it. Diet and exercise is the key to all of this.'

'Then you have been giving fruit to all the women?'

'Of course.'

'Oh,' she said, making a show of appearing crestfallen.

This amused the General. He laughed again, a sound so weak it died without the slightest echo. 'Fear not. Your work on *The Quisling Orchid* makes you more valuable to me than all the others. You are robust, and as I have said before, intelligent. That is why I have decided to include you in my Eugenics initiative, in spite of your age.'

'Thank you, General.'

'No, it is I who must thank you, for your cooperation.' He rose from his seat. 'I understand that my examinations are somewhat intrusive, but I assure you they are necessary. My aide will provide you with your fruit. Please remember—'

'They are for me alone. Yes, I understand.'

But as she walked towards the door, the General spoke again.

'Did you say you are taking a spouse?'

Silje's chest tightened. 'I did, General.'

'Mmm.' She heard him pacing around his armchair. 'And have you had relations with your intended?'

'Sir?'

'Have you been intimate with him?'

'I do not think that is a polite question, General Gruetzmacher.'

'It is not but you will answer it nevertheless. Have you slept with him?'

What did he want to hear? He wanted her to say no, that she was untarnished and pure. What would he do to her if she said otherwise?

She made her decision quickly. 'Yes.'

Gruetzmacher fell silent, and Silje thought that perhaps she had chosen unwisely.

'Frequently?'

It is too late to take a different road now, she thought. 'As frequently as my chores allow.'

'Mmm.'

She slowly turned her head to see that he had returned to his armchair, his finger steepled, his hands shaking.

'Is he pure Norwegian?'

'I am not sure what you mean, General.'

'Has he foreign blood in his veins.'

'His grandfather was from Finland, I believe. And I think there is a French ancestor who may have been related to Louis XIV. And now I think on it he spoke of distant cousins who were Swiss. No, I lie; they were from—'

'What I mean is,' the General said with a smile that could have been carved into his face with a knife, 'has your cunt been sullied by Jews?'

A surge of bile churned from her stomach into her throat. Silje swallowed it down and shivered. 'You have spent hours examining it, General,' she said. 'Perhaps you can tell me.'

The General blinked; his eyes swivelled about the room, hunting a crueller version of himself hiding in the shadows. In the end he seemed to accept that no one else could have spoken but him. 'I must apologize for my poor manners, Fräulein Ohnstad.' He wiped his brow with his handkerchief; it was the first time Silje had seen him sweat. 'I meant no disrespect.'

Then what did you mean?

He sniffed the air and looked at her, confused, as though she had vanished before his eyes and had been replaced by someone who looked exactly the same.

'Can you smell that?' he demanded. 'Cinnamon. I think it is cinnamon.'

Silje ran for the door, though she knew the General always kept it locked while he defiled her. It would have made little difference; he had hold of her when she was still more than an arm's length from any possible escape. He grabbed a fistful of her hair and held it beneath his nose, inhaling deeply.

'Sorceress!' he roared.

'General, I do not know what you are talking about!'

He let go of her and his eyes began searching again.

'The scent you wear,' he said. 'I thought I… I am sorry.'

'I am no Jew!' Silje cried. *Judas*, her soul cried back.

Gruetzmacher walked unsteadily to his armchair and dropped into it as though weighted by rocks. He wiped his forehead and cleared his throat. He breathed deeply and closed his eyes. 'Again I must apologise. You see how my encounters with them has left a stain upon my soul. I have demons, Fräulein, demons I must struggle with for the rest of my days.'

You have already lost. There was a letter opener on his desk. She wondered how sharp it was. She wondered if Gruetzmacher would open his eyes if he heard her moving. She wondered if, like Freya, she could walk across a hardened floor without making a sound.

The General opened his eyes. 'On reflection,' he said, his voice weak and fatigued, 'I think that you are perhaps too old for my eugenics initiative.'

'As you wish, General,' Silje said, unable to hide her relief.

'I will find another.' He appeared to lapse into a trance of sorts. A moment later he returned, though he seemed unsure where he was. He looked at her, surprised that she was still in his study.

'Your escort will return you to your home now,' he said. 'Please don't forget your fruit.'

'But you said I was no longer—'

'A gift.' He massaged his temples with his fingertips. 'Now leave. I have much to do.'

40

'I hate it when you go to him,' said Freya.

'I hate it too.'

She frowned because she heard Silje frown. 'Then stop.'

'It is war, Freya,' Silje said wearily. 'What can I do?' She finished counting the rafters beneath the barn roof. There were forty-three in all. When he was little more than a boy, Erik had climbed up and carved her name into the ninth beam. It had been her tenth birthday, but the tenth rafter was too far for him to jump.

She shivered and Freya began covering her naked body with armfuls of hay.

'You do not need to do that; I am not cold.'

'You are shaking.'

'I am trying not to cry.'

Freya held her tightly. 'You can cry as you like when you are with me.' Her hand caressed Silje's stomach and moved downward. Silje rolled away from her.

'You do not want to make love to me.'

'No, not today.'

'Why?'

'Just because.'

'Do you hurt?'

'No,' Silje said. 'I cannot feel much of anything.'

Freya raised herself on one elbow, her hair spilling across her jaw and her throat. Silje looked at her for what seemed like the first time in months, since her birthday. She marvelled at how much she'd grown, this thin blind waif rescued from under a floor. Her skin had lightened as the onset of autumn had begun to hide the sun; her hair had thickened and lengthened past her slim neck, the dark roots showing through the bleaching. Her shoulders had broadened under knots of taut muscle, her belly had hardened and her breasts had grown and lifted, the nipples black and swollen. Silje took one between her thumb and first finger. She drew her thumb back and forth, feeling the coarseness of the flesh. Freya closed her eyes and inhaled sharply. As her head began to fall back, Silje cradled her.

'No,' she said. 'Open your eyes. I want to see your eyes.'

Freya did as she asked.

It is the eyes, Silje thought, *so beautiful...* She pressed her lips against Freya's, forcing her tongue past her teeth. Freya seemed to fold from her.

'No, stay.' She raked her nails across Freya's skin and bit into her lip.

Freya cried for Silje to stop and pushed herself free.

'Are you mad?' she said, wiping her mouth; she was bleeding. 'I told you never to do that!'

Silje drew her legs up to her chin and gnawed savagely on her little fingernail, her thoughts suddenly assailed by images of Gruetzmacher: Gruetzmacher being shot; Gruetzmacher hanged; Gruetzmacher beheaded; Gruetzmacher raped by wild goats with eyes of burning amber. She revelled in them, or tried to. The images became more cruel, more depraved, and still she felt nothing.

'I am not him,' Freya cried, feeling through the hay for her clothes.

'I know. I did not mean to.'

'You were hurting me and you were enjoying it.'

'That is not true.'

'What is wrong with you?'

Silje hid her face between her knees.

'You will tell me, or I will leave this barn and we will never be together again.'

'You do not mean that.'

'It is the General, isn't it? It is the General who drives you to do such things. You must not go to him anymore, Silje. I mean it.'

Her words made the air seem thicker, harder to breathe; they hung there, making echoes.

Witchcraft, the General would have said. *Semite witchcraft.*

'When my mother left us,' said Silje, 'I wanted nothing more than to join her. Even though she didn't remember me for the last months of her life, I missed her terribly. Magnus could do nothing to lift me from the darkness. I didn't eat, I could not sleep. My poor father thought that I would follow her to the grave.'

'But you did not,' Freya said, putting on her dress.

'No, I found my way through.'

Freya sat by her and moved closer, so close that the scent of cinnamon was almost overpowering. 'How?'

'I became someone else: someone else who still had a mother; someone else who watched a little Norwegian girl weep day and night. This other girl was stronger, so much stronger than me.'

'But when she was strong enough to bear the pain, Silje Ohnstad came back.'

'No,' said Silje. 'No, she never did.'

'I am sorry that she chose to leave the world,' said Freya, embracing her, 'but she left someone beautiful and strong and wise and magnificent in her place. So I thank young Miss Ohnstad for that.'

'I am not strong, Freya. I never was. When Magnus came home without his eye and his soul, I became someone else again: someone who watches a young woman weep for her lost brother; someone who watches the same young woman violated by a madman.'

'You have found a way to endure, Silje. There is nothing wrong in that.'

'Perhaps you are right but how many times can I become someone else before there is nothing left of me? I feel myself slipping away. I sometimes think that no one sees me, and that I have to scream to stop myself fading into the night.'

Freya pressed her lips against hers; Silje could taste the copper in her blood.

'Listen to me,' Freya said. 'I will not let you fade. When you feel yourself falling then find me, hold on to me, and if I cannot anchor you to this world then we shall slip away together.'

The tears in her eyes made them shine, and Silje knew then that the war would break them.

'He knows you are here,' she said.

Freya blinked and wiped her eyes. 'I do not understand.'

'The General, Gruetzmacher. He knows you are here.'

'That is not possible. No one in Fólkvangr would—'

'It is me, Freya. I carry something of you wherever I go. I thought it was just your scent.' She snapped her fingers as Freya opened her mouth to protest. 'And it is a beautiful scent. When I am sad I try to imagine it and it makes me think we will be together soon and then I am happy again.'

'But you are not happy now.'

'There is something of you that drives Gruetzmacher to madness. When he defiles me he thinks he is defiling you.'

It was one of the very few moments in their lives when Freya was without the power of speech.

'He knows, Freya. He knows you are here.'

'You are wrong. It is not possible.'

'Every time I think of you, in his eyes I become you. I cannot explain it but I fear that you are in danger while we are together.'

Freya seemed to lose her. Her eyes narrowed, her jaw set. *It is such a sweet expression*, Silje thought. *She seeks the questions and answers in the same place.* As often when they fought, the answer she found was nowhere close to the truth. Still, Silje was caught by surprise when Freya slapped her face and jumped to her feet.

'You sicken me, Silje Ohnstad. Such a transparent excuse to end us, even to a silly blind girl.'

'That is not true,' Silje cried, her face stinging.

'You are using the war and its mad General as reason to leave me. That is horrible. You should at least have the courage to admit the truth!'

'And what is the truth, Freya? Please tell me because if you know then you could save both our lives.'

'The truth is that you are ashamed of me!'

'For the love of God, I do not know what to say to you when you spout such childishness.'

'Are you calling me childish?' Freya said. 'Oh Silje, if only you could see the irony in your words as clearly as I. Everyone knows about us now, everyone except your intended, Erik. Everyone knows and the only person who cares is you.'

'I am leaving,' said Silje, getting to her feet and hunting for her dress. 'I cannot speak to you when you are like this.'

'No, you stay; I shall go,' said Freya. 'Fólkvangr is your home after all.'

'What are you saying?'

'I am saying that I will not spend another moment with you, because to you there is more shame in people thinking you are in love with a Jewess than thinking you are a slut!'

Silje stopped fastening her dress; Freya's last word hung between them, burning away the last of their air.

Freya swallowed and exhaled. 'I should leave.'

'No you will not,' Silje said. 'There are things you say that change things, Freya. You can say "I do not like your goat" and "I think you have big feet" and it will be forgotten. But if you leave after telling me I am a whore then we are undone. So do not leave, not like this, not while we lie in pieces.'

Freya wavered, if only for a moment. 'If you are asking me to say I'm sorry…'

'No, I am telling you I love you.'

Silje waited, her life riding the edge of a spinning coin.

'You must marry Erik,' Freya said suddenly, finally. 'You should go to him this very night, tell him what we have done before talk of us reaches his ears. Then you must beg his forgiveness and marry him.'

'You do not know what you're saying.'

'And you must marry him before the ground grows cold. God knows Fólkvangr needs something to lift it from the darkness of the war.'

'And us?'

And it was then Freya chose to be silent.

'I see,' said Silje. 'If that is what you truly want.'

'It is what *you* want, Silje: respectability. Take it. It is my wedding gift to you.'

* * *

'I hate it when you go to him,' said Erik. He leaned across and planted a kiss on her cheek.

'I hate it too,' Silje said, staring at the rafters that held the roof of his home in place. She turned her head away from him and her eyes fell upon the painting of the ladder in the sky. A beautiful and pointless existence, she remembered.

She still ached from the General's examination, and the eager attentions of Erik whom she could not refuse without reason.

'But he never lays a hand on you,' said Erik, drawing his finger through the sparse hair that covered her groin and then down to the sore opening below.

Silje winced and sucked in air between her teeth. 'No.'

'And so what do you do in his study?'

'I have told you. We discuss the state of the war and the plight of the

Norwegian people; then we read through the articles and announcements for *The Quisling Orchid.*'

Erik, thankfully, removed his hand and turned over onto his back. 'Then he is a very odd fellow.'

'What do you mean by that?'

Silje heard him swallow. *He should stop now*, she thought. *But he is a man and so he will press on and ruin everything.*

'Well, he has one of the most beautiful women in the district, alone, in his private chambers, and all he wishes to do is… read.'

Silje rolled over and sat upright. 'Perhaps then you'd prefer it if he forced himself upon me.'

'No! No! Of course not! What I mean is—'

'Perhaps you'd prefer it if he wasn't an "odd fellow" and violates me as soon as he closes the door.'

'For the love of God, Silje, why must you always say such terrible things?'

'For the same reason you say such stupid things, Erik; I didn't think.' She lay down and turned away from him. 'I am sorry. Forgive me.'

'Always and forever.'

She felt the heat from his hand as it danced over her shoulder. *Please do not touch me*, she thought. She shivered and the warmth suddenly vanished. 'Freya says we should get married.'

'Then Freya is very astute,' Erik replied flatly.

'She says we should get married soon, before the winter takes hold.'

'Well, as much as we both love her, it is not up to her, is it?'

Silje's eyes were stinging. She realised she'd been staring at the ladder in the sky without blinking. 'I think she is right.'

It took a few moments for her words to sink through to him. 'What did you say?'

'I said she is right.' She turned around and kissed his lips, though his mouth was half open. 'Oh Erik, you look like a slapped trout.'

He clenched his teeth, afraid that if he spoke, if he made the slightest sound, then whatever enchantment had befallen her would be swept away.

'I think this is the part where you say, "Yes, Silje. I will gladly marry you at your earliest convenience."'

Erik looked doubtful. 'I thought you did not want to get married until Freya could look after herself, or Doctor Lomen had returned, or Magnus was better, or the war has ended.'

'Yes, go on; spoil it,' Silje said. 'Do you want to marry me or not?'

'You know that nothing would make me happier.' He was smiling, at last.

'Two weeks from now.'

'That is not very long.'

'Do you have something better to do?'

'No! No! Of course not! I will marry you! Yes!' He jumped to his feet and struck his head against an ornament he'd made from scraps of iron – a woman sitting on a hinged swing. The woman was supposed to be Silje, though she thought the depiction was rather wide of hip.

'We have much to do,' he babbled. 'You will need a dress.'

'My mother's will suffice.'

'Yes!' He snapped his fingers. 'Good thinking! Freya can alter it to fit your—'

'Tread carefully, Erik.'

'I will need a suit… and a ring! My God, where will I find a ring?'

He dropped to his knees and kissed her; then he was on his feet again, pacing the attic and pulling frantically at his beard. 'Flowers! Where shall we get the flowers?'

Silje raised an eyebrow.

'Yes, of course! I'm sorry; I did not think. There is so much to do! Why are you still lying there, Silje?'

'Because I am tired.'

'We have no time to sleep!' He took her hand and tried to pull her to her feet.

'For the whole fortnight?'

'You start with the invitations! We must send them out by tomorrow, otherwise people will have made alternative plans.'

'In Fólkvangr.' Silje looked doubtful.

He slid down the loft ladder, still as naked as the day he came into the world.

She had never seen him so happy. *It is a good thing. He carries enough joy in his heart for us both.*

She listened to him thrashing about in the kitchen. 'We have no paper!' he wailed. 'We are already undone!'

'Erik.'

The thrashing stopped. 'Yes, wife,' he called back.

Forgive him. He is simply trying it to see how it fits.

'When you said "*one* of the most beautiful"…'

'Clearly I meant *the* most beautiful.'

Silje smiled and pulled the blanket up to her chin. His education had begun and would endure for the rest of his days.

41

It was as Freya had said, the village needed a wedding of Jewish proportions to lift it from the mire of the war. News of Silje's upcoming nuptials spread quickly, and the villagers rallied to do whatever they could to ensure the event would be remembered in Fólkvangr for decades to come.

Though he said little to his daughter, Jon Ohnstad used his entire stock of matured goats' manure on the fifty-square-foot orchid bed he kept for emergencies (sudden births were unlikely; sudden deaths, more so).

'I barely have enough.' He looked mournfully at the orchid field. He'd had to decimate his stock for the sons of Doctor Lomen who were laid to rest at the family plot high in the mountains.

Silje squeezed his hand. 'It will be enough, Father. You'll see.'

He nodded, and sucked his lower lip into his mouth. 'You have made an old man proud.'

Silje swelled, until he grinned impishly and added, 'Finally.'

She cuffed his arm and pushed his hand away, switching quickly to an affected sulk.

Jon Ohnstad roared with laughter.

'It is not funny.'

'I have some advice for you,' he said, hunting in his pockets for his pipe. 'There are only three things you need in a good marriage: patience, forgiveness and laughter. If you have just those three then everything else will take care of itself.'

'What about love?'

Jon Ohnstad looked at her from beneath arched eyebrows and smiled. 'And what do you think love is made of?'

Silje shrugged.

'Patience, forgiveness and laughter.' He looked at her, surprised she could have gotten so far in life without knowing this. 'I blame myself,' he murmured and then glanced towards the cottage, his eye drawn by movement in an upstairs window. Magnus quickly withdrew, closing the curtains behind him.

'The sound of laughter made him curious,' Jon Ohnstad said. 'It still binds him to us, you see.'

Silje looked up to the window but did not see anything.

'And we are patient with him. We will always be patient with him and with God, and we hope that one day he will be returned to us.' He nodded, satisfied, and puffed on his pipe.

Silje inhaled the smoke until it made her nose twitch.

'I said some unforgivable things to you on Freya's birthday, the day Magnus was taken.'

'Father, please…'

Jon Ohnstad raised his hand. 'I said things that no man should say to his child.'

'I am hardly a child.'

'And to this day I remain deeply ashamed, so much so that I have been unable to apologise for my words.'

'There is no need.' Silje had no wish to be reminded of any part of that awful day.

But her father was not to be swayed. 'I am very sorry.'

'You were forgiven then. You are still forgiven now.'

He nodded again and smiled. Then he tapped her on the shoulder with the stem of his pipe. 'You see now.' He pointed the pipe at the upstairs window. 'Between the three of us, laughter.' He tapped her again and then himself. 'Patience.' He gently ran the back of his hand across her cheek. 'And forgiveness. That is the Ohnstad family. That is love. Now do you understand?'

Silje nodded.

They sat down in silence to watch the orchids grow, her head resting on his shoulder.

Laughter, patience and forgiveness, she thought. She'd always believed that love pulsed like a heartbeat at the very centre of creation. How odd it was to think it was simply made from other things. Gruetzmacher had once told her the human body was just a bag of water. She remembered thinking then that he was truly mad.

Like Freya, Erik and herself: small, simple things that had come together and made something terrible and complicated. She wondered what would become of them after she was married. Would this simple ceremony change her? Worse, would it change Freya?

Yes, they were three, but her father had just said that three things together make love. Perhaps, after a time, she could talk to Erik, explain things to him. Perhaps she could make him see that the three of them could make a life together. Would it be such a sin? If love were made of such simple things?

'Silje, listen.'

'Do not spoil it, Father.'

'It is important.'

Well, whatever it is, promise not to insult me.'

And Jon Ohnstad, being a man who was not given to breaking his word, chose to say nothing. Several moments passed, long enough for the sun to begin its slow descent behind the mountains, and for Silje's patience – one corner of love, she thought bitterly – to break.

'What did you want to say to me?'

'It is not important.'

'Clearly it is, or you would have not brought it up.'

He took his pipe from his lips and tapped out the tobacco on the ground. 'Do you remember Mrs Gyldenløve?'

'The shoemaker's wife from Kronstadt?'

'No, the other Mrs Gyldenløve.'

Silje said she did not know who she was.

'She is a seamstress in Bergen. She lives in a house a short amble from the quay. A widow. I often take flowers to her, more of late.'

'You have never mentioned her,' Silje said. 'Is she pretty?'

'That is an odd question. Why do you ask?'

'I am curious.'

'Why are you curious?'

'Why are you evading my question?'

'I am not evading your question, Daughter. I am trying to tell you something important while you seem more concerned with the notion that I have betrayed the memory of your mother.'

'And have you?'

'Have I what?'

'Have you been unfaithful to Mother?'

'I do not think that is any concern of yours and it is not what I wanted to speak to you about.'

'If you think that you indulging yourself in all kinds of harlotry behind Mother's back is no concern of mine then I'm afraid you are—'

'Silje… you remember your mother is dead, don't you?'

'That… is… a horrible thing to say.'

Jon Ohnstad sighed and shook his head. 'Mrs Gyldenløve has a daughter, younger than you, perhaps not as pretty.'

'Dear God. Not the daughter…' She remembered that her father was in the autumn of his years when he first met her mother.

Her father said, 'Do not make me raise my voice, Silje.'

And so she remained silent. *I will listen*, she told herself. *I will listen and then I will have my say.*

'Mrs Gyldenløve's daughter worked in the town hall kitchens before the invasion. In spite of her mother's petitions, she continued to work there after the Nazis took the hall for their headquarters. Gruetzmacher paid a visit to the kitchens one day several months ago, and that is where he laid eyes on Tonelise.'

'I do not wish to hear th—'

'And since then,' Jon Ohstad said firmly, 'Tonelise goes to his study every Monday at precisely four o'clock. He locks the door, and she is released an hour later. She finishes her shift, cleans the kitchens and checks the cold room stock before returning home where she spends an hour trying to remove her skin with a scrubbing brush.'

Silje remained silent.

'I fear that if it goes on then she may take her own life.' Jon Ohnstad looked at her. Silje looked away, aware that she was swaying slightly in the breeze.

'I know that you are sometimes called to the General's chambers,' he continued, though she could tell he did not want to. 'I have asked you this before—'

'And I have told you before, we discuss the newsletter. That is all.'

'And I have told *you* before,' her father said sternly, 'I am not some fool who wishes to be cosseted in a bed of your lies.'

'Like Erik, you mean.'

'Yes, like Erik.'

'I thought you liked him.'

'I love him as though he were my own son. But that does not mean he is not a fool.'

'And you are happy for your daughter to marry a fool?'

'I am happy when you are happy, that is all, and you seek to distract me, Silje, but I know you too well. I will speak and you, for once, will listen. I know that you are… familiar with the company of men.'

Silje felt her face flush bright red and then drain almost as quickly. She wanted to stamp her foot and shout 'Father, please!' so loudly that her voice would carry across the mountains. Instead, her words escaped her as a humiliated whisper.

Her father licked his lips and forced himself to press on. 'I have said nothing because…' He looked to the sky for guidance. He scored his fingers through the earth and took a deep breath. 'I took a woman, Silje, a girl younger than you are now, as my second wife without a binding separation from Marit. So with adultery as my first, bigamy became my second crime against morality.'

'It does not matter,' Silje said. 'You loved Mother. We all did. You were unfaithful to Marit, but you were faithful to Her; that is all that matters.'

Again, he licked his lips and looked down to the ground.

And in that moment of silence, Silje's world crumbled into dust.

'You are lying,' she said, though she could not think of a reason why he would tell her such a thing unless it were true. 'Who?'

'Does it really matter?'

'It matters to me! Who was she?'

'It is not important, Silje!'

'You fucked some other woman—'

'And you will mind your tongue when you speak to me!'

'You *fucked* another woman behind our backs and then you tell me that it is not important! How dare you!' Silje jumped to her feet. 'She is still alive, isn't she? She lives in the village?' Her eyes darted to every bush, every plant, every stone, every rock she could see; expecting the woman to leap out to taunt her. 'It was Marit, wasn't it? Men! You always shit so close to home!'

His face took on the aspect of a winter storm, so much so that Silje would have believed she heard thunder as he clenched his fists and the air cracked between his knuckles. They stared at each other, defiantly, as strangers. Her father said, 'It is the wife of Junges Fehn.'

Silje blinked rapidly to clear her eyes and then looked away. It was, to her, beyond all comprehension, and yet a tiny voice at the base of her skull said that perhaps it was justice, though it was likely Mrs Fehn had sinned against Silje's family long before Silje had cast her shadow over hers. She looked at her father; he seemed different to her now. Smaller.

'Were you with her when Mother was dying?' She left herself open and unshielded, dreading his reply.

'No,' he said. 'It was just once, and we both agreed it was a mistake.'

'Just the once,' she echoed.

'And there has been no one else since. Still, it haunts me, and perhaps my own weakness has prevented me protecting you from yours.'

'I am not… weak.'

'All I am saying is that you must treat Erik with more respect than I treated your mother. That is all I wanted to—'

'You are not welcome at my wedding,' she said, regretting it as soon as the words escaped her lips.

'You do not mean that.'

'I do,' she lied.

'For a mistake I made twenty years ago.'

'If you dare show your face, I shall have Gunther throw you from the church!'

To her surprise, this seemed to amuse her father more than wound him.

'Not Erik?' he asked.

She swore under her breath and got to her feet.

'I did not mean it,' he called after her. 'I know that you care for him, Silje.'

She chose not to hear him. It was a lie she could only bear to hear from herself.

* * *

The Truth followed her along the crooked road leading from her home to Fólkvangr. When she tried to run from it, the Truth sang louder.

You do not love him. You never have.

Silje tried to swear it away, but the Truth persisted. *It is the girl you want. Take her. She is yours. Take her and leave this place.*

This place.

Her universe wheeled and circled above the mountain, the cottage and Fólkvangr. Or perhaps the mountain, the cottage and the village orbited her. She thought of the ladder in the sky Erik had painted and kept hidden from her. *You should feel blessed*, she told herself. It was rare that one would know such boundless love from another, so to know such a love from two was a seldom thing indeed. She stopped running where the path split into three.

Leave Fólkvangr.

She could not. Never.

Who would take care of Magnus and her father? She had happily taken the mantle when her mother had passed away. It was her pleasure and her duty. Fólkvangr was her life.

'Perhaps they should call this place Irony.'

Silje shrieked.

'Forgive me.' Gunther stepped out from behind an oak tree that had, over the course of centuries, grown a deep smile near the centre of its trunk. 'I didn't mean to startle you.'

'What were you doing?' said Silje, fanning herself for drama's sake. 'You could have given me a seizure.'

'I doubt that.' Gunther took a few steps towards her. Silje took three steps back. 'I heard running so I took cover. Force of habit I'm afraid.' He looked back towards the tree and nodded as though thanking it for growing there.

'Is this what they teach you in spy school?'

Gunther smiled in that way that made her feel as if she were six years old. 'Amongst other things, yes.'

'And what do you mean by "Irony"?'

He shivered and rubbed his hands together. 'It came to me as I watched you standing there where the road divides, trying to decide between them.'

'I was not deciding; I will stay on this road, the one that leads to the village.'

Gunther grinned and Silje wanted to slap his face. 'I wasn't talking about the road,' he said.

'Then I have no idea what you are talking about.'

'Have it your way, as is your wont. Let us talk about Quisling.'

'If we must talk about something.' She continued briskly along the road to Fólkvangr, leaving Gunther to hurry after her.

'It is all set,' he said in a loud whisper. 'Thanks to your dealings with the General—'

'"Dealings"? Is that what we are calling it now?'

He says it so quickly, Silje thought. *Rehearsed, revised, rehearsed again, to save us both discomfort*. She was having none of it, not today.

Gunther coughed and opened his mouth to speak.

'Whatever you are thinking of saying, it will be the wrong thing, Gunther. Best leave it at that.'

He had to say something. 'British Intelligence and the Norwegian Resistance will not forget your sacrifice.'

'As I said: the wrong thing.' She stopped and took a deep breath to chill her lungs. 'What is it you were telling me?'

Gunther had turned a sickly shade of pink. *The English*, Silje thought; *they cannot even blush properly.*

'From the fragments of information you have provided,' he began, still feeling the need to praise, however indirectly, Silje's talent for whoring secrets from the enemy, 'we have pieced together Quisling's itinerary for the day. He will be heavily guarded at all times. A sniper is our best option though it is unlikely he would escape, even in the confusion.'

'I'm sure there will be no shortage of volunteers.'

'Of that I have no doubt, but Command thinks that a suicide operation would be less effective in rallying Norwegians than a clean strike with no casualties on our side.'

'Are you saying we are cowards?'

'No, I am saying that your docile aggression needs to be stoked, as it were.'

She wondered what 'as it were' meant. 'You are calling us cowards! Perhaps you should go to the cottage and explain this to my brother!'

'Why are you so difficult to talk to?'

'Why are you such an idiot?'

He seized her by the arms and pressed his lips against hers. He closed his eyes tightly; his nostrils flared as he pulled her closer. Silje watched him with her left eyebrow raised. *He should stop soon*, she thought. But he did not. It occurred to her that perhaps he was unsure how. She gently pushed him away.

'Are you quite finished?' she said.

'I'm sorry; I don't know what came over—'

'Good.' She pointedly wiped her mouth, smiled and grasped the belt around his waist.

'Silje, please; I am very flattered but I think it would be a terrible idea for us to—'

Silje pulled down on his belt and at the same time drove her knee into his groin.

Gunther's eyes bulged from their sockets. Silje noted, with some satisfaction, that her kneecap had caught him squarely in the stirring of an erection.

'You were saying,' she said as he crumpled to the ground, 'some nonsense about something coming over you? What came over you, Gunther Braithwaite, was bad manners. You think because I allow some demented Nazi between my knees I'm fair game for a hero of British Intelligence.'

'It's not like that,' he squealed like a goat at its own castration.

'Apologise.'

'I have.'

'Again, with feeling.'

'I am very sorry.'

'No, don't try to get up. Stay there and tell me what I need to know of this plan.'

Gunther rolled into a sitting position. He looked paler than usual; Silje hoped she hadn't done him a permanent injury, not that he deserved anything less.

'We are not going to kill him,' Gunther said. 'We are going to kidnap him.' Deciding that he'd been chastised sufficiently, he struggled to his feet. 'I can see this surprises you.'

'You have misread me again, Gunther; I'm trying not to laugh.'

'Well, at least you're trying,' Gunther said glumly. 'My superiors were not so polite when I first told them about the plan.'

'If you think sending a sniper is a suicide mission, then what do you call a kidnap attempt?'

'Something they are not expecting. A sniper would be unable to escape. The kidnappers will have a hostage: Quisling himself.'

He seemed to double in height.

'A while ago you told me that Gruetzmacher will present his eugenics scheme to Quisling over a late supper.'

Silje remembered. Cruelty seemed to loosen his tongue, and on that particular day he'd bled secrets even he knew he should not.

'Are you all right?'

She blinked and found Gunther was staring at her.

'The Hilton,' she said. 'You mean to take him at the Hilton.'

Gunther smiled, this time making her feel his equal. Perhaps a kick to the nether parts earned respect in the English.

'We have people working there: chefs and the serving staff. Trust me, this will be much easier than trying to shoot him. He will be surrounded by Krauts ten layers deep. A shot like that is more likely to kill one of his bodyguards than him.'

'Have you considered aiming for his head?'

Gunther treated her to the other smile, the one that made her feel like a small and slow child. 'Yes, we have. The distances involved would mean a sniper of extraordinary skill, and my superiors tell me the best ones are being held back for France.' He scratched at his moustache. 'Magnus could have made that shot,' he said. 'He had a gift.'

'And look where it got him, and please don't say anything about how his sacrifice will be remembered. Just make sure your superiors remember all of Norway.'

She set off for Fólkvangr, her steps lighter, no longer pressed into the earth by the reproach festering inside her chest. She decided this new feeling of pride and togetherness was patriotism and she very much liked it.

'Where do you think you are going?' she asked.

'I thought I might accompany you to the village. It is getting late and it would be ungentlemanly of me to allow—'

'And now you are concerned with being a gentleman. You are full of surprises this evening, Gunther Braithwaite.'

'Every time you say my name, I think you are laughing at me.'

'Perhaps I am. Go to the cottage, Gunther. Sit with my brother and tell him how the war progresses.'

He looked uncertain, perhaps even guilty.

'He bears you no ill will; no more than he bears the rest of the world anyway.'

* * *

She approached the village at twice her strolling pace, which gave the sentry very little time to signal ahead.

'What are you doing here?' Ingrid Haud cried. She rode her bicycle in a tight circle around Silje, slowing her down. 'You are not supposed to come back this way.'

'So I am no longer allowed to come to the village in the evening?'

'No! Yes! Of course yes, but not tonight.'

'And what is so special about tonight?'

The circle grew tighter until Ingrid rode to a halt, blocking Silje's path. 'If I tell you, you did not hear it from me.'

'I understand.'

'I mean it Silje; I was not supposed to tell you this under pain of a sound spanking.'

'That does sound serious, so I promise I will not say a word.'

Ingrid glanced around to make sure the trees hadn't snuck up on them, and then beckoned for Silje to lean closer. 'They are testing the lights.'

'Lights. What lights?'

'The Christmas lights.'

'But it isn't Christmas.'

Ingrid folded her arms and made a show of tapping an impatient foot. 'They are for your wedding dance. Erik borrowed them from Junges Fehn who told me to tell you "congratulations" if I saw you before he did.'

'Then you must thank him if you see him before I do.'

'He also said to tell you that he will be unable to attend your wedding because Mrs Fehn says he will have a cold that day.'

'I see.'

'I don't.'

'And I am not supposed to know about these lights.'

Ingrid shook her head so vigorously, Silje was afraid her thin neck would sprain. 'If I see you coming then I have to give the secret signal.'

'A secret signal too! This is all so exciting. I will not delay you any longer; the signal must be given.'

Ingrid saluted and cycled away, yelling, 'Silje is coming! Silje is coming!' as loudly as she could.

Silje gave the village enough time to hide whatever it needed to and then approached Fólkvangr, singing loudly. Nevertheless, when she walked through the archway, the villagers were still throwing bunting under tables and arranging themselves into lines to hide posters and signs.

'Ho! Silje!' Erik slid down a ladder from the roof of *The Mottled Goat*, and ran over to her, stuffing a hammer into his belt. 'We were not expecting you.'

She allowed him to peck her lightly on the cheek. 'So I see.'

'It's meant to be a surprise,' he said, apologetically. 'If you see anything you shouldn't then just pretend you didn't.'

'I can do that.' She cupped his cheek in the palm of her hand and smiled. 'This is all so wonderful.'

The villagers shuffled their feet and swelled with pride.

'You really didn't have to go to all this trouble.'

'Of course we did!' said Anna Haud, Ingrid's mother. 'You are the lynchpin of this village, Silje Ohnstad. We could do no less.'

'And the sooner you are married,' added Mrs Fehn, 'the better for everyone.'

It occurred to Silje that she didn't know Mrs Fehn's first name.

Rolf Lillegard was pushed in front of her. He removed his cap, pressing it firmly to his chest, and thrust a hastily picked bouquet, consisting mostly of weeds, under Silje's nose. 'We wish you good luck on your new journey, Silje Ohnstad!'

There were tears in his eyes, and in those of the group of men who had urged him to make his presentation. They nodded solemnly, and to her dismay Silje realised that at some point during the last ten years she'd had her way with all of them.

And now here they are, she thought, *to say goodbye to the woman I was*. It was quite sweet in a mortifying sort of way. Though seeing them gathered together she wondered if they'd shared stories over the last decade. Perhaps this was some kind of club and she was their mascot. She smiled sheepishly at Erik who rolled his tongue around his mouth but said nothing.

'For you,' said a thick, flat voice from behind her.

Silje turned and almost fainted away. Steadfastly looking to her left, Marit Ohnstad held out a wreath made from the most beautiful orchids she had ever seen.

'Marit. I do not know what to say.'

'Then say nothing. Just take it.'

'They are quite beautiful.'

Marit looked at her, and for the first time since she could remember, Silje did not see loathing in her eyes. 'Who do you think taught your father to grow orchids?' she said.

'And I know that he has much to answer for, and perhaps also my own mother.'

Marit stared in disbelief while she nodded, an almost imperceptible movement of her ancient head.

'But they are still my parents, Marit, and so it is my right to speak ill of them, not yours.'

The other villagers, almost unable to comprehend what they were witnessing, stayed silent.

'Hmmph,' Marit said. She gathered her skirts and looked around for a quiet route away from the town square.

'Wreaths are usually for funerals, are they not?' Silje asked.

'It is all I had spare,' said Marit. 'Count yourself fortunate.' She shuffled away through the gathering, heading west to wherever she lived. Silje did not know.

'I will see you at the wedding then, Marit?'

'Do not push your luck.'

'But I will see you. You will be most welcome.'

Marit turned and smiled, an act that seemed to cause her some discomfort. 'If I am welcome then it would be impolite not to attend.'

'And you will wear something other than black?'

'Again, Silje, do not push your luck.'

* * *

Though she suspected her aid would not be welcomed, Silje decided to spend the rest of the evening in Fólkvangr, helping with the wedding preparations. It would be good to spend some time away from the cottage, and it would give her father time to reflect on his past before she forgave him.

And so she walked into the village where she drifted regally from house to store, offering her help in biscuit-making, cake decoration, the threading of bunting and the seating arrangements for the evening meal.

She was shooed away from the church and the baker's shop and so made her way back to *The Mottled Goat* where she curtailed the huge order of ale that Grette was about to make.

'Silje, it is your wedding day,' Grette proclaimed gruffly, tearfully.

'I am well aware of this, Grette, and I am also well aware that every Fólkvangr wedding since 1929 has ended in a drunken brawl, and in one case, the death of the groom. This will not happen, not on my wedding day.'

Grette promised to police the event and ensure that no one got perilously drunk or inappropriately punctured. But Silje remained steadfast, and so the ale requisitions remained short.

Satisfied that she might have saved a life, possibly even that of her future husband, Silje went to inspect the building work for the marquee and the stand for the musicians. There she found that there was much to be learned about men while they worked, almost as much as when they lay on their backs.

To begin with there were a number of things that should not be said to a man while he was engaged in masculine pursuits such as erecting a bandstand.

She found Rodrek pounding a nail into wood using a stone when there was a perfectly serviceable hammer not an arm's length from where he toiled. When she asked him if he should really be doing that, she was sent away with a hornet in her ear.

Rodrek glared at her as she hurried away, before returning to the task in hand, whereupon he flattened his thumb with the stone.

With her ears still burning, Silje held the ladder while Erik hung the procured Christmas bunting across the roof of *The Mottled Goat*. She watched him bend the wire hooks with his teeth and asked, 'Do you not have a proper tool for that?'

Again, the familiar glare.

'Sorry, I was just trying to— Is this Mr Gundersen's ladder!'

Erik sighed. 'He said he was happy for me to borrow it.'

'But you did ask.'

'Silje, perhaps Grette needs some help inside the tavern.'

'She sent me here.'

'I must thank her for that.'

'But you did ask to borrow the ladder, yes?'

'Yes!'

Erik said the ladder was quite safe without her holding it and that perhaps she could help the Fólkvangr Embroidery Circle with the napkins…

* * *

And it was with the Circle that Silje discovered the true fount of all learning where men were concerned.

'Do not cook the same thing for him week after week,' said Mrs Schau, sucking blood from the end of her thumb. 'He forgets many things, but never what he ate six evenings before.'

The five women sat in a tight circle in Mrs Tufte's parlour, sewing by candlelight. Silje tried to oblige but found that trying to see what she was doing in the dim light gave her something of a headache.

'Keep his underwear clean,' said Mrs Tufte, peering down at her handiwork through a pair of spectacles as thick as the tavern windows. 'His shirts he will care little about.'

'In fact he will prefer his shirts to remain dirty,' Mrs Munsen added, 'so that everyone can see that he labours endlessly, without stopping – ever.'

'Do not get angry when he forgets your birthday and your anniversary, even if he becomes a small child when you forget his.'

Silje could hear Freya in the kitchen and prayed she would come through and sit with them.

'Accept all gifts, no matter how pathetic, with a grace and gratitude that is far greater than the monetary worth of the gift itself.' Mrs Schau turned Silje's napkin around and told her to pull the threads and start again.

'Never tell him why you are angry,' Mrs Tufte said. 'He must discover the reasons for himself.'

Mrs Munsen agreed. 'It is good for him to exercise his small mind once in a while.'

Mrs Tingelstaad, at one-hundred-and-one, thought to be the oldest living woman in the mountains, said, 'Only let him finish in your mouth if he has done something nice for you: fed the goats, milked the cows, cleaned out the privy and so forth.'

The old women nodded in agreement, and Silje wished she'd thought to bring a notebook.

'When Mr Tufte was alive,' Mrs Tufte said sadly, 'I always let him end in my mouth.'

Mrs Munsen used her eyes to send a cool warning to the others.

'Then you were a fool,' said Mrs Tingelstaad without looking up. 'You give the child one candy bar at a time; do not throw it the entire sweet shop.'

Mrs Tufte shrugged. 'He liked it, I liked it, and I did not have to change the sheets.'

Mrs Tingelstaad had to confess that in eighty years of lovemaking she'd never considered this.

'And you, child,' said Mrs Schau, pointing a long, gnarled finger at Silje's embroidery effort, 'should learn to sew like a real woman. His socks will not darn themselves.'

'I can sew perfectly well,' Silje protested. 'It is all these frills and laces I have no time for.'

Mrs Tingelstaad grumbled over the years she'd spent needlessly washing sheets.

'You should make time,' said Mrs Tufte. She bit through the thread, tied an impossibly small knot and threw the napkin on the pile. She had completed eight before Silje had finished her first. 'You cannot be gallivanting around the village poking your nose into everyone's business. Young Erik will be your foremost concern from now on, as you have always been his.'

'You think I will not make a worthy wife.'

'I think you will make the greatest wife in the history of this village if you grow up and apply yourself.'

Silje wondered if it was their time served on earth that granted old people some otherworldly right to be rude. 'I am sure I will try my best,' she said tightly.

'I'm sure you will. Now, that one is ruined. Start another one.'

Silje dropped the napkin in the basket and glumly picked out another plain square of cotton.

'Watch for signs of slyness in the marital bed,' Mrs Tingelstaad announced while squaring her wooden teeth with her little finger. 'For creatures of such limited imagination they can be quite craven in their attempts to engage in a spot of buggery at your expense. Do not allow it.'

The others nodded sagely.

'Unless it is a special occasion,' said Mrs Schau. 'His birthday, Christmas and so forth.'

'Not Christmas,' Mrs Tingelstaad said. 'That would be unseemly.' She crossed herself, though to the best of Silje's knowledge she was not a practising Catholic.

'And never after a heavy meal,' said Mrs Tufte. She raised an eyebrow when she noticed Silje was showing more interest in the parlour door than anything the four old women had to say. 'If he should stray then do not berate him or beg him never to stray again. Never extract promises from him that you know he is incapable of keeping.'

Infidelity was a matter always uppermost in Silje's thoughts. She turned her eyes away from the parlour door and to Mrs Tufte whose own eyes had stained pink.

'Then what should I do?' Silje asked. 'Forgive such indiscretions? Turn a blind eye to any philandering? Is that what you did, Mrs Tufte?'

Mrs Munsen slammed her hand down on the table, making everyone in the parlour jump in their seats. 'You will mind your tongue, young lady!'

Mrs Tufte raised a conciliatory hand. 'No, she may speak. The question is, will she listen?'

'I am listening,' said Silje.

Mrs Tufte passed a sharpened look to each of the women in turn, a warning that what she was about to say must go no further.

'What I did, Silje Ohnstad, is precisely what I have just told you not to do. I threatened, I begged, I tried to extract promises, and here I sit, abandoned.'

'Abandoned?' echoed Mrs Schau. 'But I thought you said—'

'Hush, Maeva!'

Mrs Tufte placed her work on the table and sat back in her chair, her arms folded across her rounded stomach.

'Then what must I do?' Silje asked.

'You must turn a blind eye and protect your sanity by extracting small vengeances wherever you can.'

Silje frowned. 'I do not understand.'

'Fill his boots with goat shit.' Mrs Munsen bit through another thread.

'While he bathes in the kitchen, you must trip and dump a pale of ice into his lap,' said Mrs Tingelstaad. She began work on her ninth napkin; she was clearly the fastest of them all.

'I have an extract of nettles and poison ivy that I used to sprinkle in his underwear and on the privy seat,' said Mrs Schau.

'It takes time,' said Mrs Tufte, 'but they can be trained. If I had known these dear ladies when Mr Tufte's eye first turned then he would still be with me today.'

The other three women blushed and took turns to reach across and pat her on the knee.

'And finish any other business before you take your vows.' She held up her napkin to the light.

Silje blinked and looked at her. Mrs Tufte ignored her, studying the lines of silk more intently than she needed to. The other women seemed similarly unwilling to meet Silje's eye.

'Why don't you go through and see her?' Mrs Tufte said.

Silje replied in more haste than she would have liked. 'There is no need.'

'I feel there is.'

Silje looked at her but the old woman still refused to look back. 'I will return shortly,' she said.

'There is no hurry,' Mrs Tufte replied. 'Your heart really isn't in it.' And then she chose to look at Silje with a thin tight smile on her face. 'I was referring to the embroidery.'

Silje felt the hairs on her neck rising. She got up from her seat and went through to the kitchen where she found Freya making the most delicate skolebrød and the most terrible mess.

'That woman is evil,' she said.

'She was speaking the truth,' Freya replied without turning around.

It means nothing, Silje told herself. *She rarely turns unless she is asked to*. 'Can we go somewhere?'

'Go somewhere,' Freya echoed, scrubbing angrily at a baking pan.

'Somewhere we can be alone.'

'And why do we need to be alone?'

'Do not tease me, Freya.'

'You are soon to be married. Perhaps Mrs Tufte is right; perhaps it is time you acted like it. Perhaps it is time,' she said, 'you put away your childish things.'

'That is not how I see you. You know it's not. Why are you being like this? You said you would be happy to share me with Erik.'

'I said I would share you, Silje. I never said I would be happy.'

'So you tell me this now, seven days before my wedding.'

'Dear God, you should really try to listen to yourself talking.' Freya tried one of the cupcakes. She wrinkled her nose and spat it into her hand.

'You should let Mrs Tufte make them.'

'I wanted to do something nice for your day.' She wiped her hands and shovelled the remains into the large pail she'd dragged in from the garden. Before she replaced the lid Silje saw it was half-filled with discarded cakes.

'They would not keep,' Silje said quietly. 'They would spoil before—'

'I am trying, Silje! I needed time to make them perfect.' She shivered and ran her fingers and flour through her hair. 'I just needed time. I wanted to show myself that I could be happy for you, but if my baking is anything to go by then clearly I cannot.' She made an odd hiccoughing sound, and then another, and then she began to cry.

Silje found herself with her arms folded around her, unsure as to how she'd arrived there.

'I thought I could share you. I thought I could wait in the dark for what affections you could spare me. I thought I could live in the shadow of the love Erik and you will share. I thought I could help look after your children while you worked the orchid fields. I thought they would call me Aunt Freya and I would love them as though they were our own. I thought I could live half a life while you lived two. But I am not strong enough, or perhaps I am not that weak. I am sorry but part of you is not enough.'

Silje kissed her and caressed her throat until she could feel her heart pounding inside her chest. She thought she'd won, but when she slid her hand between Freya's thighs, Freya pushed her away.

'No. I have much to do.'

'More baking,' Silje said, breathing as though she'd run the height of the mountain.

'Don't make fun of me.'

'I'm sorry.' She nuzzled the hair at Freya's temple, taking in her scent. It was different now: a bitter cinnamon mingled with the smell of decaying orchids. Silje realised whatever Freya felt, her heart exuded through her skin.

Again, Freya pulled away from her. 'I have errands to run.' She snatched two envelopes from the windowsill.

'You made the invitations,' said Silje, yearning for her and humbled by her in the same moment. 'I did not know. They were beautiful.'

'I have two left to deliver. Come with me.'

'You are destroying what little beauty we have found in this world, Freya. Why should I go with you?'

'Because I want us to walk together along the mountain paths, hand in hand as though we were intended. I want us to talk of our future marriage and our future children and our unborn grandchildren. I want us to close our eyes and wish ourselves at the altar of the village church. I want us to walk in the night and imagine when we are old and dying, spending our last days in front of a log fire in the cottage that belonged to your father. And I want us to do all this tonight.'

Silje remained still. She had always believed herself to be a person empathic to the emotions of others – no matter how many told her otherwise; that she could feel the ebb and flow of Freya Dorfmann with whom she shared a love that ran deeper than flesh, perhaps deeper than the essence of humanity she called a soul. Theirs was a connection that bound their bones, their thoughts, their very lives. But if this was as she believed then Silje could not understand how she had not seen this day coming.

'You are leaving.'

Freya did not shake her head.

'You are leaving Fólkvangr.'

The girl sighed and her thin body shook.

'You are leaving Norway.' Silje's heart folded and kindled into ashes. 'When?'

'The day after your wedding.'

'You are leaving *me*.'

'I am starting a new life in England, Silje. Gunther is returning to London before he is deployed to Paris. We will row out of the harbour at Trondheim and rendezvous with a British submarine in the seas to the North.'

When he forced his lips to mine, he wasn't declaring his love; he was saying goodbye. 'What will you do in England?' she asked, wondering when she had become so vain.

'I can help the Jewish refugees. Hundreds of us escape every day, even as thousands more are put to the chambers.'

'You cannot go. I won't let you.'

'There has to be more to my life than being a tiny part of yours. If you love me as you say you do then you will understand that.'

'I will call off the wedding. I will tell Erik this very night. I will tell all of Fólkvangr, all of Norway, that we will be together now and for always. You are smiling. You think I will not do this for you. I will go and tell Mrs Tufte and her coven of witches this very instant.'

Silje opened the parlour door and Freya pushed it shut.

Mrs Tufte called from the next room, asking if all was well.

'Yes, Mrs Tufte. I bumped into the door.'

'You never bump into any door, Freya Dorfmann.'

Silje began to sob under her breath.

'Very well then,' said Mrs Tufte. 'Call if you need anything, and do not waste any more flour. There is a war on.'

Freya said, 'Yes, Mrs Tufte,' and reached out until her fingertips found Silje's cheek. She ran her hands over her eyes, across her forehead, and down either side of her nose until her fingers rested on her lips. 'Still so beautiful,' she whispered. 'You will not say anything to Erik, because it is not within you to be so cruel. He has loved you for so long. He deserves the chance to make you happy in return.'

'I am dreaming,' said Silje. 'I am asleep, and when I wake you will have said none of this.' It was a childish thing to say and Silje did not want Freya to remember her for childish things. 'I do not understand; why would you do this to us… to me.'

Freya wiped away her tears and said, 'It would mean the world if you wished me luck.'

'Wish you luck.' said Silje. *I will do no such thing. I will curse you with every sinew of my being. I will pray you never know peace. You made me want you, love you, and when I see I will never want or love another, you abandon me. No, I will not wish you well. I wish you all the misfortune your treacherous heart deserves. The General is right; your kind is evil, Freya Dorfmann.*

'Silje?'

Silje opened her eyes and smiled. 'You will not need luck, Freya. I was blessed to know you even if it was for a short time. You will be safer in England and Gunther will take good care of you.'

Freya beamed with joy. 'Then tell Mrs Tufte you are going to run errands with me, and we will walk the hills together this last time.'

42

Dusk had fallen when they left Mrs Tufte's cottage. The air was warm, though Silje thought there was a bitterness to it, something she'd tasted as a child: the tears that ran down the back of her throat when her father told her her mother would soar with the angels.

It is loss, she thought, looking at Freya. *And when I lose you, it will be like losing her all over again.*

Freya took her by the hand as they walked past the Fehns' cottage. There was a light in the front parlour and a candle burning in an upstairs window.

Freya sniffed the air. 'Why do they burn a candle?'

'They burn it for Lisbeth, so she can always find her way home.'

Freya nodded and squeezed her hand. 'That is very sweet.'

'I will burn a candle for you so that you will find your way back to me.'

'I will not know it is there, Silje, not from England.'

'I will light it anyway.'

They walked in silence, a southerly road from the Fehns' home, a road that Silje seldom took. It was steep, even for those hardened by the mountains. The trees grew thick, the rocks grew larger with every step, and high above them the foliage met and conspired to shun the light of the moon. It would have been a despairing journey, but she was with Freya, and Freya travelled with light and colour in her wake. She held Silje's hand tightly and led her with an assuredness that dispelled Silje's fear. How perfect they were when they were together, and how foolish she was not to have seen it before.

Less than half a mile from the village, the road ended at a large cottage, even larger than that of the Fehns. In front of the cottage was a square containing a miniature castle and a moat. Silje remembered the castle, how its intricately carved ramparts and buttresses towered over her, blocking out the sun. Now it stopped just shy of her chest. Had it been so long since she'd visited Doctor Lomen's home?

'Why are we here, Freya?'

'Because Doctor Lomen has yet to reply to the wedding invitation.'

'Are you really so eager to see me given away to another?'

'I want this to be the happiest day of your life, Silje. How can it be if someone as dear to us as Doctor Lomen does not attend?'

The door to the cottage was shut, but opened easily when Freya pushed against it. Doctor Lomen had a hallway, a sure sign of affluence in Silje's mind. It was dark, too dark to see, so she allowed Freya to lead her, and when Freya stopped sharply she almost ran into her.

'I hear breathing. He's in here.'

Silje held her by the wrist to stop her from opening the door. 'We usually knock,' she said, rapping her knuckles against the pine. 'Doctor Lomen?'

There was no reply.

'Are you sure he is in there?'

Freya slipped past her and pushed open the door. Silje followed her inside and still could not see a thing, though now she could hear the sound of breathing, and could smell unwashed flesh and the rancid tang of urine.

'What are you doing here?' growled a voice in the darkness.

'We should leave,' said Silje.

'We are not leaving,' Freya replied. 'Doctor Lomen. It is Silje and Freya. We have come to see you.'

'Obviously,' the voice growled back.

'May we light a candle?'

'You may not. Now please leave.'

'I am going to light a candle, Doctor Lomen,' Silje said. 'Freya may be able to see you in the strange way she sees everything. But in here I am blind and I am sure you would not want me to stumble and hurt myself. I doubt you are in any state to attend to me.'

She heard him cough, heard Freya strike a match, heard herself whisper 'God in heaven' at the first sight of the good doctor in the dim light. His skin had thinned, so much so that she could see the veins and bones underneath. His eyes were hollow and had sunken deep into his skull; his hair, once the colour of fire, had dulled and greyed. His magnificent moustache had disappeared, though patches of it remained. It seemed he'd hacked at it and then decided there was no point in finishing the job. *He is killing himself,* she thought, *as slowly and as painfully as he can.* She guessed he had not eaten sufficiently in weeks, though he must have been drinking water to have survived so long.

At least she hoped it was water.

She allowed her nose to twitch, just once, and said, 'I think a good long bath is in order, Doctor Lomen.'

The doctor's eyes switched between them, and he drew his arms more tightly around a picture he held to his chest. Freya felt her way along the walls until she found the door that led to the rear of the house.

'May I take that from you?' Silje said, wrestling the picture out of his grip. Freya returned a moment later carrying a large metal tub. She placed it to one side, hearing Silje struggling.

'Can I help?' she asked doubtfully.

'There is no need.' Silje pushed the picture towards him and then pulled it back sharply, taking the doctor by surprise and causing him to relinquish his grasp.

'There's nothing here,' she said, looking at the empty frame. 'What happened to the picture?'

Doctor Lomen looked at the frame as though trying to remember something.

'Was this a picture of your sons?'

He stared blankly at the frame.

'No matter,' said Silje, throwing it to one side. 'We shall find the picture later. Before that, we shall get you clean and then make you something to eat.'

Though she did not savour the thought of seeing the doctor without attire, Silje decided that she should be the one to wash him.

'I have experience,' she told Freya.

'And what is that supposed to mean?'

'It means that I know how to wash people who – through no fault of theirs – have been unable to keep themselves clean for a number of days, or weeks.'

'You are referring to me.'

'I am. Besides, you are far too young to be seeing old men without their clothes.'

'I am not so old,' the doctor grumbled.

'Too young to—I am blind!' Freya said. She found Silje's breathing and leaned closer so she could whisper into her ear. 'And not too young for you to take me whenever you please.'

'What was that? It is rude to whisper, child!' Doctor Lomen struggled to his feet, and then collapsed into his chair. 'I am not drunk!'

'We did not say you were drunk, Doctor Lomen.' Silje glared at her. 'But you do need someone to look after you, to make sure you are well enough to attend my *wedding*.'

Freya's nostrils flared. 'I will be in the kitchen.' She stormed through to the back of the house, caring little for what she trod on or kicked from her path.

Doctor Lomen belched loudly. 'She seems angry with you.'

'She is always angry with me. Now take off your clothes while I fetch some water.'

A shallow brook ran close to Doctor Lomen's home, and it was from there that Silje filled four large pails and took them back to the cottage. She heaved them through and landed them awkwardly on the floor. To her astonishment, the doctor was already naked and sitting in the tin bathtub, staring at the window. His eyes swivelled towards her as she approached with the first pail.

'The water will be quite cold at this time of year,' she warned. 'Perhaps I should warm it first.'

'Nonsense, child. We are of mountain stock,' he said, the only explanation that the men of the mountain needed for childish and foolhardy behaviour.

'Very well.' She held the bucket above the bath and averted her eyes. 'Are you sure?'

'I am,' the doctor said stubbornly through clenched teeth.

Silje chanced a downward glance before she began to pour. His body was thin and white, and the flesh, like that of his face, was almost transparent and tempered with liver spots. She was suddenly afraid that a rush of cold water would dissolve him like salt. 'Please hurry with the soup, Freya.'

In the kitchen, several pots crashed to the floor by way of reply. Silje swallowed and allowed a tentative eye to rove towards the doctor's groin where his manhood lay coiled in a nest of red hair. By Silje's reckoning the doctor was of similar proportions to Junges Fehn, perhaps larger, though circumcised which she did not particularly care for.

'Do not just stand there, child,' the doctor barked, his eyes shut.

Silje poured the contents of the pail over him, and to his credit, he hardly flinched, though the shock forced the last mote of air from his lungs.

'Jesus Christ,' he said finally. 'That was most—' he coughed a mouthful of sputum on to the floor, 'bracing.'

Silje thought it best he did not remain in the bath for too long, so proceeded to scrub him quickly and with vigour. The second round of cold water brought a scream that rattled the cottage rafters. By the third, he was acclimatised and very much sober.

'When I said I was not drunk,' he began, 'I was lying.'

Silje scoured about his armpits.

'This is the most sober I have been since the night of Freya's birthday, the night I lost my sons.'

She wiped the flannel across his chest.

'I was prepared for the eventuality,' he said, 'no matter how unpleasant, that I might outlive one or two of them. Perhaps Jostein or Lars; they were both always so reckless.'

Silje remembered that Lars had once tried to leap from one mountain ledge to another when they were twelve years old. She'd promised him a kiss if he could do so. He'd plummeted over fifty feet, his fall arrested by the branches of the pine trees that grew below. He'd escaped with cuts and a broken wrist. Even as Doctor Lomen came bounding through the forest with her father and six others, Lars had struggled to his feet and stolen his prize: a kiss he'd planted firmly on her lips. He'd said she should forget any promises she'd made to Erik Brenna. He was braver and far more worthy of her.

'I kept them away from you, you know.' Doctor Lomen took the flannel from her and proceeded to clean his private parts. 'If you could make Lars jump from a mountain then I could not bear to think what you could make the younger ones do.'

'I said I was sorry for that a long time ago.'

'I am not chastising you, child. It just occurred to me how little I knew of destiny's cruelty back then. I thought that they were only in danger from a flighty little strumpet who lived just beyond the village.' He chuckled so Silje decided he'd spoken in jest. 'How much wiser I am today,' he said. 'And this newfound wisdom only cost me my sons.'

'You are not to blame. It was the Germans. It is always the Germans. Your sons died bravely trying to—'

'They died stupidly. They died wastefully, on a scheme that was doomed to failure and almost brought the wrath of the Reich down upon our heads.'

'You must not say such things! You must *never* say such things.'

'Do not mistake my anger for regret, Silje Ohnstad. My sons I will always love but I will always punish myself for not showing them how precious they were to me. Perhaps if I had told them then they would not have thrown their lives away. Perhaps they would not have been the cause of your brother's terrible ordeal.'

'They would have done this foolish thing no matter what,' said Silje firmly. 'Because they loved you and wanted you to be proud of them. Are you proud of them, Doctor Lomen?'

'Roy,' he said. 'He must have been so very frightened…'

'Answer me.'

The doctor whispered 'Pride' and nodded slowly. 'I hope I will be, one day.'

'Then as your friends we shall wait with you for that day.'

He nodded grimly and rose from the bath.

She leaned back on her haunches and watched transfixed as the doctor's phallus travelled endlessly past her line of sight.

'A towel, if you please.'

Silje blinked. She had not thought to find one.

* * *

The doctor consumed a whole pot of soup without offering any to his saviours. Neither of them cared; they were just pleased to see a semblance of colour returning to his flesh.

Silje found him some clothes while Freya told him about the forthcoming wedding in rapid bursts of excited exposition. She ended her monologue by thrusting an invitation under his nose. 'Please say you'll come.'

He had to cross his eyes to read it.

'Please!'

'Freya, if the doctor does not wish to attend—'

'I will be there,' he said.

'And you will be fit and you will be strong and healthy, yes?'

He nodded; Freya waited.

'Yes, I will eat plenty and stay away from alcohol.'

'And you will be clean,' Silje. said 'You will have a bath on the morning of the wedding.'

The doctor chose not to dignify her request with an answer. 'And I will return to my duties as soon as I am able.'

They left the cottage after Freya told the doctor to open wide, and then, with Silje holding her hand, placed a sugar lump on the end of his tongue. The doctor seemed puzzled for a moment, then roared with laughter.

'The pair of you,' he said. 'Stay friends, always. Things are so much better in this world when you are together.'

Silje looked at her. Freya did not look back. It was one of the rare times Silje wished she could.

* * *

'And now, your brother.' Freya waved the last invitation as they walked back along Fólkvangr's main thoroughfare.

Silje refused to believe Magnus had not said he'd come. 'He does not have to reply. He is my brother. His reply is a given.'

'Just to be sure then.'

The German curfew kept the streets empty. The Germans' fear of air-raids kept them dark. It had been many months since Freya had lit the lamps, a task she'd taken to alone since the death of Mr Kleppe. Silje had protested, of course, but found that these days she was less inclined to battle through Freya's wilfulness. She wondered if it was because she no longer saw her as the lost, blind orphan adopted by the village. She is a grown woman now, Silje thought. Less easy to influence, less likely to bind herself in an unholy triangle for something as fleeting and intangible as love.

'If you come back to our cottage then you will miss the curfew.'

'If the Germans find out I've missed the curfew then that will be the least of my worries.'

'Nevertheless, it would be wise for you to stay with us tonight.'

'Us?' echoed Freya. 'Or you?'

'I will sleep on the floor if that is what you want.'

'That will not work, Silje. It never works. We always…'

Silje waited for her to finish, soon realising she could not. 'Make love?'

Freya nodded.

'I remember when it was I who could not bring myself to say those words. It is odd how things change.'

'I suppose.'

'I will not touch you. You have my word.'

Freya sighed and for all the world looked as though she was looking for the stars. 'It is not you I am concerned about.'

'Oh,' said Silje, feeling her chest swell. 'Well, then I shall have the will for both of us.'

Freya looked doubtful but continued to walk beside her. The streets already seemed desolate. The stalls were closed and folded back into the cottages; the shops drew their shutters and the villagers began to make their way home. Silje thought it odd that Fólkvangr clung so graciously to the Germans' curfew. After all, the Nazis came to the village so rarely these days and when they did come it was often to see her.

If not for the moon they would have been in darkness when they reached the cottage. Jon Ohnstad's truck was not there. Silje thought he must still be in Bergen, selling his flowers to the few shopkeepers that remained.

Or perhaps he was still with her – the woman who is not my mother.

Freya went inside and upstairs. She waited at Magnus's door until Silje joined her, and then, for the first time that Silje could remember, she knocked.

'If that is you, Silje, I am not in the mood for company.'

'It is me, Magnus,' said Freya.

He was silent for a moment. Then he asked, 'What do you want?'

'I wish to speak to you. Can we come in?'

'"We"? Who is with you?'

'I am with her, Magnus.'

'Silje.' He sounded disappointed.

'We have come to see you.'

Again, silence. They could hear him rummaging through his bedding.

'His eyepatch,' Silje whispered.

Freya nodded, and pushed open the door.

'Freya!'

There came a cry of rage. Silje saw a malnourished wraith stumble towards the door, too weak to prevent Freya pushing her way inside.

He turned away from them, his shaking hands trying to tie the eyepatch about his head. 'Leave me alone!'

Freya took hold of his hand and twisted it back towards his wrist. Then she snatched the eyepatch away from him and pushed him down onto the bed.

'What are you doing?'

'I am inviting you to your sister's wedding.' Freya leapt on top of him, pinning his shoulders to the bed with her knees. She held his head firmly in place, while his legs kicked and thrashed uselessly.

'Hold his legs, Silje.'

Silje remained rooted to the floor.

'Silje!'

She stepped inside to do as she was told, pressing her hands heavily on his ankles. He was stronger than she imagined he would be; she pressed her weight down further, holding him fast.

'I will kill you both for this!'

It hadn't been so long since she'd seen him without his eyepatch. She wondered if she'd be less repulsed if she saw him like this more often. She turned her head away.

'You will break my legs, you fat goat!'

'I am not fat!'

'I would know what you look like, Magnus.'

'I am ugly, Freya, now get off me!'

She did not listen, which came as no surprise to Silje. Instead, she ran her thumbs across his forehead where his thinning hair met his scalp. She traced every line above his brow, working down either side of his nose.

'What are you doing? No! Don't—'

Her right thumb pressed against his left eye, and her left thumb slipped into his ruined eye socket.

Magnus howled and Silje vomited into her mouth. She ran downstairs and outside into the trees where she spat the contents of her stomach onto the ground.

'Dear Christ,' she whispered to herself, 'that damned girl.'

She doubled over and retched again, emptying the rest of her gullet. The mountain chill froze her throat, making her gasp and cough. She wiped her mouth and stared up at Magnus's window. He was so angry, more angry than she had ever seen him. Freya could not hope to pin down such unbridled rage for more than a few moments. And when he had freed himself from her then what would he do? He would beat her, definitely; kill her, perhaps.

I must go back, she thought. But her legs would not move. It was fear, and the horror at having abandoned him, her brother – and her, the love of her life.

But then another thought came to her, piercing the base of her skull and then burning its way through until it had captured her entirely: Freya, alone with him and in the darkness, astride him, her knees crushing his shoulders, her haunches pushed against his chest, her thumb inside his skull…

And so in the end it was jealousy that drove her back inside the cottage. She took the stairs two at a time and arrived at Magnus's doorway to find them both lying on his bed, Freya curved around his back, her arms wrapped tightly around him.

She raised a finger to her lips. 'He is asleep.'

Silje, her blood boiling, watched the steady fill of his lungs accompanied by his soft weeping. Freya unravelled herself from him in a fluid unfolding of her limbs and rose from the bed without causing his body to stir. 'I think he may begin to heal now.'

'What did you say to him?'

'I said nothing. I just held him until his hatred fled.'

'I could have done that. I should have done that.'

'It does not matter who did it, Silje. It is done.' Freya slipped past her without making a ripple in the air. Silje followed her downstairs, and when they reached the kitchen, she took hold of her arm. Freya shook it free.

'What is it, Silje? What is it you wish to ask me? And before you do, think carefully. I suspect your question will say such terrible things about you.'

Silje clenched her fists.

'You were gone for just a few moments. Even at our most passionate we were never so quick.'

'Please do not make fun of me, Freya.'

'I am not.'

'You wanted to though, didn't you? You wanted to have him. You always have!' For the first time in her life Silje realised what it must be like to be with her. *Poor Erik*, she thought sourly, grateful for his devotion, despising his weakness.

'For the love of Christ, Silje, listen to yourse—'

Silje crushed her lips against her mouth and felt her soul flowing into her, melding two halves of one heart. Freya's fingers crept around her throat and the heat of her broke the sweat from Silje's skin. The smell of cinnamon filled her nostrils.

'We can go to the orchid barn,' she said, searching desperately for the hem of Freya's skirt. 'We can be alone there. It will be like before, except

I will not shout at you or make you feel sad. I swear I will devote my life to your happiness.'

She slipped her hand between Freya's thighs, and Freya buried her teeth into her shoulder, clawing at the back of her neck. Even as Freya whispered 'No', Silje knew she had won. She had seized her heart's desire and would die before letting it go. Freya's hand pushed deep and turned inside her, lifting her to her toes. Silje caught her breath and closed her eyes. *God help me*, she thought. *I have won.*

43

After the massacre, the General was posted back to Berlin, where he received the kind of muted reception given to fallen heroes. The Führer kissed his cheeks then stripped him of his command. He had put down a village rebellion and birthed a national uprising. After Fólkvangr, the Norwegians met force with fire. Airfields were bombed; fuel dumps and munitions depots were raided and set alight. Collaborators were murdered in their sleep and their corpses burned in the streets.

But Gruetzmacher saw none of this; he was reassigned to a small logistics unit based in Telemark, where he rubber-stamped medical supply orders and organised the transportation of officers' uniforms to the Russian front.

I thought of him in his small dark basement, seething.

When Berlin fell he took what little money he had and escaped, travelling through Italy and Spain. Klein's notes were unclear as to how he made it across the Atlantic to Argentina, but when he arrived there, ten years and six identities later, he found the cream of the Nazi high command huddled there like 'pheasants at a country shoot', to use his own words. He was smart enough to leave before the Israeli kill squads arrived…

He pleaded with the Americans, offering his knowledge of the Iscariot Programme in exchange for sanctuary. But the Israelis were friends now, and the allies felt something akin to shame for throwing Norway to the wolves during the war. The little country that could deserved better, so they refused, and Gruetzmacher ran again.

Two years later, he arrived in New Zealand, exhausted and destitute. He made his way to the interior and built a small holding where he grew vegetables and raised, ironically enough, goats and llamas. His medical skills were revered by the locals, and though he never became wealthy he lived in modest comfort, spending his days tending his livestock, and his evenings…

Yes, it was the evenings that were his problem. 'Medical research', Mr Klein's notes said, which as a pastime for a goat farmer was going to stick out like a broken thumb.

Gruetzmacher had left a trail of shattered children from Berlin to Auckland. He'd kept himself hidden; travelled by night; slipped into new names and new lives with the ease of a seasoned actor. He'd walked across continents with his hat pulled low and his eyes to the ground, and for the most part he'd moved through the world without making waves. But there was a sickness in him, a hunger for pre-adolescent flesh that he could neither sate or control. And so his trail ended in New Zealand, at a mountain of silent, damaged children that stretched for five miles in all directions from his farm.

I wondered if he was surprised when he was disturbed one evening with a thumping at his door.

'Auckland Constabulary, Mr Szachmanowicz', he would have heard.

'Yes? Why are you here?' he would have replied, running through a checklist of alibis and lies, and if it came to it, excuses.

'I wish to ask you some questions. There have been allegations made against you, Mr Szachmanowicz. Serious allegations.'

Gruetzmacher would have put on his dressing gown, told the borrowed child to be quiet and locked her in his cellar. He would have licked the sweat from his upper lip, smoothed down the remains of his hair and opened the door with a smile.

And he would have answered the officer's questions, and he would have kept smiling and offered him refreshments, because he wouldn't have known it was Jesper Bergström drinking his tea…

I stopped reading and exhaled loudly. I'd been holding my breath, which is something I'd been doing a lot during the flight, every time the plane hit turbulence. I'd vomited three times and was grateful that the last was little more than dry heaving. I think the flight attendants were glad too. It was my first time flying but I understood the principle: several hundred tonnes of metal, plastic and wires are hurled into the air, propelled by a mixture of things that explode; it all stays aloft for several hours and then drops out of the sky under the control of one or two people who may or may not be having a lucky day.

Yes, I understood it; I just didn't believe it worked, and it was only the threat of a slow and painful end that had convinced me to take the tickets and passport and make the flight to Germany.

I slipped the papers back into their wallet. A flight attendant, the tall pretty one with grey eyes and a sharp, upturned nose, spoke my name, or rather the name given to me by Bergström. It was a strange name, one that I found hard to remember.

'Mrs Hart?' she said again.

I jumped in my seat and shouted, 'Yes.'

'I just wanted to make sure you're feeling better,' she said, with a pained smile chiselled across her dark red lips. 'We'll be landing in just a few minutes. Do you think you'll need another bag?'

I looked at the pocket in front of my seat; I'd used them all up in the first twenty minutes of the flight.

I nodded, and showed her two fingers.

She looked alarmed and hurried away to fetch them.

I was the only soul in first class. The flight attendant said short hauls were usually empty up front. I guess Bergström wanted to keep me away from the eyes of the other passengers. I wondered if I'd have a better chance at the front or the back if the plane crashed.

'We won't crash.' The sparkling flight attendant responded, a little too quickly for comfort.

'What if we do.'

'We won't.'

'But if we do...'

'Then,' she replied without letting the rictus of a smile slip from her face, 'where you sit will make very little difference.'

* * *

There was a woman waiting for me at Dresden's small and parochial airport. She held up a sign that said 'Mrs Hart,' so I walked up and down the arrival lounge several times without realising she was waiting for me. Arrivals was not particularly crowded – business types mainly, with perhaps a sprinkling of tourists and couples snatching a brief getaway. I was on my third circuit when a policeman gently took my elbow and asked me if I was all right.

'Yes,' I said dumbly, 'I think so.'

'You appear to be lost.'

I said that I was waiting for someone.

'You appear to have been waiting for quite some time.'

I asked him if he'd been watching me, which on reflection was the most stupid thing I could have said. He pressed the radio fastened to his shoulder. Before he could utter a word, a hand reached between us and thrust an ID card under his nose.

'She's with me.' The accent was soft, German, musical in a shrill kind of way. The officer took his time reading the ID card and then looked at me as though he'd found me stuck to the bottom of his shoe.

'I appear to have been mistaken,' he said, though he didn't say what he'd mistaken me for. He tapped the brim of his cap and was on his way. My saviour turned out to be a tall, dark-haired woman who reminded me of my mother when she'd been younger. She had a firm, almost masculine jaw and her pale skin was layered with a thin covering of foundation applied as a social courtesy and nothing more. She wore a slim-fitting skirt suit and heavy, flat shoes. Her lips were slightly puckered with age and her eyebrows met above a wide, broken nose. She'd chosen not to do anything about it so I knew I was dealing with someone who'd break me in two if I stepped out of line.

I said 'Thank you' and she waved the sign under my nose.

'Didn't you see it?' she demanded. 'I thought Bergström had briefed you.'

'He has, he did. I just forgot. Who are you?'

She glanced at her watch. 'We're late. We'll skip the hotel and go straight to the meeting place.'

'What meeting?

'Follow me.'

She set off at a near-march.

'I have luggage.'

'It'll be taken care of.' She walked in a perfectly straight line, forcing other people to hop awkwardly out of her way.

'My name is Brigit.'

'I don't need to know that.'

'Well, I thought I'd tell you anyway.'

'That is your choice.'

'And do you have a name?'

'Yes, of course I do.' She glanced again at her watch and left the terminal; the sliding doors barely had time to open. Her car, a BMW I think, was parked in a police bay just outside. She opened the rear door and tossed the sign onto the seat before beckoning me to get in. I hesitated for a moment, realising that for the past three weeks I'd been nothing more than a pinball: ricocheted between train stations, hotels and airports. I was back against the springs, ready to be launched again.

Dresden was an old, small town; quite pretty, with a wide river that ran alongside ancient stone buildings and evergreen trees. It was getting on for early evening, so the town was lit from beneath its spires and domes. I would have liked to have opened the window and taken in the smell of the water, but when I tried the handle it didn't work.

'Do you live in Dresden?'

She drove the way she walked – with little regard for anyone else. 'I've been stationed here for twelve years.'

'So you are with the police?'

She replied with a terse 'No.'

'The secret service, then.'

'No more questions.'

So I stayed quiet while she slipped from lane to lane, making the rush-hour traffic seem stationary.

We crossed the river and headed south. The buildings grew older and greyer. They huddled together with only narrow cobbled streets to keep them from falling into each other. The sky became a latticework of blue lines edged by grey stone.

She stopped so sharply that I was thrown forward against the headrest.

'Here,' she said by way of an apology and pulled the handbrake as though she were breaking someone's neck. 'The narrow apartment building to the left of the fish restaurant. Head for the third floor, apartment two. He is expecting you.'

I was happy to be out of the car, and if the speed she drove away at was anything to go by, then she was just as glad to have seen the last of me.

The building's interior was fairly understated though it still managed to radiate a sense of 1920s opulence; the corridors were a pale cream colour with carpets to match, and there was a tall potted plant stationed between every door. The door of apartment 3-2 was no different to all the others: a thick sheaf of solid oak in a slightly lighter cream than the walls and carpets, presumably so you could see it. I rang the bell and settled back on my heels to wait. The door opened, so quickly that I jumped away from it. A small, stout man answered. He had large, protruding eyes and there were only a few wisps of white hair left on his head. Small moles covered his neck and his nose was a bulbous mass of broken veins. He looked at me and then looked down the corridor where I'd come from.

'You are alone?'

Clearly.

'You didn't bring her with you? The woman with the eyebrows? Is she with you?' He stepped out of the way without waiting for an answer. 'You'd better come in.'

I eased carefully past him, seeing there was a gelatinous bulge under his shirt. He saw me looking at it and crossed his arms over his chest. It was a colostomy bag. So at some point during his life, my newfound friend had made the acquaintance of Jesper Bergström.

A short hallway took us through to his living room, a large hexagon with a beige carpet. There was an angle of four couches against the furthest walls and a wooden television cabinet set opposite. A collection of smooth oak and marble tables were arranged, apparently at random, in the centre of the room, while every other wall had been turned into a bookcase that stretched from floor to ceiling. There were no photographs or pictures or mirrors. There was a drinks cabinet from where he poured himself a brandy from a crystal decanter.

'Would you like a drink?'

I shook my head and thought about Mr Klein lying dead in his small, grime-laden flat. I wondered why some war criminals lived better than others.

'You wish to ask me two questions.' He sipped at the glass and closed his eyes.

More games. I was so tired of these people and their games. But at least the first question was obvious. 'Who are you?'

He opened his eyes and smiled. 'Who am I now, or who was I then?'

'Whichever will get me out of here soonest.'

He was speechless for a moment; then, keen to maintain his air of self-importance, he threw back his head and laughed. 'You have something of a fire in you. I did not expect that.'

He placed the glass on the edge of the cabinet and smoothed down his shirt before making his announcement. 'I am Doctor Altman Gust.' He looked at me as though expecting me to swoon. Instead, I raised an eyebrow and shrugged.

'I see that you have not been properly briefed,' he said, visibly deflated. 'I was one of the Reich's foremost scientists. I am surprised you have not heard of me.'

I apologised.

'My work is still used in the treatment of schizophrenia and multiple personality disorders in Europe and the United States. In fact, the research I carried out during—'

'You're another Mengler,' I said. 'I get it.'

'Mengler was a hack. I am a psychiatrist and a student of the neurosciences. And now your second question.'

As easy as the first. 'Why hasn't Mr Bergström killed you?'

His face sank and he swallowed so loudly I could hear it from across the room. So that wasn't the right question.

'You do not wish to know about Iscariot?'

'Not yet,' I replied. 'I need to know how to stay alive. He's been dismembering Nazis for years, but he didn't kill Klein—'

'Who is Klein?'

'It doesn't matter; he's gone. But when he was alive he bought time by selling out war criminals like yourself.'

Gust nodded ruefully. 'Then you know all you need to know.' He poured himself another drink, his hands shaking so violently he couldn't put back the stopper. He placed it on cabinet. 'Bergström is a practical man. He can be reasoned with, bargained with once he has taken his pound of flesh.' He looked down at the bulge under his shirt. His fingers danced towards it, then he remembered he had company. 'If you can withstand the interrogation, if you can beg when your mouth is full of your own blood, then you may be able to prove you have some future value to him.'

I saw the tears in his eyes as he moved the bureau away from the wall. He ripped the soft wood from the rear of the cabinet and felt his way inside the frame. 'Do you want to know how to be useful to him, Fräulein? Betray everything and everyone you hold dear. Ah, here we are.' He had a large envelope in his hand. It had been white many years ago, but age and handling had turned it a pale yellow. 'This is my final bargaining chip. This is the last thing I have that kept me alive. It is Iscariot.'

He placed the envelope in my hands. I couldn't close my fingers to hold onto it, so it just stayed there resting on my palms.

'Then you should keep it,' I said.

He walked back to the bottle and refilled his glass. He poured a second one for me. 'You will drink with me, Fräulein.'

I said that I would.

'There is no point keeping it. Cleaver knows I have nothing left to offer him.'

I sipped at the glass, felt the liquid burning the back of my throat. I didn't like the taste; I didn't like the burning. I took another sip. 'He wants me to betray my father.'

Gust nodded. 'And will you?'

'He says he'll kill me if I don't.'

'That is not what I asked.'

I looked at the envelope and asked what was in it.

'A secret,' he said.

'And why does he want me to have it?'

'That I cannot answer.'

I opened the envelope, and he walked back to one of his uncomfortable-looking chairs.

Documents, all stamped *klassifiziert* and bearing the Nazi eagle. There were pictures of women and children, photographed face-on and again in profile. The text was so dense it gave me a headache just looking at it. Worse, it was all in German.

'You should go now.' Gust had arranged himself so he was facing the window, away from the apartment door. 'He will be here soon.'

'Bergström is still in Norway.'

'Oh child, you understand so little. Go. You will not wish to bear witness to what comes next.'

'I'll speak to him. I'll tell him you cooperated.'

'This is the agreement, Fräulein. I live as long as I am useful. But you should not concern yourself. When I first told him of Iscariot he thought I was lying. I showed him some of those documents and he left to speak to his friends at MOSSAD. He returned two days later and told me that I was to say nothing about this to anyone. He said in return for this information I would live for two more years and would be granted a relatively painless death.'

I wanted to tell him that pain, by its very nature, is relative. What is pain to a man who was forced to eat his own flesh and blood to survive the camps? No, Gust was going to die and he would die horribly.

'I should be going.'

'Yes,' he said. 'Yes, you really should.'

I left him alone, sitting with his eyes pointing at the sky. I took the stairs down to the lobby and was not surprised to find Bergström waiting for me outside. He was leaning against a plain white Mercedes van, and he was wearing blue overalls. There were two other men with him who were unloading plastic crates.

'Do you have it?' Bergström said.

I showed him the envelope. The two men carried the crates inside the apartment building without so much as a glance in my direction.

'Good. Read it through—'

'It's in German.'

'Read it through and it will explain everything.'

'How can I do that? I can barely read Norwegian.'

'You know what a library is, don't you?'

'I don't understand why I have to do all this. Gust says you've seen the document; you know what's in it. Why do you need me?'

He looked up and squinted at the window where I knew Gust was sitting, staring out. 'I have not told you before. I will not tell you now. Just keep your side of the agreement. Deliver your father and you can carry on running around Norway, indulging your mother's persecution complex. Now, I have work to do. Contact me on this number when you have your answer.' He handed me a slip of paper.

'I'm coming with you.'

'I'm sorry?'

'I'm coming back to the apartment with you.'

He narrowed his eyes; I couldn't tell if it was rage or admiration. 'And why on earth would you want to do that?'

'I don't want him to suffer.'

'And you think that I will be less thorough in my work in front of an audience.'

That was what I was thinking, yes. He took my wrist, deforming the bone in his grip. 'Come then, Miss Fossen,' he said, half-pulling, half-dragging me up the steps. 'Let me show you what little difference you make.'

The Quisling Orchid

(13th September 1941)

‘What is this?’, you are thinking. ‘The next newsletter is not due until October!’

Indeed, you are correct my friends. This is a special edition of The Quisling Orchid published with the kind permission of our friends the Germans! The reason for this break from our standard run is twofold:

1/. Since you and I have shared so much through these hallowed pages, I thought it fitting that I use the newsletter to announce my forthcoming nuptials. Yes, dear friends; your very own Silje

Ohnstad will (as of the 27th of September) become Mrs Silje Brenna.
So who is this dashing young swain who has stolen the heart of your maiden of the mountains? Well, his name is Erik, and I have known him almost as long as I have known myself. He is a farrier-craftsman by trade, and an artist and sculptor of noted accomplishment. He is a kind and forgiving man whom I am sure will make a fine husband and a devoted father (God willing). When I asked the District Commander if I could mention my engagement in The Orchid, he said yes, provided that I make it brief. I begged and pleaded with him to allow me a few more lines, and he agreed (to get me out of his headquarters more than anything else, I fear). It is a strange thing, my friends; I now realise that General Gruetzmacher was right all along. I could have said everything I needed to in a single sentence.

His name is Erik Brenna, and I love him with all my heart.

There!

2/. Our very own Vidkun Quisling will visit Bergen on his tour of Norway. He will be with us for just one day, so you should not miss the opportunity to see and hear such a great and wise man. The rally will be held on the 1st of October. The date should be easy to remember; it is three days after my wedding (and you are all invited to the reception!).
Attendance at his rally is compulsory for all Norwegians living within a five-mile circle of Bergen. German troops will be making random checks throughout the area on the day of the rally. Please do not be found at home!

Now, as this is a special issue, we have not had time to prepare our usual fare of recipes and short stories, so I shall be running a few of my all-time favourites!

So onward, dear friends! Onward.

44

'Fair maiden?' Magnus made an unpleasant sound in his throat, part way between a laugh and a sneer. 'You are many things, Dear Sister, but a "fair maiden" is not one of them.'

Though Silje rejoiced that her twin had been somewhat restored to her, at times such as these she wished he'd been returned less his acerbity. Freya had cast her spell over him, and Magnus had left his room and stepped back into his old life. Still, he rarely smiled and seldom spoke, and some days she hated how hurtful he could be.

She snatched the newsletter from him and gave it to Gunther, who sat to her left. Freya, who was sewing yet another eyepatch for Magnus, sat to her right.

'Ignore him,' Gunther said. 'You have been a hero this day, Silje.'

'Save your praise,' Silje said, blushing. 'Just do not ask me to do it again.'

Gunther had come to the cottage in the dead of darkness three nights before. An urgent transmission had been sent to members of the local resistance group without a key to decipher it.

'Another newsletter,' Silje had said, grinding her fists against her eyes. 'Gunther, we sent out the last one but a week ago! The General will never agree to it!'

'You must make him, Silje; it is vitally important that this message goes out.'

'And how will I make him do that?'

Gunther had looked to the earth and scuffed his boot in the pebbles.

'Oh.'

'I would not ask if it were not important.' He'd looked around him, peering into the blackness. 'It concerns the Quisling operation. We need to—'

'I do not need to know. I do not wish to know. Just give me the key and I will do what I can.'

And so that night, she'd assembled another newsletter, made from articles and stories and recipes she'd previously deigned unfit for publication. She'd written her own wedding announcement, weaving the message key into the text. She'd written a courteous reminder of Quisling's visit, and persuaded her father to take her to Bergen so she could speak to General Gruetzmacher before he carried out his morning inspection of the garrison…

'I did wonder,' said Magnus, belching on his ale, 'how you managed to convince him.'

'You should not ask such things,' Freya said, always so forgiving, even when he was cruel to her.

'He can ask if he wishes, Freya.' Silje turned to him and stared savagely into his single eye. 'You wish to know if I opened my legs for him, yes?'

Magnus grumbled something under his breath and looked down into his ale.

'If you want to know, Magnus, then have the courage to ask me, instead of making cowardly attacks from across the table.'

He kept his eye down, stirring his tankard with his finger.

'He did not mean it.' Freya placed a hand on his and then her other hand atop Silje's.

'But you want to know too, don't you?'

'Why would I possibly want to—?'

'I did not have to do anything,' Silje said. 'He simply took the papers and said he'd have the newsletter ready for distribution by the afternoon.'

'He wanted… nothing?' Gunther looked at her cautiously. 'That does seem strange.'

'He is a strange man; insane, in fact.'

'What was so important that it was worth risking my sister's virtue,' Magnus said without looking up.

Cruelty, again, thought Silje.

'It does not matter.'

'It does, clearly,' Magnus said.

Gunther said, 'Let it drop, Magnus.'

But Magnus would not. He leaned back in his chair. 'You will not say because you do not trust me.'

'Now you are being ridiculous.'

'You used to share operational imperatives with me. You used to seek my aid in planning raids, sabotaging supply routes—'

'Keep your voice down, damn you!'

'And now, you do not seem to trust any of us,' Magnus flashed a self-satisfied grin and then downed his ale. 'Or is it just me. You think I broke under torture, do you not?'

'Any man would. It is nothing to be ashamed of.'

'I did not break!' His fist slammed against the table and Freya jumped to her feet in fright.

Silje gently took her arm and whispered words to soothe her while Magnus and Gunther rose from their seats to hurl insults and accusations at each other. Freya was shaking, her bare feet tapping nervously against the stone floor. If they had been alone then Silje would have taken her hand and placed it against her breast so she could feel her heart and set her world right from the love she found there.

But they were not alone, so Silje whispered to her before turning away and shouting at Magnus and Gunther. 'Enough! If this is how men of war carry themselves then it is small wonder Norway was taken so easily!'

Both men fell silent, and after a moment given for pride's sake, took their seats. Gunther apologised. Magnus did not.

'Perhaps you should tell us,' Freya said.

Gunther looked at all three of them. *Perhaps he is seeing betrayal in all of us*, Silje thought.

'This goes no further than this table.'

'Which goes without saying,' Magnus replied evenly. He joined Silje and Freya in leaning towards Gunther.

'Our training camp near Trondheim has been compromised. Many men were lost and the Germans took the coded messages, but we are confident they will be unable to decipher them. So that we may continue to prepare for the Quisling operation, we need to move our forces somewhere close, somewhere safe.'

Silje waited patiently for him to finish. Before he could utter another word, however, Freya cried, 'No! No! You cannot bring them here!'

Silje tried to calm her while Grette ushered the tavern regulars towards the door.

'In future,' Grette said, 'you should conduct your business in the church; no one goes there.'

Silje apologised and thanked her.

'Fólkvangr would never betray you,' Grette said to Gunther. 'But we are a small village of old people; do not bring this war down on us.'

'I will not; we will not. The kidnapping will be carried out when he has left Bergen.'

'Stop telling us things we do not wish to know!'

'I am simply reassuring you. The soldiers will live in the hills above the village, though they will come here for supplies and any medical treatment that Doctor Lomen can provide. After we have taken the Puppet then they will disperse without returning to Fólkvangr. Nothing can go wrong.'

Silje sighed. 'How I wish you had not said that.'

'The decision has been made. We have no choice.'

'And what about Silje?' Freya said. 'What will happen to Silje when they find out she was a part of this?'

'I do not understand,' Gunther said – and Silje would have sworn to any god that she'd seen his trigger finger twitch. 'Why would they find out?'

'Tell him!'

Gunther and Magnus looked to Silje.

'Go on!'

'Yes, I think perhaps you should tell us, Silje,' said Gunther. 'What's going on?'

'The Germans,' she whispered, hoping that no one would hear her.

'What of them,' Gunther said impatiently.

'They draw closer. They know how the code works, and they suspect the key is being transmitted in the open. Berlin has sent its best mathematicians to crack the key.'

'See!' Freya cried. 'It is only a matter of time. I said this was a dangerous plan from the beginning!'

The little colour Gunther possessed had drained from his cheeks. 'How long have you known this?'

'For three nights.'

'Jesus Christ! The General told you this himself! And you did not think to tell me!'

'They do not know *The Orchid* is carrying the key. It is the last place they will look. It is a good plan; it always has been.'

Freya was trying to stare at her. 'My God, you're enjoying this.'

'If I'd told you then you would cease the operation.'

'Damn right I would!'

'But now it is too late.'

Gunther fumed.

'They will kill you,' said Magnus, stirring his ale. 'But first they will torture you, within an inch of your life. Then they will patch you up, let you rest, and then after a day they will start again.' His voice was cold, and broken. 'It is time for you to stop seeking attention, Sister, and think of what this will do to the village.'

'Do you not grow tired, Magnus?' Silje said. 'Do you not grow weary of our friends the Germans taking our priests and our teachers, our very freedom? Do you not grow sick of the Nazis turning our entire country into a Berlin ghetto?' She dried her eyes with her sleeve. 'Well I am tired. I am tired of these animals taking us into dark rooms and doing as they see fit.'

The others protested as loudly and as sharply as they could. She rebuked each argument as it was hurled at her, and during the discourse, Gunther remained silent.

'What's the matter with you?' Magnus said to him. 'Don't just sit there! Tell her!'

Silje said, 'He won't.'

Gunther hunched down even further.

'He won't speak because he has already made his decision: we shall fight on. Isn't that right, Gunther?'

Gunther finally found the courage to look at her, look at all of them. 'If there was another way...'

The others could say nothing.

'I am going home to rest for a while.' Silje took a mouthful of Magnus's ale, and found that as heartbroken and powerless as she felt, she still did not care much for the taste. 'I would speak with you in private, Gunther,' she said, and left *The Mottled Goat* without waiting to see if he'd follow.

She walked across the street, keeping an ear for the tavern door. It still hadn't opened by the time she'd reached the shoemaker's shop, and Silje began to worry that Gunther had made her look foolish. She was about to make her way back to *The Goat* when the door burst open and he came running out after her. He stopped a few feet short of where she stood.

'I have asked many to make sacrifices,' he said. 'I wish I knew why it is so hard to ask the same of this village, of you.' He took a deep breath and gazed around the square. 'This would be easier if I had your blessing, but I will do what I have to; you must understand that.'

'I do understand,' said Silje. Then she gently tightened the noose. 'Bring them, Gunther. Your men will be most welcome here, under one condition.'

'Anything,' Gunther said. 'Name it.'

'When you leave Norway, you will leave alone.'

Gunther frowned. 'Of course. I wasn't thinking of taking anyone— Oh.'

'She stays here, with us. That is my only condition.'

'Surely Freya should choose where she wants to live.'

'She is young, and you have turned her head with stories of England and adventure.'

'I think you underestimate her.'

'I do not care what you think.'

Gunther rolled his tongue into his cheek. 'I see.' He looked back towards *The Mottled Goat.*

'When you leave Norway, you leave without her. Promise me that and your men will be welcomed into Fólkvangr with open arms.'

But Gunther was unwilling to give up on Freya so easily. 'What if I agree and then take her anyway?'

'You see yourself as a gentleman. Once you have given your word, you will not break it.'

'Then what if I tell you to go to hell and tell Erik that you are infatuated with another woman?'

Silje knew she should not have been surprised. It was his life's vocation to watch, to observe. She wondered how long he'd known, if he'd kept this knowledge as a weapon, his hand on its hilt, waiting for just this moment.

'You could do that very thing, Gunther Braithwaite, but it would not serve you.'

'Because?'

'Because it would hurt me and it would hurt Erik, and for that reason alone Freya would never forgive you. So your dream, of carrying her away to England where she would fall in love with you, will come to nothing. And mark me, Gunther Braithwaite, you would not even reach that far because if you breathe a word of this to Erik then I will bring Gruetzmacher down on your head without a second thought.'

Gunther stared at her as he would an apparition from his worst nightmares, and this pleased her; she needed him to see her like this, from this day until the day he left Norwegian shores.

'Your first duty is to your country, so it is a simple choice,' she said, suddenly aware that she was quite breathless. 'We can both leave this ground with something we both want, or we can both leave with nothing. You can have Quisling. Kill Gruetzmacher too if that is what you want. And I will do whatever else you ask. All I want is Freya in return.'

'You ask much.'

'Please.'

Gunther looked to the sky. He snarled from somewhere deep in his throat. 'I pray that one day she regains her sight, Silje,' he said as he walked away. 'Then perhaps she will see you for what you truly are.'

45

Such was their affinity that Freya could separate Silje's footsteps from the scores of others that criss-crossed Fólkvangr's square.

'I did not like this business with *The Orchid* from the very beginning. I like it even less now.'

'You have made your feelings clear, Freya, time and time again.'

'And what did you say to Gunther?'

'I have no idea what you are—'

'He tells me he cannot take me to England when he leaves. He said he could not bear to leave me alone while he fights in France.'

'Is that what he said,' Silje replied mildly. 'Did he say anything else?'

'Yes, that he would send for me as soon as he could. What did you say to him, Silje?'

Clearly not enough, she thought. 'Gunther is his own man. I have said nothing.' She marvelled at the ease at which untruths tumbled from her lips. Lying to Erik was one thing; lying to Freya was something she'd never believed she was capable of.

'If I could settle myself when I am close to you,' Freya said, 'then I would know whether or not you are telling me the truth.'

'I am not lying.'

'And I think Magnus is right. You enjoy the attention.You would endanger yourself so that people would fawn over you. And you would endanger the village without giving any of us a say.'

'You do not have a say,' Silje said, wishing she could claw back her words even as they spilled from her mouth. ‘Because you are not of Fólkvangr.’

They walked on in silence, save for Freya thanking the occasional well-wisher, and Silje saying good day to Mrs Stromme who had run the village post office until the Nazis had closed it down at the end of summer. ‘They could not even wait until Christmas,’ Freya complained. ‘Bastards. And how could you say such a thing to me?’

Silje said she was sorry, but it wasn’t enough.

‘You said you would not do this anymore. You promised that you would stop saying things to hurt me.’

‘My promise does not preclude me from telling the truth, Freya. You are not from Fólkvangr.’

‘You hurt me for the same reason that Magnus hurts you. The Nazis have tortured the both of you and you are both torturing your loved ones in return.’

‘That is nonsense.’

‘It is not, Silje. I felt the same when they butchered my father, powerless to help him or myself. It is the powerlessness that devours you and then turns itself outward to destroy your friends and your family. Do you know what saved me?’

Silje squeezed her eyes shut and tightened her jaw, letting the tears beat like a tidal wave against her intransigence; it was the only defence she had left.

‘The kindness of strangers,’ Freya said.

‘I will not cry anymore,’ Silje breathed. ‘I simply cannot. I cannot let the villagers see me weeping as though there is no hope. I am supposed to be getting married.’

‘We should go someplace where we can be alone,’ said Freya. ‘Someplace where we can cry together.’

Silje looked at her hands, watched her fingers roll themselves into fists. She was shaking. It was as Freya had said: she was casting her shame, her helplessness outward, using them to bludgeon and belittle those she loved.

They walked from the village and travelled the narrow, ice-laden road that led to the meadows above Fólkvangr, Away from the eyes of the villagers they held hands and felt the midday sun warm their bones.

‘We should have brought more clothes.’

Freya laughed and nodded. ‘You are always so practical after the fact.’

Once they reached the meadow, they lay down beneath its single tree, guarded by mountains to the north, east, south and west.

'This is beautiful,' Freya said, and Silje trusted that the beauty was carried in the sound of the winds, the scent of the grass and the air, the rustling of the leaves. She wondered if Freya's world was perhaps less ugly than her own, and as the thought struck her she began to cry. Just a mute whimper at first, and then a sniff and a breath.

'Let me hold it for you, Silje.' Freya gently drew Silje to her breast and kissed the crown of her head. 'Just for a short while.'

And so Silje closed her eyes and let her defences fall. In her lifetime, she had never known pain like it. The tears came in waves, bringing thoughts of her mother, of Magnus, of the terrible hours she spent at the hands of Gruetzmacher. She wanted him dead; oh, how she wanted to see him burned in Bergen's square for his crimes against the children of two nations, against the sons of Doctor Lomen. Against her.

Finally, her tears were spent. She slept while Freya sang softly to her to keep her warm, and when she awoke they made love under the tree.

They were frantic, unbridled. *Perhaps it is the cold*, Silje thought, *or perhaps it is because we know that our time together is almost at an end.*

And when they were done, when their skin burned to the slightest touch, they lay back in the snow and felt the mountains draw in around them.

Freya whispered, 'I am begging you; give up *The Orchid*.'

'You know I cannot.'

'You have done more than anyone has expected of you. You have sacrificed yourself in ways too terrible to think on. Do you think that Gruetzmacher will show mercy to any of us when he finds out?'

'His demons have all but claimed him. I doubt he will care.'

'It is only a matter of time. You said it yourself; they know that the secret to decoding the messages is close at hand. When Quisling is taken they will redouble their efforts to break the Resistance, and someone will speak. Someone will reveal you to protect themselves and their family. And they will come for you, and Magnus, and your father, and Erik, and Mrs Tufte and—'

'You spoke of being powerless, Freya; we are not. The newsletter gives us power. We can use it to take back our land and our honour. Do you not think the prize is worth the risk?'

'I do not prize your life over anything,' Freya said, 'not even my own.'

Silje kissed her mouth. 'I will be more careful. I promise. And if you ask me tomorrow then I will stop. I will do anything you ask, but I pray that you love me enough not to.'

'I ask because I love you.'

'Then trust me. Trust that I would die before seeing anything happen to you or Fólkvangr.'

'I do not want you to die for me, Silje! I want us to grow old in your stupid little village. I don't want to spend my life on this earth if you are not here with me.'

'And I have promised you that I will not let that happen. I will not see us apart. I will not allow death to come between—'

Freya pressed a finger to Silje's lips. She swallowed and her eyes moved back and forth as she tried to focus her senses. 'Silje, we are still alone, yes?'

'Yes, of course we are.' Silje said, feeling no warmth or presence from another. But her awareness was slowly returning, and it brought sight of a shadow across their naked forms. Silje turned and saw the shadow's keeper blocking the light of the sun.

'Erik…'

46

Freya sat upright. 'Where? Is he here?'

'Yes, Freya,' Silje said softly. 'He is here.'

Erik gazed at them without anger or grief, just sadness. There was a knife in his hand, and Silje's first thought was to shield Freya. 'Erik, please sit down. We must speak of this.'

Erik blinked and followed her eyes to the knife. Silje watched the possibilities roll in waves across his face before he settled on one. He put the knife in his pocket. 'You brought her here.'

Silje nodded.

'This is our place.'

'Yes, I am sorry.'

'I carved our names into that tree. I came back to carve the date of our wedding.'

'It is not her fault, Erik,' Freya cried. 'It was me. I seduced her. I said that I would betray her to the Germans if she did not let me have her.'

It was a desperate lie from a blind Jewess who was a desperately hopeless liar. *Having been with me for so long*, Silje thought bitterly, *I would have expected better of her*.

'I am not a fool, Freya, though perhaps I am as blind as you. I have known Silje since before you were born. I think that is love I see in her eyes, though I cannot be sure because I have never seen it before.'

Silje rose slowly to her feet, suddenly feeling the cold wind biting at her flesh. 'Please listen to me, Erik. I never meant to—'

'What, Silje? What did you never mean to do? Hurt me? Betray me?

Pluck out my heart with your fingers? And yet you have done this to me a thousand times. Do you love her?'

Silje looked back towards Freya who was dragging her hands through the snow, looking for her clothes.

'As always with you,' Erik said, 'the truth is in the breaths you take between the lies.' He looked back along the path he'd walked. 'I do not understand. Why have I never been enough for you?'

'If you would just listen to me, Erik, I can—'

The blow, when it came, took her by surprise. Erik spun on his heel, reached behind her and locked his hand around the back of her neck. He cried out and pulled her down while driving his fist into the flesh between her stomach and her groin. Silje's world blackened for a moment, and then snapped back, bringing Freya's scream with it. Erik let her go and she folded to her knees. She could not breath. She saw Freya's bare feet lunging past her, but could not find the strength to cry out. She heard a slap, a cry; Freya landed in the snow in front of her.

'Erik, please don't hurt her.'

She heard him searching through his pockets.

'It is me you are angry with, not her.'

The knife reappeared, close to her right eye. He struck her again, across her temple, sending her sprawling across the snow. He looked at the knife and then at Freya.

'Erik, please! I will marry you! I will send her away! I will never see her again.'

Erik kicked Freya's legs apart and knelt between them. Silje pleaded with him, but he was lost. And Freya, she did not move; her eyes were open but she appeared to have fainted dead away. Silje tried to get up, tried to call her name. Her voice failed and her limbs refused her.

Erik said, 'I would have spent my life making anything you wanted.' He pressed the knife against Freya's thigh and still she did not move. 'What do you say then, Silje? Perhaps I can make her into the man you have never found in me.'

'Erik, no!' Silje lifted herself and crawled towards him. 'It is me who has betrayed you. She is nothing, just a silly little girl. Take your knife to me and do as you wish. I will not stop you.'

Erik looked at her, as though seeing her for the first time, as though witnessing the birth of love itself, untouched, untainted.

The knife fell to the ground and Freya awoke. She thrust out her leg, and the heel of her foot split Erik's nose. He fell backwards and before he hit the ground she had launched herself upon him with the knife in her hand. It was only Silje who stopped her from driving the blade into his open mouth. She threw herself at her, pushing her away from him. Freya's eyes locked with hers, and for a moment Silje believed she would kill her instead. Freya blinked and her eyes misted. The knife fell from her grip.

'It is over now. It is done. All of this.'

'He was going to—'

'No, he would not. Such cruelty… it is not him. I should have seen that.' Silje held her and kissed her. 'But I thought I would lose you. I could see eternity without you and I have never been so afraid.' She kissed her lips and then between her eyes. 'I am done with *The Orchid*. No more. I will take you and Fólkvangr away from this war. And you,' she said, turning to face Erik struggling to his knees, 'I will put this right. I swear to you.'

'She will put this right,' he said to the sky. He took a handkerchief from his pocket and staunched his nose. The handkerchief stained red.

'You must put your head back.' Silje reached for him; he slapped her hand away and Freya cried out, thinking he'd hurt her.

'Do not worry, little Jew,' he said. 'I am too weak to exact justice for what has been done to me this day. Is it what you wanted, Silje; someone powerful like Gruetzmacher to treat you like the whore you are? Perhaps you despise being worshipped like a queen because in your heart you know you do not deserve it.' He got to his feet, swayed back and then leaned forward, planting his left boot heavily in the snow. Then he began to walk, away from the path, away from Fólkvangr.

'Where are you going?' Silje cried.

'In pretending you care, Silje,' he said, 'you insult us both.'

47

Bergström had a key to Mr Gust's apartment. He let himself in and pushed me into one of the large white armchairs. His associates followed; one searched the rooms while the other began moving the cases inside. Mr Gust was standing by the picture window. He was pressed and suited in black, his hair brushed and his shoes shined. He and Bergström nodded to each other and grimly shook hands.

'You know we will have to take all this off,' Bergström said, stroking the lapel of Mr Gust's jacket.

Mr Gust shrugged his shoulders. 'It is a gesture, I think. I want to meet my maker suitably attired.'

'And since when have you believed in a higher power?'

'Since I put on this suit.'

They both smiled uncomfortably, their mutual unease eventually forcing them to look out of the window.

When I noticed the suit was brand new, my legs began to shake. The sound of my shoes rattling against the floor attracted their attention.

'Does she want to see this?'

'I think it will be good for her.'

'Really, my friend, forcing the poor child to witness a murder? You are better than this.'

'Do not presume to tell me who or what I am. You are an animal, and I am not your friend. You spat on your oath and murdered innocents. I am merely here to see that justice is served.'

Mr Gust nodded sadly. 'It is a fine day for it.'

'As good as any.' Bergström offered him a cigarette which he gratefully accepted.

'I'm not supposed to smoke inside the apartment.'

'Do you think they will fine you for it?'

A cloying silence and then the apartment filled with laughter. I tried to stand up, but one of Bergström's men placed a hand on my shoulder and drove me back down into my seat. He told me not to move and then returned to moving cases from the hallway.

Mr Gust wiped tears from his eyes. 'And I am laughing,' he said. 'The last thing I expected to be doing at this moment was holding my sides. Thank you, Bergström.'

And so Bergström and Mr Gust stood by the picture window and smoked cigarettes, while Bergström's men carefully laid out polythene sheeting on the floor. Mr Gust talked about the war, the German economy and his hope for reunification.

'It will happen,' he said.

'Never.' Bergstrom blew smoke into the air. 'There is too much to forgive.'

'Not everyone is like you, Bergström.'

One of Bergström's men dropped a suitcase. It landed heavily on one corner and sprang open, spilling polished medical instruments and butcher's tools onto the floor. All of it looked brand new.

'You take care of your tools, Herr Bergström.' Gust drew on his cigarette; his hands were shaking. So were mine. He looked at his watch as though he were about to miss an appointment somewhere else. 'You said it would be quick. You promised. Why do you need all that?'

Bergström glanced at the open case, at the shining metal that skidded and slid across the floor, even as his men tried to gather it. He opened his mouth but one of them spoke first.

'It is not up to him. He had no right to make you such a promise.'

'You will hold your tongue, Yosef, or so help me I will cut it from your throat.'

Yosef, unfazed, carried on. 'The Israeli government has decreed that you must suffer for your crimes. A quick death is not in your future, Herr Gust.' To make his point, he flicked the blade of a hacksaw with his finger. The foil sang, and that was my cue to vomit as loudly and violently as I could.

'The floor,' Gust cried. 'God in heaven, the floor!' He moved from his spot and Bergström restrained him by placing his hand on his chest. Gust looked at him, enraged.

'You were running towards her,' Bergström said, 'but you were looking at the door.'

Gust began to shake, to weep; the smell of my own vomit made me retch again.

'Please,' he cried. 'I beg of you; do not do this! I have done everything you asked!'

'It is not up to him.' Yosef made his way to the bathroom, carrying four large plastic containers labelled as corrosives.

A glass of water appeared at my shoulder. I looked up; it was the other agent holding it. He was much younger and had yet to say a word.

'First time out?' I ventured, taking the glass from him.

He moved away from me without replying. He knelt down at the edge of the polythene, arranging tools at one corner – scalpels, hand-drills – before shuffling to the next and doing the same again – hack-saws, chisels and a sledgehammer. 'For his elbows and his knees,' he said when he saw me staring.

'This isn't right. You know it isn't right.'

'What he did to my countrymen isn't right,' the young agent said, but I could see his heart wasn't in it.

Gust was on his knees now, clutching the legs of Bergström's overalls as though his life depended on it. It didn't of course; he was going to die either way; the only question was how long it would take and how painful it would be.

'Get up,' said Bergström. 'The woman can see you! Be a man, for Christ's sake!'

Gust stayed precisely where he was, his tear-stained eyes following the young agent as he turned the floor of the apartment into a compact abattoir.

I could hear the shower running.

Gust was practically screaming now, and I wondered why no one else living in the building could hear him. Perhaps they were used to MOSSAD agents roaming murderously all over Dresden. Gust held on even tighter; Bergström struck him, and tried to pull away, the leg of his overalls riding up and revealing a holster strapped just above his ankle.

'I have more,' Gust pleaded. 'I have more names! I can give you—'

Bergström shouted 'You are embarrassing yourself!' and took another half-step back, his exposed ankle facing me.

'What is going on out there?' Yosef called out from the bathroom. Bergström turned his head and stared at me. *What the fuck are you waiting for?*

I glanced at the agent; he was still arranging Bergström's instruments, so I lunged from my seat, slipped in my own vomit and skidded across the floor, scrambling to reach Bergström before the agent saw what I was doing. Bergström cried out in surprise as I ripped the gun from its holster and aimed it at Gust's head. Gust thanked me as I pulled the trigger – nothing happened.

'For the love of God! Can't you do anything right?' Bergström snatched the gun from me, released the safety and shot Gust in the face. His aim was off, even I could tell, but then he had the other agent to worry about who was already reaching for his gun. The second shot was better, hitting the younger man between the eyes, and then he turned the gun towards the bathroom and fired. Yosef ran out, pistol held in front of him, and into the bullet, the impact flipping him so he landed on his stomach. A second later I heard a thud as the first agent landed on the polythene.

Bergström looked angrily at me and I thought I was next. Instead he handed me the gun and said, 'Hit me.'

'What?'

'Across the face, below the temple but above the cheek. Watch you don't crack the eye socket.'

'I'm not going to hit you! You'll kill me!'

'I will kill you if you don't. Now get on with it; we don't have all—'

I struck him as hard as I could, and he spun round, crashing to the floor. When he got to his feet, he had a tooth from Gust's shattered jawbone lodged in his cheek.

'Now, once more,' he said picking out the tooth and putting it in his pocket, 'but this time with feeling.'

The second blow was weaker than the first. By this time, he'd given up on me ever doing anything right. He snatched back the gun and told me to leave.

'The police have only agreed to half an hour for the cleanup.' He looked around and made a quick account of the blood-spattered floor and the pulp staining the walls. 'This will take far longer.'

'I'll help you.'

'You'll just get in the way,' he said, moving Gust's body away from the skirting boards. 'But your offer is much appreciated.' He muttered something about the flooring. 'Get yourself cleaned up. Use the shower, don't go near the bath.'

I did as I was told, spending only a minute in the shower; the fumes from the bath made my eyes stream, so much so that I could barely see to find the towel. I found a set of overalls neatly folded on the floor in front of the bathroom door; I put them on and went back into the living room where Bergström was rolling Yosef's corpse in polythene.

'What will you tell MOSSAD?'

'I will tell them that the operation went to shit. Gust grabbed my gun, hit me and shot the other two agents before I could stop him.' He tapped thoughtfully on his lower lip. 'I should probably shoot myself in the leg or something.'

'Will they believe you?'

'I hope so. Now you need to leave.'

I headed for the door, trying not to run.

He called after me. 'When I gave you the gun, Miss Fossen, why didn't you shoot me?'

I stood there, trembling, lost, disconnected, and after a while he smiled and said, 'Ah, you just didn't think of it.'

48

The Ohnstad family did not receive many guests, and Silje wondered if it was their distance from the village – though it was not more than a mile or so – or if perhaps it was her. The women in the village were wary of her. Perhaps the men did not come because their wives would not let them.

Well, they were here now.

She looked up, and found herself crushed beneath the intensity of her father's eyes.

'Please do not look at me like that,' she whispered.

Freya squeezed her hand.

Gunther Braithwaite cleared his throat. 'Well, we appear to have something of a situation.' It was not much, but enough to break the silence.

'That is what you call it?' growled Magnus.

Gunther had brought three of his lieutenants with him. Ebenhard Holm and Barthold Rønning had grown up in the village but had left some years ago. They were a few years older than Silje. She'd heard that Barthold was a school teacher in Oslo; she had no notion of how Ebenhard made his living, though by the looks of him, bare-knuckle boxer would have been her first guess.

The third was Carina, a woman in her forties with greying hair and eyes of steel that fixed Silje with an unwavering look of mistrust. She did not smile, not that Silje expected her to. She hardly spoke, for which

Silje was thankful. She held her machine gun in her arms in much the same way a mother would hold an infant.

'And so you have not seen him for six days.'

Silje shook her head. 'Not since that day he…' She looked at Freya, wishing Freya could look back. *If you could see*, Silje thought, *then I would not feel so alone*. 'Not since the day he saw us.'

'In the hills,' Magnus added unnecessarily.

Gunther sipped his tea and scratched his head.

Ebenhard said, 'Did he seem angry?'

'He'd just discovered the love of his life entangled with another woman,' Jon Ohnstad rumbled. 'So yes, I would venture that he would "seem angry".'

'I think the question that Ebenhard is asking,' said Carina, 'is how angry did he seem.'

'I'm not sure what you mean.' Silje's neck ached from hanging her head.

'I think you do,' said Gunther, 'otherwise you would not have contacted me. Erik is missing, beside himself with grief. You are worried what he might do.'

'I thought you might help me find him.'

'The Resistance? You thought the Resistance would help find your spurned—'

'That is enough, Magnus,' Jon Ohnstad said. He did not seem angry to Silje, just disappointed, which was a thousand times worse.

Her brother wasn't done with her. 'So what is this between you and her? What do you call that?'

'We had not thought to name it,' said Freya.

'You will be silent until you are spoken to. How could you do something like this? You are a Jew, for Christ's sake; you of all people must know how ungodly this is.'

Silje told him he must not speak to her like that.

'A woman, and another woman… together.' Carina shook her head. 'I have heard of such things but I never thought I'd see it with my own eyes.'

'It is fairly common in Oslo,' said Barthold.

Carina snorted. 'Well, that is Oslo.'

'None of this is important,' said Gunther. 'The question is, what will he do?'

'What Gunther is trying to say,' said Magnus wearily, 'is will Erik betray us?'

'No! Why would he do that?'

'To exact revenge on you both.' Magnus leaned back in his chair, giving Silje the impression he was enjoying this perhaps more than he should. 'He could tell the Germans about her. They could come for her, and then they will shoot us for harbouring her. They could put the whole village to the gun for—'

'Magnus, stop! He would not do such a thing. I have hurt him terribly, but he would not risk the lives of his friends just to hurt me in return.'

Magnus looked unconvinced. 'We should abandon the operation.'

'I told you it was wrong to trust these hill folk,' Carina said. 'The war does not touch them so how they can hope to understand the need for secrecy?'

Silje narrowed her eyes. *Hill folk.*

'We have spent too long planning this, Magnus. We cannot just give up because we suspect that—'

'If he tells the Germans that Freya is here then they will come and search the whole mountain for other Jews. That is what they did in Poland and in France. They will find them, and our camps, our training grounds, our munitions stores...'

Freya, who had remained obediently silent, decided to speak up. 'I will turn myself over to them.'

'Out of the question,' said Silje's father. 'No one will be given to those animals, not while I draw breath.'

'Take me to Bergen. I will surrender myself far from the village and then they will have no reason to come here.'

'And what if they torture you, Freya?' said Magnus. 'What if they cut the flesh from your bones to find out where other Jews are hiding? Do you think you can hold your tongue until your body finally succumbs to the pain?'

'You held on,' she said quietly.

'I knew my family would come for me.'

'We should find him,' said Carina, 'and end him if we have to.'

'If we are going to fight this war by murdering our own then we should surrender to the Nazis now.'

Carina replied, 'We are already killing our own, Mr Ohnstad, when we must.'

'Not us, not in Fólkvangr.' And Jon Ohnstad fixed her with such a look that she shrank away from him, in spite of herself.

They sat in silence for what seemed like forever to Silje. She thought that the plan should be abandoned, but if that was how she felt then it meant that she didn't trust Erik, that she had hurt him enough that he would hurt the village in return.

And still her father could not bring himself to look at her, and because she do could nothing about Erik, that became her most immediate concern. 'I did not want you to find out like this.'

Jon Ohnstad said nothing.

'Sir, this was not Silje's doing. It was I who—'

'You do not need to defend her, Freya. I know her better than I know myself. I am well aware who instigated this… this… whatever this is.'

Freya held Silje's hand so tightly she felt the bones of her fingers creak.

'Is there anything I have done in my life that you approve of?' Silje asked.

'Please do not pretend my approval means anything to you.'

'Perhaps we should return to the matter at hand,' said Barthold.

'There is nothing more to discuss,' said Jon Ohnstad. 'The Germans could be on their way while we sit here talking. You must remove your men from the village and the hills and wait for another opportunity to present itself.'

Carina said, 'Again, do you have any idea how long we have—?'

'Do you have any idea how many children there are in this village?'

Gunther tapped his fingertips against the table. His brow furrowed and Silje wondered if this was a decision she would be prepared to make, to balance the lives contained in a small village against the effort to drive the Nazis from their homeland. He looked at her, hoping to find the answer in her eyes. 'I should contact my superiors.'

'There is no time,' Ebenhard said. 'By the time the English have drunk their tea, smoked their cigars and had their cosy little fireside chats, the opportunity will be lost.'

'We have a chance to deliver a crippling blow to our enemy,' Barthold agreed. 'And with respect, Gunther, this is not your country. The decision should be ours.'

'And with respect, Barthold, this is not your village – not anymore.' Silje would have risen to her feet but she feared Freya would not let go of her hand. 'The Germans,' she said. 'I have known their kind. I know the depravity that festers in their black souls. If you do this then the consequences will be worse than you can possibly imagine. But you know this, don't you, Gunther?'

Gunther looked to his compatriots before nodding slowly.

'And yet you and your masters, thousands of miles away, believe it is worth the sacrifice.'

Again, a nod.

'Then why stop now?'

'I beg your pardon?'

'There is a chance that Erik has already told the Germans about Freya. There is a chance that they are already preparing to sweep the mountain for Jews. There is a chance that we will win this war, and a chance that we will all die tomorrow. We cannot run from whatever will be. All we can do is meet it and pray that we are strong enough to break our way through.'

'You cannot speak for the village, Silje,' said Magnus.

'There is not one person in this room, no, on this mountain, who loves Fólkvangr more than I. Without this village I am nothing.'

'You love Fólkvangr so much you would put her neck on the block for these strangers?'

'I would risk everything if it meant Freya could live free.'

Jon Ohnstad blinked rapidly and then simply stared at her. 'Well,' he said finally, 'I never thought I'd live to see the day.'

'You are being ridiculous,' Carina said. 'What possible good can come of this farce of a coupling?'

'You will grow tired of her, Silje,' Magnus said, with only sadness, and no desire to inflict pain. 'You will tire of her as you grew tired of Erik.'

'I was never in love with Erik. I wished that I were, more than anything. And I would have married him because he would make a fine husband for any woman.'

'Any woman except you,' her father said.

'Erik made me feel safe and whole. Freya makes me feel…' And it struck Silje that in all this time she'd never looked inside herself, gazed at the changes Freya had wrought in her soul.

'Standing on the top of the mountain,' said Freya, 'with the wind pressing at your back and your toes dangling over the edge. Every moment I am with her, I want to cry with joy simply because I'm alive. I want to sing whenever I hear her voice. When I am alone all I think about is her, just the scent of her, the feeling of her skin next to mine, the touch of her—'

Silje gently squeezed her hand. 'I think we have made our point.'

Jon Ohnstad gazed at them, but his eyes did not appear unkind, more bewildered.

'Two women, together.' Carina shook her head, determined not to recover from it. 'I don't even know if there is a name for that.'

'We told you,' Freya said. 'It is called being in love.'

'Yes, of course.' She laughed joylessly. 'Find me when you are both in the twilight of your lives, and then tell me what love is.'

Silje wanted to point out that when Freya and she were in their twilight years, Carina herself would be long dead and buried. It was Freya's turn to squeeze Silje's hand, pressing her to hold her tongue.

'We carry on,' said Gunther suddenly. 'We will move more men closer to the village to defend it if need be. Silje, Erik must be found.'

Silje nodded and said she would bring him home.

'Good, then let us leave the Ohnstads in peace. There is much to do and only three days left to us.'

49

They asked his friends in the village and in Bergen; many had seen him; she could tell by the looks of contempt she was given while they talked to her father.

'Packed up everything,' said Truls Bjørnebye, Erik's onetime partner in a mobile farrier business they'd started and had folded within the space of a week. He eyed Silje and snorted loudly. 'And I can hardly blame him.' He peered over Jon Ohnstad's shoulder at Freya waiting in the truck.

Silje's father chose not to defend her, focusing instead on the search at hand. 'Yes, we have already been to his home. Do you have any idea where he would go?'

'As far from her as possible I shouldn't wonder.'

That was more then enough. Jon Ohnstad stared at him until his nerve broke.

'I don't know, Mr Ohnstad,' Truls said, more respectfully this time. He glanced back towards his front door where his wife waited with her arms folded. Silje smiled at Mrs Bjørnebye, and Mrs Bjørnebye stared back.

You shall not preen and charm your way across this threshold, Silje Ohnstad. You will not steal my life from under my feet.

Silje thought of Lisbeth Fehn and realised, suddenly, how much she missed her…

'Wait,' Truls said. His eyes widened and a smile spread across his thin lips. 'He has cousins!'

Jon Ohnstad clapped his hand against his forehead. 'Of course! Two – no – three cousins on his mother's side.'

Truls nodded and Silje, bewildered, tried to remember Erik ever mentioning having cousins living within an echo of Fólkvangr.

'When did he tell you about his cousins?'

Her father ignored her; he and Tuls rattled their brains trying to remember where they lived.

'Somewhere south, I think,' ventured Truls.

Silje asked again, 'What cousins? He never told me of any—'

'Vossevangen,' Freya called from the truck.

'Yes! Voss! They live in Vossevangen!'

Silje said, 'He never told me.'

Jon Ohnstad was already halfway back to the truck. 'Of course he told you, Silje. It is more likely that you were not listening. Now come, we have a long drive ahead of us.'

* * *

Voss lay about sixty miles north-east of Bergen, an ill-advised journey during the colder months, especially in a truck that was older than Silje herself. But her father was not a fool. He returned to the cottage for blankets, food, water, shovels, the radio given to him by Gunther Braithwaite, and the oil heater that lived in the corner of the kitchen and which was, strangely enough, rarely lit.

Freya insisted on accompanying them in spite of his protests that he could take care of one of them far better than he could care for two. Silje's heart swelled to hear that he still cared; she had begun to wonder.

He climbed into the driver's seat, and Freya hurried to climb in next to him, knowing full well that Silje would want to sit by to her father to shield her.

'There is no need,' she whispered.

Silje slammed the door, and Jon Ohnstad started the engine.

They travelled the snow-laden paths in silence, Freya staring blankly ahead and Jon Ohnstad sighing at every near-obstacle and burnt-out home along the way. They had to get out three times to move a tree felled under the weight of snow, or the carcass of an animal that had succumbed to starvation in its search for food. One of the animals was a stag that lay across the path with its neck broken and its flank caved in. Silje's father said that it had probably been hit by an armoured car.

'Voss fell during the first days of the invasion,' he reminded them.

Silje remembered that Norwegian forces had gathered there and held the invaders at bay until the Luftwaffe had turned the town to rubble during a bombardment that lasted a day and a night. She swallowed and thought of Fólkvangr and of Erik's cousins, finally remembering when Erik had told her about them. She reached for Freya's hand. Her father coughed loudly so she moved her hand away.

A few moments later, having steered, with great effort, around a smashed and abandoned troop carrier, he sighed and said, 'You will be warmer if you sit closer.'

They eagerly embraced, Freya nestling her head under Silje's chin and pulling the blanket over them both.

'I thought you would be angry,' Freya said gratefully.

Jon Ohnstad said nothing.

'You must think us an abomination,' she continued, moving from brave to careless in a single breath.

'I think no such thing,' he mumbled.

'Then why will you not speak to us?' asked Silje. 'We did not mean for this to happen, and you told me once this was commonplace after the First Great War when menfolk were scarce or were crippled on their return.'

'We cannot help who we love,' Freya said quietly.

'If you think this is why I am angry then you do not know me as well as you think,' he said. 'I have always admired your spirit, Daughter; it has brought life and adventures to our village. We both know I am no saint and this is perhaps why I did not curtail you when I should have. Perhaps this is why I allowed you to… indulge yourself in ways that are unseemly for a young lady of sound upbringing.'

Silje wondered where she had been during this 'sound upbringing'.

Her father rubbed his palm across his mouth and took a deep breath. 'I saw you kissing Lisbeth Fehn once. Perhaps then would have been the proper time to—'

'That was not the same!' Silje cried.

Freya pointed her eyes at her and narrowed them to great effect. 'You never said there had been others!'

'Others? Do not say "others". There were no "others". Do you think I make a habit of seducing—' She realised this was a poor choice of phrase to use in the presence of her father. '—involving myself with women? You are my first, Freya.'

'You make it sound as though I will not be your last!'

Jon Ohnstad flushed red.

'Do not be like this,' Silje said angrily. 'Not now.'

'You always said that Lisbeth Fehn had mountainous hips!'

'I was not kissing her because I liked her; I was kissing her so she would know how to kiss…'

I was kissing her so she would know how to kiss Erik Brenna.

She did not want to speak his name here, laid raw between the anger of her lover and the judgement of her father.

Jon Ohnstad chuckled quietly as Freya snatched the blanket and swathed herself in it, turning her back on Silje, leaving her in the cold.

'Is this your first disagreement?' he asked.

'No,' said Freya, in a sulk. 'We have had many.'

Thankfully, the silence continued, aside from the occasional outburst followed by a heated and ill-thought recrimination.

By the time they reached the outskirts of Voss, Silje and Freya were seething and exhausted, and Jon Ohnstad was quite bored.

'Whatever you call this,' he said, getting out of the truck, 'the pair of you will live somewhere else if this is how you carry yourselves.'

Silje followed him and shut the door before Freya could follow her. 'What is it? Why have we stopped?'

Ahead of them the trees folded inwards, forming a winding canopy that stretched a half-mile before turning west. The road had all but vanished beneath a covering of fresh snow.

'There is a checkpoint about two miles away, but Gunther told me there is a way to avoid it if we proceed on foot.'

'Then the sooner we—'

'We cannot take Freya; it is too dangerous.'

'Father, we cannot leave her here on her own.'

'And that is why you are staying with her.' He continued to speak over a cacophony of protests. 'She is blind, a Jew, has no papers and we cannot account for who she is or why she is with us. And as remarkable as she is, if the Germans—'

'It will be dark in less than an hour,' Freya said.

Both Silje and Jon Ohnstad jumped when she spoke, as neither had heard her leave the truck. She stood facing the wind with her tongue between her lips, painting a picture of her surroundings in sound and scent.

'There are three men at the checkpoint, perhaps four. Your father is right; we will never get past them. We will move the truck into the trees and head east.'

Silje and her father looked at each other.

'When darkness comes you will need me to find your way back.'

'We need her.' Silje cast her eyes downward. Freya's feet were bare, and in the short walk from the truck had left hardly a mark in the snow.

Freya headed off towards the archway of trees. 'We are wasting time, sir.'

The Ohnstads looked at each other again and followed.

'And do not call me "sir",' Jon Ohnstad called after her.

She led them through the forest, running her fingers over leaves and branches to test her direction. Darkness began to fall and Silje wondered if they were lost, even though Freya did not hesitate in her steps.

'When we reach the town,' Jon Ohnstad whispered to his daughter, 'it is—'

'She can hear you,' Silje said flatly.

He rolled his eyes. 'When we reach the town it is important you both behave normally.'

'I am not sure what you mean.' said Silje. Finally, she could hear voices and see lights through the trees.

'I mean that you must not do anything that will draw attention to us.'

'Like arguing.'

'Yes… amongst other things.'

'What other things?' said Freya.

'Well,' he said, looking as though he was about to step into a lit kiln, 'no holding hands or… or kissing.'

'Holding hands,' echoed Freya.

'Kissing,' said Silje. 'Tell me, Father, do you think that women such as us carry ourselves differently to anyone else?'

'I was merely—'

'Do you think that women who choose to live as we do feel the need to demonstrate our love whenever someone looks upon us?'

'No,' he sighed.

'Do you think that we are such degenerates we cannot prevent ourselves from stripping naked and ravaging each other, even when in public?'

'I suppose it is too late to apologise.'

'Do you think that at the drop of a hat we will—'

'You have made your point. If anyone challenges us, you are both my daughters.'

They broke through the forest near the rear of a tavern. A narrow passageway took them to the town square – or what remained of it.

'Dear God,' Silje said under her breath.

The centre of Voss had been reduced to rubble. The church was little more than a pile of stones, and children played soldiers in what remained of the shops and town houses. Some of the lamps still stood, though most had been destroyed in the air raid, leaving the town cradled in twilight. The Germans had posted propaganda notices on any wall still standing: calls to turn in your neighbours and invitations to join Quisling's youth movement. Silje hoped the children playing in the rubble were fighting on the right side.

And there were more Germans here than on the streets in Bergen.

'Christ, we are in the den with the lions,' said Silje.

Freya swallowed and said, 'Sheep. They are just sheep dressed as lions.'

'We have little time.' Jon Ohnstad led them away from the town square.

'Do you know what his cousins are called?' asked Silje, shamed she needed to ask.

'Lunde,' her father said. 'Frida and Vildred Lunde. They own a metal-working business just outside the centre of the town.'

Although flattened, the centre of Voss was still expansive; it could easily contain Fólkvangr. They walked quickly, careful not to steer wide paths around German soldiers or avoid eye contact with them. Jon Ohnstad was especially deferent, tipping his cap to officers and enlisted men alike. An officer tapped his wristwatch as they walked past him. 'Curfew!' he shouted.

'We are on our way home, sir!'

Thankfully, the soldier did not challenge them further and returned to the task at hand: attempting to woo a young Norwegian girl who looked more frightened than charmed. Silje looked at her as they hurried away, and in the moment their eyes met, she realised that even in the near-darkness the girl had recognised her – most likely from her pictures that appeared in *The Quisling Orchid*. The girl's mouth fell open; the officer frowned and turned to see what had taken her attention.

Silje thought, *We are undone.*

But the girl grasped the officer's chin and turned him back to press her mouth against his. He returned the kiss, seemingly unsurprised, as though her capitulation had been merely a matter of time. The girl gestured with her free hand, shooing Silje and her companions away.

'She has bought us time,' Silje said. 'We must finish here as soon as we can.'

* * *

Four streets off the main square was a jewellery and trinket shop that looked as if it had been dropped on top of an old church, cutting it cleanly in two.

Jon Ohnstad knocked on the door, and when no one replied he went to the window, cupped his hands around his eyes and peered inside.

'I see a light,' he said. 'And I think I see someone moving.'

Silje knocked again while her father tapped urgently on the glass.

A moment later, the door swung open and a very tall thin woman said, 'Do you not know there is a curfew in place?'

Silje was taken aback; the family resemblance was as striking as it was unexpected. The woman could have been Erik's twin: the same waxen blonde hair, the same sallow complexion. Her chin receded, just like Erik's, though she had failed to cultivate a smile that would have alleviated this condition with attractive lines about her mouth.

'What do you want?' she asked sourly, looking past them.

Jon Ohnstad removed his hat. 'Would I have the pleasure of addressing Frida or Vildred?'

'Vildred,' she answered flatly. 'Frida is dead.'

'I… I am very sorry; I did not know.'

She looked at each of them in turn. 'And why should you? I have no idea who you…' Squinting at Freya, she pursed her thin lips and waved a hand in front of her eyes.

'Ah,' she said. 'So it is you. You'd better come in.'

They trooped obediently after her into the shop, Jon Ohnstad closing and locking the door.

Vildred led them past the living room, through to the kitchen, and finally out to the workshop which appeared to be a foundry attached to the main house. The fires were cold and the floor was covered in soot and dust.

'You make everything here?' asked Silje.

'Not since Frida was killed. Oh, and before I forget…' Vildred raised her hand and struck Silje soundly across the cheek.

'What in God's name!' Jon Ohnstad roared. He lunged forward to shield his daughter from further assault, while Freya demanded to know what had just happened.

Silje said, 'It is all right. Everything is all right, Freya.' She rubbed her cheek and took a deep breath so she would not cry. 'So, Erik has been here, I take it.'

'Yes,' Vildred said. 'Would anyone like something to drink? I have some ale somewhere.'

Silje and her father looked at each other.

'No thank you,' said Freya warily. 'We cannot stay long.'

'So you must be the famous Freya.'

'Do not think to lay a hand on her,' Jon Ohnstad warned.

Vildred moved her tools so that they could sit on the anvils or lean against the dead furnace; her guests were inclined to stay standing.

'What happened to your sister?' Silje asked.

'I told you. She is dead – killed in the air raid that destroyed the centre of the town.' Vildred began rummaging in a large trunk hidden behind the furnace. 'She was the craftsman, I'm afraid. I'm more of the bookkeeper, so now we have a shop in the centre of a ruined town, with no stock, no customers, no craftsman-in-residence…' She smashed the neck of a bottle against an anvil and poured the contents into a mis-shapen pewter tankard. Ale leaked from its seams; Silje guessed that Vildred had tried to make it herself. She drank quickly, and still only consumed half the bottle's worth. 'Still,' she said, 'at least our accounts are in order.' She chuckled to herself.

'You were going to tell us about Erik,' ventured Freya.

'Erik… Yes, Erik! My cousin, the one betrayed and humiliated by a pair of deviants.'

'If you like,' said Silje, determined not to open herself up to further attack. 'Now are you going to tell us or should we just leave?'

Vildred didn't reply until she'd drunk another half-bottle. 'He came here five or six days ago. He was upset, naturally. He said his reason for living had been torn from inside him.'

For Silje, hearing this was like being hit in the stomach all over again.

'He stayed for a few days, gave me some money, and then he was on his way.'

'Wait, why did he not stay for long?'

'Here? In Voss? Look outside, you stupid girl. Most of the people walking the streets are German. Only the despairing stay here, those without hope or any place else to go. Besides,' she added, 'he didn't come here to see me.'

'I know,' said Silje. 'He came here to get away from me.'

'Amongst other things,' Vildred said with an uneven smile. 'A woman arrived here, the day after he came to us. I let them share Frida's room. He didn't seem unhappy the last time I put eyes on him, I must say. Then, the day before yesterday, I think, or perhaps the day before that, they both disappeared.'

Silje, who had not heard a single word beyond 'woman', said, 'Who was she?'

Vildred shrugged. 'I have no idea. I never knew her name or cared to ask. She seemed pleasant enough though, and Erik clearly adored her.' The last remark she aimed squarely at Silje's heart.

'You are mistaken.'

'If that is what you wish. It makes little difference to me.'

'It is not possible. Erik would never betray me like this.'

'Well, perhaps you did not know him as well as you thought.'

'We should leave,' said Jon Ohnstad. 'Clearly he is not here.'

Freya, who had been standing motionless, deep in thought, asked, 'What did this woman look like?'

'Smaller than Erik, though many women are. Stout of build. She seemed to have known him for most of his life. I think I heard her say she'd travelled from Lillehammer.'

'Lisbeth,' said Freya. 'Lisbeth Fehn.'

Silje felt as though she had just been dropped from a great height. 'No, not her. He would never… not with her.'

'Vildred, had he come here to see her before?' Jon Ohnstad asked.

It was the question Vildred had been waiting for. 'Why, yes! Three, maybe four times, mostly in the last two months.'

'Bastard!' Silje shouted.

'Why do you care so much?' Freya asked.

'Yes,' Vildred said, getting into the mood of things, 'why do you care so much, Silje, after you and this Jew hussy—'

'Enough!' Jon Ohnstad said. 'Freya, Silje, wait outside. I would speak to Miss Lunde alone. Do not argue with me! I have had enough from both of you today! Now do as I tell you!'

Murmuring protests under their breath, Silje and Freya did as they were told. Jon Ohnstad waited for Silje to slam the door and then turned to Vildred, who would not look him in the eye.

'You have behaved poorly this night,' he said.

'What of your daughter and your charge! What of poor Erik!'

'I do not believe you care so much for Erik.'

'That is a lie.'

'I believe that you are simply lashing out because you have nowhere else to place your grief.'

'That is… not true.'

'I will make this offer to you, Vildred, because you were almost family. Gather your things and make good your affairs. Do you have transportation?'

She nodded, her eyes filled with tears. 'I have a cart.'

'Good. Then pack everything you have and come to Fólkvangr in three days. You will stay with us. We will listen to stories of your sister and you can cry on our shoulders. Is this acceptable to you?'

She did not say anything, but looked at him as though she would kill him, as though the pain she'd suffered, the loss of her sister, her home, her livelihood, were all compressed and hidden inside the man standing before her.

'Why?' she demanded. 'Why would you do this?'

Jon Ohnstad scratched his head. 'If we do not reach out and help each other then we do not deserve our—'

He took a step back when she ran towards him, but instead of assaulting him, she threw her arms around his neck and began weeping against his throat.

'That is settled then,' he said, unsure what to do with his arms. 'But at some point, I think you will need to apologise to my daughter and her – well, whatever she is.'

50

The journey home to Fólkvangr – along dark, icy roads in the freezing cab of an old truck held together with fifth-hand parts and prayers to the Almighty – should have been unpleasantly cold. In fact, it was unbearably hot. Jon Ohnstad cranked down a window to let the outside air clear the windscreen. Beside him sat Silje and next to her, Freya – both fuming with rage.

'I am just saying that I see a pattern in you, Father, and it is not a pleasant one. Is it to be that every time we run across an orphaned waif who takes delight in humiliating and insulting me, we invite her to live in our house?'

Jon Ohnstad sighed. 'And what is your complaint, Freya?'

Freya had two.

'That is what you think of me, is it, Silje? An "orphaned waif"?'

'When we met that is exactly what you were! And you did insult me! You called me fat! But I forgave you and I grew to like you and I fell in love with you and—'

Jon Ohnstad coughed loudly.

'And you,sir—'

'Stop calling me "sir".'

'Why would you invite another woman to live under your roof?'

'She was alone and frightened, as you yourself were when we found you. If I had turned my back on her then it would have been the same as turning my back on you. I wouldn't have done it then, I will not do it now.'

There was a moment's respite while Freya wept with gratitude and refused to accept Silje's embrace.

'I realise we are at war,' Jon Ohnstad said wearily, 'but must everyone weep quite so much?'

'And what will you do with this Vildred Lunde when she is living with you?'

It was a moment before Silje realised Freya was addressing her. 'Me? This has nothing to do with me! He invited her, not me.'

'You will seduce her; I know you will!'

'I see. You are jealous. She has not even left Voss, and you already think that I will bed her as soon as she drops her belongings in our kitchen.'

Jon Ohnstad coughed again.

'And why should I not be jealous, Silje? Your broken men litter the village, and now you have discovered a taste for women, I daresay you will leave me much the same way.'

Silje's jaw dropped open. 'Father! Did you hear what she said to me?'

'Unfortunately, I am hearing every word.'

Silje and Freya folded their arms and sat rooted and stiff as though nailed to their seats. Without the constant shrilling in his ears, Jon Ohnstad soon began to feel the weight of fatigue bearing down on him. He cuffed himself lightly on the cheek.

'You need to rest,' said Silje. 'I can drive for a while.'

'We do not have far to go,' he replied. 'I can make it.'

'Not on the mountain roads. Stop the truck.' The night was as cold as any she'd known, and Silje feared that without the engine running they would freeze very quickly. Freya was trembling and the silly girl's habit of not wearing shoes now made her worry for frostbite.

'Stop,' Freya said.

'We will not,' said Jon Ohnstad.

'Please stop. Can you not hear that?'

Silje glanced at her father to make sure he could not hear anything either. He shrugged his shoulders and applied the brake. As soon as the truck came to a halt, Freya jumped out and walked to the edge of the road where she stood with her toes over the precipice.

'Freya, come away from there!'

'I hear voices' – she listened to the sounds carried on the winds – 'lots of voices, all German. And machinery. Tanks and personnel carriers, I think.'

'I cannot hear anything,' Silje said.

'Stand next to me, close your eyes, and block out everything. Just concentrate on the wind.'

Silje did as she was told, holding Freya's hand and smothering all thoughts of Erik and Lisbeth and Fólkvangr and General Gruetzmacher. It was more difficult than she could have imagined, and she realised how much noise she carried inside her head: things she'd done in the past, the myriad possibilities for the future.

Freya squeezed her hand. 'Forget everything.'

And so Silje concentrated on the snow, pure and white – an eternal nothingness.

Just the snow and the wind.

Yes, she could hear the machinery, less than a mile away. And there were voices, so faint she could barely distinguish them from the sound of the air.

Jackboots on snow on gravel.

Orders being shouted.

Rifles inspected and loaded.

Tanks rolling; diesel engines breathing the frigid air.

She felt the urgency, the anticipation.

'I cannot hear what they're saying,' she whispered.

Freya did not reply, so Silje returned to the sound of the wind. She opened her ears and picked out the echoes from the surrounding hills. The hills whispered 'Fólkvangr'.

51

I can't say I hated every moment of the quest.

Was I frightened? Most of the time I was almost paralyzed with fear.

And even when we were miles apart, Bergström's cadaverous stench clung to me like a shroud cut from human skin.

Then there was the separation from my mother, who'd kept me alive – or so she said – through my hideously extended childhood. I was on my own now, being prodded and pushed along a road I was sure would end badly for me and my father.

But beyond the fear and the isolation, I found myself.

For one thing, I learned the importance of personal hygiene. I washed obsessively, three times or four times a day if I could, making up for the years I'd spent walking around layered in grime and dried sweat.

I liked to read. I was slow at first, but the more I studied café menus, bus timetables and tram schedules, the faster the symmetry of letter forms twisted and shaped themselves into meaning. At the hotel, I took to watching old films with subtitles; I even tried a book or two.

And I had a flair for languages, German especially, after spending every day for three months at Dresden's library, poring through the documents, papers and journals that travelled with me. The first piece I translated on my own was from General Gruetzmacher's journal. It was perhaps the only entry where he expressed something akin to emotion – a rare occurrence for a man who would have been driven mad if he'd had the courage to look inside himself a little more often. Gruetzmacher despaired of his fall from grace when it was discovered he'd raped a young Jewish girl, the daughter of his housekeeper:

My shame is without end, my humiliation is all-consuming. My former wife has vowed I will never set eyes upon my children again. I have been stripped of my command and the privileges it afforded me. My friends and colleagues have, understandably, turned their backs on me. I disgust them. My unholy union with this child made all the worse because she is a Jew. In the eyes of my peers, my crime is one of bestiality, nothing less.

And yet, after all she has done to me, all she has cost me, the child haunts my every thought. When I close my eyes she is there, this creature of evil. She has made me what I am, and God help me, I know I will love no other.

I mean… Jesus. He blamed her; that's how he lived with himself until Bergström found him.

And speak of the demon, he came to see me after my fourth week hidden away inside the library. He was walking with a cane, supporting himself on an arm wrapped in a plaster cast. He winced as he moved, and the bruising around his right eye was so bad I doubted he could see out of it. He gave me a large envelope full of money, and told me I should spend some of it on vegetables.

'And now you're worried about my diet?'

'You need to stay healthy.'

'So you can kill me.'

'Find your father and I won't have to.'

I was starting to believe that he wouldn't kill me no matter what, but I imagine Gust must have thought the same at some point. I asked him if he'd managed to smooth things over with his employer.

'More or less,' he said, 'mostly less. But I seem to have survived the first few debriefings at least.'

'Right,' I said, trying not to stare at the white tape stretched over his broken nose.

'And your mother is missing,' he added without taking a breath.

'What did you say?'

'Your mother is—'

'I heard you!' My voice echoed around the oak cavern. 'When?'

'Two nights ago.'

'How did you—?'

'I stay in regular contact with Doctor Nese. She likes to be kept appraised of your progress. She seems to worry about you a great deal. She says "hello" by the way.'

I didn't imagine for a moment Doctor Nese had told him my mother was missing and then added, *'And when you tell her, give her my love.'*

She'd given him a hundred messages since I'd left, but Bergström only thought to mention it now.

'Why didn't you tell me you'd spoken with her?'

'I didn't have anything to report. Now I do. Your mother is missing.'

I would've thought a man like Bergström was more accustomed to delivering bad news. He scratched at his bruised jaw and looked around for an escape route.

'I have to go back. I have to help find her. If she doesn't carry on with the treatment, she's going to die.'

He somehow managed to stop himself from saying, *She's going to die anyway*; I could see the truth of it poised on his lips. 'There is nothing you can do, Miss Fossen. I will have my men help search for her. You continue with your work.'

'You won't be able to find her. She's used to hiding. She's had us do it for years.'

He looked at me in amused disbelief. 'You do know what I do for a living, don't you? We will find her. Do not let this distract you.'

* * *

Of course I wasn't going to be anything but distracted. I left the library early, and hurried back to the hotel. The woman on reception handed me my room key as usual, and as usual she looked over my shoulder as I signed in, expecting to see a war criminal standing behind me.

Safely inside my room, I picked up the phone, called the hospital and asked to be put through to the cancer ward. Doctor Nese would be on duty; she always seemed to be.

'Brigit?'

'Doctor Nese?'

Then a long silence, punctuated by her gasping and trying to breathe. I think she was crying.

'Are you okay?'

'Yes, yes, I'm fine. It's just… I was just so worried, that's all.'

There was something strangely comforting in the way she said it. She reminded me of being four years old again, curled into a ball, wrapped tightly in a woollen blanket. It was the first time I can remember being in a bed. Monica had found us a room in a motel, after years of sleeping on coaches or on trains, or on brittle grass. She was so proud of herself, having provided something resembling normalcy for herself and her little girl.

'Are you still there?' Doctor Nese sounded alarmed, and I felt as though I was being unfaithful.

'Where is my mother?'

A pause, a deep breath, and then, 'I… I'm sorry. I don't know. I came in early a few days ago to look in on her, and she'd gone. Pulled out her lines, packed her things and left. She slipped past the nurses, the doctors…'

'She's good at that.'

'She left a note. It didn't say much, just that it was too dangerous for her to stay, that the "Friends of Fólkvangr" would find her. She said that I was to look after you.'

'I don't need anyone to look after me.'

'Yes, I know that.'

'How long can she go without treatment?'

'Brigit, I can't really answer that.'

'Just try!'

I could hear her brain working; she came up with a number and cut it in two, thinking that a harsh reality was better than a slim hope. 'She was responding well, showing signs of remission, which is extraordinary given the poor physical condition she was in.'

More than anything else, I needed a number.

'Six more months, if she's lucky, and that's not to say she won't seek treatment somewhere else.'

'She won't,' I said flatly. 'This is her endgame. This is her big "fuck you" to me and Norway.'

'Brigit, we'll find her. Your… friend, Mr Bergström said he will help.'

'I think "friend" is stretching things a little far, don't you?'

'You should come home.'

'I don't have a home,' I said, knowing how childish and obstinate I sounded.

'Yes, you do, with me. Come home.'

Home. I rolled the word around the back of my tongue, feeling the shape of it, wondering if, after so long, it would ever fit. In Trondheim, I could hear Doctor Nese tapping the handset.

'Brigit, listen to me for a moment, and please don't say anything 'til I've finished, okay?'

I said I was listening and I was, barely; I was thinking where my mother would run: someplace new, or somewhere safe, familiar?

Doctor Nese said she'd been wrong to throw me out and she was sorry. She said that twenty years after being liberated from Camp Belsen, she was still a prisoner, trapped between her need for love and her revulsion of human contact.

'Terrible things happened to women in those camps.'

'I know.'

'No, you don't. People think they do, but they don't; they fucking don't.'

It was the first time I'd heard her swear.

'I was pretty back then, if I can judge myself in such a vain way. Not that it mattered; I was a Jew and I was powerless, so like thousands of others, I became a camp favour, a reward for the kapos and the guards who'd pleased their officers. Every night, for six months until the Russians arrived. I fell pregnant twice, and the other women took care of it for me, as I often had to take care of them. As best we could, we tried to take care of each other.

'Do you know what I thought while they were raping me? I thought, How can they even bear to touch us? We were filthy, emaciated and riddled with disease. We were Jews. But every night, they came shuffling through our doors. Dirty, paper-thin, infested with lice – just like us.'

She said the older women offered themselves first; those who were already near death from malnutrition, those who were already infected with syphilis, placed themselves on the front line to protect the younger ones from the worst of whatever came into the dormitory. She said the kapos would beat them to prove to the Germans how much they could hate their own kind.

Doctor Nese told me that she had left the camp with nothing worse than pubic lice and a womb that would never carry a child to full term – and she thought of herself as one of the fortunate.

'I took you in because I thought I could help you. I thought we could help each other. And when you said what you said, about us being together, I just froze from the inside out, and I'm sorry. But I miss you. I miss cooking for you, and I miss telling you what to do, so I would like you to come home.'

Home.

'I can't,' I said. 'I can't, not until I've finished this.'

'Oh God, Brigit, you don't even know what "this" is.'

She was right, of course she was, but I'd lived my whole life like this. All this stuff with Bergström and the diaries and the decrepit Nazis he kept putting down like crippled dogs was nothing more than an extension of that life. It was just moving more quickly, and with this feeling that it would all soon come to an end.

52

I got up about eight, had breakfast and headed back to the library with my box of notes, pens and a ruler I had yet to use.

I'd been there, every day, for three months. I was aware that the reams of unread papers were rapidly shrinking away and I was no closer to the answer. Gruetzmacher's life history revealed nothing I hadn't known weeks before. He was an ambitious, handsome and gifted degenerate.

The second-from-last sheet was a cutting from *Adresseavisen,* dated 29th December 1967 – just a few years ago.

On Christmas Day 1967, Levi Szachmanowicz, a retired psychiatrist originally from the town of Telemark in Germany, opened the door of the Auckland maisonette where he'd lived since his retirement. Eye witnesses say that two policemen entered his home.

Two days later, Szachmanowicz's housekeeper returned from her vacation to find the doctor's body suspended from the ceiling, minus his skeleton which was later found in Norway. It had been cleaned and varnished, and left less than a mile away from where the village of Fólkvangr had once stood.

The location of the skeleton was the clue to the motive of such a brutal murder (the doctor would have certainly endured the most terrifying pain before dying from blood loss), and to the real identity of Doctor Szachmanowicz, later revealed as General Karl Gruetzmacher, the Butcher of

Fólkvangr, who had evaded capture having fled Germany at the end of the war.

This was the work of Israeli Intelligence (we know this because they were quite happy to admit it), aided by the Norwegian Security services, and rumour has it, a privateer.

Many would say that Gruetzmacher deserved this, but here is the question we must ask ourselves: is it right for any post-war government to be so closely associated with what amounts to execution without trial?

Bergström had drawn a circle around the word *privateer* with a red marker pen; he certainly wasn't modest about his work. The rest of the cutting was a short and unflattering obituary, which again told me nothing I hadn't known before. I put the sheets in the 'done' pile and picked up the final bundle of papers. It was much thinner than the rest, and had been coated in some sort of clear plastic to preserve it. It was a short memo, undated and unsigned. After so many months of practice, my German was good enough to read it.

Dear Sir,

Re: Recommendation for the closure of the Iscariot Project

We humbly thank you for your reply. Your concerns are, as ever, wise and well stated. The cost of this project has indeed been astronomical and to abandon it at this stage would be embarrassing to you and ourselves, but I feel that I would be doing a great disservice to you and the Reich if I did not bring my concerns into the light.
You are correct in your assessment of the nature of the project, and you are correct when you say that General Gruetzmacher has been secretive to the point of paranoid.
And you are right to be alarmed over his continued alcohol abuse. He insisted that we keep the details of the project, and its outcomes, hidden from you so as to protect you. He was wrong, and I will correct that as of now.
In short, Iscariot is a failure. I must stress that this is not Gruetzmacher's fault. Who could have predicted the fragility of the human mind, especially in our own people?
The original project was named Odin and its purpose was to create the perfect soldier: loyal, strong of mind with an indomitable sense of purpose and a will of iron. While we had some successes, we found that the mental conditioning and use of chemicals led to psychosis and schizophrenia in over 96% of the subjects. Most committed suicide on leaving the treatment, and in one unfortunate incident, one subject 'broke' while serving in Poland, killing three officers and six enlisted men before he was eventually shot.

As Gruetzmacher said at the time, there will always be setbacks when pushing the boundaries of science, and at this point the project would have been abandoned if not for the General's tenacity.
The next incarnation became what we now call Iscariot: an experiment to create spies and assassins that could operate effectively and without detection within the jewish community. It was believed that if these jews could be placed within allied forces then we could deal a crippling blow to their efforts to undermine us.
The treatment was harsh, the mental conditioning arduous, the training worthy of our own paratroops. The decision to use only children was, I believe, the correct one. They are more malleable,

more susceptible to fear. They can be moulded, conditioned, and once released back into the community, they would serve us well. We took twelve children along with their mothers, and kept them confined during their year of training. The children would spend 24 hours in conditioning, then twelve hours with their parent. This reinforced a pocket of normalcy in their psyche, even as we circumvented their bonds of loyalty and sense of morality.

I can assure you that our work in this area will, one day, be the subject of learned papers in universities and hospitals all over the world.

So where did we go wrong?

In my opinion, sir, it was the Test: the final proof that they would remain loyal to the Reich while living as jews.

I cannot begin to tell you what a frustrating day that was for us. Of the original twelve, ten survived the training, and only four survived the Test, and one of them, the daughter of Gruetzmacher's housekeeper if I recall, suffered hysterical blindness from the ordeal. She should have been executed, but General Gruetzmacher decided to return her to her father. I understand that they slipped under our surveillance and fled the country. I should have reported this at the time. I kept silent out of respect and loyalty to the General.

But I hear now that Gruetzmacher is seeking a post with the Norwegian Expeditionary Force, so I can keep silent no longer. I have grave misgivings with regard to his mental state and his continued abuse of alchohol. And 'experiments' with some of our more exotic drug treatments have left him unstable at best, psychotic at worst. I understand that to cast him aside now would be an embarrassment, but this should be considered.

I understand that Iscariot would be invaluable to the Reich if it could be made to work cost effectively and without risk of injury to our own soldiers, but we have to face facts: the jew is an inferior yet honourable creature whose unbreakable bonds with faith and family meant we would never achieve success in numbers. It would be best to cut our losses as it were, abandon the project until exotic drug treatments have advanced to the point to make it viable. Even without Iscariot we will win this war, sir. There is plenty of time.

When I looked down, the pages of the memo were scattered on the oak floor. I should have gathered them, but I knew I didn't have to. Bergström would take care of it, like he'd taken care of everything.

He'd known. He'd led me around by the nose for months, and all the time he'd known.

53

'We cannot take the main road back to the village,' Jon Ohnstad said.

Silje agreed. 'We will never get past them, not in the truck.'

'The east road then.'

'It is far too narrow. The ground is treacherous and it is too dark. You will drive us over the edge.'

'The road is passable until we reach Heimdall's Point. Then we abandon the truck and walk, though how we will find our way in this cursed darkness—'

'I will guide you,' said Freya. 'I know the way.'

The journey was indeed treacherous. The sun had melted the snow, and then, hours later, when it had fallen below the horizon, the roads had frozen and were left covered in a thin layer of clear ice. But Jon Ohnstad knew the lands and his truck well, and a few hours later they arrived at the narrowing called Heimdall's Point with him having lost control only once – an overzealous turn of the wheel that had brought them within a hair's width of the ledge. Their hearts were still in their mouths when they abandoned the truck and followed Freya into the darkness.

After an hour, Silje could not feel her toes. She worried about Freya who still insisted in walking with her feet bare. Still, the ice under foot did not seem to faze her in the least. While Silje and her father slipped, slid and danced to remain on their feet, Freya walked with a steady assuredness, following a near-perfect straight line.

'Are you not cold?'

'Of course I am cold, but we will be home soon.'

Silje narrowed her eyes, trying to pierce the darkness. She wondered if she too would have a greater awareness of her place in the world if she could not rely upon her eyes to see it.

'I can see light.' Her father pointed at four glowing pinpricks some way in the distance.

'That is the home of Doctor Lomen,' said Freya. 'We are in Fólkvangr.'

They pressed on to the doctor's house.

His door had been left open and calling out his name showed that he was not at home. They were cold and hungry so they went inside to warm themselves by the fire he'd left burning. Silje went through all the upstairs rooms, searching the wardrobes. There would be clothes to fit all of them; the sons of Doctor Lomen had varied immensely in girth and stature.

Even though she'd spent time warming herself in front of the log fire, Silje felt a cold chill as she slipped into a thick woollen shirt and a pair of dark grey trousers that had belonged to Wilfried, the middle son. She remembered seeing him wearing the same trousers at Mr Kleppe's funeral; the shirt she remembered from somewhere else…

Wilfried had been a quiet, measured man, and always polite in spurning her advances.

'You will learn much from me, Wilfried Lomen,' she'd said while unbuttoning his shirt. *'So much more than you will learn from that strumpet you are seeing in Bergen. I do not understand why you would leave Fólkvangr when everything you could possibly desire can be found here.'*

He'd folded his hands around her own and gently lifted them away from his chest. *'I am leaving because I love her, Silje. I hope that you will understand this when you are older.'*

Silje trembled in front of the fire.

'Is all well with you, Daughter?' Her father entered the room, tucking a sweater into an over-sized pair of trousers.

Silje nodded, but said 'No.'

'Hmmm.' He cast his eyes to the ceiling. Somewhere above them, Freya was rifling through a trunk of clothes, looking for something that would fit. 'If she makes you happy then everything else will fall into place. You will see. People said that your mother and I would never—'

'It is not that, Father.' She crossed her arms and shivered. 'May I ask you a question?'

'All right.' Something in her manner compelled him to take his seat in another man's armchair.

It was not a question that she'd ever thought to ask. It was not a question she'd even asked of herself. *It is best done quickly then*, she thought. *Like pulling a tooth, or castrating a goat.* 'Why is it that I cast my favours so freely?'

Silence; then from several feet away she heard him swallow.

'I think perhaps that is not a question a daughter should ask her father.'

'I am asking you, nevertheless.'

He muttered something under his breath, about the mind of a woman being a place only a lunatic would dare travel.

'Father!'

'I am thinking!' He rose to his feet and moved to stand beside her, next to the fire. 'The loss of your mother affected you greatly.'

'It affected us all.'

'Yes, but in different ways. Magnus involved himself in pursuits that were not to my liking. What was that thing he would do with the planks of pinewood tied to his feet?'

'Skiing.'

'Yes, a ridiculous carry-on. And then he wanted to be a mountaineer, climbing the sides of the mountains when we have perfectly adequate paths to the summit. Danger made him forget his pain.'

'And you…'

'Drank, yes. I drank much, for many years. Grette would send someone to the cottage and you and Magnus would come with a wheelbarrow to carry me home.' He chuckled and removed his cap to scratch his head. 'But then there is you, sweet Silje. You lost your mother and would not lose anyone else. You devoted yourself to keeping Fólkvangr as your mother left it. You have tried your best to make us happy in our little corner of the mountain. There are things you have done, Silje, things that I am sure you are not proud of, but you have done them to keep us together.'

Silje wiped her eyes with the heel of her hand. 'And after everything, I have failed.'

'We do not know what the Germans are planning, Silje.'

'I feel it, Father. We will lose Fólkvangr this night.'

Freya appeared in the parlour's doorway. She wore a set of black overalls that Silje suspected had belonged to Roald, Doctor Lomen's second eldest. Amongst his many talents Roald had been the village mechanic, and with the help of her father, had kept the family truck moving far beyond its lifetime. She wondered if her father would be able to keep it going without Roald's patience and guidance, and then she thought of the truck, abandoned in the snow and ice. *It will be fine*, she told herself. *Roald will watch over it.*

'I can hear you crying,' Freya said. 'There is no need. We will prevail.'

Jon Ohnstad opened the door, and the bitterness of the mountains blew its way through the parlour and out into the kitchen. 'Come, we must warn the village.'

* * *

'It sounds to me,' Freya said, moving her head from side to side, 'as if they already know.' She dug her toes into the snow and reached for Silje's hand.

Silje held onto it tightly and glanced at her father who lit his pipe with trembling fingers.

Fólkvangr was preparing for war.

They emerged cautiously from the woodland west of the village and were swept into the tumultuous swell of villagers and Resistance fighters that criss-crossed the main thoroughfare. In spite of the curfew, every streetlamp and every light in every home was lit to bring some semblance of daylight to the cold night. Order were shouted and obeyed without hesitation. Horses and carts rolled in and out of the village, bringing sandbags to narrow and fortify the main streets. Mr Kleppe's funeral was the last time Silje had seen every villager out of their homes all at once. Then, the mood had been one of sombre celebration; this was entirely different. There was a palpable excitement in the air, a warmth, a togetherness, a bonding in loyalty and courage.

This will never do, she thought. *This will never do at all.*

The village women were running from door to door, gathering children and lifting them into two horse-drawn carts that followed. Silje assumed that the children were being taken to the safety of the higher mountains. Some of the women joined them, but most said their tearful goodbyes and stayed to partake in the defence of the village.

They promised their children that they would see them again, very soon.

Gunther Braithwaite ran over to them. He had a rifle slung across his shoulder and a pistol strapped to his waist. 'You are here,' he said. 'We thought the Germans had taken you on the road.'

'We came east.' Silje watched in horror as a machine gun misfired, sending everyone around it sprawling on the ground for safety.

'Sorry!' Mrs Tufte called out from behind the trigger. 'I think I have the hang of it now!' She saw Silje and waved.

'She insisted,' Gunther assured them. 'They all did.'

'Will you please tell us what is going on?' Silje noticed that her father was licking his lips; he was an old soldier, as were many of the village's elders. The smell of machine grease and cordite had awoken something in him, and she did not care for it.

'We thought Gruetzmacher was planning a night exercise for his men; he's done it before to test their readiness. And then we received word from our people in Bergen. Every Norwegian working at the town hall was shot late this evening.'

Freya's legs gave way; she would have fallen had she not such a hold on Silje's arm.

'So they are coming here.'

Gunther shook his head and hunched his shoulder to reseat the rifle. 'We do not think so. We think they have discovered the location of our strongholds high in the mountains and are mounting an assault.'

'At night, fighting uphill?' It was Jon Ohnstad's turn to shake his head. 'That is madness!'

'Word has it that General Gruetzmacher is not in his right mind and hasn't been for some time.'

Carina hurried over, carrying her captured sten gun. 'I think we should send Mrs Tufte with the children. She will most probably kill us all before the Germans do.'

'We need all the help we can muster, Carina. Her distance vision is good, her hands are strong. We need her.'

Carina reluctantly allowed the matter to drop and turned her attentions to Silje. 'It would appear that you were wrong about Erik Brenna.'

'I do not know what you mean.'

'I mean he betrayed us. He knew of our bases in the hills; he knew of the Jews hiding with us in the mountains. And now, days after his disappearance, every Norwegian at German HQ is dead and there is a sizeable ground force coming our way. I do not believe these matters are unrelated, Miss Ohnstad. Perhaps if you'd learned to keep your knees together then all this could have been—'

It was less a slap, more of a punch; it caught Carina squarely on the jaw and sent her spinning to the ground. Gunther and Jon Ohnstad restrained her as she jumped to her feet and clawed wildly at Silje, who stood quietly massaging her fist while Freya demanded to know what had happened.

'Hush, Freya. It is nothing.' Silje turned to Carina who was being held fast by Gunther and her father. 'And you are not to say such things to me again.'

Carina wrenched herself free. She glared at Silje, her fingers twitching against the machine gun. 'Look what you have brought on us, Silje Ohnstad.' She swept her hand outwards, taking in all of Fólkvangr. 'Just look.'

'Go to the tavern, Carina,' Gunther snapped. 'Grette needs help with the ammunition.' She sneered and opened her mouth to say something, but Gunther was having none of it. 'That is an order!'

'Remember my words, Silje; all this on you.' With that, she shouldered the machine gun and made her way through the snow towards *The Mottled Goat.*

Before she was out of earshot, Silje rounded on Gunther. 'Why must you make your stand here? In my village? Are you mad or simply heartless? We are not soldiers!'

'Silje, there was no choice, and once I explained it to them—'

'You "explained", did you? Did you explain that Gruetzmacher's men are the pride of Germany's Expeditionary Force; did you explain to my friends, my family, that these men gloried themselves by butchering Poland?'

'He told us all this and more, Silje.' Kvist Gundersen limped towards them. He carried the ancient blunderbuss that Silje remembered hanging on the privy door behind his cottage. She wondered if it had been cleaned and serviced at least once in the last fifteen years. 'The Jews in the mountains above us? They are Norwegians, just like us. There are hundreds of them, Silje. Old men, women, children...'

'And we need to give them time to make their escape,' said Gunther. 'Six hours, that is all. The Germans will take at least two hours to get here; that leaves four.'

'And you do not think that Gruetzmacher cannot decimate us in two.'

'We are not planning to fight him,' Kvist said. 'We just need to stall him; delay him for just a few short hours.'

'And you can do that,' Freya said, her right ear turned towards the sound of guns being loaded. 'You can keep him talking.'

'She will not speak with that monster, Freya,' said Jon Ohnstad. 'In fact, it would be far safer if you joined the children in the mountains.'

'Father, I am not going anywhere.'

'Nor I.' And Freya dug her heels into the snow to show that she meant it. 'My place is at her side.'

Kvist Gundersen looked at Jon Ohnstad and raised an eyebrow. Jon Ohnstad shrugged, feeling little inclination to explain.

'Is this something akin to Ada Vetlesen and Mrs Bruun?'

'Kvist, it is none of your business.'

He tipped his cap and slid the blunderbuss across the crook of his arm. 'I shall see you all on the field,' he said and sauntered away.

'He seemed happy,' said Freya.

'Because this is an adventure for old men,' Silje replied.

Jon Ohnstad pointed to the cluster of cottages nearest the forest. 'You should move a detachment beyond the village. Hide the men in the trees and be prepared to cut off the Germans' escape route.'

Gunther said, 'It will not come to that.'

'But you will do as I ask, nevertheless.'

Gunther nodded and barked orders to his men. Minutes later, eight Resistance fighters ran from the village and disappeared into the trees.

He is wrong, Silje thought. *They are all so very wrong*. She took Freya's hand and guided her through the chaos. 'Can you find your way from home to home?'

'You know I can, Silje.'

'Then we shall help gather the children.'

With so much else to do, and with more than enough of the village women taking the children to safety, Silje knew that two more hands would make little difference, especially when she saw how Freya had to walk with more care to avoid the fighters and villagers who did not have the time to be mindful of a blind Jewess in their midst.

But it was important that she do this; it was important that Silje see it being done. The village, the stalls and the shops and the taverns and the cottages and the monument to her mother would be lost, but if the children were safe then Fólkvangr would one day rise from the earth.

* * *

Within the hour Fólkvangr's children had been sent away, with the exception of Jesper Bergström and Ingrid Haug.

'Wherever they are,' Silje assured their mothers, 'they are together.'

Mrs Bergström stood with her arms folded across her ample chest, gripping her elbows, her anguish tightly bound.

'What if they have left the village?' she said. 'What if they have taken their bicycles and are riding towards the German advance?'

'Jesper is far too clever for that, Mrs Bergström,' Silje reassured her.

'You cannot find them,' Mrs Haug said, her tear-filled eyes fixed on the archway.

Mrs Bergström agreed. 'She is right. If you call for them, then they will hide from you.'

Silje felt her heart fall to the pit of her stomach. 'That is not true.'

'Jesper hates you, Silje,' said Mrs Bergström.

'And my Ingrid hates you because Jesper hates you.' Mrs Haug looked to Freya. 'Can you find them, my dear?'

'No, she cannot. She is blind!'

'And yet she sees more than anyone else I've ever met.'

Freya said, 'I will try.'

'You will do no such thing! The village has been turned on its head; nothing is where you think it should be. You will get in the way, or worse – you could be hurt.'

Freya said she would be careful, and before Silje could speak another word, she set off towards a large cluster of Resistance fighters smoking cigarettes outside the village hall.

Mrs Haug called after her. 'Thank you, Freya! I know you will bring them back!'

Silje remembered a time when the villagers relied on her for small miracles. She watched Freya as she spoke to each fighter in turn, making gestures with her hands that described the height and breadth of Jesper and Ingrid with uncanny accuracy.

'And how will you be making yourself useful, Silje?' Mrs Bergström said.

'I will find my brother Magnus, and have him remind me how to load a gun. And what about you, Mrs Bergström? How will you aid in the defence of our home?'

'I will be away from the village,' she replied.

'I thought as much.'

'Doctor Lomen is setting up a field hospital inside the Fehn's cottage. I have some medical training so my meagre talents can find service there.'

Silje was lost for words, but Mrs Bergström was not given to pettiness. 'I will also be praying for us all, Silje. I suggest you do the same.'

Silje bit her lip and nodded. 'Everything will turn out well. You will see.'

Mrs Bergström smiled weakly and went on her way.

When Silje turned to look for Freya, she saw that the group of Resistance fighters was still there, but Freya herself had vanished. She took a breath to quell the panic rising from her chest. *She is more than capable of looking after herself. You cannot always be at her side.* Though she knew that is what she wanted more than anything else in the world, to be at Freya's side until time claimed them and they had faded from memory.

She set off towards the village hall where Magnus was running a class in weapon craft, but she had not taken three steps before a horn sounded: a signal from the forward lookouts that their time for preparation was at an end. Gruetzmacher and a small army was less than a mile from Fólkvangr.

54

The villagers and the Resistance formed an arrowhead in front of the monument to Emily Ohnstad. Jon Ohnstad stood at its point with his son to his left and Gunther Braithwaite to his right. Silje, standing behind Gunther, licked her lips and glanced across at Carina. The older woman, a born fighter by all accounts, trembled and blinked rapidly. She tensed herself and tightened her grip on the machine gun. She'd beaten back her fear; Silje wished she knew how to do the same.

The first tank rolled down the path towards the village, crushing the dwarf pines and bracken, and splitting the trunks of the trees. It demolished the archway to the village without effort and turned to the main thoroughfare. Behind it, two armoured personnel carriers and a detachment of foot soldiers uniformed in arctic combat gear: thick grey coats, hob-nailed boots, goggles and thick fingerless gloves. They had most probably marched on foot for miles, yet they still looked alert and eager for battle. Two outriders accompanied the infantry units, one of whom, despite his fur-lined hood, Silje recognised as Lieutenant Klein.

Gruetzmacher rode behind the tank in an armoured car without a roof. He had eschewed the winter gear in favour of a black SS uniform. He raised his hand to halt the advance and then leaned forward to speak to his driver. Another female, Silje noted, younger than Sergeant Krause. Silje doubted she had a drop of Jewish blood in her veins.

Gruetzmacher stepped down from the armoured car and straightened his coat. He ignored the Resistance, instead looking to the cottages and shops and then higher, at the trees that surrounded the village. He sniffed the air and let his eyes fall to the men and women standing in defence of Fólkvangr.

Something appeared to be amusing him.

'Miss Ohnstad, if you please.' He made his way towards *The Mottled Goat* without looking back. The waiting townsfolk turned to Silje, and she could see the suspicions she'd fought so hard to put to rest had returned.

She looked to her father who shook his head. 'Do not!'

'I will be safe, Father. We will be sitting in the tavern with his men outside.'

'Silje, now is not the time for bravado!' Magnus said.

'And when is the time for bravado, Magnus – if not now?' She stepped from the arrowhead and made her way to the tavern. Every eye turned, scorching a path to its door. Silje felt her stomach churn; she hardened her gait to prevent her legs from shaking.

Felix Borge swept off his cap and opened the door for her. 'God be with you, Silje.'

They had been at school together, but she could hardly remember ten words she'd spoken to him since. He lived at the far end of the village, which had seemed a hundred miles away when they were both children. How much smaller her world had become of late…

She bowed her head to enter the tavern, and Felix stole a kiss from her cheek. The kiss was warm and timid. When she turned to look at him he looked away, unable to meet her eyes. She squeezed his hand and went inside.

Grette liked to keep *The Mottled Goat* lit by candles; she said it created an air of comfort. Today, it just seemed dark. A small crowd had formed a cautious semicircle around a single table near the centre of the tavern. Gruetzmacher sat there, supping ale and eating from a small plate of bread and cheese. The crowd parted to allow Silje through. She looked for Grette and saw her behind the bar, pointing a rifle at the General. Grette lifted her shoulders slightly and gave an almost imperceptible shake of her head.

'Sit,' Gruetzmacher said.

Silje sat across the table from him with her legs turned to one side.

'Are you hungry?'

She shook her head. The crowd closed in around them. Hands slid slowly into pockets and the whispers grew louder, more foolhardy.

He is alone!

Who will stop us?

'When the world was ruled from Rome,' Gruetzmacher began, 'a citizen could travel anywhere in the conquered lands without fear of assault. Do you know why?'

'Because Rome would punish such an affront a thousandfold,' Silje replied. 'Whole villages would be put to the sword in vengeance.'

Gruetzmacher looked surprised. 'Not vengeance, justice. Those who rule decide the difference.'

He dabbed at his mouth with a cloth, and Silje dared to raise her head and look into his eyes. They were blood-red, the flesh around them wrinkled and grey. Silje suspected that the General was half-drunk before he'd sat down.

'Tell your courageous friends to leave us,' he said.

Kvist said, 'We will not leave you here alone, Silje.'

'She is not alone,' Gruetzmacher replied. 'She is with me.'

'Kvist, please, just go,' said Silje. 'I do not want you here! Any of you!'

The General looked to the tavern door, beyond which the might of the Third Reich waited with its finger on a hundred triggers.

'Go!'

The villagers looked at each other, whispered amongst themselves, and then Kvist spoke again. 'We will wait outside.'

'Yes,' Gruetzmacher said, lighting a cigarette. 'Why don't you do that very thing.'

The villagers filed out of the tavern, each one touching Silje's shoulder as they passed.

'And the barkeep,' said Gruetzmacher.

Grette said that she would stay.

'He will not harm me, Grette. He never has.'

Reluctantly, Grette lowered her rifle and stepped from behind the bar. On her way to the door, she stopped to address the General. 'One day, soon, you will all face a reckoning for things you have done.'

The General looked up and smiled. 'And one day, a week from now, you will be punished for your insolence. Now be on your way, my good woman – if that is indeed what you are.'

Grette fumed and took a step towards him, but Silje stopped her, reaching out and holding her fast by the wrist.

'Grette, just go… please.'

The General laid his sidearm on the table and pushed it towards her. 'Try this instead of that old rifle. You will have a better chance.'

Grette looked at the pistol and licked her lips.

'Grette!'

Grette did not move.

'If you try, if you fail, he will kill us both.'

And it was only then that Grette relented.

'One day, Nazi,' Grette said. 'You'll see.'

The tavern door closed, and Silje suddenly felt very cold and very alone. She embraced herself and shivered.

'I thought you'd be used to the mountain chill,' Gruetzmacher said.

'It is not the mountains.'

He stubbed out his cigarette and rose to his feet. 'I should have ordered drinks before she left.'

'I suspect that you have had quite enough already.'

His smile faded, his face reddened, and Silje wondered if perhaps she'd pushed him too far. He considered striking her, she could see it in his eyes, but that would be the beginning of his endgame, the makings of his final ploy to get what he wanted. So instead he made his way to the bar and began examining each of the caskets in turn. Silje watched him, fighting every instinct to run from the tavern, back to the safety of her father and her brother and Freya.

Gruetzmacher made his choice and filled a tankard to the brim. 'I will come straight to the point,' he said. 'Give me the Jew or I will turn everything you love to ash.'

In that moment she thought, *All is lost.* Her heart shrank, her knees began to shake and the small room seemed to pull away from her, while Gruetzmacher grew in size until she felt like a child in the shadow of a giant. 'What Jew?'

The General rolled his eyes and sat back in his seat. 'All right,' he said, 'then let us play. I have time.'

'I am sorry. If I knew who you were talking about then I would—'

'You have been harbouring a Jew in your village for a year. A blind girl, about twenty years of age.'

Silje tried to think, but when she closed her eyes and desperately sought a way out, she saw only a bright white light.

'You will give her to me, and I will be on my way.'

'Back to Bergen.'

He filled his mouth with ale and swallowed. 'Back to Germany, after a small detour into the mountains.'

'I do not know this girl.'

'Fräulein, do not make me search for her in the rubble of your village.'

'I swear, General, I have no idea what you are talking about.'

He threw back his head to stare at the ceiling, making clicking sounds with his tongue. 'You waste time for us both. I know I will find Jews in the mountains and I know I will find the girl I seek here in Fólkvangr. Why prolong the inevitable?'

For love, that is why. Silje pushed back her chair and stood up. 'I cannot help you, General, so I will be on my way.'

'And you have been using *The Quisling Orchid* as a line of communication for the Resistance.'

She swayed and sat down again.

'For that alone I should kill you, but I am offering you your life, and the lives of all your co-conspirators in this village. All I ask, in return for my mercy, is the girl. Think carefully before you refuse me again; I will not ask a third time.'

'I am sorry. I cannot help you.' She waited, for the sound of a shot and the nothingness of oblivion. She could hear him breathing, thinking. She waited for a moment more and then slowly opened her eyes. The General was staring at her, not with rage, but with something akin to admiration.

'You are brave. I will give you that.' He dropped his eyes to the table; Silje's followed, and she saw that while she'd been waiting for her life to end, he'd left a crumpled piece of paper next to the pistol.

'You should read it,' he said.

'I do not wish to.'

He sighed. 'Then let me tell you what it told me.'

'If you must.'

'Yes, I must!' he shouted, and slammed the flat of his hand against the table.

Silje crushed her thighs together so she would not wet herself. *God, please let this end*, she thought. *I care not how.*

He stared at the floor, his lips moving through some mantra she could barely hear. When he looked to her again, he appeared calm, sober, the fire of his anger having boiled the poison from his body.

'From the day we met, I could smell her on you. That scent of flowers and cinnamon. It comes from her hair, I think, though I was never sure. I hoped if I treated you kindly then you would bring her to me of your own volition.'

She wanted to blink, but was afraid the world would end if she closed her eyes again.

'You know her.'

Gruetzmacher nodded. 'Yes, Fräulein. I know her.'

'How do you know her,' Silje asked, her memories twisting and folding inside her head.

'I will tell you if you bring her to me.'

Silje's eyes fell to the pistol, the note. 'What is that?'

'Evidence.'

'Evidence of what?'

'Her betrayal, of you, your village, of the Resistance. She told me about the coded messages in *The Quisling Orchid*.'

'You lie.'

'I have no reason to.'

'You have every reason to. You think you can make me turn on her, betray her!'

'So,' the General said, lighting another cigarette, 'you *do* know her.'

Silje's hand landed on the pistol, and the General's hand landed on top of hers.

'I told you,' he said. 'I warned you when we met! I told you she is a witch who would enslave you, heart and soul!' He pulled her close and took a handful of her hair; he held it under his nose and inhaled deeply, his eyes rolling back into his skull. 'My God, yes!' And then his eyes snapped back and he stared at her in horror. 'God in heaven, you're fucking her!'

Silje grabbed the tankard and struck him as hard as she could. She heard him cry out but did not stop to see how much damage she had done. In the same moment she was out of her seat and running towards the door. A gunshot rang out and her heart skipped. The bullet splintered a wooden beam to her left and her heart began pumping again. She almost pulled the tavern door from its hinges and threw herself out into the night. She could hear Gruetzmacher swearing from inside the tavern.

Gunther and her father ran towards her.

'Silje!' Her father took her in his arms. 'What happened? What did he—?'

'Kill him,' Silje said to Gunther. 'You must kill them all.'

Gunther glanced at the soldiers who were bringing their weapons to bear. 'What did he tell you?'

'He is mad. He means to burn the village, murder every last one of us…'

'Are you sure?'

'Do you think I am lying?'

'No, of course not, but—'

'Then do as I say! Fire on them! Kill them before they kill us!'

The General appeared at the tavern door, his gun hanging loosely in his hand, blood streaming from the gash at his hairline. 'You will die this day, Silje Ohnstad!'

Before a single shot could be fired, someone ran past them; Silje's eye caught a flash of tweed, and the smell of horse sweat filled her nostrils.

He was weeping, and as he ran towards the armoured car he screamed the names of his five sons.

55

I sat on the steps of Dresden's library until the sun went down. Apparently the temperature was minus two that night, but I couldn't feel the cold. Inside my head was just a sea of black, and every so often, in the mire, I caught sight of my father drowning.

I watched the commuter swarm making its way home for the night. I tried to pick some of them out, those that stood apart, in some small way, from the rest. They were like bees: all separate, all the same. I wondered what it would be like to steal one of their lives, to slot into someone else's existence, to go home to a husband and three children (two girls, one boy), to fall asleep in front of *Gilligan's Island* with my head resting under my husband's chin. What if I could steal someone's life as history had stolen mine?

From the corner of my eye I saw Bergström limping down the steps, carrying the folders and papers I'd dropped on the library floor. I wondered if he'd been there every day, watching me struggle and curse my way through the documents and the text books. He sat down next to me, keeping his left leg straight.

'MOSSAD still not happy with you.'

He nodded and made a sound inside his throat that would have been laughter if he'd allowed it to escape. 'They have two dead operatives. They will never be happy again.'

'After three months, they still don't believe you.'

'They do not.'

'So shooting yourself in the leg was a waste of time.'

'Apparently so.'

'So what happens now?'

'I make them believe me.'

'And if you can't?'

Bergström sighed and unwrapped a packet of sandwiches. He offered one to me. I wasn't hungry. He took a bite and chewed slowly.

'You could run.'

'Israel is new to the intelligence game; she needs to prove herself, and the fastest way to do that is to pursue her targets regardless of distance and time. They would find me. It may take a decade or two, but they would find me.'

'Then I'm sorry.'

'Yes,' he said. I wasn't sure if I was forgiven or not.

He took another bite and watched the same crowds slowly being obscured by the building traffic. The smell of petrol fumes pressed down around us and the first of the car horns sounded, building rapidly to an orchestra.

'How long have you known?'

He didn't reply, not at first, so I tried again. 'How long have you known it was her?'

This time, he sniffed loudly and rubbed his chin. 'Gust was the cleverest,' he said. 'He knew how to drip-feed us information: a name here, a location there. Kept himself alive for ten years, the bastard.'

Funny thing about the way he said 'bastard'; there was no malice or venom behind it. He said it in an almost playful way, like he was talking about an old friend whom he hadn't seen for years, or a companion recently departed.

'We thought Gruetzmacher was all he had left, but no, the old fart had one more ace to play: the Iscariot Initiative. Memo by memo, report by report. Another two years of life. That note you carelessly dropped in the library – it was written by him, you know. Didn't sign it; none of them signed anything. We didn't even know that Gruetzmacher headed the project until we paid him a visit in New Zealand.' Bergström rested his fists against his chin and looked across the busy street. That was the only time I ever saw an emotion in him: sadness, such sadness.

'I saw what he did – in Fólkvangr. I was there, on the rooftops, while the fighting raged. A stupid place to hide really. I was lucky I wasn't killed when the shelling started. But then perhaps I wasn't so lucky after all.

'It started with the doctor, I think. He ran towards the tanks and they riddled him with bullets. He wouldn't stop; he just ran and ran, shouting their names, and when he reached it, he sort of… erupted. He must've have had explosives under his jacket, though I cannot imagine for the life of me where he found them.'

'His sons were in the Resistance.'

Bergström looked at me, surprised, and clearly impressed. 'You've done your homework.'

'You didn't give me much choice.'

'No, I suppose I didn't.' He took another bite of the sandwich and swallowed it without chewing. 'I knew your father. He was a good man, and when he confessed all those years ago, I thought… I don't know what I thought. It didn't make sense to me, but—'

'He confessed.'

'Yes. Why would he do such a thing?' Bergström shook his head. 'And the girl. It was not her fault. She was brainwashed, raped, tortured, beaten… No, I cannot blame Freya.'

I guessed then that Bergström had been a little in love with her. I imagined him as a small boy with a crush the size of a mountain.

I said, 'I think she might have killed the lamplighter.'

'Kleppe died of heart failure,' he said flatly, dispassionately. 'He fell and—'

'Struck his head, yes; I read it in Silje's diary.' I searched my rucksack until I found the photograph taken at the Ohnstad monument. 'Look at the stones.'

Bergström produced a pair of spectacles from his sleeve and put them on. He glanced sideways at me, a little self-consciously, then peered closely at the picture. 'What am I looking for?'

'That stone,' I said. 'Can you see the blood?'

'Yes, where he fell and hit his head.'

'Then the blood should have stained the top of the stone, not the side, unless he ran headlong into the wall.'

He looked again, still mystified.

'He didn't fall and hit his head. The rock was taken from the wall, used to kill him, then replaced – the wrong way round.'

'The wrong way round.'

'Because the person who used the stone couldn't tell which way it was supposed to go back into the monument.'

'Because the person who killed Jonas Kleppe—'

'Because the person who killed Jonas Kleppe was blind.'

He blinked, smiled and then burst into peals of unpleasant laughter.

I waited for him to get it out of his system. He wiped his eyes on his sleeve. 'So this blind woman – girl – picked up a stone, killed the old lamplighter with it, and then put the stone back. Even if what you say was possible, I knew her! She loved that old man! She would have never—'

'She loved Fólkvangr, and we both know she betrayed every one of you who lived there.'

'She could not help—'

'She betrayed Fólkvangr even though she was in love with the one woman who would never forgive her for it.'

He looked at me, his eyes trying to pierce my skin. I wanted to move away from him, but I stayed my ground, holding onto the step in case fear and common sense forced me to do otherwise.

'And if she was in love with Silje Ohnstad and betrayed Fólkvangr anyway, then it's not that much of a stretch to think she would kill Jonas Kleppe.'

He blinked and looked up into the sky, sifting through his scarred memories, piecing things together.

'The orchid shed,' he whispered.

'What?'

'I saw them… in the… in… fuck!' He closed his fists and pressed them against his skull. I hoped he wouldn't cry; I wouldn't have known what to do if he'd cried. I let him have his moment, busying myself by laying more of my scrawled notes on the steps.

Bergström was staring at me as though I were some sort of monster.

'I've been reading some stuff about mental trauma.' I had to tread carefully now that I'd realised he still saw her through the eyes of a besotted child. 'What if the Nazi experiments caused some kind of split in her personality? What if there were two Freya Dorfmanns: the Jewess and the German spy. I mean she was German, wasn't she?'

He swallowed and the muscles in his cheek twitched. It was implausible, but he wanted to believe it, to have his memory of Freya Dorfmann cleansed and sutured. But Bergström was ever the pragmatist, ever the soldier.

'You only have conjecture,' he said, 'nothing else. Certainly not enough to condemn her further.'

'The Lomen brothers,' I said. 'I've seen articles that say the Germans knew they were coming, that they were betrayed.'

'Conspiracy theorists, I'd venture. Remember, the General lost men in that attack.'

'Or did he sacrifice them to keep his spy a secret? And what about her father? What if it was Freya herself who betrayed him to—'

Bergström struggled to his feet; I guessed he'd heard enough. He glared at me for what seemed like an age and then he reached into his pocket. I knew the routine by now so I didn't leap out of my skin or scream or beg for my life; I just held out my hand and waited for the envelope to land on my palm. 'Where are we going?' I asked, 'and how many people are you going to kill when we get there?'

He forced out a smile and said, 'Have you ever been to Israel?'

'You know I haven't.'

'Good, then it will be an experience for one of us at least. Go home, get some rest; you leave in the morning.'

The Friends of Fólkvangr

(28th September 1941)

To whomever.

I woke to a foul new world this day.

Doctor Lomen is dead, one of thirty in all – men and women whom I have grown up with, or who watched over me when I was young.

I should feel the glow of victory; we drove back the invader. We forced them from our village, and my father led a group of men to reinforce an ambush on the Bergen road. It was there that Gruetzmacher learned what it was to be Norwegian.

We have given precious time for the Jews and the gypsies and the men that love men and the women who lay with women. They will make a path north-east for Sweden. A hard road I am told. I pray for them. The Resistance will move south and fight another day.

And what of us? Our ammunition is low but our spirits burn. We cannot mourn our lost because the battle is not yet done. The General will return to avenge this humiliation, and we shall surely fall.

So, if this note finds you, know that Fölkvangr fought as the vikings of old; we did not bow and we did not break. We revealed our enemy as mortals and ourselves as gods. Take our sacrifice as a call to arms, and drive the invaders from our home.

Silje Ohnstad

56

Doctor Lomen had run into a wall of gunfire – and kept running. The name of his youngest boy was on his lips when he threw himself – his clothes hanging in bloodied rags from his broken body – onto the armoured car and detonated the charges he'd strapped to his chest.

The explosion set off the grenades carried by the German soldiers nearest him.

The shockwave bowed outwards, lifting Germans and Norwegians from their feet and throwing them through the air. Then came the heat, as though hell itself had thrown open its gates. And the roar, Silje thought, was the devil himself, calling mankind to account for its folly.

She felt something burst inside her ear, and then there was silence. She breathed and the air seared her lungs. Through the fog and the dust she could hear screaming in the distance.

She wanted to sleep and so she closed her eyes and waited for the numbness to take her.

'Get up,' a voice said, while a strong callused hand took her by the wrist and hauled her to her feet.

'Father, Doctor Lomen, he—'

'Yes,' said her father, 'yes, he did.' He had a gash in his cheek that stained his beard red. Silje reached into her pocket and found a handkerchief, but he turned away from her before she could tend to him.

The villagers were slowly returning to life, raising themselves from the earth as though waking from a slumber.

Like a fairy story. Silje realised her head was in a fog. She looked around for Magnus; he was as well as could be expected, helping Gunther to his feet.

The Germans were stunned, but regrouping. She could hear Gruetzmacher shouting orders though she could not see him.

Her father called Gunther's name and in a moment he was at his side.

'This is our time.'

Gunther nodded and shouted orders to his scattered men.

Another cry split the air; they turned and saw Kvist Gundersen running towards the German line, holding his ancient blunderbuss to his eye. Silje, Gunther and Jon Ohnstad watched in horror as the old man fired the gun. Silje herself was amazed that the weapon didn't explode in his hands – Kvist had kept it clean after all.

The gun released a cannonade of metal shot, tiny ball-bearings that killed two of the Germans outright and blinded a third. Kvist threw the gun away and kept running, brandishing an old kitchen knife and heading for a cluster of six stormtroopers who were running towards him.

Silje turned to beg her father to help him, but Jon Ohnstad had gone, running across the village square, firing his machine gun. Gunther Braithwaite ran at his flank, and behind them the Resistance ran also, spreading into an arrowhead with a score of the villagers running and shouting, shielded in the arrowhead's cradle. It was a good strategy, and Silje felt a swell of pride for her father who had devised the formation, should it come to this.

It has come this, she thought, *and I am standing here, woolgathering.* And so she ran, as fast as she could, approaching the arrowhead at its right flank.

Carina saw her and grinned. 'Glad you could join us, Miss Ohnstad,' she yelled and slowed her pace so that Silje could slip inside the shield. The Resistance laid down suppressing fire, protecting the villagers who were armed mostly with farming tools. Ebenhard Holm was the first to fall; he left a space in the formation that robbed them of two more villagers. Silje wanted to turn and run back; she steeled herself and pressed on, having no idea what she would do when they reached the German line.

I will die, most likely. It occurred to her that she had not said goodbye to Freya. She felt a wooden handle pressed into her hand, and when she looked to her right, she saw Magnus grinning at her from behind his mask of scars. 'And this,' he said, passing her a large hammer. 'When we reach the Germans, swing them like you are possessed by Satan himself.' He was shouting to be heard over the roar of the villagers. 'But for the love of God, do not swing at me!'

'As if I would do such a thing, little brother!' Her words made her feel brave.

To her left, Carina began to slow before folding and collapsing in on herself; Silje cried out as Carina fell, but she ran on, feeling her tears freezing against her cheeks.

'If we hold the formation' her father had said, *'then most of us will survive until we hit the Nazi line. And then the villagers can take them. The Germans will not be able to bring their weapons to bear, not in such close quarters.'*

They hit the Nazi line, and she remembered his final words: *watch for bayonets!*

Fólkvangr pushed back the line, and Silje, as she had been told, swung and turned, and swung again. The scythe was sharp, but it was the hammer, heavy and blunt, that would do the most damage. To her right, Junges Fehn and his wife fought side-by-side, slashing and stabbing at the Germans with knives and a pair of memorial swords. Silje had visited the Fehns' home many times while Mrs Fehn was away, and she had no memory of ever seeing the swords. She offered Mrs Fehn a smile of comradeship, but received a glare of unbridled hatred in return. Some sins would never be forgiven, it seemed.

Four of the Resistance fighters had climbed up on the cottages and the tavern and were firing down into the German cluster. The villagers were surrounding them. Bodies, German and Norwegians, were pressed tightly together; it was suffocating and exhilarating.

Silje swung the hammer, cracking the skull of a young trooper, who fell at her feet, almost bringing her down as the villagers pressed forward.

The cannon mounted to the remaining armoured car opened fire, showering the fray with spent cartridges that burnt flesh as they struck. The heavy machine gun made short work of *The Mottled Goat*, and killed the men and women who had used it as a vantage point.

Grette, the tavern's formidable barkeep, met her end while firing down on the enemy.

Silje realised her life was crumbling around her; she set her teeth and plunged forward, listening for the sound of Gruetzmacher's voice.

There! Towards the centre of the Germans. He was still bleeding, his uniform torn, his cap missing. There was no fear in his eyes, simply anger and disbelief aimed more at his men than the villagers.

Have you not prepared them, Silje thought. *Have you spent so long lost in the bottle that you neglected to make them ready for the Norwegian spirit?*

He was armed only with his Luger, but he wielded it with a cold precision she found terrifying. He would shout an order, select a target, fire, kill, shout an order. He was the perfect soldier, as long as he was fighting. He ordered his men to break formation, break the circle and spread throughout the village. They would fade into the stonework and pick off this rabble one-by-one.

Silje slashed the throat of a German officer and caved in the skull of another trooper. Gruetzmacher was less than an arm's length when he saw her. She raised the scythe and he fired his gun.

She heard something clatter to the ground, and when she looked down she saw it was the scythe. A dark red stain appeared at her shoulder and spread across the neckline of her shirt. She felt herself sway, forward and then back.

Gruetzmacher raised his gun again, but the shot that sounded came from behind her right ear, and it was Gruetzmacher who fell, his left knee shattered. *And how he screams*, Silje thought. She fell into the arms of her father who tried to drag her free of the fighting.

'That was a stupid thing to do,' he said, his voice breaking.

'You saved my life,' she whispered.

'It was not me – it was her.'

Silje looked to where he pointed his eyes, and saw an old woman firing a machine gun at the soldiers who were carrying Gruetzmacher away.

'Marit.'

'Thank you,' Jon Ohnstad said.

Marit took Silje's arm and Silje felt pain, like a white hot lance, shoot through her shoulder. They carried her to a crumbling wall – the only piece of *The Mottled Goat* left standing.

'She needs a doctor,' Marit said.

'We have none.' Jon Ohnstad looked back towards the battle. The German defence was all but broken.

Marit said, 'Go. They need you.'

'She is my daughter.'

'I will take care of her.'

He hesitated, until Silje also told him to go. 'She is right, Father. They look to you. Go back and look after Magnus. I fear the smell of blood has addled his brain.'

Jon Ohnstad smiled for a moment before addressing his estranged wife. 'She is a thing most precious to me, Marit. I am trusting your hatred of me will not—'

'I have often said to you, Jon Ohnstad, that she is the daughter that should have been ours. I will treat her as such.'

He nodded grimly and embraced Silje, causing her body to tighten in pain. 'I will be back for you soon.'

And Silje felt it then, a yearning to keep him close to her, to never let him go. He wrestled himself away from her and stroked her cheek with his thumb. 'I have never been more proud of you than I am today, Silje. Your mother would—' He glanced at Marit who was pretending to look elsewhere. 'I must go. I will return shortly.'

He vaulted the rubble, with the agility of a man half his age, and ran back towards the battle line. The struggle had moved beyond the remains of the archway and out onto the narrow road, leaving corpses, an overturned staff car and two burning armoured transports in its wake.

Marit toiled wordlessly, gathering whatever wood and kindling she could find to start a small fire.

'The wound is not serious,' she said, and Silje wondered how she could possibly know this; it felt very serious from where she was sitting. 'You were very fortunate; the bullet passed straight through, though I daresay you will experience some stiffness in your arm for the rest of your days.'

She looks pleased, Silje thought. *It is hard to tell...*

Marit produced a small knife from the folds of her dress and placed it in the fire. She allowed Silje to stare at it for a moment before speaking again. 'I will need to clean the wound, stitch it, and seal it.'

'Will it hurt?'

'A great deal I'm afraid, yes.'

'Will it leave a scar?'

'Oh yes.'

Silje narrowed her eyes. 'Do not enjoy yourself too much, Marit.'

Marit turned the knife over and smiled. 'I will try my best.'

57

Silje awoke to a village that was strangely silent. The sun had risen, but there was still dust and smoke in the air.

Her injured shoulder was bandaged with a strip of chequered linen. Marit had torn it from the sleeve of her shirt.

'You're awake. Good.' Marit was sitting beside her, stirring a pail of hot water with the knife she'd used to seal her shoulder. 'You fainted as soon as I began.'

'Anyone would have, Marit.' She tried to stand and found her legs were not working.

'You will need to rest a while longer, but as you are awake and as ungrateful as ever, there are others I must attend to.' She struggled to her feet, picking up the pail of water. 'You fought well, Silje Ohnstad. I did not think you had it in you.'

Presented with a compliment leashed to an insult, Silje was unsure how to respond. She forced herself to stand up and surveyed what was left of her home.

It was much worse than she ever thought possible. The entrance to the village had been destroyed, along with the buildings that surrounded the square. Only the monument to her mother remained. She thought that she should be overjoyed, but it was simply a circle of stones, no longer the pivot of her existence as it had been a few hours before. It wasn't her mother; it wasn't her village.

The Germans had been driven back, Marit told her. 'It was glorious. Norway will tell of this victory for a thousand years.' And then she was on her way, over the rubble to where the Resistance and villagers had set up a makeshift field area to treat the wounded.

Others collected the dead.

Magnus carried Grette's body and placed it gently next to that of Eva Tufte.

'If I had not seen her with my own eye,' Magnus said, 'I would not have believed it. Old Mrs Tufte, cutting down Germans like chafes of wheat. She took six of them before she fell.'

Silje knelt down beside her, and crossed the old woman's hands across her chest. She felt numb, and then ashamed that she did not feel more. *Perhaps it is for the best,* she thought. *The time for mourning has not yet come.*

Magnus looked back towards the road outside the village. 'We could have saved her if we had Doctor Lomen.'

'Where is Father?' Silje asked.

Magnus scratched his neck. 'He took a small force to pursue the Germans back down the mountain road.'

'What of the ambush?'

'They held their position. The Germans will not make it far.'

Silje nodded. 'I wish I could have been more use.'

'You did more than anyone expected of you.'

'And I wish people would stop saying things like that.' She rose to her feet, hearing the sound of weeping from behind the monument. 'You will find me when he returns.'

'I will,' said Magnus. 'He said that you should look for Freya.'

Silje made her way across the remains of the collapsed village hall. She stumbled over the pyramids of rubble that had fallen into the street, stopping finally at the monument where she found Jesper Bergström crying with Ingrid Haug in his arms. Ingrid had been hit with a stray bullet that had left a small hole in the side of her throat.

'Jesper, can I see her?' Silje said quietly.

'There is no need,' Jesper replied. 'She has gone.'

Nevertheless, Silje sat beside him and examined Ingrid for any sign of life; there was none.

'She should have gone to the mountain with the other children,' Jesper said. 'But she would not leave, not without me. She is gone, Silje, and it is my fault. How can I tell her mother?'

Silje had seen Mrs Haug; she was one of the dead lying outside the remains of the village hall. She had refused to leave Fólkvangr for the safety of the mountains, not without her daughter. 'I will tell her myself, Jesper. Have no fear.'

Jesper nodded and held Ingrid closer. 'You should find Freya. There was so much noise last night – she will be very frightened.'

'You are right. I should go.'

'We saw you fighting last night, Silje. You are very brave.'

'And you are a good friend to think of Freya when you are so sad.' She caressed his cheek and was on her way.

* * *

For Silje, finding Freya was not a matter of searching every nook and hiding place in Fólkvangr. She knew that Freya was fearful of loud noises in the same way she grew fretful and restless if she found herself in complete silence.

The firefight would have confused her, left her disorientated. If she were able she would try to find her way out of the village, make her way to a place of tranquility, and wait until she could find her way home again.

Silje headed west to the outskirts of the village where Doctor Lomen lived – where Doctor Lomen had lived. Less than a hundred steps away from the village square, Fólkvangr became home again. The streets were clear, the winter flowers bloomed and the buildings were still whole. The Fehns' home stood untouched, along with the disused church and Mr Bergström's grocery store. The fighting had not travelled further than the monument to her mother.

Outside the village boundary, she climbed the familiar rocks that led to a small plateau and the uneven footpath which would take her to Doctor Lomen's cottage. It was not a difficult walk, but her limbs ached with fatigue and her shoulder simply ached. She wished more than anything that Doctor Lomen was alive. He would treat her shoulder, tell her that she had the strength of a stallion, tap her on the nose; she would obediently open her mouth so he could put a lump of sugar on her tongue. Quite unexpectedly, Silje began to cry.

She approached the gateway that led to Doctor Lomen's front door and wiped her eyes. Then, in a voice so soft she could barely hear it herself, she whispered Freya's name. She waited for the whisper to be carried on the wind.

'Silje! Silje, is that you?'

'Freya!'

'Silje, please go! Run!'

Germans, she thought. *The Germans have her!* She remembered that she'd dropped the scythe when she had been shot, and she had no clue as to what had happened to the hammer. It didn't matter. If the Nazis were holding Freya then she would simply tear them limb from limb. She ran to the side of the cottage and stopped cold.

Freya was there, quite safe, but she was not alone.

Erik Brenna looked thin and tired. He was holding a pistol, but it hung at his side.

'Silje,' he said and looked back towards the trees.

She was going to launch herself at him, to claw at his face, drag him to the square to face the wrath of the villagers, but he did not seem as she expected. He looked sad and lost, but there was no trace of shame about him.

'What are you doing here, Erik?'

'I... came to help. I heard the Germans had attacked the village.'

He was wearing a suit. A new suit, with an orchid in the buttonhole.

'You are not dressed for war, Erik.'

'No,' he said. 'I am not.'

'If I am not mistaken, you are dressed for a wedding.'

'Yes.'

He'd travelled all this way to try again, to give her another chance. She didn't think it possible for love to take someone with such savagery and refuse to let them go. 'Erik, listen. I am—'

'I am married, Silje,' he said quickly. 'The wedding was yesterday, in Lillegard.'

Silje's heart snapped cleanly in two. She took a breath and tried to smile. 'Lisbeth.'

Erik nodded. 'She came looking for me.'

'And so you married her, just like that.'

'The love she has for me, Silje; it is the love I have – had – for you. I would not be so cruel as to deny someone whose life depends on me.'

'Do you love her?'

'I will learn to.'

There was something else, something that had haunted her while she cut down her enemies, and now it tried desperately to claw its way to the surface.

'Is she here?' Silje said flatly. 'I should congratulate her on her victory.'

'Love is not the same as war, Silje.' He turned to Freya and told her she looked well.

Freya smiled meekly; Silje looked at her and her mind churned.

'I tried to rally the local Resistance fighters to come to our aid, but they said that they could not risk so many men for a small village of little strategic importance.'

'Does Lisbeth know you are here?'

Erik shook his head, and Silje's memory finally gave way. Her eyes widened and she spun on her toes to face Freya. 'The General knows you!'

Freya said nothing.

'He knows you.'

'Perhaps… he knows I am here. Perhaps someone from the village has gotten word to him.'

'No, it is much more than that. When did you meet General Gruetzmacher?'

'I have never met him, I swear it.'

She had sworn herself to the truth far too quickly.

'I was with him before the battle; he spoke of you. He said things about you that I thought only I knew.'

Silje approached her, and Freya took a step back. 'Silje, please listen to me. I can—'

'Dear God, it was you.'

'No, no, it—'

'How could I have not seen it. It was you. You betrayed us.'

'No!'

Silje lunged towards Erik, pushing him off his feet and snatching the pistol from his hand; she turned the gun towards Freya and released the safety catch. Freya backed away until she could go no further, her escape blocked by the cottage wall.

Silje grabbed her throat and pressed the muzzle of the gun against her head. 'I gave you everything! I gave you a home; I gave you my friends!' The rage subsided as quickly as it had come, replaced by tears she knew would never end. 'I gave you myself. All that I am, it was yours – for the keeping.'

'If you believe I betrayed you, Silje,' Freya whispered, 'then kill me; my life is already over.'

'Oh, Freya; can you not see? You have killed us both.'

Silje closed her eyes and pulled back the hammer, and it was then that Erik Brenna scrambled to his feet and cried, 'No! It was me! It was I who betrayed you, Silje!' He lurched forward and tried to take back the gun. 'I know how much you love her! If you kill her you will surely take your own life! Not today, perhaps, not while your village still needs you, but you will. Your grief will consume you and you will wither and you will die. So I am telling you, Silje; it was me. I betrayed Fólkvangr because you hurt me, because you destroyed me, and I wanted to destroy something you loved in return.'

Silje wrested the gun from his grip and pointed it at his eyes. 'You are lying. You are lying to protect her. Why would you lie, after what we have done to you?'

'Yes,' he said, raising his hands. 'Why would I say this if it were not the truth? Think hard, Silje.'

There was shouting coming from the village, but the voices were too far away to hear clearly. Silje looked to Erik for signs of deceit, and it occurred to her that if he were lying, she would not recognise it.

'You want to believe me,' he said.

The voices from the village grew more urgent.

'What are they saying?'

Freya shivered.

'Freya, what are they saying!'

'The Germans have regrouped. Reinforcements have come. They are heading back towards the village.'

'Then I must go,' said Silje.

'Take me with you!'

'If the Germans overrun us, you'll be killed. You must head for the higher mountains, as fast as you can.'

'I am not going anywhere without you.'

'Go to the mountains.'

'I will not.'

I will come for you.'

'No.'

There was no time for them to fight, for Silje to make her see reason.

'Freya, I will miss you.'

'Silje, no! Don't do th—'

Silje struck her as hard as she could with the stock of the pistol. Her prayer was answered; Freya fell, unconscious. She would not have to find the strength to hurt her again.

Erik swallowed and looked to Silje.

'Take her to the mountains,' she said. 'You will take care of her. Do you understand?'

'You trust me? After I betrayed you?'

'Well, you are unlikely to do so again.'

'You do not believe me, do you?'

'What I believe does not matter anymore. Whatever you are, whatever you have done, I will always trust you with my life.' Silje knelt beside Freya and caressed her. 'Whatever she is, whatever she has done, she is all that matters.' She kissed her mouth. 'So you will take her to safety, and when she wakes you will tell her that I love her and I forgive her.'

Erik lifted Freya from the ground. 'I will take her to the Resistance, and then I will return here. You will need every man you can—'

'No, Erik. You will stay with her until she is safely in Sweden.'

'Silje, I cannot just—'

'I trust no one else to do this. Stay with her; make sure she does not make contact with anyone.'

He protested, saying his place was at her side, defending the village they both loved, and for once in their lives she let him speak; she let his love pour forth and she accepted it with grace and humility. And when he was done she said, 'You will do this for me, won't you, Erik?'

And though it would scar his soul, he agreed.

'Then go, please.' She kissed him and left a crescent of blood on his lower lip. 'And remember you will always be mine, Erik Brenna.'

58

For most of the night I lay awake staring at the ceiling, trying to draw the pieces together inside my head. There were still parts of it that were untidy, hanging threads that had to be pulled and tied to make the whole thing neat and watertight.

If Freya had some kind of multiple personality disorder then how were her episodes triggered? Coded messages? Stress? Maybe it was a sound or a smell.

According to Silje's diaries, Freya became a different person when they were fucking, 'like a thing possessed' were her exact words, so maybe sex was the trigger.

And how did she contact the Germans? Their spies used message drops, so perhaps there was one somewhere in Fólkvangr. The Germans were there often enough, delivering supplies and picking up drafts of *The Quisling Orchid*.

I smoked three cigarettes and got up to take a shower. It was five in the morning; I was still wired, so I smoked two more and climbed back into bed.

The deeper question was why Bergström needed me. He had all the answers, so why this pantomime? Why not just let me bring my father home?

An hour later there was a knock on the door. I got up and pulled on my bathrobe.

I was expecting Bergström, but it was another faceless MOSSAD agent: dark hair, tanned skin, dead eyes.

'Get dressed,' he clipped. 'Your plane leaves in two hours.'

He waited in the corridor, while I brushed my teeth, put on my clothes and packed a small bag. Then he walked me down to the lobby, sticking so close to me that I could feel his sweater against my shoulder. He held my wrist as I paid the hotel bill.

I told him I wasn't going to bolt. He carefully checked the receipt and then squinted at me. For a moment I thought he was going to question my raid on the mini-bar; in the end he just shook his head and tucked the receipt in his back pocket.

'Come,' he said, 'car waiting.'

The car, a white Alfa Romeo, was driven by a thin dark woman who could easily have been a taxi driver or another MOSSAD operative. She diligently checked the roads at every turn and every change in speed, and also used the mirror to look at me when she stopped at traffic lights. She didn't say anything for about twenty minutes, but then suddenly piped up, 'You don't look like much.'

I had no reply to that, but Mr Dead Eyes next to me smiled into his magazine.

She whisked us to the outskirts of Dresden while most of the town slept, to an airfield where a small plane waited on the tarmac with its engines running.

The car pulled up next to it and I was frog-marched up the steps. I hadn't been through passport control and I doubted a plan had been filed for the flight. The word 'kidnap' buzzed loudly inside my skull.

I sat down near the rear of the jet and recited my mantra. *If they were going to kill you, they would have done it already.*

The driver was also the co-pilot; she went through to the cockpit, and while the door was open I caught sight of Bergström running through a checklist. The cockpit door closed, leaving me to wonder if there was no end to his talents.

Ten minutes later, the sound of the engines rose in pitch and then throttled up to a dull roar. The plane lurched forward and accelerated so quickly I was pressed back into my seat.

Bergström shouted 'Short runway!' from the cockpit by way of an apology. The plane took off into a steep climb that left me grinding my teeth. God, I hated flying.

* * *

Bergström woke me up during the flight. I looked out the window and saw only ocean. The sky was a clear blue around us and we were riding on the clouds.

'I have good news,' he said indifferently. 'We have found your mother. She is on her way back to the hospital.'

I felt guilty that I wasn't more relieved. She'd always accused me of being self-centred and here was the proof.

Bergström threw himself down in the seat opposite. 'I have persuaded the Norwegian authorities to lend us a few police officers, just to ensure she stays put.'

'You can't make her stay if she doesn't want to.'

'Yes we can.'

He poured himself a large vodka and offered me a cigarette. I took it and allowed him to light it. He took one himself and sat back with his eyes closed, blowing smoke through the side of his mouth. 'You have no idea how long we have been planning this.'

'I have no idea what "this" is.'

'True,' he said, and that was it. He seemed to fall asleep, so I took the chance to watch him carefully. Not a twitch or murmur. His eyelids didn't flutter and he didn't appear to breathe. After fifteen minutes I reached forward to shake him and his eyes snapped open.

'What are you doing?'

'I thought—' To be honest, I didn't know what I'd thought.

'Hmph.' He looked out the window, shielding his eyes from the sun. 'We're almost there,' he said, more to himself than to me. He reached down the side of his seat and picked up a small brown folder. 'We will be landing at Tel Aviv. From there you will take a bus to a kibbutz called Ein Geidi, a few miles west of the Dead Sea.' He handed me the folder. 'There is your bus ticket, and some money. Do not spend it all on cigarettes.'

I asked him, 'How do you do it?'

'Do what?'

'Kill people. How do you kill people?'

He scratched his nose and gathered his thoughts. 'Well, there's quite a few different ways. I suppose we can split them into three basic groups: close-quarters, distance, deferred, though I suppose the deferred methods, such as poisoning and car bombs, are really just distance methods which—'

'I meant, how can you bring yourself to kill people?'

'Ah.' Clearly this was the first time he'd been asked. Still, to his credit he didn't have to think too long. He leaned forward and looked earnestly into my eyes. 'When you have decided you must kill someone – I mean really decided – then do not dwell on it. Do not spend days thinking whether or not you are doing the right thing, or if there is another course of action you should take. Put it out of your mind until the moment arrives and then…' He smiled, pleased to be on familiar ground.

'And then what?'

'Commitment. Remind yourself of the righteousness in what you are doing. Celebrate the sacrifice you are making of yourself, the sliver of your soul you give to the devil so that justice be done.'

He poured us both a drink. I hadn't the heart to tell him I hated vodka.

'What am I supposed to do when I reach this place?'

'You are going to pay a visit to an Israeli national hero.'

'Freya Dorfmann.'

'That's right.'

'And what am I to say to Freya Dorfmann?'

'Whatever you want to say.'

I dropped the envelope on the floor. 'No.'

'Excuse me?'

'You heard me. No.'

He leaned back in his seat and tapped his fingertips together. His eyes sharpened and his nostrils flared. He was thinking of breaking something off me.

'Did you just… refuse?'

He could just lean across and snap my neck.

'Just tell me what the fuck this is all about. You have all the answers; you always have. Why are you making me do this?'

Or he could just shoot me, though I'd read firearms on a plane tend to end badly for everyone onboard.

'Look, I've done everything you've asked. You've dragged me across Europe, killed people in front of me, threatened me, my mother, my mother's doctor who also happens to be the only friend I have in the world' – he looked hurt – 'and now you're taking me to meet the woman who betrayed Norway and fucked up my whole life! Don't you think I at least deserve—'

'Politics,' he said. 'It's just politics. Let's leave it that. And I killed one person in front of you.' He held up a single crooked finger as though the number was really that important. 'Just one!'

I sat back and folded my arms. He quietly smoked a cigarette.

The sea below us became a desert, bright and barren. Small pockets of life began appearing as we flew east. Ancient monuments sprang from the sands and soon gave way to small cities.

'The less you know, the better you play your part.' He fastened his seatbelt.

'That's not good enough,' I said. 'I've trusted you not to kill me. The least you can do is tell me what I'm doing here.'

'No,' he said, and closed his eyes.

A few minutes later he opened them to find me still staring at him. 'Knowing will do you little good,' he said, closing his eyes again.

He wasn't going to tell me; I certainly couldn't make him. I looked out the window and wondered how Monica's battle was going, and how much time we'd have left together once this was all over. 'I shouldn't be here,' I whispered. 'I should be with my mother.' I looked back at him and said, 'Did you hear me? I want to go home. I won't do this anymore.'

Bergström stared into space with his lips screwed tightly together. He was seething, but not at me. He unfastened his seatbelt and took four folders from the wallet next to him. He leaned forward, spreading them out.

'Iscariot left four survivors,' he said. 'Four from twelve who made their way to Israel soon after the war.' He pushed the first folder towards me.

'Aliza Dantzig was taken in by a legal clerk and his wife. In spite of her ordeal, she excelled at school and studied Law at the University of Jerusalem. She became a barrister specialising in human rights, and later a judge. She left the legal profession five years ago and entered politics. She is now a minister in the Department of Justice. She is married and has two children, one adopted.'

He slid the second folder next to the first.

'Irwin Gantz entered politics straight out of university. A doctor who has never practised medicine, if you can believe that. He is currently leader of one of our smaller opposition parties, and is an outspoken critic of settlement policy and security operations abroad.'

A mouthful of vodka and then Bergström moved on to folder number three.

'Chaim Schultz,' he said, wiping his mouth. 'Ex-MOSSAD.'

I choked on a cashew nut.

'Yes, I thought that would surprise you. Mr Shultz is a close friend of Irwin Gantz, and is currently serving as the Minister for Defence.'

He didn't move the last folder; he just stared at it.

'Freya Ilana Dorfmann,' he paused and took a deep breath, 'came to Israel from England in 1954, having aided in the resettlement of refugees during and after the war. She studied Agriculture at Jerusalem, becoming firm friends with Aliza Dantzig.' He stopped and looked down to his right, his eyes narrowing as though something had just occurred to him. 'Hmm, anyway, she started a network of orchid farms and a flower delivery business, sold both companies and went to live at the fledgling Ein Geidi kibbutz. She is using her wealth to launch a new political party which aims to curb Israel's expansion at home and abroad.' He sat back in his chair and finished his drink. 'Our sources tell us that Aliza Dantzig will defect from the government and join her as soon as the party's formation is announced.' He lit another cigarette. 'So you see our dilemma.'

'Yes,' I said. 'You have four people who may or not be victims of a failed Nazi experiment, and who may or may not be spies for an enemy that doesn't exist.'

'The enemy still exists, Miss Fossen. It is alive and thriving.'

'Then why don't you just kill them? It's not like MOSSAD to be squeamish all of a sudden.'

'Had we discovered Iscariot several years ago, before the four had amassed popularity and influence, then that may have been an option, but now…' He shrugged his shoulders. 'As I said. Politics.'

'Right.'

'We are not animals, Miss Fossen. We have approached them, told them what we know. We have offered them the opportunity to step away from public life and slip into anonymity.'

'Under MOSSAD's watchful eye of course.'

'Of course, and wouldn't you agree that is far better than the alternative? If we were to dispatch such outspoken opponents of our operations, no one would believe they were accidents. The fallout would tear Israel apart. We know it; the four of them know it.' He leaned forward and frightened the life out of me simply by taking my hands.

'MOSSAD cannot be seen harassing its political enemies, neither can the police or any other branch of the security services, especially when all we have as evidence is a memo written by a man I recently dissolved in a bath.'

The plane's wheels touched down and rumbled across the tarmac.

I asked him what any of this had to do with me.

'If I told you that, Miss Fossen,' he said, 'then you really would run.'

* * *

I wasn't surprised when he abandoned me at Lod International. At passport control, he pushed through to the front of a very angry queue and showed his passport to the immigration officer. The officer looked him up and down and then made a phone call, switching his eyes between Bergström and me. Finally, he nodded and waved us through.

The airport was hot and crowded, a glasshouse that caught the heat of the sun on all sides. The locals didn't seem to mind. They fanned themselves with their newspapers, lying back in their seats with their eyes shut, thankful their God had drawn a home for them in the sand. The rest of us drank water and perspired in equal measures. I turned to ask Bergström if we could find some place cooler and he'd disappeared. I didn't panic, though I think I would have done a few months before. I'd picked up a few words of Hebrew during my time in Dresden, enough to find a bathroom and the nearest bus station. I asked one of the dozen soldiers keeping watch inside the terminal building. He didn't say anything. He just pointed to a sign showing a bus and an arrow.

It was cooler outside; the sun still baked the earth and the people under it, but at least there was air, hot and dry as it was. The airport was just a terminal and a runway; it had a thin, doll's house feel about it, as though it would disappear inside a sandstorm one day. It certainly didn't appear as robust as the Israelis who went about their day while keeping a wary eye on foreigners. Israel was a young country, born of a people in perpetual flight. It showed.

I found a bus heading out towards the Black Sea, paid the driver and took a seat near the back. The windows were tinted to screen out the worst of the light, but it didn't help too much with the heat. The bus sat on the tarmac for another twenty minutes before we moved away, the seats only half-full.

We skirted the edge of Tel Aviv, rows of white stone houses and markets that gave way to the desert. The road, such as it was, stretched out ahead of us, disappearing where the earth curved, swallowed by the low sun.

I tried to stay small, curled up in my seat with my arms folded and my knees pressed high against my chest. It was supposed to be a cocoon of invisibility, but I was surrounded by a people who looked for the invisible, for enemies in the light.

The woman a few seats in front had been stealing glances at me since the journey began. An hour later she moved, rocking and bouncing her way to the back so she could get a better look. She dropped into the seat on the other side of the aisle and positioned her knees under her chin so she could wrap her arms around her legs. She was mimicking me while trying to look as though she wasn't. I smiled graciously, at least I hope I did. She didn't smile back; instead she just asked me where I was travelling to.

I asked her something in return. 'Are you the police?'

She smiled, finally, and asked me if it would bother me if she was. I said that would depend on what, as a police officer, she would do next.

She laughed, a little too loudly for my liking. 'I'm not the police,' she said, leaning back and pressing her head against the window, 'so maybe we can both relax and have a conversation.'

'What if I don't want a conversation?'

'Then we'll both sit here, very quietly, for a long and boring ride on a very hot coach.'

She looked familiar: middle-aged, slim with ringlets of silver hair and shining eyes to match. Perhaps in her forties, or a little older, and dressed for the heat in a white linen trouser suit and a large-brimmed hat thatched from lacquered straw. She had no hand luggage with her, and when I dropped my eyes to her arms I could see they were clear.

'If you're looking for a tattoo,' she said, 'I don't have one. I grew up in England during the war.'

Her accent agreed with her. She was still smiling, and I couldn't shake the feeling that I'd seen her before.

'You're not from here, I can tell,' she said. 'Me neither, in a way.'

'You're not Jewish?'

'Oh, I'm Jewish, just not Jewish enough, not for the new homeland anyway.' She drew her knees up further, pulling herself away while inviting me in. She was flirting with me; when I didn't respond she unfolded, moved across and extended a slender hand. 'Pasha,' she said. I looked at her hand as if it were loaded.

'Go on; I won't bite.'

Her hand seemed much cooler than it should have been, but the handshake was strong and self-assured. She let go and launched into a life-story that I only half listened to. She was a nurse, she told me, working with the terminally ill in some place called Coventry. She had no husband. 'Which is almost unheard of for a Jew of my age. But I love my work, and the men I've known never seem to understand that. They all seem to think it's all rather ghoulish.' She stopped and smiled at me as though I was supposed to say something. 'Anyway, it was important to me, and I wasn't about to give it up just to spit out children for the rest of my days.'

She took two cigarettes from a silver case, lit them and offered one to me.

'So is this a vacation?' I said, taking the cigarette from her.

'No.' she said, shaking her head. 'I left my job.'

'Why? I thought you said you—'

'Cancer.' She blew a ring of smoke into the air. 'Talk about life's irony.'

'I'm sorry,' I said, because that's what you say when someone tells you they've got cancer.

'I think I took my diagnosis pretty well. The doctor said that most people just cry and never stop; others just thank him and leave the office and he never sees them again. Me? I just lit my cigarette and asked him how long.' She seemed fairly pleased with herself.

'So,' I said, 'how long?'

'About twelve months. That's not a hard and fast number, mind you. Depends on a lot of things they're not really sure about yet, but what they do know is that at some point, in the very near future, I am going back to the ground.'

She shivered and closed her eyes, savouring a long draw on her cigarette that almost burned it down to a stub. It was the first time I'd seen the mask slip. She wiped her eyes and forced a smile to her face. 'I went back to work the next day, but I knew I didn't want to wait this out. So I went home, told my sister the house was hers, and left.'

I tried to think of something to say and I was grateful she didn't let me struggle for too long.

'I'm just venting. You don't have to join in unless you want to.'

I didn't, not really. 'I'm sorry, I'm just not very good with—'

'Death? You're not supposed to be. You're supposed to shuffle through your days as though it'll never come to you. You're supposed to believe that if you live a good life, another life will be your reward. That's bollocks. My shot's been cut short, so I'm going to burn through the rest of it.' She lit another cigarette, more as a statement than a need.

'That doesn't sound very Jewish.'

'Then the plan is coming together.'

I wondered if this was a genuine belief or just anger that she wasn't ready to admit to. I wasn't about to ask her. It wasn't any of my business, and though she was talking at me like an old friend, I didn't know her.

And then I realised why she seemed so familiar.

'I reckon you've got about ten minutes to tell me all about yourself.'

'I don't think so.'

'Oh, I do. You see, I think you could be the most fascinating person I've ever met.'

'I haven't said two words to you.'

'And you don't think that makes you fascinating?'

I felt myself blush. She was wearing me down, grinding my defences into the sand. I swallowed and stepped out from behind what was left of them.

'My name is Brigit Fossen. Well, it's really Brigit Brenna. My father is Norway's most notorious traitor, and my mother has been driven half-mad trying to run from that.'

She didn't even blink, just sucked on her cigarette and narrowed her eyes.

'And for my whole life, I've run with her, until I got mixed up with a Nazi hunter working for MOSSAD who's dragged me halfway around the world to expose a blind war criminal. Your country is too hot and too dry. I stand out here, and I don't like to stand out. I hate it; I hate all of this. I want to go home and that's something I never thought I'd say because "home" hates me too.'

She looked at me thoughtfully for a moment, and then went for broke. 'All you're missing is company. Here's an idea; you and me hook up for a while. I can show you—'

'And if things weren't bad enough, there's a MOSSAD agent trying to be the two people in the world who mean anything to me. A repressed lesbian working in medicine who also just happens to be suffering from cancer? For God's sake, it's like you stitched my mother and her doctor together and left a big ugly seam.'

She stubbed out her cigarette and blew the last of the smoke out through her nostrils. She regarded me coolly, but did me the courtesy of telling the truth. 'I told him we were overcooking it. "Let me be myself," I said. "I'll have her on a leash by the time we reach the Dead Sea."'

I wanted to hit her, but she'd probably kill me. She looked like she could. 'Where is he? Where's Bergström?'

'On his way. I'm just the babysitter.'

After all this time he still didn't trust me. 'I have done everything he's asked.'

'Reluctantly.'

'I don't remember anyone saying I had to like it.'

'None of us "like it", these things we have to do. But we do them.' Her eyes hardened, staring at something locked away in her past. Whatever it was wanted to consume her, but she wouldn't allow it, not yet. 'Look around you, Brigit. What do you see?'

'A bus,' I said. 'A bus and six MOSSAD agents.'

She tried to look unimpressed. 'Further than that.'

'Sand then, lots and lots of fucking sand.'

'He told me you were smarter than this,' she said impatiently. 'The Germans tried to wipe us out, erase us from history. Six million of us went to the chambers while the rest of the world looked on. And after the war, when we begged for a home of our own where we could live in peace, the rest of the world put us here, surrounded by countries who would happily finish the job the Nazis started. I look out there and I see our enemies hiding in the sand. We had to temper ourselves; force ourselves to do things that were against our nature.'

'And that's what you're doing, is it? When you send animals like Bergström after old men?'

'What we are doing is sending a message. We are showing the world that we are no longer sheep who will stand in line to be butchered. And Jesper Bergström is a hero, remember that.' She stabbed a finger at me, and I could see something more than admiration. She was giving away more than she intended, so she changed path, turning my focus elsewhere. 'Do you know why he left Norway?'

I didn't imagine I'd leave this bus without her telling me.

'Because it sickened him. The Nazis violated your country, and what did you do? Nothing. You did nothing during the war and you did nothing afterwards. This… weakness nauseated him and so he came to us because he understood what we were trying to do. While Norway seeks to make itself into some kind of socialist utopia, we seek to make ourselves the most feared nation on earth. We will return hatred tenfold; we will do whatever it takes to protect our land. We will take power here and abroad so no one will dare wash their hands of us while our enemies exterminate us.' She sat back in her seat and took deep breaths, apparently exhausted. I wondered if this was a daily mantra that Israeli agents recited to themselves, in place of their prayers.

'Norway is not weak,' I said. 'We just chose not to let the war define us.'

'A noble choice to make,' Pasha snorted, 'when you're not surrounded by nations that hate you.'

59

Pasha and I made a silent pact and didn't utter another word until we reached Ein Geidi. The bus pulled into an unmarked area of flat sand in front of an archway made of white stone. It looked very much like the one that had once stood at Fólkvangr. Beyond the arch were rows of squat white buildings surrounding an area of tended grassland.

'This is where we part company,' Pasha said. She walked me to the front of the bus and down the steps where she checked that I had the address and a map.

'Through the arch and keep the sun to your left; you'll find her house. You can't miss it.'

'All the buildings look the same.'

'Don't worry; you'll know it when you see it.' She took off her hat and jammed it down tightly on my head. 'You're in the desert; you'll need this.'

I thanked her and she squeezed my cheek. 'You came this far,' she said, 'so I suppose there must be something to you Norwegians after all.' She climbed back on the bus.

I watched it pull around and head back the way we'd come until it was lost in the sands. I looked at the map, and tried to decipher the address which was written in Hebrew. Classic Bergström; I was going to have to work hard for this.

I think I understood the Israelis better, and Bergström's attachment to them. They were bitter and vengeful – perhaps rightly so. They saw a necessity in what they were doing. They needed this land and they needed to become this thing they despise so they could hang on to it. This is why they did terrible things, and did them so openly that it attracted revulsion from the rest of the world. I wondered if they could see the irony.

Still, there was a peaceful, clinical beauty in what they'd built here. An oasis of plants and wildlife, music and art living in and amongst the white stone buildings. I took the first street, listening to the musicians playing to a small group of tourists. The street opened out into a garden and a small circle of water. Beyond it, acres of lush green ran alongside a wide path of colours divided into smaller squares of perhaps a half-acre, each stocked with flowers of every hue.

Orchids.

Acres and acres of coloured orchids.

But it wasn't the flowers or the smell of cinnamon that held me paralysed; it was the man who stood in the very centre of the third square. One man of many, whose skin was paler and whose hair was long and blonde and whose arms had grown thick and heavy through years of penitent toil.

Even with so much distance between us, I could see my own square jawline and high forehead; I could see the line of my neck and the angle of my chin.

I didn't walk around the pond; I just ran through it with the protests of the locals ringing in my ears. He heard the commotion and turned his head, seeing me running towards him. Tears clouded my vision making the colours of the orchids bleed into each other. The others working the field looked at him and he just shrugged back. He took a long handled scythe and came running towards me. The others followed, spreading out to form an arrowhead with my father at its point.

They thought I'd come to take her, and then I remembered that I had.

60

Silje stumbled from the copse and ran towards the sound of voices. She found the survivors of the first assault were erecting new barricades and making repairs to what remained of the old. Magnus and her father were sitting near the rubble that had once been *The Mottled Goat*. Magnus's head was in his hands, and her father simply stared straight ahead. She knelt down and gathered them both in her arms.

'We won,' she whispered.

'Yes,' Jon Ohnstad said. 'I suppose we did, for now.' He struggled to his feet, using the length of a captured rifle to steady himself. Magnus followed, getting up and searching his pockets.

He asked if she had found Freya.

'She is safe,' Silje assured him. 'I found someone who will take her to the higher mountains.'

'We need to prepare ourselves,' said her father. 'They will be back soon and we must be ready. Magnus, help with the barricades, and I will strip the dead for anything we can use.'

'And what should I do, Father?' It was the first time she'd seen him as anything other than a farmer, a cultivator of fine flowers and a goatherd to their small holding of livestock. But here he was, the man before her birth, a soldier: calm, deliberate, ruthless.

'Do whatever you can, Silje.'

And so she did much as she had when Fólkvangr was whole. She moved from one place to another, helping here and there without feeling she was making a difference.

She missed Freya terribly.

And whenever she found labour, bandaging a wound, or helping mount a machine gun to a barricade, her mind wandered and filled itself with images so horrifying she could barely draw breath.

Freya standing at the right hand of General Gruetzmacher, wearing an SS uniform.

Freya standing over the bodies of the Lomen boys.

Freya standing before a firing squad.

'You did well today,' Gunther said.

She stopped applying axle grease to the machine gun and turned to face him. He was covered in grime, sweat and blood. He assured her the blood, at least, wasn't his.

'But you are hurt,' she said, looking at the bandage wrapped around his forearm.

'A flesh wound,' he said. 'It is nothing.'

Silje smiled. 'And how long have you waited to say something like that?'

Gunther grinned back. 'My whole life, I think.'

They sat down and shared the last of his bread and an apple which he cut into pieces with his combat knife. They chewed slowly and looked for the sun to appear from behind a cloud that Gunther swore was shaped like a goat.

'You have been in Fólkvangr too long,' Silje teased. 'You are seeing goats everywhere.'

He laughed loudly, perhaps just to hear the sound, Silje thought.

'We are not going to survive another assault, are we?'

Gunther's smile faded. He turned his eyes to the ground.

'You should go,' she said. 'You, your men; you can still make the mountains.'

He was silent for a moment; he slowly flexed his fingers, cracking each knuckle under his thumb. 'I am insulted, Silje Ohnstad,' he said. 'You will make no such suggestion again.'

'Your bravery does you credit, Gunther. But the time for noble gestures is long past. You should escape while you can. To stay would be to waste yourselves when you can survive to fight the Germans in a battle that can be won.'

'Then you should come with us.'

'This is my home. I cannot live anywhere else but here.'

'You have not tried.'

'I do not need to try. I only need to know.'

Gunther sighed and scratched his cheek. 'I never thought I would hear you speak like this, Silje. I thought that you would sacrifice anything to protect your village.'

'The village is lost, and now that I have seen the godlessness of our enemy I know the world is far larger than Fólkvangr.'

Gunther stared at her and shook his head. 'Silje, what is the purpose of resistance?'

'To fight them.'

'But why do we fight? Why not surrender? Surely that would be far easier.'

'Then we fight for freedom.'

'We fight for Norway. We fight for the Norwegian people: their freedom, their lives. If we were to abandon you then that is simply surrender without formality. I will hear no more of it.'

At the sound of raised voices Gunther was on his feet and running towards the remains of the archway with Silje at his heels. They arrived to find Magnus already organising the men and women into groups. Barthold was with him, doubled over, clutching his knees.

'What is it? What's wrong?' Silje demanded.

'The Germans,' he gasped before Magnus could open his mouth to answer. 'They have regrouped; they are on their way back. We have ten, perhaps fifteen minutes at the most.'

Silje locked her knees to prevent herself from falling. She felt empty, as though everything inside her had been suddenly clawed out.

'That is not possible,' Gunther said. 'That is not enough time for reinforcements.'

Still gasping for air, Barthold said, 'No reinforcements. It is the same group that attacked before.'

Magnus and Gunther exchanged glances and that was enough to tell Silje that something was wrong. 'What? What is it?'

'It makes no sense,' said Gunther.

Magnus agreed. 'He has very few men left, and we have more weapons now. To attack us without reinforcements…'

'Perhaps he seeks to hold us at bay until his secondary force arrives.' Barthold stood straight and accepted his machine gun from Magnus.

'It is a poor strategy, and nothing about this man suggests an officer who makes poor choices.'

Silje disagreed. 'He made an uphill assault on a village that lies at the end of a road too narrow for his troops and his tanks to travel in anything other than single file. That sounds like a poor choice to me.'

Magnus tapped his front teeth with the stump of his thumb. 'He wasn't expecting to fight. This was supposed to be a show of strength.'

'Then why did he come here?' said Gunther. 'What is it that makes him so desperate?'

Silje answered quickly. 'It doesn't matter. All that matters now is that he came, and now he is coming back.'

'You are right. We have much to do, far too much to waste time talking.'

Silje said she would hasten the evacuation of the injured; Gunther said he would move his men into a half-circle – they would attempt to ensnare the returning troops and finish them before they reached the pass to the higher mountains.

Before he left to check the heavy machine guns, Magnus took hold of Silje's arm.

'I will see you behind *The Mottled Goat*,' he said.

Silje looked over her shoulder, at the smouldering pile of dust and stones that used to be Fólkvangr's first tavern. She thought of Grette and how all the time that she'd known her now seemed shrunken, compressed into a single second, the time taken for a shell to reduce the tavern to rubble.

'Behind the wall, Silje,' Magnus said again. 'I will see you there with Father when the battle begins.'

Silje nodded and tried not to cry.

'Have no fear, Sister,' he said. 'God will be with us this day.'

They parted company as Barthold cried out from the remains of the arch. 'They have returned!'

Silje and Magnus ran towards the wall where their father waved frantically and shouted to them to keep their heads down. And as she ran, Silje felt the rumble beneath her feet.

Another armoured car, she thought. Gruetzmacher had held one back.

'An armoured car,' she said as she slid to a halt and lay down flat between her father and her brother. She aimed the machine gun at the north road and felt herself swallow.

Magnus cursed under his breath. 'Where did that come from?'

'He held it back,' Jon Ohnstad replied. He looked to his left and waved. Gunther signalled back, and the sound of dozens of rifles and pistols being loaded and cocked echoed around the village square.

So few of us, Silje thought; *so very few*.

61

Never let them surround you. The first rule – drilled into me since the day I could walk.

I saw the circle forming, farmers armed with scythes and threshers coming in from all sides. Someone shouted 'MOSSAD!' and more of them came from behind.

What if I'm taken? What then?

I dropped to my knees and clasped my hands behind my back. I shouted that I wasn't with MOSSAD.

The circle drew tighter.

'I need to speak to—' What would his name be? Monica said they'd changed their names so many times it was hard to remember who they were when they first ran. 'I'm looking for Rodrek Fossen!'

My father stopped in his tracks and looked around as if he were waiting for someone else to come forward. I doubted he'd heard anyone speak Norwegian in years. Two of his companions spoke to him. I couldn't understand what they were saying, but it sounded quite heated. One of them pointed an accusing finger at him and then took off in the direction of a large house at the edge of the orchid field. My father turned back to me.

'If you are not MOSSAD then who are you?' His Norwegian was stilted, the words jumbled and uncertain.

I didn't reply. He either trusted me or he didn't.

'I asked you a question!'

I raised my head and tried to muster a look of defiance, something of my mother he might see in me. His companions watched as his face contorted its way through a cacophony of memories and impossibilities. One of his men tried to take hold of his wrist. He spoke softly to him; my father pulled his hand away. His eyes darted left and right, looking for some place he could hide from the truth slowly dawning on him. He dropped his scythe so he could cover his mouth with his hand. He looked as if he was going to stumble; he threw his weight onto his toes to steady himself and then he came towards me, slowly at first, before breaking into a slow ungainly run, limping slightly on his left leg. He slowed down when he was less than a yard away from me and his legs just seemed to give way. He staggered the last foot and fell to his knees, taking me in his arms.

How can I say what I felt? As if there had been a hole in my life and I'd had no idea it was there. An emptiness, a blackness that I hadn't realised had possessed me until he closed himself around me and wept.

'What are you doing here? How did you—?' He ran his hands through my hair, separating the strands, running each one through his fingers. 'My God, you are beautiful.' He crushed me to his chest, and I said nothing.

What I could have told him began a lifetime ago, a lifetime without him. I told myself I would hate him for it, hate him forever, and that promise I'd made to myself when I was ten years old, and cut myself with a stone to seal it in blood – that promise withered and died. And all it took for me to let it go was for him to hold me tighter.

'Your mother. How is she? Is she back in the hospital?'

'You smell of cinnamon.' My voice sounded hollow and meek, like a child's.

He nodded, made a small swallowing sounding in his throat. 'It's the orchids,' he said. I wasn't sure it was.

'You left us.'

'To protect you; to protect both of you.'

His men turned away from us. I could hear the sound of cars approaching from the west.

Someone leaned over me and whispered into his ear as though I wasn't there. My father nodded. He clipped instructions in broken Hebrew and his men began to disperse, taking positions on the paths leading to the orchid fields.

The car engines grew louder. I could hear three of them, maybe four. It was Bergström; it had to be. My blood froze, but it wasn't fear; it was understanding.

'You knew.' I was in awe at how quickly my father had forgotten me.

'You knew Monica was sick. You knew she was dying and you never came.'

His nostrils flared and he ran his tongue over his teeth. There was somewhere else he needed to be, other than here – with me.

'I left to protect you both.' He pushed me away so he could point back towards the archway. 'To protect you from him.'

Bergström limped through the arch, flanked by two men I'd never seen before. The three of them were dressed in brightly coloured tie-dye shirts and flannel trousers. I was starting to think everyone north of Ein Geidi was a MOSSAD agent.

'Did you bring him here?'

I almost lied and said no. I didn't want to disappoint him, though he'd made it his life's work to disappoint me.

'He's not here for you,' I said. 'He promised.' Though Bergström had promised no such thing. 'He just wants Freya Dorfmann.'

'Then he'll have to kill us first.'

'Or you could just let him have her.'

He looked at me as if I'd just pushed a knife between his ribs.

'You could let him take her, come home, and be a husband to your dying wife and a father to me.'

'Brigit, listen—'

'Or you and your men can die here, and they'll take her anyway.' I couldn't let that happen. I hadn't come this far to see him torn from me in the middle of the desert. 'You know what she is. You know what she's done. Just let them have her!'

'Brigit, I can't. I made a promise.'

'Then break it!' He didn't look as though he might, not even for a moment. And I realised then that it wasn't Freya Dorfmann who was holding him here. 'She's dead. You owe her nothing.'

I felt a hand slip under my arm and haul me to my feet. My father rocked back on his heels and stood up. It was supposed to be a show of vitality, though he winced and I heard his knee pop. 'Hello again, Jesper.'

I wrestled my arm away from Bergström and moved to stand next to my father. Bergström seemed surprised, disappointed even. 'A few short months ago you were going to help me kill him.'

Was I? It was so long ago I could scarcely remember.

'Things change,' I said and took my father's hand. I squeezed it but he didn't squeeze back.

Instead he said, 'You can't have her, Jesper,' and I could see that I'd already slipped from his sphere, cast aside – again. Why was everyone else more important to him?

'Erik, please don't make this more difficult than it has to be.'

As if on cue, Bergström's men slowly reached into their jackets.

'Oh, it's already "difficult", Jesper. You really think Israel will let you do this? Drag a national hero – a blind national hero – from her home, and kill her workers in the kibbutz she helped build? You will destroy Israel, Jesper, before it has even begun.'

'We do not intend to kill anyone.' Bergström glanced at me, pushing reassurance, seeking approval. He cared what I thought more than my own father did.

'And when the people learn how MOSSAD pursued her to face crimes that she had no idea she was—'

'It wasn't us,' Bergström said sharply. 'MOSSAD has not pursued anyone inside Israel's borders. That is not our mandate. These men,' he nodded towards the gunmen he'd brought with him, 'are police officers who are here to take a suspected war criminal into custody, following information passed to them from a foreign third party.'

Shit.

My father said, 'You expect anyone to believe any of that? No matter how you play it, Jesper, the people will see this for what it is: MOSSAD spying on Israeli citizens when they're supposed to be looking outward for threats beyond our borders. You're just the SS by another name.'

His companions whispered and nodded.

'And where is this mysterious third party of yours, this investigative genius that uncovered a Nazi mind-control experiment buried for a quarter of century?'

Please don't tell him. You don't need to tell him.

Jesper smiled and looked pointedly at me.

My father's eyes switched between us, waiting expectantly for an answer already laid out for him. His eyes stopped moving, finally settling on me. 'Brigit, did you... did you help him?'

I didn't have to answer. He blinked slowly and looked to the ground. 'Oh Bright, you have no idea what you've done.'

And that was it. Whatever dream I'd had of bringing him home, of reuniting my family, of living a normal life – it slipped away and I let it go.

'What I did,' I said, 'what I tried to do was build a life for Monica and me, while you hid yourself here so you could keep promises made to the dead. Don't you dare judge me.'

Bergström scratched his chin and smiled.

The orchid workers had become restless while my life, which I'd sought to piece together, unravelled further. They nudged one another and pointed in the direction of the house. The circle began to widen. They laid down their makeshift weapons and took a step back. My father turned. Bergström followed his gaze, and for the first time I saw fear in him. He wrung his hands in front of his waist and chewed at his lip.

So I turned too, and I saw her.

She'd walked from the main house, gliding across loose stones and sand in her bare feet without making a sound, finding her way with long deliberate strides and echoes none of us could hear.

My father called out to her, 'Go back to the house.'

'I will do no such thing, Erik Brenna,' she called back.

She was tall, a shade under six feet, slim and almost royal, her thin white dress long enough to sweep across her feet. She carried a bouquet of orchids in the crook of her arm. She climbed the steps that led to the square, pinching the dress at her thigh to keep it from dragging on the ground. Even as she approached I could see that everything Silje Ohnstad had written about her was true. She was much older but as radiant as I'd pictured her; her skin, darkened by years under the desert sun, had taken only a few deep lines around her eyes and shallow ones around her mouth. I suspected she rarely smiled. Her hair was bound in a thick braid that showed only a few strands of white woven through the shadeless black.

She stood between Bergström and my father, momentarily inclining her head in my direction. 'Jesper,' she said. 'Back again so soon.'

'It's been six months, Freya.' He was nervous, off-balance. Something about her had stripped him of his self-righteousness. He glanced down at his feet, just in case his courage had fallen between them.

'Time and the sand,' she said airily. She handed him the bouquet. 'For Pasha,' she said and then she turned to me. 'You smell familiar.'

'My daughter,' said my father.

Freya's face lit up like the sun, and a wave of guilt swept over me. 'This is Brigit? My God! What are you doing here? I never thought I'd ever get the chance to… Let me look at you.' She reached forward, and without asking me she swept her hands across my forehead, across my nose and cheeks, down to my chin… Her fingers were strong yet gentle, though the skin of her fingertips was rough and calloused, and in spite of the heat her hands were oddly cold.

I tried to feel offended.

She stepped back and smiled, her eyes boring into mine. 'You are as pretty as your mother, Brigit. Welcome.'

Bergström laid the orchids on the ground and cleared his throat. 'Brigit has become quite an expert on you, Freya.'

'Don't, Jesper,' said my father. 'Just don't.'

Freya slipped into her quizzical mask and pointed her eyes at him. 'Don't what?'

While my father shook his head and dropped in frequent 'Lies, all lies', Bergström recounted and embellished, speaking the truth while twisting it out of shape.

Freya nodded occasionally, tilting her head towards me, listening to my heart breaking.

Bergström finished with a flourish; his final word was 'traitor'. I caught it though I'd stopped listening some time ago.

'Well,' Freya said to me, her chest heaving. 'You've turned out to be quite the clever little detective.' She managed to keep the loathing from her voice, which I was grateful for.

'When she started this she could barely read,' Bergström said with what I could have sworn was pride. 'No education, no social skills, no sense of personal hygiene…'

Please stop talking.

'Little more than a street urchin really.'

Well, fuck you then.

'And yet she managed to piece all this together by herself,' said Freya. 'With no help from you or MOSSAD.'

My father smiled and shook his head.

'If you had stayed quiet, Freya,' Bergström said, not caring whether or not she believed him, 'if you had just lived out your life here with your fucking flowers, if you had not attempted to seek political support abroad—'

'You mean if I had built a prison for myself.'

'If you had just lived out your life in the desert then we would have let your part in all this stay buried. We could have found a way to deal with the other survivors that did not involve you. We would have let Silje Ohnstad's memory of you stand for all time.'

Christ, I thought, *you as well?*

Freya smiled, something she clearly wasn't used to. 'You know, I remember you as a lovesick little boy who'd spend hours following me around the village.'

Bergström trembled, both enraged and off his guard. 'You are seeking office. If you succeed then that will be four Iscariots holding high positions within the Israeli government. MOSSAD cannot allow that.'

My father said, 'I had no idea it was up to MOSSAD.'

'MOSSAD's sole purpose is to protect Israel.'

'From foreigners.'

'If you do this, Jesper, then Israel will think you are simply trying to remove one of your most outspoken opponents – which is precisely what you are trying to do. There is no evidence Iscariot even worked.'

'You and the other three,' Bergström said, turning to Freya, 'all seeking to castrate the secret service, all seeking to stop our operations to eliminate Nazis in hiding, all opposing our attempts to occupy territory to secure our borders. Have you ever asked yourself why all four of you hold such dangerous ideas and parade them publicly? Do you not think that you say these things because you are still in the thrall of your Nazi masters?'

His words wounded her, but she made a brave attempt to hide it. 'Or is it perhaps those of us who have suffered the most under the Germans have no wish to see Israel emulate them.'

Bergström stared at her and then snapped his fingers. The police officers came forward. The orchid farmers stepped up to block their path.

'No!' Freya raised her hand.

My father said, 'You are not going with them.'

'Yes, Erik; I am.'

'I cannot let you.'

She stepped towards him and caressed his chin, pressing her forehead against his. 'Once again I release you, Erik Brenna.'

'And I've told you; you cannot do that,' he said. 'Only she can do that.'

'Oh Erik. She is gone.'

And I thought I was the only person who saw this. Silje Ohnstad held so much sway in death, I couldn't imagine what it must've been like sharing the mountains with her when she was alive. I could barely imagine there being room in the mountains for anyone else.

'Freya, the promise I made to her remains.'

'Listen to her,' I said glumly. 'She's gone. Has been for more than twenty years. Even she's accepted it and she loved her just as much as you did.'

There was an entry in Silje's diary about the day my father had discovered them in the hills. She'd described how mechanical he was; how he'd thrown Freya to the ground, forced her legs apart; how he was going to mutilate her with his knife, before he came to his senses... There was a flash in his eyes; it only lasted for a moment, but he turned it on Freya and I imagined the way he was looking at her now mirrored the way he looked at her then, back on that mountain when the two women he loved more than life itself had ripped him in two.

I was glad Freya couldn't see it, even for the moment it lasted.

She placed a gentle hand on my arm, but it wasn't enough to stop me. 'You don't love us,' I said to him. 'Not like you loved her.'

'Brigit,' Freya began, 'that's not—'

I pushed her hand away; it was enough to silence her.

'I get it, but you have to leave this place. If not for Monica and me then do it for yourself.'

'I'm going with them, Erik,' said Freya. 'I cannot hide here anymore. If they want to fight me, if they're willing to use your daughter to do it, then let's do it in the open.'

He said, 'Then let me fight with you. It's what she would have wanted.'

'She's dead!' I shouted. 'Don't you understand that! Jesus! She's dead and the only reason you've been this woman's slave for the past twenty years is because you think being close to her is the same as being close to the woman who betrayed you for her!'

I wish I'd spoken more quietly. The orchid farmers tried to look elsewhere. Bergström coughed and ordered the police officers back to the cars. He turned and spoke to Freya. 'If you are not back here in fifteen minutes I will come for you.' Then he limped away, back towards the arch.

The farmers began to protest, and Freya had to calm them, tell them that this was best for everyone. They finally began to disperse, still protesting as they returned to the fields.

That left the three of us. The Fólkvangr triangle.

Freya must've felt the discomfort in the air; she announced she would return to the house and pack her things.

Which left my father and me. We looked away from each other. He scuffed his feet in the sand, and I tried to think in which direction Scandinavia lay. I was of a mind to walk home.

'I know I haven't shown it,' he said. 'But I'm happy to see you.'

'Did you ever love her? My mother, I mean.'

He was silent for a moment, trying to decide between mercy and the truth. 'Not as I should have.'

The truth it is then.

'She knew this, and she accepted it for a time. Lisbeth and I were both so… broken. Silje Ohnstad broke me, and every day I was with your mother, my despair broke little pieces from her.'

'And that's why you left?'

He whispered 'Mostly' under his breath.

'And what about me?'

He had no answer for that, neither of us did. Even in death, Silje Ohnstad was too powerful a force to be reckoned with. I looked away from him and I thought I could see an ocean beyond the archway, but it was an illusion, the sky reflected in the sand.

'I have never known her as Lisbeth,' I said. 'Only Monica. Monica Fossen.'

'We had to change our names. Many came to believe I had betrayed Fólkvangr, and there was no one left alive to tell them otherwise.'

'No one aside from my mother.'

He nodded. 'She couldn't. In a way, she believed I deserved it.'

'Perhaps she was right.'

'Yes,' he said. 'I think that perhaps she was.'

'You're not going to come home with me, are you?'

'You're staring at your dreams, Brigit, like you're staring at the sun; and they're blinding you to the truth that is as plain as day. You don't want me back in your life. You don't need me.'

'And she does?'

'I made a promise.'

'You made a promise to my mother, your wife! You said that you would love and honour her until your last breath. Why does one promise mean everything to you, while another means nothing?'

His blood rushed to his face, a sudden anger that reminded me of Monica, but held rigidly in check. He wanted to tell me something; his lips moved slightly, mouthing the words to exorcise them from his conscience. 'You should go home,' he said. 'Your mother is ill. You should be with her.'

'And where should you be?'

He looked towards the house and that was his answer. So instead of being led by the nose I decided I should find answers of my own.

'Where are you going?' he called after me.

'Where does it look like I'm going?' I shouted back. 'I'm going to the house. I want to talk to her.'

62

I walked past the acres of orchid fields, the scent changing with the colours. The flowers closest to the house smelled like ground vanilla, strong and sweet. I guessed these were her favourite, while the ones that carried soft cinnamon were furthest away.

A flight of narrow steps took me to the main house. The door wasn't locked so I pushed it aside and stepped into a wide hallway painted white along two walls and the ceiling; the third wall was painted blood red. The paintings and photographs were mostly of Fólkvangr and the Ohnstad family.

Seven pedestals stood at equal distances along the left wall, each carrying a small ornament that seemed strangely out of place in such a grand hallway: a wooden mixing bowl and spoon; an ancient sewing machine; a Luger pistol; a woodsman's knife with JO carved into the handle; a goatskin eyepatch.

The next pedestal was for a thick book with a grand leather cover labelled, in French, as the Old and New Testaments. When I flipped over the first few pages, I found it wasn't a bible at all; it was a huge book of erotic pictures. The furthest pedestal carried a glass case containing a neatly folded wedding dress.

The Ohnstads were a complicated family.

I expected to see more about Silje Ohnstad; she had been her lover, after all, but then I remembered that the woman was blind so why would she need pictures? All the photographs she would ever need were kept safely inside her head. So all this was for us: mortals whose memories of Fólkvangr would fade with time. The house was a museum as well as Freya Dorfmann's home.

'What do you think?'

I spun round and almost knocked the mixing bowl from its pedestal. She'd managed to get within three feet of me without making a sound.

I made excuses and apologies which she graciously waved away. 'Would you like something to drink?' she asked. 'Strange thing about the desert; people in it don't seem to know when they're thirsty.' She moved gracefully through to the drawing room without waiting to see if I was following her. There was a sensuous pull about her; I could see how Silje Ohnstad had lost herself.

The drawing room carried the same pattern of décor: two sides and the ceiling painted cream, and then a garish blue for the right wall. There were more pictures, mainly of Norway. I recognised a painting of the mountains above Bergen where Fólkvangr used to be.

She poured water from a pitcher full of melting ice and then cut a lemon in half, squeezing the juice into both glasses.

'You remind me of your mother,' she said.

'I hope not.'

She smiled, and the room became lighter.

'How is she?'

'Dying.'

'Yes, Erik told me. I'm very sorry.'

'I think you should be sorry for a lot of things.'

The remark was meant to wound her but she didn't even flinch.

'I read a lot about you,' I said, taking the water from her, 'in Silje's diaries.'

Her glass stopped, poised close to her mouth, and she appeared to look straight into my eyes. 'Then you know things that very few are privy to.'

'You and her...'

'Yes,' she said, sipping at her glass, 'her and me.'

'Did you love her?'

Her eyelids started twitching; she was consumed by memories that had burst free from wherever she kept them imprisoned. 'You have no idea,' she said. A tear escaped her right eye; she quickly wiped it away.

'You never married.'

'No.'

She fell silent so I asked her about the orchid fields that surrounded her home.

'Silje's father taught me,' she said, brightening slightly. 'She never seemed interested. He bred an orchid in memory of his late wife, you know.' She pointed through the window. 'The acre closest to the house.'

I'd seen them as I'd approached. They were a deep cream colour with a single black spot at the bottom of the cup. The wind brought the smell of vanilla into the room.

'I think there is something else you want to ask me.'

'Yes,' I replied.

She placed the glass on a table and seated herself in a wicker chair. She folded one leg under the other. The muscles in her neck tensed.

'I've pieced things together. I know that your mother was Gruetzmacher's housekeeper before the war began. I know that he—' The words locked in my throat. It was fine talking to Bergström about it; then it was remote, flat words typed on a plain sheet of paper. And now I was standing in a room with her, the woman whom this had happened to, the woman I was already growing fond of no matter how hard I tried not to… The flat, clinical words suddenly sprang into life.

'He raped me,' she said. 'From when I was seven years old. Every three months, on the third day of that month. You could mark a calendar by him.' She shivered. 'It felt like he was testing me; seeing what had changed in me every quarter year. And between the attacks, I couldn't breathe, just waiting for the day to come around when it would happen again.'

'Didn't you tell anyone?'

Freya shook her head. 'I should have done. Easy to say now I suppose. But it was 1936. The Germans had been persecuting Jews for years by then. My father's millinery business had burnt to the ground, and my mother had to give up being a cellist and take whatever work she could get. She cleaned houses for some of the party members, but as Hitler's influence spread, the work disappeared. In the end, the only employment she could find was with him.'

'Gruetzmacher.'

'Yes, and I was the reason why.'

She picked up a box of cigarettes from the dresser and lit one. She offered one to me, but the heat was punishing; I didn't want to smoke.

'His wife found us in the end. She was a member of *Nationalsozialistische Frauenschaft* and attended meetings almost every day. But she was taken ill on that third day of the third month, so she was driven home. He didn't hear her enter the house, or walk upstairs, or open the bedroom door. I heard her though, and I didn't warn him because I thought that if he was discovered then it would stop. She reported her husband for having carnal relations with a Jew. He lost everything: his position, his home, his family. My mother lost her job, but at least I was free.

'But then he came back, a year later, restored, aside from his sanity. He found us living in the ghetto. He beat my father within an inch of his life and took my mother and me. He said we were going to be part of a grand plan that would help Germany win a war that hadn't begun.'

'Iscariot.'

'I think it was called Odin back then. After a year and six days, I could dismantle and assemble a machine gun without light. I could build a radio from scratch. I became fluent in three languages. I could run five miles in sub-zero temperatures carrying a field pack that weighed more than I did. I could kill a man twice my size with my bare hands. They forged us into murderers during the day and then returned us to our faith at night. It sounds like you need more water.'

I said I could get it myself, wondering what 'needing more water' sounded like to a blind woman.

'And then, after a year and six days, came the final test of loyalty,' she said matter-of-factly, stubbing out her cigarette. 'We were taken to an old aerodrome and each child was ordered to shoot its mother. Two of the children shot themselves. One shot someone else's mother. I don't know if he didn't understand the instructions or hoped that it would be enough. Anyway, he failed the test, so the guards killed him.'

She stopped, uncertain if she was remembering it correctly.

'Yes, one shot three guards, before she was cut down.' She smiled distantly. 'I don't think Gruetzmacher saw that coming.'

I didn't doubt it.

'Ivan and Sol were the bravest of us. They didn't cry, they didn't beg. They stood up straight and held each other as they were executed.' Again, she offered me a cigarette. I took it, too numb to do otherwise.

'Three did as they were asked, one without hesitation. I think Aliza hated her mother though I cannot think why. She'd always been kind to me.'

'But you survived,' I said.

'I was spared,' she replied. 'I couldn't do it. No matter how much my mother begged me, I couldn't bring myself to pull the trigger. She shouted at me, told me I was weak, a godless daughter; then she told me she loved me more than anything else on earth and if I loved her then I would do this one simple thing: I would grow old. And I failed her. In the end she put the gun in her own mouth and put her finger over mine to pull the trigger. It was the last thing I ever saw.'

She straightened her legs and flexed her toes.

'Gruetzmacher let me go. I don't know why. He argued with another scientist and then had me taken back to the ghetto. I never told my father what had happened, and he never asked me what became of my mother. But I think he knew I had done something terrible. He was just happy to see me again.'

'And then Norway.'

'Yes, with help. A lot of help from people who gave up their own chance of escape so we could make the journey. We wouldn't have survived in Berlin, not a penniless hat-maker and his blind daughter.'

She rose from her chair and settled her eyes on my right shoulder.

'But that isn't what you wanted to ask me, is it?'

I said no, it wasn't.

Freya sighed, and looked for all the world as though she were watching me. She turned and walked from the room. 'Bring the water and the glasses,' she said. 'It's very hot outside.'

I picked up the tray and followed her to the rear of the house, to a large garden that grew wild with thorns and roses. Bamboo plants grew crookedly from two corners, and bindweeds threatened to choke the life from the orchids growing in an uneven square of dry grass that hadn't been cut in months.

She'd had gone to considerable effort to make her personal garden as grotesque as humanly possible.

Freya smiled and apologised for the heat. 'There are microphones in the house,' she said. 'I can hear them.'

I put down the tray and sat next to her on a love seat wrought from iron gargoyles. I wondered if my father had made it for her. I doubted it; according to Silje's diary, Erik Brenna was incapable of making anything that wouldn't be loved.

'This garden,' I said. 'This is how you punish yourself.'

Freya inclined her head towards me, and for a moment, in her eyes, I could see someone else. I slid away from her.

'Iscariot took my sight but left dreams in its place. I remember when they started, two nights after I met Silje for the first time, I dreamt I betrayed my father to the Nazis. Every night, the same dream. And when I was rescued and taken to Fólkvangr, I dreamt of messages to the enemy hidden in the stones of the Ohnstad Monument. I thought it was just the guilt because I'd let them torture my father and take him away from me. '

'You were young. There is nothing you could have done.'

She smiled again, but not at me. 'That's exactly what Silje used to say.' She poured out two glasses, and didn't drink until I'd finished mine.

'There was an old man called Josef. Josef Kleppe. He was a widower, a lovely, tragic man who lit the street lamps around the village when night fell. I used to walk with him every second night of his rounds. I wasn't much use to him, but he liked my company. He was lighting the lamps closest to the Monument, the night after one of the dreams. I could hear him breathing, singing, facing away from me, and I was so close to the Monument… I didn't expect to find anything, not really.' She closed her eyes. 'But the dreams were driving me mad, and I thought if I just searched the flagstones then I'd know I was imagining it, and I'd be free of them.' She covered her mouth with her hands, and her shoulders began to shake. But she held herself together and her composure returned after three deep breaths. Like me, she could cry quickly and silently. I wondered if this was something Iscariot had taught her, as Monica had taught me.

'There were scores of them,' she whispered. 'I couldn't see them, but I could feel their shape, their weight. The paper was from the supply the Germans had given to Silje, torn into quarters and then folded in half. I could taste the charcoal in the air. I didn't remember writing them, but the touch felt so familiar. That's when I knew. The dreams about the message drops, about betraying my father… They weren't dreams at all.

'And then Josef found me weeping on the ground, trying to hide the notes in my dress. He saw what I was doing, and he started crying too. He said I'd betrayed the village. He didn't understand I was hiding them. I was going to burn them. I thought he would tell the villagers, and Silje would find out, and she'd be so ashamed of me. I would lose her, and that's when I lost myself… I just disappeared. I thought I was buried for days, trapped in the darkness. And when I came back, I was still at the Monument, with a flagstone in my hand and Josef Kleppe dead at my feet.'

I realised Freya was sitting closer to me now, and I hadn't seen her move.

She raised an eyebrow and turned her head towards the house. 'Jesper is coming – with… six… seven men.'

'Does he know any of this?'

'No.'

'Then why tell me?'

'Because you remind me of her. Because if I had your courage I would have told her what I'd done. I would have saved her life, and Magnus's, and Mr Ohnstad's, and all the others.' She leaned across and gently stroked my ear between her finger and thumb. 'Tell Bergström if you must.'

Bergström pounded on the front door.

'What'll happen to you?'

'Oh, they won't hurt me. They'll make sure I never hold office. They'll use Iscariot to mount a witchhunt and sweep away their enemies. They'll say the information came from elsewhere so they don't look like the secret police force they are. And thanks to them, you, dear Brigit, will become an Israeli national hero.'

I told her I didn't want to be a hero of anything.

'That is MOSSAD outside, my darling. You'll be what they tell you to be.'

63

The Ohnstads lay flat with the rubble of *The Mottled Goat* pressed against their chests. Silje turned to look at the other survivors less than ten yards away, hiding behind whatever cover remained. Gunther Braithwaite licked his lips with a tongue that Silje was sure was as dry as her own. He caught her eye and gave her a thumbs-up.

The tremors became unbearable, and Jon Ohnstad turned to whisper to his children, 'I want you to go. Both of you.'

'No,' they both said.

'I am your father. You will do as I say!'

Neither Silje or Magnus moved, so he tried something else, something brutal in its truth: 'I do not want the Ohnstad name to die here.'

'Then send Magnus away,' Silje said. 'It is with him the family name will endure.'

'And leave you?' Magnus shot back. 'Even with one eye, I shoot a hundred times better than you.'

'You lie or jest or you are mad. I have not decided which.'

'Ah, yes! You are right, Dear Sister. I am lying!'

'I am glad you see it.'

'Yes, I shoot a *thousand* times better than you!'

'Father! Tell him to stop!'

Jon Ohnstad chuckled and ruffled their hair.

'I fail to see what you find amusing,' said Silje.

'I am simply thinking, My Daughter, how proud your mother would be of you both; of all of us.'

The rumbling halted, and Silje realised how much the vibrations had been hurting her chest. 'What is going on?'

'The armoured cars have stopped.' Magnus raised his head over the wall, only to have his father pull him back down.

Gunther was signalling.

'They have stopped advancing.' Jon Ohnstad scowled at his son. 'At what point in your life did I raise you to do something so stupid?'

Silje chuckled.

'And your mother is growing less proud by the moment, Silje.'

'They have stopped,' Gunther shouted, 'about twenty yards from the arch.'

'Can you hear that?' Silje turned her head so her good ear pointed to the sky. 'What is that?'

'I cannot see anything,' said Magnus.

The sound grew louder, a thrum and low drone, like a million angry wasps.

'There!' Magnus pointed at what looked to all the world like a giant bat flying out of the sun.

'Luftwaffe!' Gunther cried and opened fire.

And then the ground erupted around them. Silje covered her head with her hands and searched her memory desperately for the word *Luftwaffe*.

The dust began to clear, and in the silence, she saw Gunther and his company lying shredded across the rubble.

Luftwaffe, she thought. *Death from the skies.*

'The coward,' Jon Ohnstad said through his teeth. 'Gruetzmacher has called for air support! The spineless—!'

'We are too exposed here,' Silje cried. 'We have to move!'

Beyond the square, every shop, cottage and stall suddenly erupted in fire and stone.

The Ohnstads ran from their hiding place and joined the survivors who had left doorways, crumbling walls and teetering homes that would surely have been their tombs.

'We must run for the copse,' Jon Ohnstad shouted. 'We will find cover there!'

And so they ran, beneath the steady hum of an aircraft engine.

'I cannot see it!' Magnus cried.

'It'll come from behind us!' Barthold shouted. 'Hiding in the sun!'

They could hear it now, low and so very close.

And the copse, Silje thought. *It is so very far away.*

She heard her brother say, 'It is too far. We're not going to make it.' And so she grabbed her father's arm and pulled him to a halt.

'Father…'

He looked at her and then at the sun, the aircraft's wings stretched across its breadth. He nodded, and raised his machine gun. As he opened fire, his comrades-at-arms stopped, turned, and did the same.

'Keep running!' Magnus shouted, his gun crackling into life. 'Keep running! We will give you time!'

Silje fired too, aiming at the beast bearing down from the sky.

But the others did not run. They stood their ground, shoulder to shoulder with the Ohnstads.

She heard her father cry out 'Ohnstad!' again and again, so she cried out too, joining her voice to his.

And there were other voices. Names Silje had known all her life.

'Soren!'

'Kolsberg!'

'Von der Lippe!'

'Staffe!'

'Nilsen!'

So many names, she thought; *so many brave friends.*

'Ohnstad!' Magnus cried, and was cut to the earth.

'Ohnstad!' her father roared, and vanished inside a storm of hellfire.

She whispered Freya's name, and when she closed her eyes the young Jewess once more wandered blindly into her heart.

And Silje Ohnstad could not have been happier.

64

MOSSAD moved quickly; the following morning every Israeli newspaper covered the story of a young Norwegian woman who had unmasked Nazi spies wielding power within the new Israeli state. Aliza Dantzig was arrested straight away, so I guessed she was a particularly uncomfortable thorn in MOSSAD's side. The other two, Irwin Gantz and Chaim Schultz, were rising politicos, though they served on opposite sides. They stepped down; there was no need for arrests. Gantz shot himself a week later, leaving a note addressed to his dead mother.

Freya had been right. She was far too popular to be dealt with harshly. She confessed that she had been conditioned as a Nazi spy. She admitted to the blackouts that left spaces in her memory in which, she admitted, she was capable of anything. She even said that she may have unknowingly brought about the tragedy at Fólkvangr.

Yes, it was no longer a massacre; it was a 'tragedy'.

But Freya was a national hero. She'd aided refugees during the war and continued to help survivors of the camp when the war ended. She'd worked hard to secure medical aid for Jewish veterans who came into the country.

If not for MOSSAD and me she could have been Prime Minister one day.

Instead, she announced her retirement from public life and returned to her orchid farm, under the watchful eye of her nation's security forces.

But at least she was alive, and free – after a fashion.

I tried hard not to enjoy my six minutes of fame. I was paraded on Israel's radio stations, telling my carefully rehearsed story and taking great pains to point out that I'd uncovered the nest of Nazi spies on my own, without any help from MOSSAD. The country applauded me warily, sceptically. I was offered the freedom of three towns, and there was even talk of planting a tree in my honour somewhere. The accolades and praise continued to trickle in for the next two months, and then I think someone at MOSSAD got a little jealous. It was just small hints at first, leaks to newspapers suggesting that the secret service *may* have helped in breaking the insidious ring of Nazis, as they called it. Then a few more leaks, suggesting that I had been accompanied by MOSSAD officers during my investigation.

Many in the government said that the secret service was simply trying to take credit for the hard work, determination and diligence of a near-illiterate foreigner. They should be ashamed of themselves. Why hadn't they discovered this? Why was so much funding diverted to fools who couldn't even find spies under their own roof?

For shame, the newspapers said.

On the day that Tel Aviv's main heavyweight published an article calling for MOSSAD's disbandment, Jesper Bergström came to my hotel.

'Pack your things,' he said and started throwing the contents of my closet onto the bed. 'You're leaving the country.'

'When?'

'Today. Now.'

'I'm supposed to appear on a radio show.'

'It's cancelled. Here's your new passport.'

I took it from him. The exit visa was already stamped.

'Seems the plan to distance ourselves from this operation has blown up in our faces.'

'Are you in trouble?' I said hopefully.

'No more than usual. Your popularity is not sitting well at the top. Best you leave before the less intelligent and more excitable members of our esteemed organisation decide to deal with you somewhat less secretively.'

I was ready to go in ten minutes.

* * *

He took me to the airport and waited with me until my flight was ready to board.

'No private jet?' I asked.

'I thought it better to put you on a flight with other passengers. It's slightly less likely to suffer a mid-air mishap with other Israelis on board.'

'Good thinking,' I said weakly.

'Besides which, our budget has been cut.' He looked at me sourly as though it were my fault.

They announced that my flight was boarding, so he picked up my bag full of books and handed it to me. 'It wasn't supposed to be you,' he said. 'We were going to use Klein.' Another sour look. 'But for the most part you played this very well, very professionally. Thank you.' He gave me a small plastic card with a phone number etched into it. 'In case you should ever need my help.'

I couldn't imagine a universe in which I'd ever want to see this man again, let alone seek his help.

He shook my hand, and then as a strained afterthought, he pecked my left cheek. 'Safe journey. Stay out of trouble.' He cleared his throat and then he left, making his way through the crowds as though wading through water.

65

Before takeoff, the pilot left his hiding place to shake my hand. He said I'd done a great service to his country and that Israel would never forget it. The stewardesses followed; a handshake, a few words of gratitude and then a kiss on both cheeks.

The flight was delayed so that every one of the one-hundred-and-fifty-three passengers could form a line to shake my hand. I made the best job I could of signing autographs; a readable signature was still something I had to work on.

We finally left the runway an hour-and-a-half later than planned, the passengers content, and me with an aching wrist, feeling a complete fraud.

I tried to sleep once we left Israel's fortified air space, but guilt had taken hold, so I just sat in my seat listening to the thrum of the engines. Night came and brought with it an almost violent restlessness. I took Silje's diary from my bag and began to read it through. MOSSAD had let me keep it though they'd taken everything else I'd gathered concerning the Occupation and the Iscariot experiment. I imagined they weren't bothered with the ramblings of a young mountain woman living the last year of her life.

I realised why I couldn't sleep. I was out of Israel; I'd slipped free of MOSSAD's yoke. I could think for myself without pressure or preconception or what Bergström laughingly called 'guidance'.

I had met the great Freya Dorfmann and I'd realised that she held nothing but a profound and reluctant love for Silje Ohnstad. And no matter what the Nazis had done to her, that love would never allow her to harm Silje, or Fólkvangr.

I couldn't sleep because I knew it wasn't her.

And my father? He'd sacrificed everything – his future, his wife, his daughter – so he could honour the memory of a woman who'd died thirty years before.

I couldn't sleep because I knew it wasn't him.

So I pored through Silje's diary again, one year during the war.

Her last year.

And it was only when she wrote about the funeral of Jonas Kleppe I realised that it wasn't a love triangle at all.

It was actually a square.

66

The plane landed in a rainstorm. The wind lashed black water across the window in opaque horizontal sheets. I should have been terrified.

Instead I was just numb.

Instead I wished I'd just left well enough alone.

I said goodbye to my inflight fan club and went through passport control on the fake documents Bergström had given me.

I left the airport without going through baggage reclaim. I'd brought two suitcases back from Israel, the sum total of everything I owned.

I should have cared more. I didn't. I didn't care about anything. I should have let everything stay dead in Israel.

The rain soaked through my clothes while I waited for a taxi. I closed my eyes and clamped my jaw to stop my teeth from chattering. She would have lashed out at me for this. *Keep your eyes open, Brigit! Danger can come from anywhere at anytime! You have to be aware of everything around you!*

I opened my eyes and there was an old man standing next to me, holding an umbrella over my head.

'Thank you.'

He just nodded and lit a pipe.

I wondered what had happened to all the taxis.

'You're something of a hero these days,' he said suddenly. 'Been following your adventures on the radio.'

'I'm not really a hero.'

'You exposed all that business in Israel and cleared your family name. What's not heroic about that?'

'I had a lot of help' – in throwing an innocent woman to MOSSAD's wolves. A *blind*, innocent woman.

When the taxi finally arrived, the old man opened the door for me and shielded me from the rain until I was inside. He raised his hat and closed the door.

'Where to?' the driver clipped. He looked at me through the mirror, his eyes growing steadily wider.

'Ohnstad Memorial Hospital,' I said, the first time I'd been able to say its name out loud.

* * *

I was a different person by the time the taxi swung into the hospital car park. The driver hadn't said a single word to me and when I tried to pay him he refused.

'It's on me,' he said.

I asked him why and he just shrugged. 'Because.'

I thanked him and shut the door. He skidded on the wet asphalt in his haste to get away. There was a sticker on the back of the taxi, a swastika cleaved in two with a knife: the Friends of Fólkvangr. I guessed my family wouldn't be hearing from them anymore.

A few people stopped to say hello and shake my hand when I signed the day book. They said I was courageous to take on the whole Israeli government like that. A nurse asked me if my father was coming home.

'He should,' she said, and the doctor standing next to her agreed. 'He should come home and he should be pardoned.'

'Yes, the King himself should pardon him,' one of the orderlies said. A few others joined them; doctors, nurses, visitors and patients. They spoke warmly, apologetically, and with each kind word the cloud over me grew darker.

I made my excuses and freed myself from the circle, just catching the lift before the doors closed. I made my way to the fifth floor where there was another unwelcome surprise waiting for me.

It wasn't much, but it was more than I deserved. A banner over the reception area that read, *Welcome Home, Brigit!*

There was a huge ring cake standing on a low table close to the floor. It was so tall it would have left almond paste on the ceiling if they'd put it on the reception desk.

The doctors and nurses clapped and cheered, and I felt my cheeks burning.

Dagrun stood near the nurses' station watching me in that disquieting, intense way that she sometimes does. She'd changed. Her hair had gone from grey to white in a few short months, but she'd had it cut into a very business-like bob. She was wearing a dress I'd not seen before, a Warhol print of Marilyn Monroe that was cut surprisingly high above the knee. Not quite a minidress, but quite daring for Dagrun, and she was wearing makeup. I wondered if it was for me.

She'd lost weight too; enough for me to notice, anyway.

'Definitely not a diet,' she said, handing me a Coke bottle. 'I can't eat properly when I'm stressed, and I've been pretty fucking stressed since you left.'

And still swearing, My God.

'I was worried.' She looked around to make sure no one else was watching us; the staff and patients were enjoying the unscheduled break and seemed to have forgotten I was there.

Dagrun struggled for something to say. 'You still travel light.'

'Sorry?'

'No suitcases.'

'I left them at the airport.'

'I'll call reclaim, have them brought to the apartment.'

She searched my eyes for a sign: joy, revulsion… 'If that's okay. I mean if you have somewhere else to stay…'

'No, your place is fine. Thank you.'

'You can stay for as long as you want,' she said. 'Just don't trash the place.'

I tried to smile.

'Sorry. Bad joke. Not used to humour.'

'You'll learn.'

'I hope so.'

She held my hand, forgetting we weren't alone.

'How's Monica?'

And for a moment she'd forgotten she was a doctor. My hand fell back to my side.

'She's doing far better than we expected. She's responding to treatment, eating well, but, Brigit, please don't get your hopes up. The prognosis hasn't changed.'

'She's doing okay though, yes?'

She nodded. 'Yes, she's doing fine. I'm sorry about all this; I should have taken you to see her straight away. I just wanted to—'

'I know. It's all right.'

She rubbed the back of her neck and murmured something about professional conduct. 'You unsettle me,' she said. 'You always have.'

We left the party and walked the corridor towards my mother's room. I could almost hear her thinking.

'I'm not young, Brigit,' she began, 'I'm not that pretty and I'm not exactly svelte.'

I said I wasn't sure what 'svelte' meant.

'I'm overweight and I'm not good with people. I can be intense, bad-tempered and sometimes I say things that a minute later I wish I could take back. I scream at night and sometimes I can't bear being touched. I've been getting help with that, but I don't think I'll get much better. I really don't have anything to offer you except—'

'We should talk about this later,' I said.

She looked to the floor. 'I shouldn't have said that. Any of it.'

'No, I'm happy you did.' I pressed my mouth against hers. 'We'll talk later.'

'Dinner,' she said, her face glowing. 'I'll cook. Or you can.'

'We'll both cook.' I eased open the door to Monica's room.

'Call me.'

'I will.'

'Promise?'

'I promise.'

I closed the door behind me and waited until I couldn't hear her footsteps anymore. Then I pressed my head against the back of the door and began to cry. Monica gave me exactly one minute.

'So you're back.'

I turned and saw Dagrun's idea of 'doing well'.

She looked greyer than ever, like the colour of stone. Her bones showed through flesh that had worn to the thinness of tissue paper. Tubes and feeds snaked in and out of her, and there was the smell I remembered from before: chlorine and decay.

I'd hoped she'd be stronger.

'You don't have a kiss for me?'

I watched her, feeling my heart pounding in my throat. Then I walked around to the other side of the bed and leaned in close. She turned her cheek towards the ceiling. I pressed my lips to her ear and whispered.

'I know it was you.'

Then I drew away so I could see her eyes.

'Fólkvangr,' I said. 'I know it was you.'

She swallowed and waited. Her breathing deepened, her lips curled into a snarl. She entered flight mode and her eyes began hunting for an escape route. There was none; she'd be wired to this hospital until the day she died. When she realised she was going nowhere, she slowly calmed down. I stood and waited.

'I saw you on television,' she said airily, 'telling the world it was Freya Dorfmann. Are you now telling the world you lied, Brigit?'

And still so very clever…

'There were four of you,' I said. 'Freya, Erik, Silje – and you. I didn't see it because I've only ever known you as Monica. Monica Fossen, my mother. But before you were her you were Karoline Vennerød, and before that you were Hilde Eriksen, and before her you were Ruth Bondevik, Mabrit Strøm, Lisbeth Brenna.

'And before you tried to bury her with all the others you pretended to be, you were Lisbeth Fehn.'

Monica's eyes hardened.

'You betrayed your home, just to break her.'

She swallowed and wrung the sheets in her hands, wondering if there was anything of us she could salvage. There wasn't, which only left the truth.

'You have no idea what she was like,' she whispered. 'She was a bitch, a childish, self-centred narcissist. She treated your father like something she'd found under her shoe – and he always went back to her. Time and again she'd betray him and time again he'd return and beg for more.

'Even after he found her fucking that Jew; even after I married him; even when I thought "Finally! At last! He's mine!" she was still there, over my shoulder whenever he looked away from me, on his lips when he slept. He would have gone back to her again, Brigit. He would have gone back to a life of betrayal and misery.'

'So you thought the answer was a betrayal of your own. God, all those people…'

'I saved him!'

'Are you even sorry?'

She turned that look on me, the same unblinking eyes that drilled into my being when I said I was tired of running. *Listen to me, Brigit. This is how it is. This is how it will always be. But if you want to leave me, then fine. I'm a survivor; I thought I'd raised one too.*

'Brigit, listen to me. I did it for him. For us.'

She put her head back and closed her eyes. I was trembling. Every inch of me rattled and shook.

'If you tell Bergström, he'll kill me.'

'Yes.'

'And is that what you want? You want that animal to butcher your own mother?'

He'd do that. I knew he would.

'Is that what you want?'

'No, of course I don't.'

She exhaled and smiled. 'Good.'

She beckoned for me to come back to her. I stayed rooted to the floor. Her hands dropped down to the bed.

'We'll forget all this nonsense, Brigit. We have our traitor: Freya Dorfmann. We'll leave it at that.'

I blinked, and then I nodded.

'And perhaps you're right. Maybe it's time to stop running.'

I said 'Yes' without even thinking.

'God knows I don't want to spend what little time I have chasing around this fucking country. I'll leave the hospital. We'll get a little flat someplace near the dock.'

'I don't like the docks.'

She laughed. 'Fine, wherever you want.'

And that was it. She'd absolved herself of blame, of guilt. We could have a normal life now.

'Come on. Lie next to me.' She opened her arms.

And so I went to her, knocking over a vase on the way. Her eyes followed it to the floor, where it shattered, while I took a cushion from the chair without missing my stride. By the time she realised the vase was a distraction, I was on top of her, my knees on her shoulders, pinning her to the bed. I pushed the cushion over her face and pressed it in close about her ears, with the weight of my body on top of it.

Bergström told me that when you've decided to kill someone then don't dwell on it. Don't think about it. Don't question whether or not you are doing the right thing. Don't try to convince yourself there must be some other way.

Don't think about it, he'd said, not until the moment arrives. And then…

Commitment. Remind yourself of the righteousness in what you're doing. Celebrate the sacrifice you are making of yourself; the piece of your soul you give in order that justice be done.

I wept and pressed down harder. Monica struggled. Her arms flailed, her fingernails scored lines in my wrists. I pressed harder and felt her right shoulder pop from its socket.

But she was still struggling.

'Mother, please… just stop.'

I counted softly to myself. O*ne, two, three, four…*

If the treatment and the illness hadn't weakened her then I don't think I could have held on. She lashed out with her legs, trying to throw me to the floor. I just thought of Bergström and how many times he'd done this with his mind clear of everything except the righteousness of his action.

Eight, nine, ten…

She worked her good arm free and sank her fingernails into my cheek. I could hear her weeping.

Thirteen, fourteen…

At sixteen she stopped. I don't know why. Perhaps after years of carrying her secret alone she'd finally had enough, or perhaps the thought that her own daughter would take her life was too much for her to bear. She stopped fighting and used the last of her air to curse me.

Her arms slid away from mine and she lay still.

I pressed down for a minute longer until I heard her neck break.

I didn't regret it. There was no point in condemning myself for something I'd sworn to do from the moment I stepped from the plane.

Remorse was for the runners, the people who tried to escape the justice they knew they deserved, people like Klein and Gust and Gruetzmacher.

That's not what what I wanted for Monica.

It's not what I wanted for me.

So I sat on the edge of the bed, lit a cigarette and waited for Dagrun to find me.

I wouldn't run.

Not anymore.

* * *

The fantastic front cover

was designed by Janet Robinson

http://www.scribbleleaf.com

I'd also like to thank Mollie Baxter and Sarah Quigley for their tireless effort in editing the original manuscript.

James Major for giving the book the final once-over

Alan Stokes for saying something rather amazing and poetic about a ladder that got the ball rolling about two years ago

Richard Warrick, whose determination to pursue his dream fuelled my own

And my partner Helen for… well… putting up with me really!

I was told once that writing a novel is a solitary, lonely business. Over the past two years I've learned that it doesn't have to be!

15267921R00287

Printed in Great Britain
by Amazon